MANCE HEARD SOMETHING SNARL.

His breath caught, and despite the chill in the house, sweat skated down his rib cage.

A nebulous gray form stepped from the wall. The form grew more distinct. And larger. Mance squinted, but there was no mistaking: it was a huge, wolflike creature. Fully emerged from the wall, it turned and looked at Mance, its eyes wild. Then it snarled again, revealing its long, sharp teeth.

Mance couldn't move. The wolf creature kept its eyes on him for a half dozen heartbeats before swinging toward the dark hallway, loping away into the shadows.

Mance's body quaked, and he closed his eyes. And when he opened them seconds later, it was pitch dark in the room. Someone . . . or something had snuffed out the candle.

TERROR LIVES!

THE SHADOW MAN (1946, $3.95)
by Stephen Gresham
The Shadow Man could hide anywhere—under the bed, in the closet, behind the mirror . . . even in the sophisticated circuitry of little Joey's computer. And the Shadow Man could make Joey do things that no little boy should ever do!

SIGHT UNSEEN (2038, $3.95)
by Andrew Neiderman
David was always right. Always. But now that he was growing up, his gift was turning into a power. The power to know things—terrible things—that he didn't want to know. Like who would live . . . and who would die!

MIDNIGHT BOY (2065, $3.95)
by Stephen Gresham
Something horrible is stalking the town's children. For one of its most trusted citizens possesses the twisted need and cunning of a psychopathic killer. Now Town Creek's only hope lies in the horrific, blood-soaked visions of the MIDNIGHT BOY!

TEACHER'S PET (1927, $3.95)
by Andrew Neiderman
All the children loved their teacher Mr. Lucy. It was astonishing to see how they all seemed to begin to resemble Mr. Lucy. And act like Mr. Lucy. And kill like Mr. Lucy!

THE LIVING DARK
DARK

Stephen Gresham

ZEBRA BOOKS
KENSINGTON PUBLISHING CORP.

ZEBRA BOOKS

are published by

Kensington Publishing Corp.
475 Park Avenue South
New York, NY 10016

First printing: May, 1991

Printed in the United States of America

Part One
A Darkness Calling

Chapter One

1

Shadows covered most of her face.

"You taste good," said Mance, maneuvering on the pallet so that he could kiss Jonella full on her pillowy lips. Candlelight pierced the angle between his head and shoulder, spawning a crowd of shadows, one of which divided Jonella's face. He wanted to see her clearly; his life had too many moments blurred by confusion.

Each tentative, yet steadily more eager kiss evoked a soft moan from her, and Mance felt the familiar surge of emotion he could never quite understand.

"You smell good, too," he said, touching his nose against her chin and throat and finally against the rabbit fur on the collar of her coat.

He believed that one day he would marry this girl, whom he called Johnnie.

"It's Tanya's perfume," she whispered, the shadows stealing back most of her face.

"It never smells this good on your sister," he said.

Jonella tensed.

"When have you been sniffing around my sister?"

"Oh, Johnnie, hell . . . I don't have the hots for your sister."

"Don't you think she's pretty?"

"Not so much as you."

She hesitated. Giggled. Touched his cheek tenderly.

"Just the right answer," she said before pressing her lips firmly to his and tickling him with her tongue.

His stomach showered sparks. Momentarily he pulled away. A bit breathless, he said, "You getting us started, sweet Johnnie?"

"Maybe."

"Still wanna marry me someday?"

"Someday."

She shivered and snuggled closer to him on the threadbare pallet they had arranged in the middle of the floor of Guillo House, a long-abandoned Victorian mansion a few blocks from downtown Soldier, Alabama.

"When?" he prodded.

"When we're eighteen instead of sixteen, and when . . ."

Guillo House groaned.

A high-pitched whine slithered from the fireplace where no fire burned.

"Only the wind," said Mance.

They had become accustomed to the various sounds of Guillo House: the creaking of floors, the settling of joists, the rattling of windows, many with broken or missing panes, and the keening of the wind whipping around corners, seeking ingress wherever possible.

"Someday this old house will fall in on top of us," she said.

He shook his head.

"And then *what?*" he said.

"Huh?"

"You said we'd get married when we're eighteen instead of sixteen and when . . . and then you didn't finish what you were going to say."

"Oh."

She shivered again and buried her face in the cheap fur collar of her coat.

"Tell me, Johnnie," he persisted.

"Nothing," she said. "Keep me warm. It's not easy making out in the middle of January in a haunted house."

"It's not haunted."

"It is, too."

He pulled her closer.

8

"Listen. Forget about everything but me and you." He reached behind him and moved the candle so that the light would bathe his face and she would see his smile. He brushed at his shoulder-length hair and said, "Let me kiss your rose." His smile was that of a mischievous young boy. "Come on, Johnnie, I wanna kiss your rose."

She frowned.

And he continued.

"If you let me kiss your rose, I'll let you lick my fang."

As usual, his proposition caused her frown to shatter and her laughter escaped like the sound of broken glass falling to the floor.

He rolled up his sleeve. The pale skin on the underside of his right forearm sported a two-inch tattoo: a single, vicious-looking fang, its blue outline intensifying the whiteness of the surrounding skin. Shifting herself, Jonella smiled her sexiest smile and shook her springy, nondescript brown curls. She took his arm. Her gesture was part of the ritual—a stage before the heavier making-out.

Her tongue flicked against the fang like a serpent tasting its prey.

"Jesus, that feels good," said Mance.

She sucked gently at his skin, raising goose bumps all the way to his shoulder. He lowered his face and softly kissed her cheek.

"Hey, it's my turn," he followed. "Let me have the rose."

She shivered again and raised her head.

"Don't you think it's cold?" she said.

The scowl on her pretty face meant one thing to Mance: nothing more would happen until he had obeyed her veiled demand.

"Damn it, Johnnie, you do something like this every time." Frustrated, he pushed to his feet.

"I brought a blanket," he added, hoping to assuage her.

"It's not enough. Start a fire. Please."

He threw up his hands. Frustration edged into anger.

"OK, but I'm telling you. One of these days we're gonna burn this old firetrap to the ground."

He located a crowbar—their protection against intruders, he

9

claimed — near their stash of supplies: a six-pack of Rebel beer, a bag of pretzels, and his jam box, and began tearing at one of the walls, removing plaster to get at the narrow strips of lath.

"I don't think it has to be a big fire," she said. "Just enough to take off the chill."

Mance stacked some old newspapers onto the grate and then heaped the strips of wood on top of the paper and lit the small pile with a cigarette lighter.

"Did you hear that scratching sound?" Jonella whispered.

"It's Sting," said Mance. "He's probably hungry and thirsty."

Shaking back his long brown hair, the young man lifted a white rat by the tail and set it in front of the flames. The rodent, squeaking in rapid beats, promptly raised itself on its back legs and sniffed the smoky air.

"I don't think it was Sting," said Jonella. She had removed her coat, and Mance was disappointed and not a little irritated that she had stopped there.

"Of course it was. Here, look, you feed him junk and he'll stop fussin'. Watch."

Into a grimy saucer he placed a pretzel and then poured a third of a beer around it. The rodent immediately ceased its tiny racket and plunged into the snack.

"I just don't think it was Sting," Jonella mused as she studied the shadow-strewn wall behind her.

"Who was it then — Jason or ole razor-fingered Freddy?"

"No. I think maybe it was 'Eleanor'."

" 'Eleanor'?"

Mance continued building the fire; he didn't like her other-worldly tone of voice — it definitely sent out the wrong vibrations when he had his heart set on kissing her rose.

"Something tells me that was her name. You know, the woman I've always imagined staying in the upstairs bedroom. She was very sad. Something tells me she was very unhappy. But I don't know why. I call her 'Eleanor' because that was the name of the woman in that old paperback your Uncle Thestis gave me to read. I think the title was *The Haunting of Hill House,* and it was written by some woman."

"All of Uncle T.'s books are strange."

" 'And whatever walks there walks alone,' " said Jonella, moving her fingers to animate the wall with new shadows.

"What the hell are you talking about?"

Mance was trying to get a rein on his frustration as he stoked the fire. Sting munched contentedly on the pretzel and lapped at the beer. The wall above the fireplace creaked and popped.

"About the ghost," Jonella replied absently, "or . . . or whatever caused Eleanor to drive her car into that tree at the end of the story and kill herself."

"You shouldn't read books like that."

Mance noticed that she was wearing her black sweater, his favorite, and while it hugged her body deliciously, it also concealed the rose.

"Such a sad woman. The Guillo House woman, I mean," she murmured. "Do you think we'll ever know her story?"

"Will I ever get to kiss the rose? Got a pretty good fire going."

Jonella brightened. And in one swift motion she tugged herself free of the sweater and smiled at him, and the glow of the fire seemed to burnish and bronze her skin. And there was the rose—a tattoo about the size of a quarter—resting innocently just above her left breast. A lesbian friend of Sparrow, the Vietnam vet who ran the pawnshop and soup kitchen downtown, had been the tattooer for both the fang and the rose, and she, in the judgment of Mance and Jonella at least, had created works of art.

At the sight of Jonella's breasts, Mance went to his knees and shuffled toward her.

"Would you look at this, Sting," he said. "This is our woman."

An erection bulged his jeans. He reached out to cup her left breast, and then he began to angle his lips down at the rose. But his lips never met skin. A whoosh and thrum filled the air; a loud clatter traced across the roof just above them. Jonella shrieked and covered her breasts. Syncopated cooing sounds filtered down from the ceiling like a heavy fall of dust.

Mance wheeled around; Sting circled his saucer nervously.

"What was *that*?" said Jonella breathlessly.

"Pigeons," Mance returned, a little shaken himself and not

11

completely certain he was correct. "The fire probably excited them. Maybe I got it too hot. Better let it burn down," he added, turning to glance at the flames, which were already diminishing.

"I'm sorry, Mance, but I just don't think I'm in the mood for this." Jonella pulled on her sweater and ran a hand through her hair.

"Aw, damn, Johnnie, come on."

"My mind's not on it."

"The pigeons have flown off . . . they won't make any more noise."

"It's not the pigeons or nothing like that."

He edged closer to her and tried to hold her hand. She jerked it away.

"Why'd you have to quit?" she said, her jaw assuming a hard line.

"Quit? Quit what? Oh . . . oh, I see what it is. You're still upset about me quitting school. Well, that's tough, because I'm sixteen, and in Alabama I can quit school and I did because it was useless and boring as hell and I'm glad I quit. So's now I can work more hours and we'll have money one of these days to get married."

"I don't think you should have quit and neither does your Uncle Thestis."

"Johnnie, it's none of Uncle T.'s goddamn business what I do. He can sit up there in his hole of a room with his silver cup and his jars of marbles and all those old stinking magazines that are rotting and he can rot right along with them for all I care. The weird ole fart."

Jonella seemed mildly shocked and resolutely angered.

"You told me once that your Uncle Thestis was the best friend you'd ever had, and I think it's a crying shame you've let something like this come between you. You know how important he thinks a good education is. You've disappointed your parents, too."

"My parents?" Mance felt his anger heating up while the fire in the fireplace — and in his jeans — continued to dwindle. Sting, unnerved by the tenor of their exchange, climbed up his master's arm and sought refuge beneath his long hair. "Are

12

you serious? My parents haven't cared what I did for a long time. Not since . . ."

"Not since Karen was killed? I know. I've noticed that. Your Uncle Thestis has, too. Your big sister must have meant an awful lot to them."

"Her death turned them into zombies," Mance said, his tone bitter. "You wanna know how pathetic they've become? Right before Karen's car accident they had this trip all planned to the Great Smoky National Park up in Tennessee—it was supposed to be the honeymoon they couldn't afford to take when they first got married. Well, they still haven't taken it. Claim they can't leave Scarlett's—as if their nothing of a restaurant would fold up without them around for a few days. They're going to decay and die just like this whole fucking town—they don't give a shit what happens to me or anything else."

"I don't think that's true. They know that if you don't finish school, you'll never get a decent job."

Mance freed one of the beers, popped the top angrily, and listened to the dusty echo of her words before taking a sip. Guillo House was locked in a crouching silence. The fire burned low.

"I've a got a decent job—couple of them, in fact, and you know it. Loading trucks at the beer warehouse is good money, and if Boom—your son-of-a-bitch of a brother-in-law—would get them to bend the rules down there, I could drive one of the trucks this summer. I pick up a little work at Austin's furniture store and at Fast Track's lounge—I make as much as some guys who're supporting a family. And you're earning money, too."

Jonella shook her head and looked squarely into his eyes.

"I'm not going to work as a waitress in your parents' restaurant for the rest of my life. Mance, you and I deserve better than fly-by-night jobs. It would be just like Tanya and Boom. I see what they have. It's nothing. I don't want to end up like them."

"Maybe I'll join the army," said Mance, scooting around so that he could lean his head against the wall. He heard Sting's protest and then glanced again at the dying fire. "Be all that I can be. They have training programs."

13

"Join the army and be another Sparrow?" said Jonella, incredulous.

Slamming his beer down, Mance spoke through gritted teeth.

"Sparrow's the way he is 'cause he got sprayed with Agent Orange over in Vietnam. There's no wars these days 'cept safe little bombing missions over deserts. The army would be safer than walking the streets of Soldier at night."

His anger relented a notch. Neither spoke for a few moments. The scratchings and skitterings of Guillo House seemed to inch closer.

"Here's the thing, Johnnie—we gotta get outta this town. It's bad for people. Look what it did to Punch. He was the best black policeman Soldier's ever had and the town was ready to string him up by the balls for something I'd swear he was never involved with."

"I think maybe that was racial," said Jonella.

"But that's my point—Soldier's got no respect for people. It's like . . . it's like a big, ugly wound that never heals."

They fell silent again, and the walls of Guillo House shifted and moaned, and downstairs a hunk of plaster thudded to the floor, and beyond them, somewhere among the many dark and empty rooms, they heard a faint growl.

Jonella stood up and put on her coat; her eyes registered exhaustion and a touch of fear.

"Some of us have another school week ahead of us tomorrow, and I have to stop by Scarlett's and pick up my check. Tanya buys groceries on Monday."

Mance reluctantly nodded, but his attention was drawn to a darkness calling through the years of secret emptiness which Guillo House had jealously guarded.

2

Mance followed Jonella down the dust-laden stairs, the beam of his flashlight spilling over a broken spoke or two in the banister and through the thick accumulation of cobwebs. In the foyer they carefully avoided a missing floorboard.

14

"Do you think the fire was all the way out?" she asked, turning to look up at the second floor as if she expected to see flames licking at the doorway to their special room.

" 'Fraid so," he groaned.

She jabbed at his ribs.

"I mean the one in the fireplace."

"Yeah, and I left our pretzels and beer for the ghosts."

"You're wasting money."

"No, I'm not. I get all our goodies and all our beer from the warehouse—what you call *gratis* if you work the four-to-midnight shift."

"Stealing's what you mean."

Mance chuckled despite a lingering residue of anger and frustration.

As they walked away from Guillo House, he glanced back at the once imposing residence and wondered, vaguely, whether Jonella's theory of a sad and possibly crazy woman inhabiting the old abode could be true. And the thought gave him a slight shiver.

"Did you know that Uncle T. hates that place?" he said.

"Yes," she replied, "but he's never told me why. Maybe you should ask him?"

Jonella was not, apparently, going to let the rift between him and his uncle remain a closed issue; but Mance had no inclination at the moment to pursue it further. He gave the old mansion one last glance: Guillo House was situated in an aging neighborhood of sprawling two-story structures, several vacant, some having been converted to boardinghouses or apartments, while others remained in the hands of an elderly couple or perhaps an elderly widower. The street was Chrokinole Street, which angled into North Street, once the town's main drag, but now only a ghost of its former self.

At the merging of Chrokinole and North stood Scarlett's, a hulking, two-story frame building of no particular attractiveness, complemented somewhat by pseudo-Greek columns to create an antebellum facade. Mance could see by the parking lot that business late that Sunday night was slow.

In the two blocks from Guillo House to Scarlett's he and Jonella had not exchanged a word. Sting, so it appeared, had fallen asleep—beer always made him drowsy. Inside the restaurant, the temperature was only slightly warmer than the January night.

"Hey, sweetheart, how you?"

Mance saw how easily his mother smiled at Jonella from behind the cash register, but he saw in that smile just how cosmetic it was, concealing a raging sadness beneath it.

"Hey, Mom, you look tired," said Jonella. "You have much business after the lunch shift?"

"Oh, a piddling of folks. Some reg'lars for dinner, don't you know." She paused to arch her eyebrows and wrinkle her nose as if she smelled something disagreeable. Then she whispered, "Truth is, we're fixin' to close up a might early. Mance's daddy has a back actin' up on him again."

"Has he seen a doctor about it?" said Jonella.

"That man see a doctor? Oh, when mules sing in the choir at the Sunday service, he might. Don't believe he's seen a doctor but oncet or twicet in his life."

Mance had to admit that he enjoyed seeing the relationship that had developed between his mother and Jonella, how Jonella called her "Mom" and how sometimes they chattered together like schoolgirls.

"A vacation to the Smokies would help that back," said Mance, probing not so tenderly at an old sore spot.

But his mother instantly shooed at him as if the suggestion were absurd. Then the woman directed her attention at Jonella.

"I'm 'specting you came by for your check, didn't you, sweetheart?"

"Yes, ma'am, if it wouldn't be no trouble."

"Goodness, no. I have it right here somewhere jist waitin' for you."

Out of the corner of her eye she noticed that Mance was leaning impatiently toward the dining area. He had set his jam box by the counter. "Uncle Thestis asked ta 'bout you today," she said to him. "He's losing ground, it seems to me. So blue, don't you know. Would be a tonic to him if you was to visit to him . . . and, you know, talk 'bout things."

Her voice trailed off and she busied herself searching for

Jonella's check amidst the chaos of the register counter. Without a word, Mance turned and met Vivien Leigh's stare. It was slanting down at him from her portrait above the fake fireplace and mantel—she was all in all Scarlett O'Hara and that fire and determination in her eyes had once been in his mother's eyes and, occasionally, he saw it in Jonella's. Perhaps it was the legacy of every southern woman. Certainly that look of "I will" had been in his Aunt Rosamond's piercing glare when forty years ago she had opened Scarlett's and nurtured it as a shrine to her all-time favorite movie, *Gone With the Wind*.

Everywhere one looked, photos, drawings, memorabilia of every sort imaginable met one's gaze, including a first edition copy of Margaret Mitchell's legendary bestseller that was proudly displayed on the fake mantel. Rhett and Ashley and Melanie lurked in every nook and cranny of the restaurant and on a far wall the Culleys had commissioned Tanya to paint a mural of Tara replete with Gerald O'Hara galloping forth on his white steed and Scarlett in the shade of a massive oak surrounded by beaus, while Mammy shot daggers of reproach at her from an upstairs window.

Scarlett haunted the restaurant—its colors, texture, its ambience. Or perhaps the real ghost was Aunt Rosamond, for this was the temple of her familiar and had remained so until her death in the late fifties, at which point her brother, Thestis, had become owner and manager. In the early sixties, the restaurant had suffered under his management, and he had agreed to sell it to Royal Culley and his wife, Clarene, with the understanding that he, Thestis, be allowed to occupy one of the upstairs rooms as his living quarters until such time as the gods removed him to Valhalla.

While the history of the place might not have been of interest to Mance, its future was, and that future seemed bleak. The glory days of Scarlett's had passed, and he knew it and assumed that in their own way so did his parents. Passing the buffet, he sniffed at the offerings—only the fried okra caused his mouth to water. He noted, disappointedly, that all the barbecue was gone. On weekends his dad would call upon a black man by the name of Slow Eddie to come in and prepare big vats of barbecued ribs. Continuing on into the kitchen, Mance discovered a stray rib or two; Slow Eddie fed him a toothless grin. And then Mance's dad slipped in from the back, his face sweaty and laced with pain.

"I heard your back's hurting you again," said Mance.

Royal Culley scraped at the central grill with a metal spatula.

"I'll live," he mumbled.

"That's debatable," said Mance, instantly regretting the words, wishing instead that he had shown some compassion. Or, better yet, that the man would say something, *anything*, about his quitting school.

The distance between them seemed greater than ever.

Mance finished the ribs, licked his fingers, and headed back to collect Jonella. They said good night to his mother and pressed out into the darkness, Mance hesitating at the front door to pick at a fresh onslaught of dry rot in the clapboard siding.

"This dump isn't in much better shape than Guillo House."

Jonella did not respond; they walked in silence down North Street past the courthouse, and at the next corner Jonella stopped and said, "Don't you think you should reconsider quitting? There's a new counselor at school you could talk to." She hunched her shoulders and sighed. "Would you do it for me?"

"Johnnie, damn it . . . no."

She spun away from him and walked off at a rapid pace.

"Hey," he called after her, "don't you want me to walk you home?"

He ran and tugged at her coat, but she pulled away, slapping at his hand.

"Johnnie, why can't you try to see my side of this? You're being a real little bitch, you know that?"

But she was marching on at full clip, and he knew that he would be wasting his breath to say anything more. Tomorrow or the next day or the next, he assured himself, they would make up.

The hurly-burly had awakened Sting; he nosed around to Mance's throat. Mance cradled him in front of his face and the rodent's red eyes caught the amber of the sodium streetlamps.

18

"Sometimes I hate to admit this my friend," he said, "but I love that woman. Damn . . . I really do."

3

Mance felt empty as he watched Jonella descend the slope of North Street toward the railroad tracks. Since it was a Sunday night, the streets, not surprisingly, were deserted; there was no traffic; even the blinking yellow caution light had extinguished itself — or had vandalism claimed another victim? Jonella would, in two blocks, reach the railroad tracks, then continue on for another several blocks as North Street gained elevation near the Rebel Beer warehouse; eventually she would reach an uninviting-looking trailer park where she occupied a double-wide with her stepsister, Tanya, Tanya's husband, Boom, and their two children.

Across the street to the left of Jonella's path, the white-washed building housing Austin's Used Furniture caught Mance's attention; through the front window he could see a nimbus of light issuing from the rear where Mr. Austin would, no doubt, be settled into an overstuffed chair in his "reading room," curled up with a good book — probably one of the classics. Next door, orange neon scripted out the words Fast Track's, with the visual suggestion that the letters were racing across the night. Neon ads for Miller, Budweiser, and Rebel beers hung in the front window like misshapen puzzle pieces. Inside, Fast Track himself would be singing and wiping down the surface of the bar while his coterie of regular customers, most aging black men like himself, would be playing dominoes or nursing hours-old drinks. And Fast Track's son, Punch, would likely be at a table by himself and in his cups. Past the next two buildings, both abandoned, was Sparrow's pawnshop and soup kitchen; there were no lights, but Mance knew that if one were to knock on the front door, Sparrow's scruffy face and half-maniacal eyes would soon appear to welcome you.

"Come in before the bastards get ya," he would likely say, or possibly something incomprehensible.

Beyond Jonella to the right, at the distant corner before the

19

street crossed the railroad tracks, sat a scab of a building the first floor of which housed the Soldier Holiness Temple, an all-black church where even at that hour gospel songs and a fiery sermon were being belted out and Satan was being held at bay.

This was Mance's world: home for the beggared, broke, destitute, dirt poor, don't-give-a-damns, fortuneless, impecunious, impoverished, indigent, low, needy, penurious, and poverty-stricken, strapped, and unprosperous. But not dreamless. Furthermore, Mance knew that the denizens of North Street were his friends. He knew that he could carry his crippled heart to any one of those doors and someone would listen to his tale of love and woe.

"Sting, you know anything about women?" he joked with the rat before the critter crawled back into its den on Mance's shoulder. "I need advice. I'm hurting, friend."

And he was.

Jonella was nearing the bottom of the street, and his only urge was to run after her and tell her how much he hated it when they fought, how close the great fabric of life came to unraveling when they hadn't shared a good night kiss.

"Damn it," he whispered. "Try to understand me, Johnnie."

With that, he turned from North Street onto Jefferson Davis, another dimly lit and unpromising street clustered with buildings that resembled tombstones, gutters filled with wind-blown trash, and parking slots occupied by a number of abandoned cars. Mance thought about the rose and Jonella's breasts and how she was defiantly holding out to retain her virginity until they were married. And his erection returned, and the notion of her virginity seemed hopelessly old-fashioned, but it was among the many trivial things that made him care so much for her, care beyond their differences—that she was all thought and intuition and he was all feeling and sensation.

Up ahead, a pair of stray dogs beat night tracks in a hustling, scavenging lope, starved, probably mean, and utterly on their own. Mance found himself watching them and identifying with them. Life handed some people an empty plate with no guidebook for putting food on it.

"I'll live," he whispered to himself, then inwardly cringed

20

at hearing an echo of his dad's earlier words.

The strays had picked up his scent. Ears pricked, they momentarily halted their foraging and gave him the once-over. Hands jammed into his pockets, Mance strolled along fantasizing about how it would be that first time—that first time making no-stops love to Jonella. God, it would be good. The thought of losing that chance stung him, numbing his senses, sending an arrow of regret down his spine. He paused to kick at a beer can and to muse on the cosmic reality of how the fates occasionally ganged up on a guy to kick him figuratively in the balls.

Something had roused Sting.

He was suddenly squeaking off signals of alarm like a smoke detector. Mance looked around. No one in sight. Nothing moving except the strays.

"Don't shit on my shoulder," he warned the rodent. "What's your problem anyway?"

One of the dogs stepped into a pool of light. It was a plain white pit bull, heavily muscled in the shoulders despite showing a washboarding of ribs. The animal growled low; Sting danced a feverish jig behind Mance's right ear. Then Mance slowly turned. Behind him the other stray, a matching pit bull except for a splotching of black, had taken root on the sidewalk.

Breath caught high in Mance's chest.

The dogs were trying to corner him, their bodies stiffened, tight, as if wound, ready to spring into action.

Don't show them you're scared.

Mance reasoned that whoever once upon a time had first offered that advice had probably never been stalked by pit bulls that looked as if they hadn't eaten in three, four days.

He decided to bluff his would-be attackers.

"Hey!" he suddenly shouted, flapping his arms as menacingly as possible and stomping the heel of his boot. "Get the fuck outta here!"

The pit bull to his left took a tentative step backward and growled thickly; the other one, however, held its ground. Mance looked over his shoulder into a grassy alley between two vacant buildings, surveying his chances for survival. The

21

more aggressive dog to his right charged a few feet and barked a throaty, blood-on-its-mind bark and followed it with a long, low, very serious growl.

"Oh, shit," said Mance.

In the shadows at the end of the alley was a city trash dumpster half the size of a pickup truck, but Mance couldn't see whether its cover was open or closed. *Be open or I'm dog meat.* He was scared and being scared torched his anger, and yet he had no weapon to protect himself. By the dumpster there appeared to be a heap of broken bricks . . . and it occurred to him—one of those crazy, boyishly heroic thoughts—that he was glad the pit bulls had chosen to stalk him rather than Jonella.

He tensed his body for flight.

A long string of foamy saliva dripped from the mouth of the dog to his left. The other dog wore a mask of featureless insanity—there was a deadly space between its eyes. The animal gave every indication that at any moment it could launch itself at his throat.

So he mentally coached his escape: *ready, set* . . .

He pumped his arms and knees, his boots slipping ever so slightly on the grassy surface. His running fired a furious round of barking. He could feel the dogs at his heels as he closed in on the dumpster. Twenty yards to it. Ten. Five. He slowed to dive over the lip of his redeemer.

Be open, goddammit.

It was.

But he crashed through a miasma rising from putrescent accumulated trash, stagnant rainwater, soggy, discarded clothing reeking of oil or gas or worse, and the squishy, smelly remains of a dead cat. Mance nearly gagged, and yet the snapping jaws of the pit bulls stayed safely at the edge of the dumpster.

"Yeah, go to hell!" he screamed at them.

Then he noticed that the back of one pantleg had been ripped; one of the dogs had missed dicing up his leg by a fraction of an inch. And suddenly he noticed one thing more: Sting had leaped from his shoulder to the rim of the dumpster. Hardly had a shout of protest risen to Mance's lips before the rodent, disoriented by fear, cast its fate to the shadows

22

of the alley. The dogs, naturally enough, gave chase.

Mance climbed awkwardly out, slipped, fell hard on his bottom, swore, and saw a blur of white shuttling along the edge of a building, dogs in hot pursuit.

"Beat it, Sting!"

And the frightened rodent did, easily losing the canine chasers, both of which, after a brief but frantic search for their prey, returned their attention to Mance—who felt naked and rather foolish except that he was standing near a pile of bricks. He loaded his hands, stood his ground, and waited for their next move. He figured he had two chances: one, they would attack together, which would spell disaster for him; or two, they would attack one at a time, thus giving him a prayer.

He got lucky—for the second time, he had to admit.

"Try some of this!" he yelled as the one to his right charged. He threw the brick with all the strength he could muster; it wasn't a direct hit, but it landed squarely enough against the dog's shoulder that the animal spun around and began to yelp as if in its death throes. It tore away from Mance, its cries apparently so terrifying to its companion that both dogs were soon streaking west on Jefferson Davis Avenue.

Mance was trembling so violently that he sat down in the alley and buried his face in his hands until he could get a grip on his emotions. Then he began to look for Sting.

4

Jonella had been several blocks away when she heard the barking and the shouts; she gave no special consideration to them at first, for she had entered a labyrinth of thought, a dark and twisting realm in which her desire for a seashells-and-balloons relationship with Mance led her deeper and deeper into confusion.

He needs to grow up.

There was no escaping that conclusion. He was stubborn, she admitted, and he was no more ready to get married than earth was to collide with heaven. Quitting school was symptomatic of his immaturity in so many ways, and it had been a purely insensitive act for him to toss aside his long-standing friendship with his Uncle Thestis. What would Mance ever amount to? What kind of provider could he be?

But I love him.

And that admission hit her like a fist of thorns.

She slowed, and thought a moment about going to him, confessing her love despite being resolutely put out by him. The labyrinth of thought overwhelmed her; she leaned against the corner of the nearest building to compose herself. She didn't see the black pickup parked under the overpass bridge a half a block away to her left. The easy, rolling strains of gospel music drifted out over her—the Soldier Holiness Temple had popped its cork and the music was flowing.

Jonella sighed, unable to avoid a wave of self-pity.

She thought of Tanya—*at least Mance isn't mean like Boom*—and she began to anticipate what she would find when she reached the trailer. Would Tanya have locked herself and her two little girls in the bathroom again? Would Boom be sitting on the sofa, watching TV, brooding darkly, smoking, drinking, stoking the volcano of his abusiveness? Would Tanya have bruises tonight? Or would everything be sweetness and light?

Why doesn't she stand up to him?

Why doesn't she leave him?

In the distance there was yelling; a dog cried as if it had been shot.

Jonella thought of her mother.

Tanya doesn't leave Boom because some women are spineless.

Like Momma. God rest her soul. The woman had ricocheted from one man to another like a bullet that never accurately struck its target. Had those failings at love driven the woman over the brink, or had schizophrenia precipitated her disastrous romantic forays?

The yelping of the dog penetrated Jonella's thoughts, forming yet another link with her mother, who, in her waning days, would often look up from her sewing or some other domestic chore and ask Jonella to quiet the dog barking beyond the window—when no dog was in sight. Such an essentially inno-

24

cent form of neurosis would have been tolerable, but her mother's affliction gradually reached a deeper level. One day she began to hear voices speaking to her from the neighbor's dog or from any mangy mutt that happened to cross her path.

"They tell me things, Jonella. Secret things. Things I must never tell another soul, and I have so many secrets in my head I'm afraid it will explode. Do you think my head is swelling up? Will my brain start leaking out my nose?"

One day apparently it did. They took her away. And she wasted into nothingness in a hospital.

Please, God, don't let me ever get like Momma.

Out of the corner of her eye she could see the black pickup easing into the intersection.

I want Mance and me to have a good life together.

The singing escalated. Jonella pushed away from the corner and strode toward the railroad tracks; the pickup approached, but she chose to ignore it.

Until it blocked her path.

There were two young men, white, with dark beards and baseball caps and big, ear-to-ear grins on their faces and a vaulting glee in their eyes. Jonella started to step around behind the truck when the driver backed up. The young man on the shotgun side rolled down his window.

"Need a ride, sugar?"

She shook her head only slightly and headed around the front fender; the driver performed another blocking maneuver, and she felt a tiny, ice-cold snake of fear squirm in her bowels. At the same time, she was angered, a throat-tightening anger.

"My buddy here needs company tonight, sugar. Had a blow up with his woman, and I sorta promised I'd find us a woman for the both of us. You're on the young side, but hell, you look good to me—don't she look good to you . . . ?"

When he turned to address the driver, Jonella ran toward the door of the Holiness Temple. Behind her the truck roared into gear, and its headlights sprayed across her. She pulled on the doorknob and found—*God, please no, this can't be*—it was locked.

Bouncing over the curb and virtually pinning her against the plate glass window of the temple, the truck clattered and growled.

"Them niggers don't want you, sugar—not like we want you. You come on and get in with us—just let's have us some fun is all we want."

With surprising quickness, the two men jumped out.

"My boyfriend's coming to pick me up," she said, and wondered to herself why she had offered such a stupid, naive remark.

"We'll get you ready for him," one of them said. She couldn't tell which, for they had become faceless, moving shadows. The cold snake of fear in her bowels threatened to sink its fangs into her. One of the men must have had heel taps on his boots because she heard a muted scraping and then the grip of a callused hand on her wrist as they tried to drag her into the truck. She spun away, fell, got to her feet, and scrambled a few frantic yards before one of them tangled his fingers in her hair and yanked hard.

She saw stars and cried out. The other one positioned himself in front of her and drove a fist into her stomach. She doubled over, crippled by pain and loss of breath. Her knees gave way. She was shoved and pushed and dragged through the doorway of a defunct business establishment—it had been known as Your Hidden Beauty Salon—and into a dark and dusty room.

Gasping for breath, she pleaded, "Please . . . don't . . . do . . . this."

She heard them panting and chuckling excitedly, and then she issued the start of a long, desperate scream for help. It, however, gained little momentum before a fist hammered into her jaw, breaking two back teeth; her head snapped to one side. She saw winking points of light similar to the ones her mother used to place on their hapless Christmas tree.

The cold snake of fear was striking viciously.

And then she felt her body going limp. Consciousness swirling away.

Fingers and a knife tearing and cutting away at her jeans.

* * *

26

"Come on, Sting. Hey, ole friend, where are you? Dogs are gone."

Mance surveyed the area closely in case his attackers might have a mind to return and finish their business. He was still trembling slightly from the episode. *What kind of a fucking town is this that has wild dogs running loose in the streets?* Well, it was Soldier, Alabama. Things could have been worse. He had been lucky. But had he not been calling for his frightened rat, he might have heard a muffled scream rising from Your Hidden Beauty Salon; so might have any member of the congregation of the Soldier Holiness Temple, but they were singing the second chorus of the invitation hymn, and folks right and left were being attacked by the holy spirit. Amen and praise the Lord.

"There you are," said Mance, suddenly locating the fiery dots of Sting's eyes beaming out from a hole in one of the derelict foundations. He lifted the rat onto his shoulder and glanced around again for any sign of the dogs.

"Let's you and me head home. This has been quite a night, huh?"

Chapter Two

1

Mance's dream reeled on lucidly; he was in the alley off Jefferson Davis once again and he was searching for Sting, calling out the rat's name as he looked along the foundations of the lost to shame buildings. Something stirred within one of them; the ground quaked around him, and suddenly he could see Sting, or at least his huge red, glowing eyes, eyes the size of billiard balls—the outline of the rat ghosting through the holes in the foundation indicated that he had grown to the size of a Great Dane. Even more peculiar and unsettling, Sting was *talking*, at first in no intelligible language, then gradually in something like English. Rat English?

Mance was amazed.

When his mother knocked on his door, he shook himself from the web of the dream with difficulty. His light came on. He rolled over and saw that Sting was in his cage, nose stuffed into his nest of excelsior and rags. Mance felt relieved.

"Mance? Mance, honey, are you awake?"

The dream released him, and he blinked at the harsh light.

"Mom, it's not my day to work early anywhere."

"I'm aware of that. I am. But . . ."

She had slipped quietly into his room, closing the door and leaning against it as if she needed support. She was wearing a faded pink housecoat and was clutching nervously at the collars of it.

"I need some more sleep, Mom. What do you want?"

The woman took a deep breath; one hand jerked spastically toward her face.

"There's trouble," she said, no energy in her voice. "Bad trouble."

Instantly alarmed, Mance threw his covers off and sat on the edge of the bed; his mother was usually cryptic like this when there were health problems or an accident.

"Is it Daddy?"

"No," she said. "No, he's some better, I think."

Mance cleared his throat; there were lines of shock and fear in his mother's face he'd never seen before. Impatience seeped into his tone.

"Would you go on and tell me what it is? You're acting strange."

She batted her eyelashes and gathered herself.

"It's Jonella. She's in the hospital. She's been . . . *attacked*." Her emphasis upon the final word was punctuated by the bulging of her eyes, but for Mance the word seemed to be in a foreign tongue—Rat English?—and it held no meaning for him.

"Attacked?" he whispered, glancing down at the floor, puzzled. Then he looked up at his mother. "Attacked? What do you . . . she's in the hospital? What do you mean?"

Tears had started to trickle down his mother's cheeks.

"She's in sorry shape. Our sweetheart, Jonella. That's according to Tanya. She jist called."

"God damn it, Mom, what happened to her?"

The woman flinched.

"Don't curse at me, Mance. I'm upset enough as it is. Do *not* curse at me, please."

Mance was up pulling on his jeans and boots—*the dogs*—that had to be it. The pit bulls had attacked Jonella. *Jesus, no.*

"It's these times, son," his mother exclaimed. Her fingers were tugging at her collars again. "You read about it nowadays, but you think—no, it won't never happen to me or nobody I know and love—but it has."

Suddenly Mance realized that she wasn't talking about a dog attack; he felt the skin on his forearms tingle.

"Mom?"

29

The woman momentarily choked as if she were trying to down a large piece of Sting's nest.

"I'm trying to say it." Her eyes pleaded with him. "Jonella, she's been . . . raped."

The word twisted her face as if it were fresh dough, rearranging the muscles, tendons, and cartilage, and delivering a heat which appeared to singe her skin and scorch her tongue.

A bubble of disbelief closed around Mance: For a moment, he felt as if he had forgotten how to breathe or how to walk. He stumbled forward. His mother said something—more foreign terms. A heavy, cold lump of anger had lodged itself near his heart. His fingers were so numb he could barely button his jeans.

"I'm taking the van," he said, pushing past her, her hands fluttering helplessly. Out in the hall he saw a block of shadow, the figure of a round mole of a man in a robe. As light sliced from his room into the hall, Mance focused upon his Uncle Thestis; sorrow patched over the man's eyes as he watched the predawn scene unfold.

Mance's mother whispered something to Uncle Thestis as Mance thundered down the stairs and through the kitchen, where he became vaguely aware of his dad preparing for another day at Scarlett's. But the two of them didn't exchange a word.

Keys wrested from their customary hook, Mance climbed into the dirty gray van, which, in better times, they had used for catering. It coughed to life, and the cold lump of anger near his heart seemed to be growing, sending sharp pains across his chest. Out on Soldier Road, he sped toward the Catlin County Medical Center between Soldier and Goldsmith. Traffic being light, he ripped through yellow lights and one red one and ignored the speed limit entirely.

Johnnie. Johnnie's hurt.

It was beginning to sink in. All of the horrible ramifications began to parade through his mind despite his lingering unwillingness to believe.

This couldn't have happened to Johnnie.

He felt the first vibration of the physical and emotional pain she must be experiencing. He gritted his teeth and pounded on the steering wheel. More than anything else in the world he wanted to hold her in his arms and exorcise the demons of her nightmare.

If . . . if they hadn't fought . . . if . . . if he had walked her home . . . if . . . if he hadn't quit school . . . if . . . sweet Johnnie . . . sweet Johnnie.

2

In the clean and shining waiting room, eerily quiet except for the occasional paging of a doctor, Tanya greeted him.

"Oh, Mance, I'm so sorry. Just so sorry I can't know what to say."

She threw herself against him and he reflexively held her, smelling the perfume that had smelled so good on Jonella last night, but that now was much too pungent.

Tanya sobbed.

"Where is she?" said Mance as he began immediately to unwrap himself from her embrace. "I gotta see her."

He looked beyond to some chairs where Tanya's two small daughters, Crystal and Loretta, were sitting as soberly and maturely as their young bodies would allow. Crystal, five, was trying to keep Loretta, three, in check, but the younger one was eager to explore this strange new world into which they had been thrust. The girls had their mother's blond hair, blue eyes, and pale skin.

Wiping away tears with her fingers, Tanya stood back from him and forced a ridiculous smile.

"The po-lice and a doctor—two different doctors really— been in and out to see her. And this nice lady officer, she's black, but she's nice—she's talked to her. She, you know, this lady officer, *specializes* in helping women deal with, with . . . what Jonella's gone through. I think everybody's trying to take real good care of her, Mance. They really are."

"I got to see her," he said. "I got to see Johnnie." His words seeming to echo as if they hadn't come out of his mouth.

"Well, they told me—they said: she's resting fine and recovering and needs rest and time for the bruises and things to

31

heal. Her jaw's pert ner't broken and her whole face . . . she's probably not gone be so pretty to you right this minute."

"Where'd this happen? Who found her?"

"Down by the tracks. And nobody found her. We's all sleeping, you know, and sometimes I hear Jonella come in if she's been out late. She has her own key so's she can come and go as she pleases. Well, middle of the night, I hear somebody fumbling and pawing at the door, and Boom, he's dead to the world asleep and I definitely didn't want to wake him if I didn't have to, so I went to the door, and Jonella, she just sorta fell in on the rug crying and told me she had to go to the hospital. When I got her inside and over by a light, I could see she'd been beat up bad and her clothes, they was all tore—and I think I knew right away what'd happened and it like to broke my heart on the spot."

Mance paused to imagine the scene, and Tanya turned to shush at the girls, and when her shushing received little response, she dug into her purse and said, "You girls want a candy so's you can have something to occupy you?"

They did. Tanya gave some change to Crystal and directed her to a vending machine against the opposite wall of the waiting area.

"Boom's here, too," she explained to Mance. "He's in the men's room."

"Did Johnnie get a good look at the guy?" said Mance, his fists clenching and unclenching.

Tanya looked up at him, surprised, it appeared, that he knew so few details.

"God damn it, I'll get the bastard that did this. Did she recognize him?"

Tanya's mouth drew up into a peach pit.

"There was *two* of 'em," she said.

That revelation left Mance in too much of a daze even to notice Boom entering the area.

"Helluva shame, boy. Life can be a royal shit pile sometimes, can't it?"

Mance felt long bony fingers on his shoulder. Boom was tall and angular and smelled of smoke; his black hair was slicked back and greasy like a juvenile delinquent from the fifties. He had hollow cheeks and thin lips and a protruding brow over dark eyes that seemed to be dilated most of the time.

He leaned closer to Mance and added, "Women got to learn about certain kinds of men," he said.

Pulling away from his grasp, Mance said, "What do you mean by that?"

He had never cared much for Boom, so it took only the slightest provocation for him to feel something like hate toward the man. At that moment, he would have loved to smash a fist into his face—into *somebody's* face.

"He don't mean nothing by it," said Tanya.

Boom reached out and locked his wife's arm behind her back, then shoved her so hard that she nearly fell to the floor.

"Shut your bitch mouth," he exclaimed, pointing a finger at her as she stumbled away from him. "If I need your help to talk, I'll give you a kick in the ass and you'll know. Till then, keep your shithole shut. Y'hear me? Tend to those damn kids—one's got chocolate all over hell."

Mance stepped away to gain control of his anger. A nurse ducked her head into the waiting area to check on the commotion. Boom gestured that everything was fine, and then he sidled over to Mance.

"What I'm saying is—sometimes women have a way of getting men they don't know—strangers, you know—of getting them excited. Hell, boy, things like this—my opinion is women bring it on themselves, and my advice to you is to put that girl of yours on a short leash and don't let her go walking out by herself at night. You can't trust her."

Mance wheeled to face him; mentally he had to restrain himself from planting his fist in the dark cavity that passed for Boom's mouth.

"I don't care about your opinion, and I don't need your god damn advice."

He wished that he had sounded tougher, more defiant, but most of his energy and concentration were directed to Jonella and her condition—and to retribution for what had been done to her.

"OK, smart boy," said Boom, smiling, raising his hands

33

palms up and backing away. "Just trying to help you out. I *know* how to handle women."

Mance found a chair, sat down, and dropped his face into his hands. Across the room Boom and Tanya began to argue; one of the little girls was crying. Wearily, Mance looked up in time to see Boom viciously twisting Tanya's arm; the scene began to take on an air of the surrealistic: the antiseptically clean and colorless area pulsing suddenly with fantastic shapes, balls and spirals of orange and red and velvety blue and deep purple, and he thought he saw the figure of Boom transform into a pit bull, then into something even more savage and beastly.

Mance had taken about as much as he could stand. He sought out the nearest nurse's station.

"Which room is Jonella Withers in?"

A middle-aged woman wearing too much makeup eyeballed him suspiciously.

"Room two-thirteen. But she's not to have visitors just now—young man, I said . . ."

Mance scrambled along the hall, dodging laundry carts heaped with sheets and whisking around an ancient little man who was navigating an inch at a time using a metal walker. His hospital gown had come untied in back, revealing a pale, wrinkled prune of a bottom.

Room 213 seemed to jump out at Mance.

3

In the meager light, he could see an empty bed. In the far corner another bed was surrounded by a gauzy curtain; the bed was occupied.

A nurse appeared behind him at the door, and to her, in a soft voice, he said, "I'm her boyfriend. All I'm gone do is sit here so's she's not by herself. I won't disturb her."

"Are you Mance?"

"Yes, ma'am."

The nurse reluctantly relented: "Well then . . . she's asked for you. I suppose we could allow it."

For a run of indefinite seconds, perhaps a minute or more,

Mance simply stared at the gauzy curtain; shadowed behind it was an apparently sleeping figure. Jonella. His Johnnie. Seeing that shadow, knowing it was the girl he loved, Mance felt the bubble of disbelief burst. The cold lump of anger near his heart heated up rapidly until it began to glow hotly with a hatred beyond anything he had ever felt.

Two of 'em.

They were somewhere out there. And they would have to pay for this. It was the only way.

He took a deep breath and tugged at the curtain. It whispered aside. A small table lamp gave off a weak pool of light, enough to reveal Jonella's bandaged face.

She looked delicate and helpless and somehow diminished.

Emotion squeezed hard at Mance's heart.

"Oh, Johnnie . . . sweet Johnnie," he said, the words barely audible.

Her eyelids fluttered, and for a moment he was afraid he had awakened her. He studied her face; there was an ugly, purpling bruise on her left cheek, and one bandage near the left corner of her mouth and another low on the right side where jaw met throat.

She's tough. She'll make it through this.

The thought materialized, reassuring him to an extent. And yet . . . and yet something had been lost. It was like being in a familiar room and sensing that one piece of furniture is missing, but you can't determine which one it is. Only, no — this was worse because whatever had been lost could not be retrieved.

He stood very close to the end of the bed and glanced down at his hands, hands which appeared to be so useless in combating the evil that had put Jonella in that hospital bed.

"Mance?"

Her eyelids fluttered again, and Mance's legs went watery. He eased around to her side.

"Mance?" she repeated, her voice filled with cotton. She could talk only out of one side of her mouth.

"Yeah, Johnnie, it's me."

She struggled to offer a smile.

"I'm glad you came."

35

"Hey, I'm not really supposed to be in here. The nurse says you need rest, so maybe I better go and let you get some."

She reached a hand toward him.

"Please stay."

He took the hand—it felt clammy and weak, but if it had been possible he would never have released that hand again.

"OK. Not too long. I better hadn't hang around too long."

She moved her lips. Pain wrinkles traced across her forehead.

"I'm thirsty," she said.

"Oh, I'll get the nurse."

She squeezed his hand to stop him.

"On the lampstand. My cup."

The plastic cup had some clear liquid, ice, and a straw. He held it near her mouth and she sucked at the straw.

"What is this?" he asked.

"Sprite, I think. It helps because I don't have any spit."

"Your jaw hurt?"

She nodded.

Then he said, "Sorry . . . you probably don't wanna talk much. Guess it would be too much pressure on your jaw."

Smiling feebly, she gazed off to one side. Suddenly they had become like strangers. Silence claimed the space around them.

Eventually she said, "Did you bring Sting?"

"No. Last night, you see, these two dogs, pit bulls, they . . . oh God, Johnnie, I'm so sorry, so sorry, and God I promise I'll get 'em for this, I'll get 'em, I'll get 'em for this."

At his outburst, her expression darkened. She began to talk as if nothing serious had occurred, nothing more significant than a cold or the flu.

"Looks like I'll miss the English test today," she said. "On *Macbeth*." Between sentences she paused to wet her lips. "I know that play. I studied. I coulda got a good grade."

"Don't worry about it," said Mance. "Don't worry about nothing."

With effort she raised one hand to her hair.

"I bet I look like one of the witches, don't I?"

Before Mance could respond, a nurse clattered into the room and gave her some kind of a pill. Then Tanya tiptoed in to say good-bye—the girls had become too rambunctious to wait around longer, and Boom had to go to work.

When they were alone again, Jonella talked on distractedly about school, trivial stuff—to Mance at least it was. He was holding her hand; she was obviously exhausted, but each time he cautioned her that she should try to sleep, she clung to him almost desperately. In her eyes he could see that she was building to something. In the midst of her description of her plane geometry class she suddenly said, "I can't be no virgin for you no more."

Tears followed, trickling into her bandages.

"No, Johnnie," said Mance, "no, this . . . this doesn't count."

It sounded stupid, but he had no idea what else to say. He felt as if a strong wind were tossing him along like a piece of paper.

The bandage low on her jaw had worked loose; tears were stinging the surface welt. Mance started to press it back into place, but when he saw the marks on her skin he froze. He bent closer to make certain he was seeing what he believed he was seeing.

Jonella self-consciously smoothed the bandage down.

"Mance?"

They were bite marks.

Human teeth had broken and bruised the skin.

Mance wanted to feel a rush of blind anger; instead, he felt that at any second he would burst into tears. And, strangely, something almost whimsical occurred to him: the memory of a story he had read in junior high—"The Birthmark"—about a man obsessed with a mark shaped like a hand on his wife's cheek. Mance remembered nothing else about the story.

"Mance?"

The question in Jonella's voice was a question about all the evil in the world. Cosmic evil. Why? *Why* had it been visited upon her? Mance pressed her fingers to his lips. For a passing of seconds, she appeared to relax. But then a storm of thought seized her. The little girl in her, frightened, confused, wanting reassurance, timidly asked, "Mance, will I get pregnant? Will I get some kind of disease?"

37

She might as well have asked him how many particles of dust the wind would blow down North Street that day. He shook his head. She closed her eyes.

In a few minutes, she fell asleep.

4

The local police caught up with Mance later that morning at Scarlett's for routine questioning. He told them what he recalled of Sunday night, but, no, he had not seen a black pickup and, no, he had not seen anyone else that night. Only pit bulls. Unfriendly pit bulls running loose—and why didn't the city deal with such a menace? And most of all: why hadn't somebody stopped the men in the black pickup from attacking his Johnnie?

Mance came away from the discussion somewhat less than confident that her attackers would be hauled in soon. As a result, he convinced himself that he would have to deliver whatever justice might be forthcoming.

For that he would need a weapon.

A gun.

In a far corner of the restaurant, his mother brought him a late breakfast. He wasn't particularly hungry, though his stomach had been churning, gnawing upon itself. She insisted he eat something. Work awaited him at Austin's used furniture store and at the beer warehouse. He would need his strength.

"Jonella pretty bad off?" his mother asked, after watching her son push grits away from his scrambled eggs.

Mance felt his chest tighten. Images of those grotesque teeth marks on Jonella's jaw held him as if spellbound.

"They smashed up her face," he said.

His mother sat down by him, keeping one eye on the cash register. She appeared to be repressing tears.

"All of us is praying for her and thinking about her, you know. I might could get away this afternoon to visit her, and we just sent her some flowers—a pick-me-up bouquet. Doesn't hardly seem like enough, does it?"

"Johnnie's tough," said Mance, more to himself than to her.

38

"It's gone be hard, but she's gone recover from this. I feel like she will, and . . ." He really didn't know what else to say.

The scrambled eggs had lost their flavor.

"I know she'll be fine, just fine after a while. But Mance, a mother can tell when her boy's ate up with bitterness, and I can see it in you, and it's not good."

"God damn it, Mom, how you expect me to feel? Long as those guys are running free and haven't paid for this—paid hard—I'm gone feel the way I feel."

His mother picked at her fingers quietly, then said, "I wisht you'd speak to your daddy. Talking to a man could help some. Your daddy . . . or your Uncle Thestis. He, you know, your Uncle Thestis, he thinks the sun rises and sets on Jonella. Him and her, they's thick as fleas. Why, Jonella took a liking to him the first day she knew him. And this morning he sent her a big bunch of flowers and wrote a note to her on one of them little cards. Sanders Florists sent the flowers, and, you know, if Uncle Thestis could get up and about better, he'd go see Jonella today. Maybe you could bring him there. He'd like that. He's been so worried about her. Could you maybe talk to him? It'd ease his mind a mile."

"No," said Mance. "No, I'm not talking to daddy or Uncle Thestis."

"You not . . . jealous of your Uncle Thestis, are you? I mean, of his friendship with Jonella?"

Mance's jaw stiffened. His mother seemed to shrink when she saw the vaulting anger in his expression.

He managed somehow to calm himself enough to finish a few more bites of his breakfast before he said, "Promised Austin I'd help him unload some furniture."

He pushed away from the table.

"When you coming back?"

He shrugged and headed toward the door, glancing up once at Vivien Leigh; something in her eyes told him that Scarlett O'Hara understood what it meant to fight against one's fate—to fight to recover what had been lost.

Before he left, Mance detoured back to his room to get Sting; the furry creature was overjoyed to escape his cage.

"Thought I'd forgot about you, huh? Johnnie . . . she wanted to know where you was, but I can't carry you into a hospital. Hey, it could be trouble. They use rats like you for experiments."

Sting secured a position under his keeper's long hair. In the hallway, Mance paused by Uncle Thestis's door. Part of him wanted to knock and enter that cluttered room and melt into the company of the man who had been his almost constant companion while growing up. Uncle Thestis would be deeply interested in news about Jonella.

But . . .

Hard feelings. Misunderstandings. Mance wasn't ready to face him. So he swallowed his regret and rustled off to Austin's. The day had become overcast, threatening rain. It had been a wet and mild winter. The gray clouds matched his mood.

Austin's Used Furniture greeted him with its usual legion of items designed for lower-middle-class shoppers who looked upon soiled mattresses as potential bargains. As he entered the store, he found, as usual, that only one pathway wended through the stacks of bedsteads, mattress springs, coffee tables, overstuffed chairs, kitchen tables, lampstands, lamps, sofas, love seats, recliners, water beds, dressers, ottomans, and various and sundry quite possibly unsaleable pieces. At the rear of the store, he ducked under a row of wall hangings on a clothesline—garish creations in orange, turquoise, yellow, and purple on a velvety black background, depicting unicorns, eagles, and, most popular of all, icons of Elvis Presley and Jesus Christ.

The store was empty except for Mr. Austin.

"Good morning, Master Culley."

It was Austin's typical welcome to him. A large hand reached out to shake Mance's. A genuine smile accompanied the welcome. Kelton Austin had operated the furniture store for a year or so, and in many ways he did not fit among the derelicts on North Street. He was tall and thin and rawboned; a wonderful shock of white hair crowned his head. He had a serious face, warm, hazel eyes, and a wise expression. He was a well-educated, well-read man with a vocabulary out of keeping with his surroundings.

He had come to Soldier from Georgia. And no one seemed to know why he came. One day Mance had asked him, and Austin had merely replied, "It was time." That seemed to be his philosophy for nearly everything. Mance respected it, and, for that matter, so did everyone else along North Street. If a man had secrets . . . well, he had a right to them.

"Come to help you unload your truck," said Mance.

Hands on his hips, Austin paused. Mance could feel how the man was sizing up the emotional texture of the moment. There was kindness and sensitivity in his eyes and in his voice.

"Work is always good therapy. I appreciate your willingness to come help me, especially under the circumstances."

So he had heard about Jonella. Mance was glad he said nothing more about the matter.

In the alley behind the store, Austin's truck, an oil-burning monster that a local transfer company had junked, was filled with furniture and appliances he had purchased in a nearby town.

"Sing out when you get to the larger stuff and I'll lend you a hand," said Austin, who then returned to the store.

To Mance's surprise, it felt good to work up a sweat, to strain his muscles, lifting, carrying. Meanwhile, the physical labor allowed his mind to open to memory. His visit with Jonella in the hospital commanded his thoughts. He could see her bruised face, feel the clammy touch of her hand, and hear her crushed voice.

Mance, will I get pregnant? Will I get some kind of disease?

He began to work faster, lifting, carrying, straining. Sting, inundated by his keeper's sweaty locks, sought refuge under an old wringer-type washing machine. Finally, he could no longer hear Jonella's desperate words; instead, the image of the bite marks jabbed at him like a spear.

His anger burned on a short fuse. When the leg of a coffee

41

table broke off in his grip, he felt the explosion build inexorably.

"God damn it!" he screamed.

Austin arrived on the scene just as Mance began smashing the table against the rear of the truck. He watched until only shards of glass and splinters of wood remained. Then he placed his big hands on Mance's shoulders.

"Go ahead and break something more if you need to. You can't bury your rage. Be like King Lear—sound your displeasure to the gods."

Mance continued smashing at the truck until his knuckles bled, and when the gust of anger had spent itself, he did a peculiar thing: he laughed. Perhaps because he was feeling so miserable or perhaps because of Austin's odd remark—*sound your displeasure to the gods?* It was definitely not east Alabama talk. It struck him, even wallowing in self-pity as he was, as incredibly funny.

But tears crowded close in line behind the laughter.

"Come on into my office," said Austin. "We can talk in the company of my myriad friends."

Mance hesitated.

"I don't want nobody else around, OK?"

Austin smiled warmly.

"You won't mind these friends, I assure you."

"What about the truck?"

"There will be time later. Your tribulations are more important."

The man's office was in a back room of the store; it was lined with floor-to-ceiling makeshift bookshelves spilling out foxed and musty hardbacks and stacks of paperbacks. Nestled in one corner were an overstuffed chair, a free-standing lamp, and a threadbare footstool.

As Austin led him into that lair of words, he said, "Good, good. See, the gang's all here."

Mance saw no one—only sour-smelling books, their odor mingling with the legacy of Austin's last pipe, which rested on a shelf close to the reading chair. Austin picked up the pipe, but did not light it.

"Introductions would be appropriate, wouldn't they?" Austin followed. "On the wall to your right you'll find some of the older crowd: Plato, Virgil, Homer, and Ovid. Wise, wise fellows despite their hoary aspects. Just above them, some British gents—always good company: Chaucer, Shakespeare, Milton, Mr. Swift, and crusty old Samuel Johnson."

As Mance listened, he couldn't hold back the beginnings of a smile.

Austin was in his element.

"Over here," he continued, "some British lads who've been called Romantics: Coleridge, Wordsworth, Byron, Shelley, Keats; and on the shelf above them the Victorians: Dickens, Browning, Stevenson, and the vampire man, Bram Stoker."

Turning toward the other side of the room, he tipped his pipe at one particular shelf.

"Some fine Americans, too: Emerson, Thoreau, Poe, Hawthorne, Melville, Twain, Hemingway, Faulkner; the list could go on and on. You see, I'm never truly alone. These gentlemen, a few ladies, too, offer me their stories and images and ideas anytime I request them. They don't pay rent for rooming here, but the compensation they provide is . . . shall we say, timeless?"

Mance surveyed the canyon of books.

"Have you read all these?"

"Most of them. Some, many times."

Austin gestured for him to sit on the footstool while the man himself eased his lanky frame into the overstuffed chair.

"If I read some of these books," said Mance, "would it make me quit feeling so shitty?"

Austin rocked back and delivered a hearty laugh. Yet, when he saw the pain in Mance's eyes, he sobered, allowing a dignified silence to steal into the scene.

"These great writers and thinkers, they have written about every conflict the human heart has ever experienced. But nothing they or I can say will ameliorate your suffering or Jonella's. To live is to suffer. No one escapes it. Evil, in one form or another, touches our lives. We are, it seems, each forced to confront it."

"I'm gone confront it with a gun," said Mance, determination tensing his body.

43

"No solution," said Austin.

"*My* solution."

Austin sucked thoughtfully a moment on the unlit pipe.

"Do you . . . *love* Jonella?" he asked.

"Sure. Yeah . . . sure I do."

"I used to believe that books were the greatest gifts of the ages. But I was wrong. The greatest gift — the only true gift — is to find someone to love and care about. It's having someone besides yourself to live for. I *almost* missed that. But would you like to know what I've decided? One of these bright and handsome days I'm going to ask Miss Adele Taylor to be my wife. To be my companion."

Over the past several months, Mance had noticed that Austin would close early some afternoons and stroll a few blocks north to the two-story brick boardinghouse where Miss Taylor would meet him on the wide front porch and they would talk, or, on occasion, walk to Scarlett's for dinner. Mance had never considered that romance was an issue — and certainly not marriage. Why, both Austin and Miss Taylor were in their sixties, weren't they?

"Why are you telling me this?" said Mance.

"Because. Because it's time you understood something: love is the only response to evil. A pound of love for every pound of evil."

"That from Shakespeare?"

"No," Austin smiled. "No, it's from Kelton Austin, lonely, warmth-questing soul. Forget about the gun and revenge and creating more violence in response to violence. Don't do it. And something else: be aware that there's a particular kind of power in women. Men don't have it. Men need women in order to be complete and whole. Loving a woman can be like taking a piece of broken furniture and fixing it, making it functional again. Hold on to the love you have — don't immerse yourself in hatred."

Mance listened, but he disagreed.

He needed a fierceness in his life to strike at the darkness that threatened to consume him. He needed it for Jonella, too. Violence was the only way, he felt, to deal with her attackers.

To Austin he said, "I want a gun. That's what I want now."

The man with the glorious mop of white hair shook his head
sadly.

6

That afternoon Mance visited Jonella briefly in the hospital.
Flowers semicircled her bed; Mance felt guilty for not bringing
her anything, but Jonella forgave him—she was in good spirits, though her jaw remained very sore and her stomach ached
from the hard punch she had received from one of the attackers. She didn't, however, mention it to Mance, choosing instead to show him where the cotton had been removed from
the two lost back teeth.

They talked, or rather Mance listened, as Jonella mumbled
on about how well the nurses and doctors and Miss Prince, the
black policewoman, had treated her; she also read Uncle Thestis's card to him.

> On wings of love and care my thoughts fly out to you,
> for life is sometimes darkness, but you are always light.
>   From the central fire of my heart, Uncle Thestis.

Reading the card misted Jonella's eyes. Mance said nothing.
He couldn't keep from staring at the bandage covering the bite
marks, and even though Jonella had told him that the two men
were strangers to her, he wanted desperately to ask her for anything that would help identify them.

As their conversation waned, Jonella seemed to read his
mind.

"Don't ask me no more about those men," she said. "I just
want my life to get back to normal—we can't change what
happened, Mance."

She tenderly touched his face and then allowed her hand to
slide down his arm and linger at the fang, rubbing circles
around it with her fingertips.

"The rose has missed you," she added, but Mance looked
away, bitterness and frustration clawing at him.

45

Clocking in for the four-to-midnight shift, Mance felt tired. He hoped the Monday night loading demands would be as light as usual. Being the youngest worker at Rebel Beer, he had been afforded a somewhat special status; he was known to his co-workers as "the kid," and most admired his willingness to work hard without complaining.

At the shift change, it became evident that many of the men knew about Jonella. Mance reasoned that Boom may have told them. It wasn't that he minded, but their efforts to console him would likely make him feel self-conscious.

"Hey, kid, hang in there," said one, patting him on the shoulder.

"Sorry to hear 'bout this," said another. "Lotsa mean, damn bastards out there."

"Hope they catch 'em and neuter the sons-uh-bitches," remarked a third.

To each awkward gesture of sympathy, he nodded and smiled weakly.

A few of the men speculated openly on who it could be. Somebody from out of town, one or two concluded: "Trash drifting through." Inevitably, several maintained the attackers "had to be niggers"—but they were told that Jonella had reported the two assailants as being young white men with dark beards.

Most of the men chose to be quiet around Mance; it was their way of letting a man suffer on his own, which was the way they felt it had to be. Throughout the evening, however, Mance became aware of another element at the warehouse: a scattered handful of men, the lowlife of the shift—friends of Boom mostly—who deliberately let slip a joke or a salacious observation about women and the male sexual appetite. But Mance avoided those clones of Boom by plunging himself into his work.

Basically he got along fine with the other men; like him, they, too, had quit school, seeing a more satisfying life in using their backs than in using their brains. Possibly a few had, over the years, regretted that decision. At Rebel Beer there were two groups of men: one, the older guys, forties or older, with teen-aged kids Mance knew; some even had grandchildren. These men had worked years and years with the company and gotten stuck at various levels, harboring little hope of supervisory or management positions. They were merely counting the days to retirement. Mance felt sorry for them. What if he ended up the same way? Such a thought was discouraging.

The second group was the younger guys, late twenties and early thirties, married and yet still boys in many ways. They thrived on drinking, cheating on their wives, hunting, fishing, getting up to their eyebrows in debt, and developing profanity to an art form. They thought of themselves as studs, dipped snuff, and, occasionally, snorted cocaine, though the drug was much too expensive for most of them.

Equal opportunity had made some headway at the company; there were three black workers, and the four-to-mid-night shift boasted one woman, a flirtatious redhead named Della who supervised inventory. She was always looking for a better job—or a better *something*. Mance shared her attitude; saw Rebel Beer as a stepping-stone job for something better down the road—what that would be, he couldn't be certain. All in all, what he had wasn't a bad job; good, honest, hard, physical labor. He could do worse. Mance knew the huge ware-house intimately: the mountainous rows of beer cases stacked to the ceiling—regular Rebel, Rebel Lite, Rebel Pride, and Rebel Yell—neatly arranged on thick, wooden pallets. In addi-tion, the company had its own line of pretzels and pork rinds and beer nuts, thus necessitating a separate wing of the ware-house just for boxes of the snack items.

Mance's job was loader, which simply meant that he and two other men loaded cases of beer into trucks parked along the dock area. It was monotonous, sweaty (always warm de-spite the concentrated air-conditioning needed for the beer), terminally boring work, punctuated with mindless conversa-tion. Sometimes he got to run the "goose," the nickname for the forklift, to vary the routine. Midevening the crew took an hour break for dinner, and on that particular Monday evening, Mance stole away among the lofty stacks of boxes with a soft drink and a bag of pretzels and his radio to be alone and to think about Jonella. And getting a gun.

Sting ventured out onto his shoulder for a helping of pretzels. Mance shoved a tape of Metallica into his jam box and let the heavy metal group bombard him with the rough-hewn lyrics of "To Live Is To Die." And he fantasized. What would it be like to have a gun in his hand and confront Jonella's attackers? Yeah, it would be a trip—watch 'em sweat, make 'em beg, make 'em suffer—just as they had made Jonella suffer. They would plead for mercy, and then: would he haul them into the police? Or would he enact a more complete revenge? He savored the possibilities.

When the shift came mercifully to an end, he found that he did not want to go home. So he swiped a warm six-pack and climbed out a back air vent into the alley and began to walk up North Street, images of Jonella, her breasts, and the rose keeping him company. Not surprisingly, his after-midnight ramble led him to Guillo House.

To *their* room.

He lit a candle and sat on their pallet and drank one of the beers, though every sip tasted sour. He felt like hell. Mostly, he felt alone. The silence of Guillo House seemed to offer no consolation, no comfort. But the shadows brought back memories. One especially: the first night he secreted Jonella to the second floor room which became their very own. They had been fourteen at the time and had fled the scene at a junior high dance one warm spring evening, and Jonella had gotten her dress dirty. They had comically smoked a cigarette, leading Jonella to promptly announce that she wouldn't marry a man who dipped snuff or smoked because, to her, those were nasty habits. And no hard drugs either. Drinking beer, however, was OK. And Mance had kissed her and felt her breasts, and that first night they had talked about tattoos well before the rose and the fang came into being.

They returned to Guillo House again and again.

Jonella had held on tenaciously to her virginity.

Without warning, the memory faded.

Mance guzzled most of a second beer, then noticed how deadly still the room was. He listened to his breathing, and,

48

ever so faintly, he could smell the perfume Jonella had been wearing Sunday night. Suddenly he hated the silence.

"Wake up!" he shouted over and over. He slapped a tape into his jam box and Metallica's "Harvester of Sorrow" filled the emptiness; the rock music shook the walls, and Guillo House came alive: the rooftop pigeons took flight in a thunderous rush; the scream of guitars echoed from room to room.

Mance found his crowbar and began directing the sounds as if he were an orchestra leader, but with every swish of the crowbar he grew angrier. No amount of noise could drown out his thoughts of Jonella and her attackers.

Love is the only response to evil.

"No, goddamn it," he cried. Not even the wisdom of Kelton Austin could sway him. He turned and saw something on the wall. It was his shadow, and it disgusted him. The crowbar smashed again and again at his exaggerated figure; chunks of plaster exploded from the wall and white dust drifted free until an eerie, snowy fog choked at the theater of shadows.

Mance brought the crowbar down hard upon the jam box, and Metallica skidded into silence.

"Somebody help me!" Mance called out.

And he pictured Boom as he had seen him in the hospital waiting area—the man as a pit bull and then as a savage creature tearing at Tanya and the children. Mance threw the crowbar at a far wall; it bounced, stirring more dust; and then he dropped hard to the floor. He whispered, "Somebody help me."

It was chill and dark except for the candle.

But Guillo House had been awakened. The walls shuddered. The white fog of plaster dust swirled.

On Mance's shoulder Sting cowered, squeaking as if frightened out of his mind. After a moment or two he became as motionless as a ceramic figure on a whatnot shelf.

Mance clutched at another beer, but never opened it.

To his right, the wall bubbled. He scooted several feet away from it. It pulsed. Mance felt he was imagining things.

Then he heard something snarl.

His breath caught, and despite the chill, sweat skated down his rib cage.

A nebulous gray form stepped from the wall.

"God," said Mance. It felt as if something had pulled the word out of his mouth.

The form grew more distinct. And larger. As large as an old Volkswagen beetle. It gained detail, and Mance squinted, but there was no mistaking: it was a huge, wolflike creature. Fully emerged from the wall, it turned and looked at him, its eyes wild yet curiously not vicious. Then it snarled, revealing its long, sharp teeth.

God oh God.

Mance couldn't move.

The wolf creature kept its eyes on him for a half dozen heartbeats before swinging toward the dark hallway and loping away into the shadows.

Mance heard it pad down the stairs. He rushed to a window and peered into the darkness below. Nothing. No sign of the creature. But it took Mance several minutes to convince himself that what he had seen had been a hallucination.

So damn real.

Wouldn't Uncle Thestis have freaked, he thought to himself, what with his interest in the supernatural and the occult?

Mance's head spun. He had vented his anger and it had been replaced with fear. He thought of Jonella, but this time when he imagined the teeth marks on her face, he also saw the fangs of the wolf creature.

His body quaked.

He closed his eyes.

When he opened them seconds later it was pitch dark in the room. Somebody or something had snuffed out the candle.

Chapter Three

1

"I loss it big time on Denver. What I'm sayin' is big time. An' you never seen a sorrier team on the field. Su-u-u-uper Bowl — hey it was de Stinker Bowl, an' ole Fast Track Johnson loss it big time."

"So why don't you quit gambling?" asked Mance.

"Hush yer mouth, boy. Gam'lin' makes ole Fast Track's blood run like a creek affer a heavy rain. I do like gam'lin'. I shorely do."

Mance had to smile despite the blue funk that continued to set its hooks in him. It was late morning, he had a headache and he couldn't get the image of the wolf creature out of his mind.

"Fast Track, can two beers make you see things?"

The heavyset black man, hair and sideburns and mustache tinged with silver, busied himself cleaning behind the bar, humming some jazzy ditty as he prepared for the one o'clock opening.

"Shoo-we, I know dat's right. Some folks only gots to sniff atta beer an' dare head wobbles an' snakes slither 'tween dare legs an' dare chins fall to de floor."

Mance chuckled, but it cost him.

"Damn, my head feels like it has a pinball game going on inside it."

"Drink yer masher," said Fast Track as he polished a few

51

beer mugs. "Dat stuff'll straighten out what ails you—gots my special formula."

Mance examined the steaming glass of yellow liquid.

"Looks like piss," he said.

Fast Track's laugh was surprisingly high-pitched.

"Naw, sir, boy," he returned. "Nuthin' like dat. Shoo-we. De masher gots lemon juice, orange juice, egg yolk, mustard, an' a secret ingredient."

"Cat shit?" said Mance, playing along.

Fast Track laughed harder.

"See dat—you feelin' better jist breathin' de fumes of it."

"Not really," Mance followed. "I'm kinda having a hard time. I need to borrow something from you."

"Hep me wit dis first," said Fast Track, but when Mance saw the old man slap a bettor's sheet on the bar, he groaned.

"No way, man," he said. "Last time I gave you advice I told you to bet on San Francisco and you didn't listen."

"But dis is basketball, boy. You know, hoops. Two games— dat's all I need. I got Vanderbilt an' Tennessee an' Florida an' LSU. Tennessee by four an' LSU by ten. How'd you feel? Hep a ole nigger out."

"Fast Track—come on. I don't know shit about basketball. I hate basketball."

"Thing is, boy, I needs to hit," he said, his voice taking on a somber air. "I shore do. I'm down some big money. I shorely am."

"OK, OK . . . go with the underdogs," said Mance reluctantly.

"Spots on de dawgs," the old man sang out. "Gots it covered."

Mance watched him happily tuck away the bettor's sheet.

"Now you got to help me."

"Fast Track alwis heps his friends."

Leaning closer to emphasize the seriousness of his request, Mance said, "I need to borrow a gun. I need to get whoever attacked Johnnie."

Fast Track's head snapped back.

"A gun? Who-o-o, no, boy. When you carries a gun, somebody gets a bullet. I know dey do."

"Just let me borrow your shotgun. Please, man."

"Sweet Lick, you mean?"

From beneath the counter the old man brought out a double-barreled shotgun. "I gots to keep dis around for fights. Stops de fights like throwin' ice water on humpin' dawgs."

"I need a gun against these guys," Mance continued. "The police aren't gone be no help."

"Dey would if'n my boy, Punch, was still on de force. Dees guys like butcher men, are dey?"

"What are butcher men?"

"Toughs sent out by de big bookies when you can't pay yer debts. Dey sneak down yer alley some night an' slit yer throat an' cut out yer heart an' you bleed till de ground's gone soft."

"You scared of butcher men?"

"You got dat right—ole Fast Track wants no part a butcher men."

Head continuing to pound, Mance took a sip of the masher and spit it back into the glass. He wiped his mouth.

"I want revenge for what happened to Johnnie," he said. "I want it bad."

"Know what I wants bad? I want my Punch to get his job back on de po-lice force. He gots framed—I know dat for a fact."

Mance nodded, but he was impatient.

"So you won't let me borrow your gun?"

"No can do, boy."

"Maybe Punch will," said Mance, and he sought out the game room area.

2

The pool cue was a master craftman's tool in his hands; when he was only thirteen, Mance could whip most adult players at eight ball. Word had gotten around. No one took him on anymore. Only strangers who didn't know they were stepping into a hustle.

This was Mance's turf.

He scattered the balls with a loud break. A second or so

later he heard a moan – the reaction he had sought. He pocketed three balls and started to run the table, though the clatter thumped painfully at his temples.

"Christ almighty, knock it off, would ya?"

The voice came from a closetlike room only a few yards from the pool table. Someone who had been lying on an army cot stirred, coughed, and then rose unsteadily from the shadows.

"Need to talk to you, Punch," said Mance, crashing the cue ball into a cluster, sending a sharp, plastic clamor bouncing off the rails.

"Hey, goddamn you. I'm up. Christ. Find my socks, would ya? Silly-ass white boy."

Mance found his socks for him, had Fast Track pour him some tomato juice, and helped him to a table near the bar. Soft overhead lighting revealed the handsome, masculine face of Odell "Punch" Johnson, a young man in his late twenties who looked like a cross between Carl Weathers and Billy Dee Williams. But instead of being an actor, he was an out-of-work police officer taken to drink and self-pity. Still, he remained in decent physical shape, his fists every bit as rugged and powerful as they were ten years ago when he nearly made the U.S. amateur boxing team, and earned the nickname "Punch."

Mance got right to the point.

"I need a gun."

Punch frowned.

"Like hell you do. Whatchoo gone do, shoot that damn rat that lives on your shoulder?"

"You know what I'm gone do – you heard what happened to Johnnie, didn't you?"

"Yeah, I heard, and damn you know I feel for both of you, but what good's a piece gone do you? Good chance you'll get your silly-ass head shot off."

"Listen, Punch, aren't you the one that always told me about if somebody takes a man's pride away from him he's got to do what he has to do to get it back?"

Punch leaned back and let his head roll on his shoulders. He winced, still in the painful thralls of his hangover. He nodded.

And Mance continued.

"Getting *your* pride back's gone mean getting back on the police force—for me, it's making those bastards suffer who trashed Johnnie."

Punch's gaze drifted past Mance toward the bar, where Fast Track was pouring peanuts onto saucers.

"That ole nigger there means the world to me, Mance. He took me in when my folks dumped me on the street. You hear what I'm sayin'? I want my job back for him and for me. I lost my job and my wife *and* my pride. But I was framed—two of 'em on the force set me up. Gone be hell provin' I'm tellin' the truth long as they're gangin' up on me."

"A gun," said Mance. "What about a gun? You gone help me or not?"

Punch focused on the boy and shrugged his shoulders.

"I'll help you any way I can. But not a gun."

"You know I can buy one if I have to do it that way," said Mance. "I can buy one from Sparrow. I'll get one."

"You probably will. And I understand why you think you have to—to get your pride back. I understand that. But I don't want no part of handin' you a gun. I don't want the blood of the best pool player in Catlin County on my hands."

He reached over and squeezed Mance's neck and then made a fist and playfully jabbed at him.

Mance sighed deeply.

"I'm not gone give up," he said.

3

To understand the enigmatical figure known as Sparrow, one had to acknowledge three important points.

First, the man could be exceedingly humane. These assertions of humanity were primarily directed at the homeless and discarded souls who periodically appeared on the streets and byways of Soldier. Black, white, male, female, old, young (though mostly old), religious, heathen, conservative, liberal, sick, crippled, retarded—it mattered not to Sparrow, a fortyish man with flowing locks of blond hair partway down his back, garbed in army fatigues with the name Sparrow stamped in black letters over the breast pocket. He took in everyone who knocked upon his door, and even a few who didn't but should have. He gave them food—there was always a cauldron of Brunswick stew simmering at the rear of his pawnshop—and he gave them a bed—a scattering of cots and worse-for-wear mattresses (some donated by Kelton Austin)—and, in his own inimical way, he gave them hope. In their presence, he was gentle and kind and soft-spoken and would listen to a chorus of hard-luck stories and probably even shed a tear or two and offer a pat on the back and the same words to each and every derelict piece of humanity: "Don't worry; you got a friend." Sparrow called his street people "burdens" and "crosses," but he used the terms affectionately.

Second, the man was sometimes crazy. This was a legacy of combat duty in Vietnam and one of the manifestations of exposure to Agent Orange. If one looked deeply into Sparrow's eyes, one could see the madness—it was rather like looking into a kaleidoscope and finding that its shards of glass never quite formed a consistent pattern. His actions often gave evidence of his mental aberrations; for example, during a rainy, three-day stretch he once tethered himself halfway up the flagpole in front of the courthouse, an act in protest over the city fathers ruling that while his pawnshop might be allowed to operate, his soup kitchen would not be. Sparrow literally ran himself up the pole. And stayed there. The city fathers backed down, officially proclaiming him crazy, but not wanting to deal with all the adverse publicity. As an adjunct to his occasional protests, he talked crazy—as if possessed—showing all the classic symptoms of the paranoid schizophrenic. His sentences would often start off coherently only to dissolve into gibberish or something sounding very much like jabberwocky. At such times, it was best simply to give him the floor and stand back and listen.

Third, it was rumored that Sparrow was psychic—another side effect of Agent Orange, some speculated. A few had witnessed and later testified that he could change his facial countenance into horrific shapes, that he could read minds, and that he could affect animals and even influence the weather. In short, he was by turns humane, crazy, and weird. Yet, everyone on North Street seemed to like Sparrow, even though everyone seemed a little frightened of him.

Including Mance.

He entered Sparrow's pawnshop early that afternoon after having struck out in his attempts to borrow a gun from Fast Track or Punch. He had gone home and raided his money pouch, stuffing $126 into his pocket. It was only after he entered the shop that he suddenly realized he'd never actually carried on an extended conversation with Sparrow. Still, this was his last chance to get a gun. He had cold cash — it would do his talking for him.

The same items you would see in countless other pawnshops graced Sparrow's: jewelry (especially rings), watches, cameras, radios (Mance was painfully reminded of having smashed his jam box), golf clubs, a guitar or two, and, of course, guns — shotguns, rifles, and handguns. Mance leaned over a glass display case and saw immediately the one he wanted: a used Rossi .38 Special, silver with a brown, woodgrain handle. Price — $149.50. Mance bit his lip. Maybe Sparrow would take less.

"Dingledodies!"

Mance looked up.

"Piss call before lunch. Every last one of you wash your hands and drain your bladders or no stew. Cornbread. Hear what I'm sayin'? Cornbread today for every burden."

The man called Sparrow shambled toward him, directing the gathering of old men at the rest room door. Then he focused on Mance, and the boy saw twin lightning streaks shatter the placid blue eyes.

"Whatcha need?" he asked.

For a twinge or two, Mance was silent, and when he jump-started some words, Sparrow interrupted him.

"Had a dingledodie of a dream last night. Dark and fluctuant, crystalline it was; spirals sucked me up into a black and vacant eye. I had a vision. Hear what I'm sayin'?"

He leaned conspiratorially close, and Mance timidly acknowledged that he did.

"I witnessed," said Sparrow dramatically, "the birth of the Final Chaos. It has been loosed upon the world, not in a fire-

57

storm, but frimsied in a narsteltic brenting of barmoostered efflestilence."

Mance stepped back. He couldn't keep his eyes from Sparrow's face. Would this be the moment? Was some weird metamorphosis about to take place? Two seconds stretching toward eternity passed; Mance swallowed, a bit disappointed that Sparrow's eyes didn't pop out or that his nose didn't transform into a snout.

"I came in to buy a gun," he said.

"Oh," said Sparrow, apparently disappointed, perhaps wanting the boy to be more impressed with his dream. "Your name's Mance, right?"

"Yeah, and I really need a gun."

"Word on the street has it the bastards got to your girl."

Mance felt his body tensing.

"I brought cash. I'm interested in that .38. Could I hold it?"

He pointed down into the handgun case. But Sparrow made no move to unlock the glass; instead, he studied Mance closely for an uncomfortable span of seconds.

"You ought to kill your enemy with your bare hands," he said, flexing his fingers. "Only a man who's scared of his enemy uses a gun. I'll give you some advice. If you're that scared, go ahead and get a gun, but take the tip of the barrel and worm it into your ear. Click. And poof you're gone. Hear what I'm sayin'?"

Mance looked away nervously. The only other person in the shop was an old man slumped over asleep in a chair.

"There's two of 'em, and the cops aren't gone do me no good—I'll give you a hundred and twenty dollars cash money for that .38."

Sparrow smiled. Was it kindness or madness glimmering in his eyes? Mance couldn't be certain. The man tapped a finger at his temple.

"The mind can kill. It has power. Hear what I'm sayin'? Dingledodie power."

"Hey, I just want to—"

Sparrow's face drew up as thin as an ax blade.

"You don't believe me, do you?"

Mance felt the air around them grow colder. But, no, he had to be imagining that.

"It ain't that I don't believe you . . ."

Sparrow became as animated as a roman candle.

"See old Rollo? See that old frizzlemadick? One of my burdens. He's not dreaming because all his dreams died long time ago. Watch what I can do. I'll put Rollo naked between clean sheets . . . in his mind, you see, and I'll have this gorgeous young blond . . . oh, she'll have breasts as big as Indian River grapefruit and legs that lead to heaven, and she'll slip into bed with him and she'll have better hands than the best wide receiver in the NFL and she'll . . . well, you watch Rollo's face."

So Mance did. But out of the corner of his eye he also watched Sparrow, the man's concentration so intense it seemed to suck all the breathable air from the room.

In ten seconds Rollo smiled.

In twenty seconds something like ecstasy spread across his face.

In thirty seconds he had an erection that threatened to split his soiled old dungarees.

Sparrow snapped back. That's the way it seemed. Like a giant rubber band, he snapped back to reality, and in a few seconds Rollo's smile faded; a few more and the erection was history.

Suddenly Mance wanted to leave, forget about the gun, and never come into Sparrow's again.

"It's the power of the living dark. I've only shown it to a few other souls, and I wouldn't have shown it you except I thought for a second you doubted me, but what I see now is different—you've been near it, too, haven't you? Seen it. Touched it. The living dark. Oh, I won't press you. I understand. I do."

Mance felt his intestines squirm, then growl. Best strategy, he decided, would be to ease away from there and see whether someone at Rebel Beer would loan him a gun—or maybe he would forget about it entirely.

Sparrow was surveying the ceiling of the shop.

"Our own fucking planes sprayed that orange whimsy on us. Burned me. Like tiny, tiny particles of sand or glass heated up in hell, only I never knew what it was till later. Made me dizzy.

Made me puke. Rearranged the wiring in my brain is what I'm sayin'. Power of the living dark. I've got it and I'm gone need it against the Final Chaos because, like I said, I dreamed it's out there. So you be careful on the streets. It's out there. But I don't have to tell you because you know, don't you?"

Mance let his gaze drift out the window. He considered running. Nosing along the gutter on the other side of the street were the two pit bulls that had tried to corner him and rip him to pieces. Sparrow apparently saw them, too.

"Watch this," he said. "I can scare the fuck outta them and not say a word."

Folded within himself so as not to get in the man's way, Mance witnessed the darkening of Sparrow's face; it constricted and his eyes glazed over like ice on a pond. The results came almost immediately: the pit bulls yelped and cried as if they'd been sprayed with buckshot. They ran in opposite directions, and when Sparrow heard their flight, he chuckled softly.

"Still have it," he said.

Mance had his hands jammed in his pockets.

"You . . . you can sure do some cool tricks," he said, his voice laced with fear and awe and confusion.

"Tricks are for pricks," said Sparrow. "We have to be ready for the bastards."

Uncertain of the reference, Mance backpedaled toward the door.

"What about your gun?" Sparrow exclaimed.

Mance halted.

"Oh . . . yeah. Guess I forgot. What about that .38?"

He approached the display case cautiously, warily.

Sparrow scratched at his beard.

"How old are you, Mance?"

"Sixteen."

"Humph. Dingledodies. See that little sign behind me? You got to be twenty-one in the state of Alabama to purchase a handgun. You got to fill out a Firearms Transaction Record Form 4473 and then two or three days while they check to see if you're on the Most Wanted list. And if I get caught selling a handgun to someone under twenty-one, they fine me five thousand big ones and throw my ass in the brig for five fucking years."

Mance shrugged.

"Guess I won't be buying a gun."

Sparrow unlocked the case and placed the .38 on the glass.

"The Final Chaos is coming," he said, and then, to Mance's surprise, he pushed the gun toward him. "I'll take your hundred and twenty if you think you need some fire to keep the bastards from walking all over you."

"What about the law?"

Sparrow grinned. Humanitarian? Maniac? Nothing in his face gave him away.

"Don't worry," he said. "You got a friend."

4

Night on North Street.

A light rain falling.

Kelton Austin is in his office reading Melville. Fast Track has cranked up his gang of jazz musicians, filling his lounge with mellow vibes. Sparrow is preparing to bed down all his burdens. Mance is at work at Rebel Beer.

Business at Scarlett's is slow.

Guillo House is silent except for drops of rain leaking through damaged parts of the roof.

But among the abandoned buildings on North Street something moves furtively, searching dark, dusty corners and watching, watching the street for signs of the prey it will recognize instantly.

Stray dogs whimper and cower at the scent of the wolf creature.

It is feeling stronger with each passing hour. It is an avatar of blood and savagery. It has a task to perform.

And it hears the darkness calling.

5

Several days later.

Jonella thought: why is it that winter rains can set in and

gray-wash a day until it can't be used for anything except pondering your own sad state of affairs? She had thought leaving the hospital would improve her spirits. Having argued convincingly that she was physically *and* mentally able to return home, she soon wondered whether she hadn't made a mistake.

She didn't belong at the hospital and she didn't belong at Tanya's and her jaw was nearly as tender as before and she could not, *could not,* look at herself in the mirror. She had been swallowed by grayness, an all-encompassing depression that made everything and everybody seem dead. She tried to tell herself that she was merely worried about the hospital bill, but that was a weak and thin lie.

Truth number one: she could only bear each passing moment while curled in a fetal position with her eyes glued to the fake wood paneling in her tiny bedroom, a bedroom the walls of which—oh, *God, I've got to be wrong about this*—appeared to be moving steadily inward.

Truth number two: she decided that she hadn't been attacked by men, but by animals—large, ursine creatures that had clawed at her with a primitive lust. Her decision was based on a strange development: she could no longer envision their faces; and she had the bizarre sensation that some dark force had stolen into her memory and erased every detail connected to the identity of the two men. But how could that be? she wondered. And hadn't the force a voice? And hadn't it whispered something to her? Something she could not recall? *Please, God, don't let me get like Momma.*

Truth number three: Miss Prince's counseling had lost its magic. For a few days, the "positive image, self-worth" pep talk had worked. Then—a wall. A gray wall like a wall of steely rain. Miss Prince had warned her: "You'll hit some real low points, lower than you've ever been. Just keep reminding yourself that you did not bring this upon yourself. It is *not* your fault. You have the same personal worth as before. You are strong and attractive and intelligent and *alive*—and you will put this behind you, and your life will be as full as you ever imagined it would be. You will be wiser than before. You will understand in ways that others cannot about evil as a real presence—about human beings who have a sickness—violence is a sickness—and when that sickness is out of control, they will turn it upon someone else. Don't allow this to destroy your personal integrity. Don't allow it."

But Jonella feared that it had. She felt dirty. She had replayed the events of that night dozens of times to determine, to satisfy herself, that she had done nothing to provoke or in any way deserve the attack. But always there was the torture of self-doubt. She began to behave compulsively: she took long showers and scrubbed herself raw, she found that no amount of soap could remove the imaginary grime. So she would douse herself in perfume, leading Boom one night at the supper table to remark, "Hey, what is this? We turning this trailer into a goddamn cathouse?"

His comment related indirectly to truth number four: Jonella was finding it difficult to be around men. To sit in the same room with Boom was to be enclosed in a small space with a poisonous reptile. Boom obviously could sense her discomfort and appeared to delight in it. Tanya offered poor consolation. Worst of all, Jonella did not want to see Mance. He had come to visit her twice and called her numerous times, but she had been cool to him and he, of course, could not fully understand why. At times she would break into tears when they said good-bye—she wanted him to leave, and yet she wanted him to stay; she wanted him never to touch her or kiss her again—thoughts of the rose and the fang had soured—and yet at other times she wanted desperately for him to hold her in his arms, and make the gray-wash of depression disappear, replaced by a bright and shining world in which she would feel strong and whole and . . . clean.

Into her dark reverie Tanya and the girls clamored.

"School books, missy. Those teachers won't have you falling behind," said Tanya, bouncing on Jonella's bed, her voice tremulous with a false glee. "I brought algebra and your lit book and—this big brown one is biology, I think—and, oh, that new health teacher is a hunk. Somebody said he played football at Auburn."

Tanya paused.

"Hey, what kind of day you havin'? A good'n? Things is better, huh? I told you they would be."

63

"I think I'd like to die," said Jonella.

"Oh, what kind of talk is that? In front of my baby girls, too. Can't you just try to cheer up, honey? Are you real sure you're trying?"

"I am," said Jonella, and turned her face away.

"Everybody at school says hey, and they ask about you and hope you'll be back soon, and I told 'em you're doing just fine. Just fine, and . . ."

Tanya's carousel monologue rattled on. Jonella rode on the words a revolution or two before she saw the walls inch closer. She was afraid they would crush her before she mustered the courage to scream.

6

The rain had slackened to a mist.

Through the gray curtain of the afternoon, Thestis could see the rough, dark outline of Guillo House. Was there something different about the meeting of its angles? Some clue in the juxtaposition of roofline and chimneys? What is it? he asked himself. What mysterious imperative had prompted him to leave his room and follow the wiles of his intuition?

Something told him (warned him?) that he must go to Guillo House.

The mist flecked his cheeks and brow.

Deep within him the pain, a snake of razors, slithered into new territory. He winced.

How much longer, Conqueror Worm, how much longer do I have?

Guillo House reclaimed his attention. Was it brooding?

He could never bring the edifice into view without feeling a mixture of love and hate for it. How could the same house at one point have welcomed him, providing him warmth and security, and, at another, spread horror through his veins?

Unconsciously Thestis tapped his cane on the sidewalk. Would he ever crack the mystery of Guillo House? He thought of his final night in that house years ago and . . . did he hear footsteps just then? Was it his cane?

"Pardon me, but would you care to share my umbrella?"

Thestis visibly shuddered.

"Oh, do excuse me. I certainly didn't mean to startle you."

Thestis gained his bearings and discovered a tallish, white-haired gentleman at his shoulder, maneuvering a black umbrella so that it sheltered both of them.

"I must have been lost in thought," said Thestis, slightly embarrassed. "Thank you. It was careless of me to come on this walk without my umbrella."

"I see you've been admiring Guillo House," said the other man.

"Yes, in part, you're quite right. At the same time, well . . ."

The other man sought to bridge the awkward trailing off of the sentence. "I have heard it said that a house of such obvious antiquity is a repository of memories rather like a good library—if one only knew how to read the secret text of walls and floors."

Thestis gestured his awareness of that particular idea. "Guillo House transcends even that—it is, I believe, of that class of rare phenomena known as sentient structures, or would appear to be. It has, essentially, a life of its own."

"Intriguing concept—especially if true. You seem to have a close acquaintance with Guillo House."

"Yes . . . I . . . I lived there once."

"I see. Most interesting. I would like to hear more about that one day. By the way, my name is Kelton Austin. I own the used furniture store down on North Street."

He extended his hand.

"I'm Thestis Sinclair. I live at the rear of Scarlett's with the Culleys."

"Of course, yes. Mance has mentioned you. Would seem unusual that I haven't met you before this."

"I don't get out and about much," said Thestis. "I've been ill."

"Sorry to hear that."

"Mance is my nephew. Good kid at heart, though having a tough go of it these days. I know his young lady friend, Jonella, and I'm deeply troubled about her horrible experience."

"Yes. Yes, indeed."

The mist thickened into a light but eager rain.

Both men grappled with a passing silence before Thestis said, "I'm afraid I'm going to have to excuse myself. This cold, wet air mucks up my old bones. They'll bite me all night if I don't send them home and warm them up."

"I should be on my way as well. I'm meeting a friend. Miss Adele Taylor. Perhaps you know her."

Thestis hesitated.

"Yes. Yes, as a matter of fact, I do. Please send her my regards."

Austin escorted Thestis back to Scarlett's; they chatted along the way, expressing further concerns about Mance and Jonella, and when they parted they agreed that they should talk again — it had all the earmarks of an instant friendship.

But as Thestis burrowed into his room, pain shattered his insides, stealing momentarily the good feeling surrounding his chance meeting with Austin. Before sinking into his chair, he reached for his pacifier, a silver cup he valued above all of his other treasures — above his numerous jars of marbles, his photographs, and his stacks of old magazines and newspapers. He clutched the cup to his chest and waited for the pain to pass.

And he thought about Guillo House.

How would Gottfried Sücher solve its mystery?

Suddenly he rose and began rummaging through an old wooden file cabinet of manuscripts and sleeved copies of magazines.

"Yes, here we are," he said eventually.

It was a copy of *Weird Tales*, a fantasy pulp magazine, this copy being from the early fifties. Among its contents: "The House That Spawned Shadows," original fiction by Thestis Sinclair, featuring a magnificent header drawing of an old manse from which shadows flowed in fantastic shapes like Lovecraftian entities or Jungian archetypes. The story had netted him five dollars; more importantly, it continued the adventures of his fictional psychic detective, Gottfried Sücher, a creation in the tradition of Algernon Blackwood's John Silence, William Hope Hodgson's Carnacki the Ghost-Finder, and Dion Fortune's Dr. Taverner. Sücher, a "ghostbuster" par excellence, parried with his knowledge of the occult one dark force after another, failing only once to best his foe or to untie the Gordian knot of enigma—the House That Spawned Shadows (modeled upon Guillo House) had been that single blemish on his record.

Whenever Thestis pondered a difficult matter, he would imagine his brilliant detective, a man whom he envisioned as looking much like Peter Lorre in the movie *Mad Love,* head shaven, dressed in a heavy, fur-lined coat, with those tragically sad and sensitive eyes attempting to penetrate the darkness of the human condition.

What now Herr Sücher?

Guillo House and Mance and Jonella—was there a connection?

Thestis Sinclair did not know. Perhaps Gottfried Sücher would.

Against the chill of the winter twilight, Thestis poured himself a cup of hot coffee from his ever-present pot, heaped six spoonfuls of sugar into it, and tucked a coverlet over his aching legs.

Give me time, Conqueror Worm, give me time.

7

The weekend arrived.

Having Saturday night off, Mance had hoped to spend time with Jonella, but she was on some new medication that made her lethargic and sleepy—being with her, Mance decided, was rather like having a date with a zombie. Worse yet, they had fought. Mance had told her about the gun, showing her how he had it concealed within his jacket and telling her of how Sparrow had risked his neck to see that he got the weapon.

Jonella had not been impressed.

In fact, she had cried—perhaps because of the gun or perhaps—to Mance at least—for no good reason at all.

"Johnnie, you were doing better the first day or two I saw you in the hospital—what happened?"

She had attempted to explain that the real depression had set in as a delayed reaction; however, she faltered somewhere in the middle of it, breaking into a fresh round of tears and burying her face in a pillow.

Frustration reigned supreme.

Harsh words were exchanged.

Mance stormed off. Even Sting had become upset.

And thus Mance stared into the dull, lusterless eyes of an unpromising, lonely evening that could only stare back haplessly. He went to Fast Track's. A covey of old black men had fired up their instruments and were sending out easy, mellow jazz notes with the confident air of a good dealer dealing cards.

At the rear of the lounge Mance found Punch shooting pool. He wasn't drunk. A good sign.

"Let's go somewhere," said Mance. "Put this pissant town in our rearview mirror."

"Sounds like a take. Give me two more shots to finish off this sacrificial lamb."

It took him four more shots, and even then he barely defeated the young black man he was playing. But once inside Punch's Toyota (paid for before Punch had been kicked off the police force) Mance didn't mind the extra wait.

"Where'd you get the gun?" Punch asked.

Self-consciously Mance wrapped his jacket more tightly against his chest.

"You notice it that easy?"

"Hey, I used to be a cop. Remember?"

"Sparrow. He felt sorry for me."

"He could get his ass in all kinda trouble."

"You wouldn't turn him in, wouldya, Punch?"

"Not me. Sparrow might find out and cut my throat some night when I'm laid out stone drunk."

Mance breathed a sigh of relief, and on the way out of town Punch described a better way to conceal the weapon, advising Mance to shift it closer to his armpit.

They drove along a back road south of Soldier; Mance knew where they were headed: a scab of a town called Providence—simply a gathering of houses, no post office or bank but two churches and a heavily frequented bar known as Jimmy's. The town was also the residence of Punch's ex-wife, Chantel, a tall, willowy, model-like beauty with coffee-colored skin who, after leaving Punch, moved in with her mother and grandmother and younger sister who had three kids and no idea who fathered any of them.

"You feel like you'll ever get back together with her?" Mance asked as they pulled in among the other pickup trucks parked at Jimmy's, many of them sporting gun racks and high-powered rifles in their rear windows.

"Who? Oh . . ." Punch's fingers tap-danced on the gearshift knob. "I'd cut off my arm if she wanted me to . . . if that's what it would take for that woman to be mine again. Is that pussy-whipped or what?"

He laughed, derisively at first, then more genuinely. And Mance joined in, though he felt he understood some of the man's pain.

The namesake of the bar was a sow's ear of a white man, lost somewhere in his sixties, with purpled veins forked across his nose and cheeks. He ran a good bar, however, reasonably clean, the draft beer cold. He catered mostly to young whites, couples as well as stags, and a sprinkling of blacks. Punch was welcome because he had helped Jimmy curb what had become a serious drug trafficking situation at one time.

Mance had been in the bar before, and while he couldn't be sold beer, he was allowed to shoot pool. On this particular night he saw something above the bar he hadn't seen before: an air-brush-on fabric depiction of a lone wolf against a twilit forest; the animal was turned to face every viewer, its yellow eyes wary yet unafraid. It put Mance to mind of the creature he had imagined at Guillo House and of the uncanny sensation he had experienced all week — a feeling that at the farthest edge of his peripheral vision the wolf creature lurked. But, no, of course, like the afterimage of looking directly at the sun, the creature would, no doubt, fade eventually.

As the evening wore on, Punch and Mance played pool; Sting moved about as if in discomfort. Country-western music irritated the rat, and the jukebox offered no alternatives. Surrounded by the familiar *clack* of pool ball against pool ball, Mance began to relax and to forget about his troubles with

Jonella. Punch set up a few hustles, delighting in the ease with which Mance defeated the unskilled challengers. By late evening, Punch had settled in for some serious drinking; Mance accepted the fact that he would have to drive them home, but he allowed himself to take on one final opponent, a bearded fellow who obviously knew his way around a pool table.

They played five rounds of eight ball, Mance winning four.

"You had enough, John Mack?"

The bearded fellow's companion, slightly older and also bearded, seemed eager to leave.

"I'm comin', Raybert." Then he turned to Mance and smiled broadly as he rolled his cue across the table. "Kid, you're fuckin' good with that stick."

But as Mance acknowledged the compliment, he found himself staring at the man's smile.

At the man's teeth.

It was an odd moment; the room tipped as if a cartoon giant were beyond the walls lifting the building to peek within. John Mack's smile disappeared, replaced by a hesitant grin. There was nothing more. No incident. No words exchanged. Mance helped Punch away from his latest beer, fished the truck keys from his pocket, and trundled out of Jimmy's.

8

"I'm gone to see Della," said Raybert.

"Come on, man . . . wouldja just forget that fuckin' broad?"

John Mack Davis was caressing his deer rifle; they were in Raybert Ford's Cougar speeding toward Soldier. No more joy-riding in Raybert's black pickup, for it might be easily recognized.

"I'm only gone talk to her one more time. She's about to get off work."

"One more time, shit . . . I've heard that before."

Raybert drove on in silence, hunched over the wheel with grim determination, his mouth twisting and ticking.

70

"Why don't we breathe some air we ain't never breathed? We could go to Alaska. You and me's always talked about goin' huntin' for Alaskan brown bear. Hell, Raybert, what's keepin' us here? Not smart for us to stick around . . . and downright fuckin' crazy to be cruisin' into Soldier."

But if Raybert was moved by John Mack's eager monologue, he gave no indication. Minutes later they dropped down North Street, slowing at the tracks long enough for John Mack to remark, "Wouldn't mind takin' another poke at that sugar we took turns on last Sunday, would you?"

The other man said nothing. He was grinding his teeth and picking at a nasty pimple on one nostril.

"Raybert," John Mack continued, "you know it ain't exactly like there's no other women in the world—what's so fuckin' special 'bout Della? Hell, I mean, you and me needs to go off huntin'—Alaska, Canada—pick up work along the way, get the fuck outta—"

"Shut up," said Raybert. He did not shout. "Shut up. Shut up. Shut up." The words flowed like molten lead, intense and burning, yet controlled. The Cougar rolled into the employees' parking lot at the Rebel Beer warehouse. John Mack grumbled something inaudible. Raybert switched off the engine and took a deep breath.

"I got to do this," he said. "I only wanna talk to her. Straighten out some shit. My mind's just not hangin' level on some things. Wait for me."

John Mack shook his head as if completely exasperated and disgusted.

Mance got them home safely. Fast Track met them at the back door to the lounge; his face collapsed in disappointment when he saw Punch's condition, but he thanked Mance and chortled over his son like an old mother hen.

Envy. That's what Mance felt. There was a strong father-son bond between the two black men. Yes, Punch was drowning his troubles and that wouldn't solve anything; and yet, someone he called Pop was around to pull him out of deep water.

Mance had no reason to believe that he and his own father

71

would ever have that kind of relationship. Swimming against that current of disenchantment, the boy headed home. It was a clear night; several days of rain had ended; there was a high, star-clustered sky and a three-quarter moon.

North Street seemed preternaturally still.

He walked slowly at first, glancing over his shoulder down toward the railroad tracks. He thought of Jonella—fantasized momentarily about holding her naked in his arms—then he stopped. He had the feeling that someone was watching him—no, not simply watching him—a prickly feeling inched up his spine and nestled on his shoulder. Something or someone was letting him know that he was being monitored. Sting shifted his position as if he had experienced the sensation as well.

Mance swung around, scanning the area for signs of the pit bulls. He patted at the gun beneath his jacket. He saw nothing. And yet, he couldn't shake the feeling: *something's out there.*

What does it want?

He walked briskly home.

John Mack had grown restless. He had exhausted a string of imaginary hunting expeditions in which he successfully bagged every big game animal known to North America and had the head or hide or both to prove it.

He played the radio and blankly followed the exit of the four-to-midnight shift until the parking lot was empty save for the Cougar and Della's small foreign car. The tall wire gates to the back dock had been closed; beyond them was an almost palpable darkness.

"Come on, Raybert," John Mack whispered, "ole Della's got somebody else dipping his wick in her candle. You're history far as she's concerned."

John Mack sat squeezing at the trigger of his rifle and commending himself for avoiding a manhood-leeching entanglement with any woman. No, sir, he hadn't allowed himself to be led along by his dick—no sweet young thing had set her hooks in him. No way.

"No way that'll ever—"

72

It looked as large as a cow. Something gray and thick with fur was nosing along the side of the warehouse.

John Mack sat up.

"Sweet Jesus."

His hands tingled as he watched the creature—it had pointed ears and a tail and yellow eyes that glinted in the meager lighting of the parking lot—move toward the gate leading to the back dock.

"Oh, sweet Jesus."

John Mack jammed a fistful of cartridges into his rifle, though some dribbled onto the seat and floorboard.

His mind scrambled: *Too fuckin' big for a dog. Or a coyote. Can't be a bear. It's like some kind of fuckin' wolf. And where the fuck is Raybert? He oughtta see this.*

The creature hesitated at the wire gate, and John Mack could have sworn that it turned and looked right at the Cougar—right at *him.* He swallowed icy needles that gathered in a lump in his groin.

Then the creature stepped through the gate.

Not through an opening—John Mack was certain of that even at a distance of forty yards—but *through the wire.* And into the darkness.

Nerves burning, rifle in hand, John Mack pressed himself quietly out of the Cougar and scuttled to the gate. But the darkness concealed everything except the outline of a beer truck and the solid line of the dock. He examined the gate; it was latched but not padlocked.

I saw what it did, he told himself, his heart beating much too fast.

He glanced around, thought about going after Raybert, then decided against it. Some wild creature on the prowl for food had roamed away from the woods and ended up in town—some creature he'd never seen in this part of the country, but a creature soon to be his trophy, and he would make the front page of the local paper and be the subject of special articles in all the hunting magazines and the best-looking women would . . .

He swung open the gate.

"Hey, big sugar, show yourself," he said.

Rifle readied, he duck-walked toward the truck. He concentrated, believing he would catch a glimpse of it as it tried to escape the dock area.

Probably more afraid of me than I am of it.

But John Mack was wrong about that.

He never saw precisely where it came from; he heard gravel skitter beneath its back paws as it leaped; he heard its snarl, an unearthly sound. It seemed to have materialized out of the blackness, rushing at his face as if catapulted by the night itself.

He was slammed to the ground. His rifle flew to one side. Fangs tore at his throat and jaw as the creature landed full upon him, crushing the air from his lungs, bouncing him against the hard gravel. And as the creature's momentum carried it beyond his body a few feet, John Mack rolled away. He scrambled wildly, thudding into a front tire of the truck.

He tried to cry out, but the wind had been knocked out of him and blood seeped from his throat and jaw and mouth and nose. The creature was on him again as he crawled desperately under the high clearance of the truck. Fangs ripped at his right calf; he heard something pop. Felt fire. Yanked hard and freed himself minus a baseball-sized chunk of his leg.

The creature lowered its head to peer in at its prey.

John Mack scrambled near the transmission housing; he continued to struggle to catch his breath so that he could scream for help, but the only sounds he could manage were pathetic gasps. He grabbed at his leg and felt the warmth of his own blood and muscle and . . . *sweet Jesus, is that bone?*

Yellow eyes, seemingly as large and bright as flashlight beams, glared at him.

The darkness began a slow, inexorable swirl.

Somehow the creature was making itself smaller; he could hear its eager, raspy, predatory panting, and, at last, he screamed.

Sharp teeth closed upon his left hand.

He dug in the heels of his boots and struggled to pull away. His arm twisted in the socket; he heard another pop and a snarl, and with his free hand he swung at the creature, his fist glancing off its shoulder.

74

He felt the creature's jaws crush several fingers.

He screamed and punched until the creature released his hand.

And came for his head.

The world faded to black as a steel trap shut tightly upon his throat, severing the jugular.

Mance woke.

He was having difficulty breathing. Sting was squeaking like a rubber doll.

The boy massaged his throat a moment and then pushed the covers away to check on the rat.

"You doin' OK?" he whispered.

Gradually Sting calmed down.

"Maybe we had the same dream," said Mance, though he recalled no dream, only the sensation of the stars cutting away savagely at the flesh of the night.

"It's OK," he said. "Everything's gone be OK."

And somehow he really believed it would be.

Raybert followed the blinking red lights of Della's small car as it accelerated out of the parking lot. Moments earlier he had actually begged—*good God, what's wrong with me?*— begged that woman for another chance.

His actions sickened him. John Mack had been right: *fuckin' broad.*

"Damn you!" he shouted into the night. "Damn you! Damn you!"

He ran back to the Cougar, half thinking he ought to chase her down and teach her a lesson—and let John Mack help him. Except that John Mack was nowhere to be seen. So Raybert got out of the car and began calling for his friend. And then he went looking for him.

He found him at the tall, wire gate.

John Mack's torn, bloodied body had been dragged a number of yards, and someone had attempted to pull him through the wire, succeeding only in stuffing the head, or parts of the head, through the large mesh. At least, it appeared to be John Mack, for the body caught in the gate had no facial features. No face at all.

Raybert stumbled twice on the way back to the Cougar.

His mind was a white-hot blank.

His hand trembled so severely he could barely manage to jam the key into the ignition. He rocked gently against the steering wheel, his chest heaving in a series of dry retches. The Cougar began to shake. The engine groaned once, but failed to start.

Raybert heard a rattling of breath. Then felt it warm and moist upon his shoulder and neck. He turned to look into the backseat.

The wolf creature leaned closer, yellow eyes staring intently into Raybert's as if studying what terror can do to a man's face.

Chapter Four

1

He woke relieved.

Yet, he could not, despite extreme mental exertion, connect with the source of relief. Some problem had, during the night, been solved. Too many webs of sleep held his thoughts. Shaking free to clarity seemed impossible.

"Sting?"

His pet was in his cage, uncharacteristically calm and relaxed.

Mance looked over at his jacket on the arm of a chair—the gun, why didn't it compel him as it had?

"Strange night," he said, scratching at his scalp.

In the shadows of his room, he glanced down at his darkly stained hands.

Blood?

He suddenly rushed out into the hallway and slipped into the bathroom and switched on the light. No, not blood. No stains whatsoever. Again, he experienced the sensation of relief. No blood on his hands and yet . . . he washed them, soaping them up and rinsing them several times. No appearance of blood, but rather the *feel* of blood. The odor of blood.

He thought of Eugene, a boyhood friend. And the railroad tracks.

He definitely smelled blood, slightly pungent, suggestive of lawn mower oil.

Mance dried his hands; the unnerving sensation relented and the odor began to fade.

Puzzled, he returned to his room.

"We gotta go walk, man," he said to Sting, lifting him from his cage. The rat scampered up his arm and scurried under his long hair.

It was a partly cloudy Sunday morning. Nothing out of the ordinary stirring on North Street. Scarlett's was opening for breakfast. A few old men would saunter in for coffee. A few churchgoers would invest in the breakfast buffet.

But North Street was wearing a different face somehow. What was it? The morning light? Was the street not as dusty? Not as many pieces of loose trash skittering about? Purged—it was a word with which Mance was only vaguely familiar, but he felt that it fit the freshly washed, curiously new air he was breathing at every step.

Mance had left his gun at home. He did not miss it.

Crossing the tracks, he smelled blood again. Eugene's blood. He could, if pressed to, identify the very spot where the accident had occurred years ago. How old had he been? Five? Six? He pushed the memory aside.

Up the hill toward Rebel Beer he saw a police car and an ambulance, neither running lights or sirens.

"What's going on, Sting? A break-in, I bet."

But, no, not likely that an ambulance would be on the scene with a simple break-in.

Mance jogged to the side parking lot, where he saw Boom talking to three police officers and one man in a coat and tie. Rebel Beer was closed Sundays, but Mance knew that Boom, as day shift dock supervisor, routinely checked on the trucks and loading dock on Sunday.

A slight breeze was kicking up pellets of dust.

The police had ribboned off much of the parking lot, and an ambulance attendant was wheeling a body along, a blood-ied sheet covering its entire length. Mance happened to be close enough that when the wind tugged the sheet free of the person's face he saw the head of a bearded man—the companion of the man he had played pool against. Of that he was reasonably certain.

"God . . . what is this?" Mance whispered to himself.

One of the policemen was motioning for him to keep his distance. Mance smelled blood — lawn mower oil — and stepped back instinctively. Boom ducked under the bright yellow police ribbon and came toward the boy. The man looked grim and deflated. He was staring at the ground and had his hands in his pockets.

"What happened?" Mance exclaimed. "Jeez, was there a fight? What's with all the blood?"

An involuntary shiver seized Boom. He glanced apprehensively over a shoulder.

"Been a killin'," he said, his voice tremulous and weak. " 'Bout thirty minutes ago I was checkin' the dock, same way I do ever Sunday morning and . . . goddamn . . . two of 'em, and the one at the gate . . . goddamn, I mean . . ."

He shivered again and walked on past Mance.

"Boom, hey, who did it? What happened? Boom?"

But the man crawled into his truck and sat there staring through the windshield.

Mance pestered the police, but to no avail. They appeared shaken, too, though not to the same degree as Boom. The ambulance carried two bodies away, and Mance continued to smell blood, and then he thought of Eugene and train dodging.

As a small boy, when he wasn't doing something with Uncle Thestis, he had a companion whose name was Eugene — last names are never important to small boys. Slightly older — eight or nine — Eugene was blond and chunky and retarded, with a droopy mouth and slow eyes and feet and ears that stuck out pathetically.

Eugene loved trains, but his grandmother, with whom he lived, expressly forbid him to play near the tracks. Such an order naturally fueled the boy's attraction for the metal monsters, and so it frequently happened that Eugene would tow young Mance secretly to the tracks where they would wait patiently for a manifest freight to roar through. These freights, of course, would have reduced their speed as they approached Soldier, but not enough to dampen the spirit of Eugene. Seasons of joy would pass across Eugene's face as the train neared; his body would quake, and he would hop excitedly from one foot to the other and screech like an owl. But as the cars rolled by, he would lapse into a ministate of Nirvana, mouth open like a carp feeding along a creek bank. Ecstasy would flow in the boy's veins instead of blood.

One day it chanced that the two boys created a game—Mance could not remember whose idea it was—a game of "dodge the train." It was simple: wait until the engine had reached within fifteen yards or so of their lookout spot and then dash across the tracks screaming like wild Indians and loving every death-threatening instant. It was a crude game—as the best ones often are—but they had virtually no opportunities to refine the basics, for they only played it twice. The first time proved exhilarating; the second time . . .

Mance never understood exactly what occurred. Or why. When the slate gray face of the monster engine thrummed and growled close to their lookout, Mance sprinted over the tracks, his bare feet dancing, a shiver worming its way across his shoulders. He shouted with glee. And Eugene followed, matching Mance's vocalization of triumph. And then—maybe he'd become confused? Maybe he wanted to spice up the game?—Eugene turned and tried to make it a second time.

All Mance saw was the pink tumble of Eugene's bare legs; all he heard was the train's brakes hiss and the wheel housing scream and the engineer's futile yank of the horn. Mance did not shout or cry or run home. He waited and watched as various men flowed to the scene. The train carried Eugene's body for nearly a hundred yards.

At one point in the aftermath, Mance saw a man pick up pieces of Eugene and place them in a wheelbarrow. For weeks the area along the railroad tracks smelled like lawn mower oil. It was an odor that Mance could not forget; and he could not bear, from that day forward, to be around a wheelbarrow.

2

Mance went home and ate a late breakfast. The memory of Eugene released him, but the shock he had encountered at the

Rebel Beer warehouse remained, like a sharp pain which appears to have no precise location. The face of the bearded man . . . all the blood . . . a dark collage was forming, generating a feeling that somehow he knew something about the circumstances of the murders. Yet, how could that be possible? Yes, he had seen the two men in Jimmy's. That, however, meant virtually nothing.

At Scarlett's, Mance pulled his parents aside and told them the news: his father grumbled something and shook his head; his mother clasped her hands to her face and exclaimed, wide-eyed, "No, you don't mean it!"

The news would spread up and down North Street and throughout Soldier from Scarlett's.

After eating, Mance called Jonella; Tanya answered and explained that Jonella had taken some of her new medication barely an hour ago and had gone immediately to sleep and was likely not to awaken until early evening. Then Tanya asked whether he'd seen Boom, adding that the man had come home very upset, had been abusive—"a real mean and scared look in his eyes"—and had left the trailer, giving no indication where he was going.

Doubtful it was the best course, Mance went ahead and told Tanya about the murders. She squealed a string of "Oh, my Gods" and breathless exclamations of horror before he could extract himself from the conversation.

He had a bad feeling about Jonella being in that trailer. It obviously wasn't safe for Tanya and her girls—Boom was a time bomb.

Restless, Mance started off on another walk, fully intending to visit Austin or maybe see whether Fast Track would unlock the lounge and let him shoot some pool. But his meanderings led him instead to Guillo House, to the second-floor redoubt he had so often shared with Jonella.

Despite the bright sunshine splashing through the broken windows, the room wasn't the same without her. The walls showed evidence of his rage the night he had hallucinated the wolf creature. Scattered pieces of his jam box mocked him. He sat down on the pallet where he and Jonella had shared each other's embrace. He leaned his back against the wall and

81

closed his eyes. And listened to the language of abandonment, that secret code tapped out by every empty house, but especially inscrutable at Guillo House.

One question persisted beyond the others: who did it? Had the men killed each other? From what little he had squeezed out of the police, that seemed unlikely. He knew that the two men did not work for Rebel Beer. What had brought them to the warehouse? Was someone at Rebel Beer a killer? There were enough candidates, men violent enough to commit murder—chief among them Boom himself. Yet, Boom claimed to have found the bodies. Did the police suspect him? If so, wouldn't they have held him?

The bearded men.

The smile of the one. His teeth.

Mance suddenly felt the temperature of the room drop ten degrees.

A snarl jerked him fully awake. He glanced around. Was there someone else in the house? He felt a presence. A curious warmth layered itself over the chill. Mance could feel Sting quivering.

"Who's here?"

Silence.

But the presence felt even stronger.

Mance pushed himself to his feet.

The evil ones are dead.

The voice spoke into his consciousness, a masculine voice, yet not quite resembling any other he had ever heard before.

"Who are you?"

Mance spun around.

But the voice issued no further words. He sank back down upon the pallet. And the rush of an epiphany seized every muscle and nerve, every emotion and thought.

Jonella's attackers had been killed.

Every fiber of his reason told him that he had only imagined the voice—it could not know—but yet it did. Somehow it did know. And Mance believed it.

"They're dead," he whispered.

But who killed them?

He closed his eyes and a scene materialized in which two pit

82

bulls ran yelping in fear from some invisible enemy.

When Mance opened his eyes, he felt he knew the identity of the killer.

3

In the dream, she witnessed the death of two large, bearlike creatures with human eyes. A shadow so deep, a blackness beyond darkness, stalked them and killed them, and though the scenes were horrifying she did not look away. She woke from the dream relieved and inexplicably calm. She switched on the lamp by her bed and examined her hands—they no longer felt dirty. Was it the dream or Dr. Colby's medication?

As she yawned and stretched and felt refreshed, the dream lost some of its resonance. She thought about her only visit to Dr. Stanton Colby's office, a dark, womblike room lined with bookshelves and wood paneling. Colby himself, a psychotherapist, surprised her; he did not look like a doctor, choosing to wear jeans and a plaid workshirt and a baseball cap. A wad of tobacco bulged one cheek.

"Not feelin' so good, pretty little lady?"

Those were his first words to her. Then he asked her to describe what she was feeling, whether she was eating and sleeping well. What if any dreams she was having. The pills he prescribed for her gave her back her appetite, but made her crave sleep.

She had awakened early in the evening. Tanya brought her a tray of food and Crystal and Loretta brought her "happy" crayon drawings which they had, no doubt, slaved over all afternoon. Jonella made a pleasant fuss about the crude drawings; and, in fact, she had decided the medication was pulling her out of her depression. She took a tumble, however, when Crystal pointed to the bite marks on her jaw.

"Did you get bite-ed by a dog?" she asked innocently.

"My Lord," Tanya exclaimed, and hustled the girls from the room. "I'm so-o-o sorry, Jonella. Can't imagine what'd make her ask such a godawful question, can you?"

Jonella smiled wearily, her fingers touching the mark.

"She's just a little girl, and besides, I can't keep the bandage on it forever—makeup doesn't hardly cover it, though."

She noticed that Tanya was fidgeting even more than usual.

"Hey, don't worry about what Crystal said," Jonella followed. "She's just curious. Probably wondering when I'm gone get straightened out. Those little yellow pills Dr. Colby gave me really zonk me—and I had the strangest dream. . . ." She paused. Tanya was trembling.

"What is it, girl?"

Jonella reached out to touch her shoulder.

"Just godawful news. It scares me. Boom . . . I'm 'bout sick scared."

"Tell me. Tell me, Tanya. What is it?"

Tanya opened up and told her what Mance had relayed about the murders at Rebel Beer, and she talked about Boom's behavior and her apprehension about his return. Jonella listened, and in her thoughts she once again witnessed the deaths of the bearlike creatures.

But this time they had human faces.

And she recognized them.

4

Jonella taped a fresh piece of gauze over the bite marks before Mance arrived that evening. Still groggy from the medication, she stayed in bed to greet him.

"Hey, Johnnie," he said as he ducked his head cautiously into the room.

She smiled, feeling as shy as if they were suddenly strangers. Were they? she wondered. The attack, she believed, had changed her, and could change her further, though the last doctor to examine her at the hospital seemed to rule out any diseases transmitted by sexual contact. Odds were, thankfully, not good on pregnancy either—wrong time of the month. These realities cheered her, and yet . . .

"Sorry I'm such a sleepy wart," she said. "It's those yellow pills."

"Sleepy wart?"

Jonella giggled, and it made her self-conscious of sounding like a little girl.

"Momma would say that, you know, when I was slow getting up . . . 'sleepy wart,' she called me."

Mance chuckled nervously, then toyed with something behind his back.

"Brought you some of them chocolate mint patties you like."

He handed her a small bag which contained three foil-wrapped patties.

"Thanks—seems like I'm always hungry anymore."

He sat on the edge of the bed.

"So you feelin' better?"

"Some."

She lifted her hand to the patch of gauze because she could see that, now and then, his eyes would rest upon it. To anticipate his concern, she said, "This bothers you, doesn't it? I've tried, Mance, all kinda ways, you know, to cover it."

He looked away.

"Oh, hey . . . it's . . . don't mean to stare at it."

He was embarrassed, and their conversation thudded along a few minutes like a car with a couple of flat tires.

Eventually he said, "Guess probably you heard what happened at the warehouse?"

She nodded. "Tanya told me . . . and it's got her worried. Boom, she says he's acting weirder and meaner than usual. Hope all this doesn't set him off."

"I wish you weren't staying here," said Mance. "Maybe if I talked to my folks . . . maybe we could find some room for you with us."

Jonella smiled hesitantly.

"I'll be fine, but I worry about Tanya and the girls."

Mance appeared to be working up the courage to deliver a speech about an issue weighing heavily upon his mind.

"I feel like," he began, "well . . . there's something we can both stop worrying about."

He was uncertain how to proceed.

"I think I know what you mean," she responded.

Surprised, Mance said, "You do?"

"Did the two men who got killed have beards?" she asked.

Mance looked at her; he felt the pressure of a cold emptiness in his chest.

"Yeah. Yeah, they did," he said slowly.

"It's them," she said.

"Jeez, that's what I was gone to say. Why do you feel it was them?"

She shrugged and knotted her fingers and frowned.

"I think . . . I think maybe I dreamed it."

She related the dream about the bearlike animals being killed, and he followed with an account of what he had experienced at Guillo House, though he stopped short of telling her who he suspected the killer was.

When they had finished exchanging stories, something curious, something a bit magical, passed between them. Something like muggy August air being broken by a storm, leaving the atmosphere clean and rain-sparkled and pleasant to smell. They felt relieved. They felt, though they could not have articulated it, that a strange form of justice had been served.

They did not understand precisely what had occurred, but they smiled and embraced and kissed—they were a couple again. And they laughed when Tanya rapped timidly at the door and said, "Hey, you guys decent in there? I'm comin' in with bowls of ice cream."

5

Two days later, Jonella had suffered her self-imposed cloistering long enough—she had to get away from the claustrophobic walls of the trailer, the incessant chatter of Tanya, and the brooding menace of Boom, and because Mance was helping Austin, she had to find other companionship. She set about preparing to "go visiting" in as cheerful a frame of mind as she could muster, cutting back on her dosage of the yellow pills the night before so that her eyelids wouldn't droop all day. She dressed in jeans and a sweater, and Tanya flitted about fixing her hair for her, producing a style she had seen in some women's magazine. Jonella wasn't

86

thrilled about it, but she let it ride.

A more major task awaited her: how to cover the bite marks.

A heavy coating of makeup *almost* did the trick; however, if one looked directly at the marks, a shadowy outline of them emerged.

"Does it show real bad?" she asked Tanya.

"I can't see it no ways, honey. No, and well, maybe when you turn your face a certain way . . . no, and it's not so's you'd notice. Least, I wouldn't. Maybe if you kept your chin down and didn't smile. Honey, it's fine. Or you could put some blush on it—I got some called Purple Fire—we could try that, but, honey, really, you look fine."

Jonella sighed exasperatedly and soon after began walking to Scarlett's.

Mance's mother met her at the door and hugged her and clucked over her excitedly and announced to the clientele that Scarlett's "sweetheart" had returned. Embarrassed but gladdened, Jonella soaked up the welcome.

"Thanks, Mom," she said.

"Oh, and wouldn't Uncle Thestis be overjoyed to see you—like a rainbow in his rainy life. Would you mind goin' up to visit to him?"

"Of course not, Mom. I'd like to."

And Mrs. Culley clasped her hands together as if a prayer had been answered.

Moments later, Jonella was standing outside Uncle Thestis's door. She knocked hesitantly.

"Entree," a voice echoed.

A shadowy, almost comically cluttered room opened before her. A somewhat rotund, molelike man—Jonella always thought of the creatures in *The Wind in the Willows* when she saw Uncle Thestis—struggled to free his body from an overstuffed chair.

"Hey, Uncle Thestis—it's me, Jonella."

The man's eyebrows pumped up and down; he steadied himself with his cane, and his smile imitated the motion of a tidal wave.

"Miss Jonella, as I live and breathe, the sight of you gives my heart a reason to continue beating—I can't describe how delighted I am to see you, dear."

She stepped forward to embrace him; he smelled musty and stale, and his coffee breath was a little offensive, but she did not mind. He was so sincerely happy that she couldn't possibly have been repulsed.

"I'm really glad to get out of my sister's trailer. Those walls . . . I was going bonkers, you know, and I needed some fresh air."

"My thoughts have been with you every day."

"Thanks for the flowers and the card—did you get my thank-you note?"

"I did. I most certainly did."

He pointed to a tall dresser, the top of which was a jungle of old sepia-toned photos in tarnished frames, a silver cup, and jars and jars of marbles. She giggled at the sight of all the marbles. Her thank-you note was nestled among the clutter.

"Uncle Thestis, how many do you have? How many marbles total?"

"Oh, marbles, you say?" His face inflated a fresh smile. "People have been known to say, 'Thestis Sinclair has lost his marbles,' but as you can plainly see, there they are in all their shining glory—not a one lost. How many, you say? Well . . ."

He adjusted himself in the chair so that he could study the jars. His face dropped a curtain of seriousness, and it struck Jonella as almost comical. And, to herself, she thought: There's a boy inside him.

Yes, inside this man a boy lived, still alive to the wonders of the world, both its complex ones and its simple ones. The eager, otherwise meaningless joys of boyhood had not faded for him, and she admired the fact that he continued to pursue them unabashedly.

"But you see," he followed, "those represent only the tip of the iceberg of my collection. Look under the bed, if you would."

She lifted the corner flap of the chintz spread covering his small, lumpy bed, and there she beheld mason jars jammed with winking lights of every possible color and type of marble she could imagine.

She issued a tiny squeal of surprise.

Then, with his cane, he pointed to the closet.

"And . . . and there, too, if you will."

"Uncle Thestis, you could have a marble museum," she said as she opened the door cautiously, almost as if she expected something or someone to leap out at her. Among the shadows were reinforced shelves crowded with jar after jar, each filled to the brim with cat's eyes and shooters and steelies and types she did not recognize.

"A million," she exclaimed. "You must have a million."

He chuckled as she sat down again.

"Um, more like ten thousand, I should guess. One of these days I shall recount them. But not while the Conqueror Worm has me in its sights. I've not been in the very best of health."

"I've felt better myself," said Jonella.

And suddenly they looked at each other and the starting gun for an old, familiar game had been sounded. Almost in unison, they said,

"I give you the world's smallest violin."

Forefingers rubbing gently against thumbs.

And then laughter.

"You remember, don't you?" said Thestis, eyes outsparkling any of his marbles.

"Couldn't forget that," said Jonella. Images of much earlier days flooded her thoughts—moments when she and Mance would traipse into Thestis's room complaining of a skinned knee or a scraped elbow or an upset stomach from eating too much candy. The man's response was ever the same: forefinger rubbing against thumb, a feigned sadness in his eyes, and the words, "I give you the world's smallest violin." And a lesson: never complain about your health as long as your heart is beating and your eyes are open to receive the great light of the world.

"But this time," said Thestis, bringing her back to the present, "*you* truly deserve the sympathy and compassion. The world has been unimaginably cruel to you, and I deeply, deeply regret that."

Jonella lowered her chin—she thought fleetingly of Tanya's advice.

"Mom tells me you've been poorly and that you oughtta see a doctor," she said.

"Fie on it—wouldn't do a drop of good. We outrace the Conqueror Worm for many years, but in the end he catches up. Always has. Always will."

"The Conqueror Worm?"

"An old term for death. Poe was fond of using it, I seem to recall."

Jonella nodded. Feeling uneasy with the topic, she looked around the room again, her eyes resting upon stacks of old magazines.

"Uncle Thestis, do you ever throw anything away?"

He raised his eyebrows.

"Why, every last piece of stuff in this room *belongs*," he joked. "Well, I should put it this way: I never throw away good memories of people—people like you . . . and like Mance."

The mention of Mance's name sent an electric shock through Jonella.

"Will you and he ever, you know, be friends again?" she asked hesitantly.

"One day perhaps. You must understand," he explained, "that Mance is trying to find himself, to discover a way to shape the shadow side of himself into something he can live with."

"Shadow side? Is that something real bad? It makes me scared thinking what he might do. Did you know that he bought a gun because he wanted to shoot the men who attacked me? He does lots of things without thinking. Is that because of his shadow side?"

"In a way, yes. A person's shadow is rather like a separate personality formed of all those aspects of ourselves that we've rejected. But just because we've rejected or repressed them doesn't mean they've disappeared—Mance is wrestling with a defiant shadow. Many boys his age do. The only option for me is to sit patiently and wait until he needs me again. One day, perhaps he will."

Jonella thought a moment.

"I think I've got one, too. A shadow side. But I can't believe you have one."

90

Thestis chuckled.

"Oh, but I do. Over the years a person, unfortunately, projects that shadow onto other people or even onto things. Would it surprise you to learn that my shadow is concentrated in Guillo House, the very house where you and Mance go for your trysts of youthful affection?"

She blushed, then touched self-consciously at the bite marks, hoping they weren't ghosting through her makeup.

"Why Guillo House?"

Thestis issued a deep sigh.

"You see . . . but, no . . . such a long story, peopled with mystery and better suited for another time."

"I've got a mystery of my own," she said. "I mean, Mance and I together do. It's about the murders at Rebel Beer."

"Oh, yes, Mance's mother told me of them. What has happened to Soldier? Why, it appears to be returning to the bad old days of the thirties—violence and attacks and killings. Are drugs somehow involved?"

Jonella hesitated.

"I don't think I know anything except . . . I think . . . and Mance, too . . . we think the men who got killed were . . . we think they were the same men who attacked me."

She recounted her dream as well as Mance's feelings and sensations about the experience at Guillo House.

"Interesting, yes, very much so," said Thestis.

"Could we be right? It doesn't hardly seem like we could be."

"Dreams and psychic voices—yes, it's quite possible I suppose. I've written stories about such unusual occurrences."

Jonella rolled her shoulders as if they had knotted up.

"I thought maybe I should go to the police, you know. And maybe identify the bodies. I thought about it, and I just can't do it. Can't bring myself to do it, so if it was them, well, then they're dead and won't hurt nobody else. If it wasn't, well, I don't want to think about that. Mance and I believe it was, and it's a relief to us and so . . ."

"Now, you did say, didn't you, that Mance heard the voice while he was in Guillo House?"

"Yes, sir."

91

Thestis patted her hand, but she could see that he was distracted, voyaging upon some strange sea of thought. Alone. She had touched a nerve of some kind with her account. But she decided not probe into his reaction.

"It's a mystery for the likes of Gottfried Sücher," he said, reconnecting with her and smiling benignly.

"Your psychic detective?"

"Yes—how wonderful that you remember him."

"I read about him in some of your stories. He could figure out anything."

"*Almost* anything," he corrected her. "Did you know that in German, Sücher means searcher?"

Jonella shook her head, and for another hour or more they allowed the real world to recede from consciousness as Thestis waxed on about occult mysteries and the supernatural and the fun of imaginary horrors.

Reluctantly Jonella rose to leave when it became evident that the man was growing weary.

"Please come to visit again soon," he said. "I've missed you."

"I'm fixin' to go back to school next Monday," she said. "Plan to anyway. Back to work at Scarlett's, too. So I'll be seeing you."

He squeezed her hand and winked.

"Oh, but that rascal Mance is a most fortunate fellow to have such a lovely ladyfriend."

Jonella ducked her chin, but then leaned forward and hugged the man. She believed that somehow he knew about the bite marks, and yet had not once betrayed his knowledge.

"Thank you, Uncle Thestis," she whispered.

He returned her embrace.

"The thanks is mine to you for bringing beauty into an old, ugly dog's life."

6

A cool but sunny afternoon greeted Jonella as she negotiated North Street. She walked without fear, and yet she had

92

been careful to leave Scarlett's well before dark. The visit had lifted her spirits. She would make it. She would try not to complain. She smiled at the image of Uncle Thestis—boy and occult scholar and writer all in one lumpish, lovable man.

Few cars or pedestrians were evident; by the courthouse a few old black men loitered, and near Austin's, a dilapidated truck had parked, its hauling space stuffed with mattresses and box springs.

Jonella strained at the window of the furniture store to catch a glimpse of Mance, but he was nowhere in sight, so she crossed the street and headed for the trailer she called home.

And the eyes of the wolf creature followed her.

From an abandoned building at the bottom of the street it watched her approach. No stray pit bulls dared step into view to confront her. They knew better. They had been warned. The creature was learning Jonella's scent, her ways, the nature of her fears, the texture of her thought.

At the corner, before North Street crossed the tracks, Jonella slowed at the Soldier Holiness Temple; she glanced toward the empty store next to it. The creature pricked its ears— it sensed her apprehension in the form of a cold, heavy, wet fear. The creature readied itself to emerge. Then Jonella raised her chin determinedly and began walking again, quickening her pace.

The creature relaxed. It made itself completely invisible.

And followed her to the door of her sister's trailer.

At no time was she aware of its presence.

Chapter Five

1

Later that week Rebel Beer continued to be a hive of excitement. The police had conducted routine interviews with nearly everyone; the parking lot and dock area had been combed for clues, and rumors, naturally enough, had seemed to pour from the very walls of the warehouse. Mance had listened disinterestedly to all the speculation, the chief theory being that Raybert Ford and John Mack Davis had engaged in a lovers' battle over Rebel Beer's own Della Wilson, leading to the demise of both.

One of the men on the four-to-midnight shift put the kibosh on that reading of events.

"Boom hisself," declared the man, "seen the bodies, and he told me they's so far torn up that only one of them nuthouse fuckers you hear about that cut up people an' eat 'em coulda done this. Naw, sir, they didn't kill each tuther. No gun done the killin' neither."

Another on the shift seconded the view.

"It's a psychopath—betcha a fiver. Lotsa wild bastards out there these days. Slightest little thing sets 'em off. Mostly sex. Betcha 'nother fiver sex is at the bottom of this—some bastards shoot their rocks off sticking their pricks in warm, fresh blood."

At that point Mance, disgusted by the tenor of the claims, plunged into the nightly task of loading the trucks.

The killings had caused everyone who worked on the dock

to look twice at shadows; increased security—two uniformed Soldier police officers patrolled the parking lot area during the shift—did virtually nothing to ease the tension.

"They say Boom's gone strange. Didja hear that, Mance? Day shift guys been complainin' about how he's so . . . so edgy."

The speaker was a young, dark-haired co-worker named Spivey who was small but strong and had bulging eyes which, when he discussed anything stimulating, threatened to escape their sockets.

"You think Boom killed 'em?" he followed, eager for Mance to respond.

"No," he returned quickly. "Boom's mean all right, but . . . it wasn't him."

"Ole Della's the cause of this," Spivey continued, eyes receding slightly. "What man wudn't fight over her—those knockers and the way she flirts up to ever'body. She ever flirt up to you, Mance?"

"No."

"Well, word has it she'd dumped on Raybert—Raybert Ford. You know him?"

Mance shook his head.

"I knowed both of 'em boys—Raybert Ford and John Mack Davis. They's from over around Providence. Raybert, he went to school with my older brother. In an' out of trouble, you know, but nothin' like John Mack. Car theft, drugs, rape— John Mack had served time at Limestone."

Mance suddenly became more interested in Spivey's chatter.

"You say, rape?"

"Yeah, a little gal in Providence, only he got outta the charge is what I hear."

Mance felt a welling of satisfaction.

"Somebody got him this time," he said.

"Yeah . . . yeah, sure the fuck did," said Spivey.

At the meal break Mance secreted away to a far corner of the warehouse to share a bag of chips with Sting. And to think. As usual, pleasant wisps of thoughts about Jonella stirred feelings of desire—things were going to be better between them now, now that the attack had been avenged. He had come to believe without question that Raybert Ford and John Mack Davis were the men who raped Jonella. They had been killed. Mutilated, if you gave credence to the rumors. By . . . someone.

Mance sat on a case of beer. He wasn't hungry. Sting gorged himself on the chips and had trouble climbing back onto Mance's shoulder.

The evil ones are dead.

The words materialized in his thoughts as a mere echo of what he had heard at Guillo House. Whose voice? Who had killed them? Who could project his voice into another person's consciousness? Mance thought again of old Rollo at Sparrow's pawnshop. The old man's smile. The old man's erection.

It's Sparrow. Sparrow did it. Sparrow killed Ford and Davis.

He brought up an image of Sparrow's face.

Lightning streaks danced in the man's eyes. And Mance heard a replay of his voice.

It's the power of the living dark.

But why? Why would Sparrow have killed them?

Don't worry. You've got a friend.

And how? How had Sparrow done it?

You ought to kill your enemy with your bare hands.

Mance looked down at his hands. He flexed his fingers and shook his head.

"The living dark," he whispered to himself.

Then it was time to return to work.

The remainder of the shift crawled by at an agonizingly slow pace; Mance and Spivey were sent from the loading dock to the snack food packaging wing for some stacking of back inventory. Spivey dusted off the topic of Della Wilson, iterating his secret or not-so-secret longings for her. The transition from there to a related issue proved an easy one for Spivey, but it took Mance somewhat by surprise.

"You're not a virgin, are you, Mance? See, I know you ain't 'cause you and that girl of yours—Janet—well, you've been goin' together for a long time, and if you've been together with the same girl for a long time, well, it just figures you ain't just holdin' hands no more."

"Her name's Jonella," said Mance, but he decided not to correct Spivey's assumptions about his virginity. What young man would?

"Jonella—right. I've seen her. Real damn pretty. Real fine. Me, I ain't got a girl. I'm twenty-two years old and don't got a girl. Worser than that . . ." He paused as they moved to another pallet of boxes and Mance repositioned the forklift. When a moderate silence fell into place, Spivey continued.

"If I told you a secret, Mance, would you promise to God and Jesus you wudn't never tell another body?"

"I guess so," he said, not particularly interested one way or the other. He was mentally walking around a difficult matter: should he go to Sparrow and thank him for killing Ford and Davis? Or, should he go to the police? Or, should he say nothing? And was he, in fact, one thousand percent certain it was Sparrow?

"I'm a virgin," said Spivey. He gritted his teeth and looked a little pale. "That makes me a real sorry ass, don't it? Look at it—you're just a fuckin' kid and you've already . . . and me . . . I think maybe there's a reason for it, Mance."

Mance shook his head. He felt uncomfortable and couldn't believe that the big clock purchased last year by their union office showed another half hour to quitting time.

"You're not a sorry ass for that," he said. "You're just . . . saving yourself."

Embarrassment rushed through him; it sounded like a wimpy thing to say. Spivey, however, didn't appear to have heard the remark.

"When I was 'bout twelve," he began, as if he were talking to a psychotherapist rather than a co-worker, "in the seventh grade, I think, we had this neighbor woman, Mrs. Ruddock, Lila Ruddock, and her husband got killed in an accident at the mill and 'bout two weeks after it happened she asked my mom if I could help her move some furniture . . . swear to God I'm not making this up. She got me in her bedroom, and she was wearing this robe, and she really didn't have anything for me to move. She asked me if I thought she was 'desirable'—hell, I never even knowed what the word meant, and then she opened

97

her robe and—swear to God—she never had on one stitch of clothes. She said I could touch her and do whatever I wanted to and she would never, never tell anyone . . . and I was so scared I ran like hell."

Mance couldn't hold back a chuckle.

"Guess I would have, too," he said.

Spivey suddenly looked relieved.

"You would have? Hey, glad to hear it." He hesitated before adding, "You think Mrs. Ruddock scared me away from women forever? You think women know I'm scared of 'em?"

Mance shrugged. "I doubt it. I don't feel like they would. Don't worry about it."

Near quitting time they were sent back to the loading dock and finished the shift there. And Mance found himself staring into the shadows beyond the warehouse, the very same area in which John Mack Davis had been savaged.

"You scared?"

Mance jumped. He hadn't noticed Spivey approach.

But this time Mance decided to level with his co-worker.

"Yeah. Yeah, I guess maybe I am."

Spivey nodded. Halfway smiled. And for a few heartbeats he had the face of a twelve-year-old.

The squad car patrolling the Rebel Beer parking lot pulled away shortly after midnight. As Mance walked up North Street, he wished he had told Spivey the truth about being a virgin. But then again, it was nobody else's business, and he wasn't especially eager for Spivey to be a close friend. He had enough friends: Punch and Fast Track and Austin. And Sparrow. An image of Uncle Thestis materialized, then dissolved rapidly. No image at all of his father.

And there was Jonella.

She was returning to school next week, and he had a plan, a sort of "welcome back" evening at Guillo House. Next Wednesday would be Valentine's Day—perfect. Buoyed by pleasant anticipation, he crossed the tracks. Sting scratched at his neck as if to remind him that he had forgotten to call to mind one other friend.

"Hey, good buddy. You're cool, you're cool."

He jerked affectionately at the rat's tail, and then the varmint settled into his resting position.

Mance began to hum a lyric from Metallica.

And that's when he saw the figure shamble from beneath the overpass bridge.

Whoever or whatever it was, it completely arrested Mance: some fifty yards away, the figure was moving toward him, its eyes drawn to the ground, its shoulders rocking as it lurched along. Mance likened it to the movement of some kind of ape, and yet even at that distance and even with shadows dominating his view, Mance believed it was a man.

Fascinated, he continued to watch as the figure scrambled into an abandoned building. There was a suggestion in the movement that the figure was searching for something—no, not precisely *searching*. More like *hunting*.

A chill spread across Mance's shoulders.

Sting squirmed.

Two blocks away a car passed.

Mance had not moved for thirty seconds when the figure emerged and slid among the shadows, directing his path away from Mance.

Curiosity overcame reason, and the boy followed.

Who in the hell . . . ?

Closer, Mance could hear the figure talking low, a babel of words as if in distress. Occasionally the figure would stop and Mance would press himself against the nearest building to remain out of sight; the figure would appear to scratch at the sidewalk; or, a time or two, he stood more erect and clawed at the air.

Jesus, what is this?

The figure's clothing gradually became more evident: black or dark blue shirt and trousers—not jeans—and a black stocking cap and black tennis shoes. Mance could not see the figure's face; in fact, he hoped the mysterious individual would not suddenly reverse directions and catch him on his trail.

Deeper into the shadows, where the last streetlamp failed to extend its pool of light, the figure turned left up an alley, an alley Mance knew well, for it led behind Sparrow's pawnshop,

Fast Track's lounge, and Austin's furniture store.

Mance stayed as close as possible, hesitating at the mouth of the alley, which had no illumination save for a meager light at Fast Track's back door. The figure pressed forward, and once during the tense moments in which Mance pursued him, he thought he heard the man snarl. In a duck walk, Mance gained ground until he was no more than twenty yards from the figure.

At that point, the figure appeared to raise himself on his toes and sniff the air.

Mance crouched low.

But he knew that the figure had sensed his presence.

God, what am I doing?

One impression dominated the boy's senses: whoever he was, the figure up ahead was dangerous — and he might at any second turn and attack.

Mance tried not to breathe.

He waited, carefully eyeing the shadowy outline. He was prepared to run if necessary, because his instincts told him not to challenge the menacing figure.

The tension wound the night like a strand of barbed wire.

A minute or longer had passed when the tension was broken by a voice, not spoken aloud, but rather one which entered his thoughts clearly, distinctly.

Keep away, friend.

Mance gasped.

The figure groped his way forward, and there was enough light from the rear of Fast Track's to reveal that he had stopped at the back door of the pawnshop. The figure paused there for only an instant and, in one swift, fluid motion, removed the stocking cap.

Long, blond hair rustled free.

And then the man known as Sparrow slipped from view.

2

"But I *know* it's him."

"You don't *know* shit, boy."

100

"I followed him, Punch. After the night shift at Rebel, I was coming home and I saw him. He was acting weird, you know, walking pretty fast, and sort of swaying like a monkey, you know, a chimpanzee or a gorilla. He'd been under the bridge — I got no idea what the hell he was doing. And he shuffled in and out of here — this old hotel — like he's lookin' for someone. I started following him, but I couldn't tell who it was at first 'cause he was wearing dark clothes, you know, and a stocking cap — it was Sparrow, no shit. And that's not all."

Punch thrust his fists violently at the large leather bag hanging from the ceiling; dust puffed away from it, and it groaned and popped in response to the onslaught. Right, left, right, left. Punch hammered and jabbed and slammed. Sweat glistened on his forehead and upper lip; his biceps rounded into hard mounds and his feet whispered and scratched at the thin layer of dust on the floor. With each punch, the man issued a harsh *tuk, tuk,* his breathing controlled as if regulated by some machine housed in his lungs.

A final flurry. One last vicious uppercut.

The bag swung away and when it swung back Punch embraced it, pressing his sweaty face against the leather surface. His cheeks bulged; he blew out air in a ragged pattern and hawked a wad of spit off to one side. Out in the street, a late morning rain fell.

Punch squinted through his partial exhaustion and said, "So how the hell does that make Sparrow a murderer?"

"I explained it all," said Mance, a touch petulant. "He's been talkin' about the Final Chaos and about killing enemies with his bare hands and — and, more than that, Punch, he knew, he *knew* I was after the bastards that attacked Johnnie."

"Sparrow's a vigilante — that what you're saying?"

Mance hesitated.

"What's a vigilante?"

Punch shook his head disgustedly and gave the bag one more hard jab.

"If you'd stay in school, you'd know the meaning of words. A vigilante is like someone, say an ordinary citizen, taking justice into his own hands, going after criminals. You remember that movie *Death Wish*? Had Charles Bronson in it?"

"Sure, I loved it." Mance playfully shaped his hand into a gun and fired it.

"Well, that dude was a vigilante."

"OK, so that's what Sparrow is. He killed those guys. Tore 'em to pieces with his bare hands—he did. Punch, he's crazy as hell, but he says he's my friend. And last night he talked into my head. Back there in the alley. The other night at Guillo House he did it, too. It's like he makes a telephone in your head and says things to you over it."

Dumbfounded, Punch studied Mance carefully; a smile was flickering lazily at the corners of his mouth. Mance looked away.

"I know this sounds like bullshit, Punch. . . ."

Softly, slowly, Punch said, "You better believe it does. . . . You on something, boy?"

"Damn it, no. I'm serious. This is important to me. I came to you 'cause I thought you could tell me what to do. It's got me, you know . . . kinda scared."

"Telephone in your head? Does it ring? Ring-a-ding-a dingy?"

Punch began to laugh, a deep, rolling laughter. Then he motioned for Mance to come sit by him on a bench in the near corner of the otherwise empty room.

"Man, I'm sorry," he said, "but your story's nuttier than any I ever heard when I was on the force."

"But it's true."

"OK, let me ask you a couple of questions: first, how would Sparrow have known those two guys were the ones that attacked Jonella—if, *if* in fact they were?"

Mance gestured helplessly. "I guess 'cause he's psychic. It's what that Agent Orange shit did to him. The 'living dark' is what he calls it—I told you what he did to ole Rollo and those stray dogs."

Punch draped a towel over his head and held out one of the boxing gloves for Mance to untie for him.

"Second question: my inside contact on the force claims those two bodies were ripped up by what must have been some kind of animal—claws and sharp teeth—they weren't beaten with a tire iron—now how exactly did looney

102

tunes Sparrow do that?"

Mance clenched and unclenched his fists.

"Bare hands is all I can say. Punch, he was like an animal when I saw him last night. Maybe it's something he learned in Vietnam—some kind of weird martial arts."

Punch cocked an eyebrow skeptically. Mance freed him of one glove and started on the other.

"Third question: what in the hell do you expect me to tell you? You've given me the biggest line of cowflop in the history of this county. Believe me, what you've told me couldn't begin to form a case against Sparrow."

"See, that's just it. I don't feel like I want anybody to catch him. I'm not going to the cops. Not doing that. I've been figuring and figuring on this, and the only thing I come up with is that Sparrow's like . . . don't laugh at this—he's like my guardian angel."

Punch did, however, laugh.

"Guardian angel? Boy, you're really full of it today."

"No, my Uncle Thestis used to tell me people have guardian angels, but most of the time you never see 'em. Maybe Sparrow's mine."

"Go ask him."

The audacity of Punch's return threw the boy off-balance. Recovering, Mance said, "Sparrow has me spooked."

"I'll let you in on a little secret about your man, Sparrow," said Punch. "When I rode night beat I caught Captain Midnight—that's what we called him—several times on his nocturnal ramblings. Way I read it was that every once in awhile he got a wild hair and went on 'patrol,' reliving his Vietnam days. He was out hunting for gooks."

"You feel like he should be arrested? Guess maybe he's not safe."

"Officers Lawrence and McCants are on the North Street beat these days. They're damn good at framing people. We'll see how good they are at protecting folks from a psychotic killer—though I doubt Sparrow's one."

"They the pair that framed you, huh? I saw 'em last night—black lady and a white dude. Which one's Lawrence and which one's McCants?"

Punch picked up a jump rope and stood.

"Vanetta Lawrence—no lady, a first-class bitch. Got pissed 'cause she didn't turn my head. Clay McCants—he saw me as an easy fall guy. But I get another review this spring. If they'd back off on their story, I'd be reinstated."

"You want it for Fast Track, don't you?"

"That's a take. For myself, too. And Chantel . . . and what we coulda had together."

Mance watched as Punch began to jump rope, the rhythm of the exercise mesmerizing; the black man's thigh muscles rippled and a sheen of sweat covered his chest and throat after a few minutes. The rope sang. Punch jumped higher. The repetitions increased until he winced in pain and collapsed on the bench.

"Why you doin' this?" Mance asked. "And who's letting you use this building?"

"Wanted to see . . . what a heart attack . . . felt like," he said, breathing heavily. He coughed and rubbed at his knees. "John Hummert, you know, the retired doctor, owns this place . . . like he owns most of the empty buildings along the tracks. With all his money, he doesn't care. I'm just borrowing the space to get back in shape."

"You gone to box again?"

"I've thought about it—might have to if a certain old man keeps running up gambling debts."

"Fast Track in trouble?"

"Fraid so. It's like a sickness. I've tried to help him. I've tried to deal with the big boys in Montgomery. They're starting to apply some pressure. They can get rough when they feel like it."

Mance saw the worry clouding Punch's expression.

"Can't you put the finger on their whole operation? Can't you get your dad out that way?"

"Me? Think about it. How much clout does a suspended cop have?"

Mance realized he was right, and yet he hated for their conversation to end on a down note.

"I know what Fast Track needs."

"Yeah, what?"

"A guardian angel."

Punch chuckled.

"Would you loan Sparrow to us?"

"Hey, no . . . I might need him again. Get your own."

The worry in Punch's face evaporated; Mance readied to leave, and as he started for the door, he said, "Thanks for listening."

Punch saluted him with a taped wrist.

"You want one last piece of advice?"

Mance stopped. "Sure, why not."

"Next time that phone in your head rings," said Punch, "don't answer it."

3

It was proving to be the wettest February in Catlin County history. For three straight days moist air from the Gulf of Mexico had streamed into Alabama. Each day possessed a grainy, misty-gray cast so that late morning was indistinguishable from late afternoon. Night would arrive early, and, ironically, would bring relief; blackness broke the hammerlock of grayness.

The rain continued on Valentine's Day. But that night Mance and Jonella returned to Guillo House for the first time since Jonella's attack, and Mance, at least, was determined that the wet stuff would not spoil their evening. He had everything in place, including a fresh blanket to spread atop their pallet. He had candlelight and music (the latter pouring from an old transistor for which he had bought new batteries) and food (leftovers from the noon buffet at Scarlett's) and drink (Diet Coke for Jonella; Rebel Pride for him).

He had purchased a fancy, splashy red card for Jonella—For My Sweetheart, it read—a large heart pillowed out of the front with saccharine-sweet words inside, words Mance would never have thought of. In fact, they embarrassed him somewhat, but he wanted her to be impressed by his having paid a buck seventy-five for the card—the sentiments on paper weren't as important as their being together, he reasoned. He signed the card affectionately, the Fang. In addition to the card, he had emptied his wallet of a twenty-dollar bill for a special box of chocolates in which each piece of candy was in the shape of a rose. For *his* Rose.

So the Rose and the Fang exchanged cards, and Mance then eagerly pressed the box of candy into her lap.

"I haven't finished reading my card," she said.

She was wearing his favorite black sweater and she looked terrific; the swelling had disappeared from her cheek and a sparkle had returned to her eyes. An extra coating of makeup succeeded in covering the bite marks, though Mance knew, unerringly, where they had been. They remained the only suggestion of a blemish in her appearance.

"Well, hurry."

She giggled at the overwritten card and fingered its cushiony heart. Then she opened the box of chocolates. The roses were a big hit. She prodded him to tell her how much he had paid for them, but he held on to his secret. Hugging his neck, kissing him warmly on the mouth, she thanked him.

"I love you, Mance," she said.

"I love you, too, Johnnie. Happy Valentine's Day . . . and welcome back to our place."

"Our place," she whispered, and then, to Mance's surprise, she began to cry.

"Hey, what's wrong?"

She never said. It was one of those inexplicable emotional displays women put on — crying when they're happy, bitching at you when they love you the most. Who could figure it? Best not to try, he reasoned. So he said, "Want some leftover chicken?"

And, magically, she stopped crying. She looked at him as if incredulous.

"You're so romantic," she teased, laughing through the dissolving tears; then she playfully poked at his ribs.

They ate chicken wings and macaroni salad and cold baked beans and something that was supposed to be blueberry cobbler but had disintegrated into something resembling lumpy grape soda. It mattered little. They were together.

The rain continued. Mance built a fire in the fireplace, and

106

they repositioned their pallet closer to it to avoid several leaks from the roof.

Aided by the extra light, Jonella contentedly looked about the room like a new bride assessing decoration possibilities.

"Mance, what happened?"

He followed her surprised expression as it drifted from one damaged wall to another, alighting eventually upon the remains of his jam box.

"I just got . . . upset, you know. I was so damn mad and frustrated about what they did to you . . . I lost my head. It was weird. This whole place seemed weird that night."

Jonella hooked an arm lovingly through his.

"It's your shadow side."

"My what?"

"Uncle Thestis explained it all to me."

Mance groaned.

"You could learn a lot from him," she added.

"About shadows? What's there to know?"

"I'll tell you, smart britches."

And she did.

When she finished her summary of Uncle Thestis's theory, she tacked on a postscript: "He'll be waiting for you when you need him."

Mance visibly stiffened. "That ain't gone happen."

"You think you know everything, but you don't," she said.

"I don't need Uncle T. 'cause I've got a guardian angel — we both do."

Jonella blinked. She cocked her head.

Mance smiled. He had her puzzled.

"A real guardian angel," he continued, not bothering to mention that he had borrowed the idea from Uncle Thestis. "You'll never guess who it is."

She couldn't, and when he shared his notion, she scoffed. "Sparrow? You've got to be kidding."

But there was one thing she couldn't deny: something very, very strange had occurred. Coincidence? Possibly. Otherwise, she had to admit that someone had been almost preternaturally aware of their situation.

"He claims he's my friend, and, you know, I feel like he really is crazy enough to kill somebody. The way it was done, though . . . the condition of the bodies . . . like some wild animal did it. Out by the back gate to the dock you can still see blood . . . it's like it's down in the grain of the asphalt and won't never come out. One of those guys musta bled buckets."

"Don't, Mance. Don't. Stop talking about it, please."

"Sure. Yeah, sure. Sorry."

He lifted Sting free from his shoulder and offered him some chicken and some macaroni salad, but he opted instead for the soupy cobbler.

"At school today," said Jonella, "we talked about tests performed on rats—they experiment on them. Vaccines for AIDS and all that kinda thing. Next week in biology we're supposed to cut up a starfish."

She wrinkled her nose.

"So did you get caught up with your work?"

"Some. In English we're reading *The Glass Menagerie*. It's about this girl with a bad foot who collects little glass figurines and her favorite is a unicorn. And this older boy she kinda likes comes to her house and accidentally breaks off the unicorn's horn. She's really lonely and reminds me of the girls at school who don't never have dates."

"So what's the point of reading a story about a girl that never has dates?"

"It's not a story—it's a play. It's drama."

"Same difference."

"Mrs. Franklin says it helps you understand the inscrutable possibilities of human behavior, or something like that."

Mance frowned.

"Shit," he said, shaking his head. "School's a waste."

"Not if you want to make a better life for yourself. This morning in biology I was thinking I might like to go to college."

She set her jaw defiantly as if she expected Mance to object. And he did.

"College? Jeez, Johnnie . . . folks like you and me don't go to college. We're getting married, and then we'll have children and you won't have time for college even if you could get in. Besides, college costs a lotta money."

108

"I can think about it," she responded. "Thinking about it was kinda exciting because I thought maybe I could do it. Maybe I could. Momma was smart enough to if things hadn't gone wrong with her mind. It was real interesting listening to all that stuff about the experiments on rats, you know, making them sick so real people could benefit one day from the research."

Mance scooped up Sting and tucked him away.

"Hey, I wish you'd stop talking about that. Sting knows. Somehow he knows what you're talking about and it makes him nervous."

Jonella laughed softly. But then her eyes misted and her chin quivered.

"I had such good thoughts and . . ."

"Hey, what're you cryin' about?"

He touched her shoulder. She leaned toward him, and he held her in his arms.

"You don't wanna spoil your welcome back, do you?" he added.

It was a soft, almost soundless crying. He rocked her, and the rain pattered, finding holes in the roof or creating new ones. Guillo House seemed to be hushed as if viewing the couple like a concerned friend. Creakings and poppings and secret tickings broke the background silence intermittently.

Jonella's crying did not continue long; she snuffled and pressed her fingertips into her eyes to wipe away the tears. Her mascara smeared into black commas, and Mance smiled and hugged her firmly and she said, "At times at school I'm fine. I think good thoughts. I want to learn things. But when I read about that girl and the broken unicorn I had to leave class. I went to the rest room and bawled my eyes out, and I thought to myself: you'll have to go back and see Dr. Colby a lot more."

"Just don't read no more sad stories," said Mance.

"I think maybe I'm not stable. My emotions . . . I think it's like I swing back and forth. I'm OK. Then something happens. Like at school I saw this man with a real dark beard. One of the teachers I haven't met, and I was scared. I didn't want him to pass close to me in the hall."

109

"I wish you'd quit school," said Mance. "Seems like it's making you worse instead of better."

"It's not just school. It's everywhere . . . but only sometimes. Like this room. You know what I hate about it?"

"Probably it's too cold. I can fix the fire, Johnnie. It won't be no problem."

He started for the fireplace, and she said, "It's the dust."

He hesitated. "Dust?"

She timidly lowered her fingertips until they almost touched the surface of the floor.

"When those men attacked me, the floor was dusty in that building . . . just like this floor. Dirt. And the dirt . . ." She rubbed at her wrists, and her face twisted into a grimace. "I thought it got beneath my skin. Sometimes it comes back and I can't wash it away."

She stared into Mance's eyes.

"Sometimes I just can't wash it away," she repeated.

Mance could feel his heart beating in his throat.

"Don't talk like this, Johnnie. It really bothers me, you know."

"I can't help it."

"Have you ever been scared you would go crazy?" she asked.

In her eyes, Mance looked suddenly younger, smaller, not capable of protecting her.

"No. Not really," he said.

He had one arm around her, and one hand was touching her hair, and she imagined that his grip on it was tightening. Neither his advances nor the glow of the firelight comforted her.

What's wrong with me?

Why can't I get well? Why can't I be like before?

"I think it's what maybe scared Eleanor," she said. "Maybe . . ." She paused to survey the shadows and to listen to the wind skirl across the roof. The rain had ended. "Maybe it was this house. It made her sad. It scared her. It made her feel alone. And different."

"Probably never was anybody like that Eleanor woman," Mance said. She could tell that her mention of the imaginary person troubled him. Yet, she couldn't avoid thinking of her, projecting her existence into the scene.

"We would have been friends. Eleanor and me," she said, smiling ever so slightly at the thought.

"She ain't real, Johnnie."

He held her by the shoulders and then began to push her backward onto the pallet.

"Something must have tried to hurt her," she said, looking beyond Mance at the jagged shapes on the ceiling where plaster had fallen away.

"I want you, Johnnie. Forget about everything else."

"I tried not to show them I was scared," she continued. She bit at her lip. Mance's face blurred once, then cleared. She blinked.

"The door was locked," she whispered. "Why would a church lock its door?"

"You're beautiful, Johnnie. You're the most beautiful girl I've ever seen."

"I ran, and one of them pulled my hair."

"Sh-h-h . . . sweet Johnnie, don't talk."

She felt him press down upon her. Felt the air being forced from her.

"I . . . couldn't scream . . . hit me so hard . . . and the dust on the floor."

Mance's face darkened as it blotted out the firelight. He lowered his lips, and when they touched against the soft underside of her jaw, she struggled.

All of the pain, every intense, sharp-edged moment of it returned.

Jonella screamed.

Mance fell away, surprised, shocked. He reached for her as the screams issued from her in rapid bursts and echoed throughout the emptiness of Guillo House.

"I don't never want to go back there," she said.

They were halfway between Scarlett's and the railroad tracks. It was chilly. Jonella had her box of chocolates tucked under one arm. Mance had eventually calmed her, and she had

111

asked him to walk her to the trailer and he had agreed to, and he felt that, mysteriously, she had been taken away from him—he couldn't understand what had happened—and he had no idea how to possess her ever again.

"Sure," he said. "No, we don't have to. We can find us a better place."

He thought he heard her sob once.

"I spoiled the evening," she said matter-of-factly. "Be patient, Mance," she followed. "I won't always be like this. I'm not gone be like Momma." And in that last remark, he heard her voice firm a resolve he couldn't begin to understand.

"Sure," he said. "I mean, I can wait till you're better. That doctor will help you . . . and I . . . well, the only thing I can say is . . . I love you."

She bumped him hard with her hip.

"You better," she said. And he wondered whether she was on the verge of laughing or crying.

They walked on in silence until they reached the trailer and stood by the door.

"I think I'm going to be all right," she said.

"Could I kiss you good night?"

She smirked.

"Of course you can, silly." But then her expression hardened. "Don't give up on me, Mance. I've been thinking that maybe you're my only reason for living. Without you, I'd be in really sorry shape. Sorrier than now." She hesitated. "I'm going to be all right. I am."

She forced a smile.

He kissed her.

And that's when Tanya, her movement jerky and spasmodic, reached out and pulled them inside.

4

Her eyes pulsing like neon on a marquee, Tanya gathered Mance and Jonella into the living room of the trailer.

"Was Boom out there?" she asked, her glance snapping back and forth between them.

Mance looked at Jonella and shrugged. "No, haven't seen him," he said.

Tanya closed her eyes tightly, and as she rocked forward on the edge of the sofa she leaned her forehead against a clenched fist.

"I'm so, so scared," she said, her voice cracking.

Jonella slid over beside her and draped an arm over her shoulder.

"Boom been after you? Has he? Has he hit you or the girls?"

In a tiny, tremulous voice, Tanya said, "No. But he's gone all cold. All cold so's I can't know who he is no more. Cold talk. About bodies and blood."

Mance sandwiched her opposite Jonella. He saw that the two girls, Crystal and Loretta, were playing at a low table near a model truck, an eighteen-wheeler constructed of what appeared to be pieces of wire coat-hangers. Covering most of the floor were sheets from a sketch pad. Charcoals and pencil drawings, figure studies, sketches of the girls—Tanya's talent was evident in each of them.

"What do you mean, 'all cold'?" Mance asked her.

"It's not Boom no more," she said, her voice gaining strength. "At supper tonight he looked at his food and said, 'If I could just get those bodies out of my mind.' And then he said he was leaving to go think about what he could do to stop seeing those bodies and all that blood. His voice . . . his voice was so-o-o cold."

Tanya shuddered, and it struck Mance oddly as almost comical.

"He'll probably get over it," he said. "It shook him up, but he'll get over it."

"How long has he been gone?" asked Jonella.

"Several hours—I better pick up my drawing things. He wouldn't like it if this room's cluttered when he comes back."

She continued rocking. Neither Mance nor Jonella said anything more until Tanya spoke again.

"It could be bad. When he comes back, you know. I've been telling myself not to be so scared. I mean, Boom's my husband, and he loves me, I think, and loves the girls, and so why would he want to hurt us? It's those bodies—they've turned his

113

mind cold. And I've been wondering if I . . . if I should keep living with him."

She glanced quickly at Mance and Jonella for their reaction.

"You shouldn't have to live scared, Tanya. No woman should be scared of her man."

"That's right," said Mance, though he knew that in Tanya's shoes he would also be scared.

"But on my wedding day I said I would love, honor, and obey him. And where would I go and take the girls if I did leave? And what would happen to you?" She directed the latter remark to Jonella, adding, "You've had things a lot rougher'n me lately. I can't leave here. I have to be here—it's what I'm supposed to do, isn't it?"

Jonella shook her head. "Not if Boom's going to hurt you or the girls. Over by the mental health center they have what's called a safe house, a place for battered women. Miss Prince told me about it. Women who've been abused and raped can go there for a while and be protected. A woman named Twylla runs it."

"Is that Sparrow's friend?" said Mance. "The one that tattooed us?"

"Yes, and Miss Prince told me she's a big help to women in trouble."

Suddenly Tanya brightened.

"Oh, I'm gone be fine. I just gotta buck up—if I'm a good, loving wife it would make a difference for Boom. This is maybe my fault. A good wife, you know, can make a man's life work out for him. It's my duty to make things better for him."

Jonella frowned. "Don't think that way—not if he's threatening to hurt you. He needs help you can't give him, Tanya. Bein' a good wife won't make any difference if he's emotionally disturbed. He'll need professional help. It's hard. I know how hard it is. The counseling and the doctors—you go through hell. But I think Boom needs it."

Mance studied the two young women: Tanya, a little girl in so many ways, trying to act like a woman, but struggling to find sensible boundaries for her role; Jonella, vulnerable to her own state of depression, was obviously stronger when she attempted to lend support to

114

someone else—in this case, her stepsister.

Mance felt out of place. Over by the low table, the two little girls, both dressed in short, pastel nighties, their bare legs firm and innocent, were admiring the model truck, probing at it with their tiny fingers.

How could anybody hurt them? he wondered. Then he turned to Tanya.

"Hey, I better get going. Jonella has some homework, and I wanna beat it home before it starts raining again. I don't feel like Boom will do nothing bad." He wanted to believe what he said, but he had doubts.

Tanya jerked; her smile dissolved and she clasped her fingers onto his wrist. The tips of her fingernails cut into his wrist.

"No, don't," she exclaimed. "Don't go. Stay around till Boom comes. Please, Mance. Jonella, make him stay, OK?"

There was a thin lining of desperation in her voice.

Crystal and Loretta gazed at her, frown wrinkles creasing their foreheads.

Jonella gave him a look which said that maybe he should stick around for a while longer. So he agreed to.

"Thanks," said Tanya. "You're a good guy, Mance." Then she clapped her hands as if giddy at having her way. "OK, girls, happy faces. Let's put on our happy faces till bedtime."

And they followed their mother's lead when she maneuvered her face into an exaggerated smile. Mance exchanged looks with Jonella; she seemed somber and tired. Minutes later, she had set up at the kitchen table to complete a short analysis of the character of Laura in *The Glass Menagerie*.

Mance helped Tanya pick up the loose sketch pad sheets. To pass the time, she had him pose for a head-and-shoulders portrait.

"Your chin's hard to do," she observed after several minutes.

"It's the only one I've got, Tanya. Give me a break."

"Maybe it's the way you're holding your head. You're slumping your shoulders too much."

Mance hissed some impatience.

"If I straighten up, it pinches Sting. OK, here, wait a second." He deposited Sting on the floor; the rat sat up and gave the room a thorough, once-over sniff. Crystal and Loretta

115

squealed happily at the sight of the creature. And Sting went to check them out; his arrival caused the squeals to escalate toward cries of fear.

"Sting, get back over here," said Mance.

But for the model truck, it was too late. In pressing themselves away from the rat, both girls stumbled, then tumbled into the table and onto the truck. Under their weight it bent severely at the juncture between tractor and trailer; the crush snapped a couple of the soldered joints.

After Mance had secured Sting, Crystal, the older of the two girls, skipped away from the disaster, firing an accusatory line at her younger sister: "Lookit what you done — broke Daddy's truck."

Loretta's face crumpled. She ran crying to Tanya, who was approaching the truck as if in a trance, her fingers tapping nervously at her throat. Loretta tackled one of her legs, but Tanya seemed not to notice.

Mance stared at the woman, surprised by the sharp glint of fear in her eyes.

"Here," he said, "maybe we can fix it."

But his words were drowned partially by Loretta's wails. He knelt by the table and examined the truck. Tanya joined him; her breathing was irregular; she appeared to be trying to swallow — her tongue was generating soft clucks.

"Two of the joints broke," said Mance. He attempted to bend the truck back into shape and partly succeeded. "I could try maybe to resolder it." Beneath the table was a soldering iron and coil.

"Will he notice?" Tanya whispered. She was frightened; the area around her eyes blanched. "Since those murders he's spent hours on this. Will he see it's broke?"

She searched Mance's eyes for reassurance.

"I don't know."

The incident had drawn Jonella away from her homework; she took Loretta in her arms and soothed her with soft talk and a few kisses.

Tanya cocked her head to one side and surveyed the truck; she bit her lip and mumbled something inaudible. Mance continued to fiddle with the tangle of wires, straightening some,

116

positioning others so that they wouldn't be as noticeable.

"It's 'bout as good as it's gone be," he announced.

Tanya blinked out of her daze. For a moment or two Mance had toyed with the impression that she was drunk—inebriated by fear? Was that possible? Once again, however, she appeared suddenly normal, or as normal as Tanya was capable of being, and she looked at him and said, "You've waited around long enough. You could go on home if you want to."

Beyond Tanya's shoulder, Jonella was holding Loretta and showing further signs of exhaustion.

"OK, sure. Maybe I should," he said.

He scooped up Sting and had the rat squeak a good night to the girls; they responded with weak, tentative smiles. Jonella followed Mance out the door. It was misting and cool.

"She gone be all right?" he asked.

"I hope so," said Jonella.

"How about you?"

She smiled. "I'm a tough little rose, remember? I've got thorns to protect me. But I wish I hadn't spoiled Valentine's Day."

"No, hey, it wudn't no big deal. I'll see you later."

They kissed.

He rambled toward home, wondering if that kiss would ever again be as warm and exciting as it was once upon a time.

5

The scary part for Jonella was that Boom wore a strained smile. He had walked through the door with it on his face. It was the kind of smile that changed the atmosphere of the room, something akin to learning that a corpse is hidden behind the sofa.

It was a more enigmatic smile than Mona's famous one.

And certainly more potentially deadly.

Tanya bubbled over Boom the minute he came home, smothering him with wifely concerns about what she could do for him: get him a beer or coffee or a sandwich or turn on the television or God knows what else.

117

Jonella fought hard to keep from retching as the scene unfolded.

But all Boom said was, "No, I'm fine."

He sat down on the sofa and to Jonella he said, "Hittin' the books, huh? Good girl."

She acknowledged him.

"Some of them hit back."

It wasn't exactly the wording she would have deemed appropriate for the moment.

Crystal and Loretta were in a rocking chair, thumbing through a big picture book of butterflies. Tanya, nervous as a cat, said, "I wonder why I've never done a portrait of Boom?"

She offered the comment to no one in particular. She was just thinking aloud and praying that he hadn't noticed the broken model truck. Had he?

Jonella tried to keep one eye on her concluding paragraph and one eye on Boom. No, she believed he had been too preoccupied with his own dark thoughts to give any attention to the truck. Thank goodness, she thought. Could it be resoldered one day when he was at work? She was lost in the apparent tangle of that thought when Boom sprang up from the sofa and said, "I need to do some exercises."

With that he sprawled on the rug and, like a caterpillar, inched toward the model truck on his knees before turning onto his back. His head was no more than two feet from the low table.

Jonella glanced at Tanya in time to see her stepsister virtually swoon in horror.

"Oh, Boom, do you think you should?" said Tanya, obviously deathly afraid of his short distance from the model truck.

"Yeah, I'm tight. Sit-ups will help me relax."

Hands behind his head, he began.

"But Boom," said Tanya, getting down on her knees beside him, "you work so hard at the warehouse, won't this wear you out some?"

"It's helping me," he said, his body locked into the up-and-down, back-and-forth rhythm, ". . . helping me relax . . . and think."

118

In her peripheral vision Jonella watched him snap off the sit-ups, his energy flowing freely, the strained smile on his face still there, tight and cold. And Tanya sat by him helplessly, like someone near an out-of-control machine, with no understanding of what it might do next.

6

Mance had just slipped Sting into his cage when he heard the voice.

Go back.

Sparrow's voice? He believed it was. No way to be certain. Just a feeling. More importantly, though, he understood the reference. Yes, go back to the trailer. To Jonella and Tanya and the little girls.

Take your gun.

The voice wasn't necessary for that thought. He realized he shouldn't have left them.

"Sit cool, Sting. Gotta go out again."

He loaded the .38 and concealed it in his jacket. Out into the night mist he made his way. North Street was empty as usual, but more ghostly and eerie than it had ever appeared to him before. He cleared his mind of every thought except of Jonella. The voice materialized once more, causing Mance to break into a run.

He felt the fear tighten his muscles.

"I'm coming, Johnnie."

The voice had spoken only one word, but it was enough to send him racing toward the tracks and up the slope past Rebel Beer.

One word.

Hurry.

7

Boom and his sit-ups made Jonella nervous. Not being able to concentrate on her essay, she decided to go to bed.

119

"I'll see you in the morning," she said to Tanya, giving Boom a wide berth as she walked past the sofa.

"OK, honey," Tanya mumbled. She was still on her knees next to Boom; she reminded Jonella of a timid, half-frightened animal—a doe, perhaps, anxious to avoid predators.

Jonella leaned down to Crystal and Loretta and saw that they had secreted two chocolate hearts into the pages of the book. It made Jonella think of her chocolate roses, and experience a pang of guilt that Mance's welcome-back evening had not gone well. Someday, she vowed, she would make it up to him.

She smiled at the girls and said goodnight to them. Crystal caught her arm.

"Does Daddy know we broke his truck? Is he mad at us?" Her whisper was so soft that Jonella had to ask her to repeat what she had said. She saw a storm of apprehension in the little girl's eyes.

"I think it'll be all right," she whispered back, giving each a kiss on the forehead.

Such angels.

She glanced once more at Tanya and Boom; the sit-ups continued apace, and Jonella felt a knot tighten in her bowels.

Eventually Boom eased off on the sit-ups; sweating, huffing and puffing, he slapped his stomach, causing Tanya to jump. He smiled at her.

"Now I'm ready," he said.

He was sitting akimbo; one trickle of sweat escaped through a sideburn. Tanya wanted to wipe it away, but she was afraid to touch him.

"Ready for what?" she asked cautiously.

"For whatever it's gone take. Ideas are comin' to me."

His comment puzzled her, so she shifted gears. "Sorry I didn't even get you a Valentine's Day card—guess it shows we're an old married couple when you forget 'bout Valentine's Day."

She rocked gently and giggled.

"Hearts and initials," said Boom distractedly. "Remember

120

how kids used to cut or burn their initials in trees or spray-paint 'em on bridges?"

Tanya nodded.

"Kids trying to be romantic," she said. "Me, what's romantic is a fire. Boom, you think someday we could have a house with a fireplace? A fire sometimes would be nice."

Boom was staring at the opposite wall.

"A fire would be good. A good idea. Burning. If I could burn those bodies out of my mind . . ."

Tanya's breath caught in the back of her throat. Her thoughts scrambling, she looked over at her daughters.

"Girls," she snapped, "bedtime. Say good night to your daddy, and then go brush your teeth and use the bathroom and I'll come tuck you in di-rectly."

Her voice quavered, but she couldn't help it. She felt close to a victory of sorts; Boom apparently hadn't noticed the broken wires on the model truck.

The girls scurried out of the rocker. Loretta said, "Good night, Daddy."

Boom said nothing; he seemed to be staring through her as if she were a ghost.

Crystal hesitated, twisting her fingers nervously.

"Daddy? Daddy . . . I'm real sorry we broke your truck."

Tanya never took her eyes off Boom; she felt as if she were falling through a deep, dark night into nothingness. *Dear God, what will he do?*

"It was an accident, Boom," she said. "Really it was. You see, Mance put that white rat of his on the floor and—"

"Hush," said Boom. "You girls come here to your daddy. See," he told them, "just about the moment I walked in tonight I saw that my truck had been broke. Makes me sorta wish you and your momma hadn't tried, you know, to hide it from me. But you come on over to the table here and I'll show you what we're gone do."

"You're not upset?" said Tanya.

"Upset? I have an idea of what would work." He rapped his knuckles gently at the side of his head. "I think maybe I can get rid of these awful pictures in my mind, you know—the bodies and the blood."

121

Then he got up and went to the door leading into the hall-way and the bedrooms beyond; he closed it and locked it.

"Boom? Why did you . . . why did you do that?"

A nervous laugh seeped into Tanya's voice.

Boom returned to the low table where his daughters hovered near the model truck. He winked at Tanya.

"This is gone be a family matter," he said.

He plugged in the heating coil and took his soldering iron and some tweezers from a small box.

"Mance bent it some back into shape," said Tanya. She inched closer to the table. "I know how much work you put in on that. But it was an accident, you know—really nobody's fault."

From the box containing the soldering iron and tweezers, Boom lifted out a pair of wire cutters and snipped off two pieces of the truck. To the girls he said, "See what your daddy has? I'll bend this one into a C for Crystal, and this one into an L for Loretta."

The girls giggled innocently. Tanya smiled.

The heating coil blazed a bright orange. Boom carefully placed the C on it and waited.

"Don't get close, Loretta," said Tanya. "Burn, burn." Then to Boom she said, "Can you solder those pieces back on?"

"Not gone to," he said, his smile so thin it showed no teeth. "Gone put initials on my girlfriends."

For a moment his comment failed to register with Tanya. She watched as with the tweezers he raised the C from the coil and held it out to admire it.

Suddenly he grabbed Crystal and pulled her close; before Tanya could react, he pressed the red-hot wire onto the tender flesh of the girl's thigh.

Her scream was immediate and sharp and intense.

"Boom!" Tanya cried out and lunged at him. The flat of his open hand caught her perfectly at the curve of her jaw. Her head snapped as if it might spin an entire revolution. With a groan she fell away and was silent.

Crystal, continuing to scream, scooted away from her father on her bottom. Loretta began to cry, too.

"Everything's gone burn," said Boom.

122

And he reached for Loretta.

Crystal's screams jerked Jonella from near sleep. The high-pitched sounds tore into her like dozens of knives piercing her chest. Twisting out of bed, she slipped on her robe and hurried into the hall.

Boom. It's Boom. God, those little girls.

She switched on the light and was surprised to find the door to the hallway closed. Another round of screams had assaulted her ears; this one was even higher pitched than the screams that had awakened her—*was it Loretta? First Crystal, then Loretta?*

And what about Tanya?

She turned the knob and found the door locked, and, instantly, she began beating upon it.

"Tanya? Tanya, let me in? What's going on?"

She twisted the knob frantically, pulling at it, then slapping at the door with her palms and then her fists.

"Tanya!"

More screams. She tried to imagine what was happening to the little girls.

"God, oh my God," she whispered.

She stepped back and thrust her shoulder at the door; it seemed to give some, but did not pop open.

"Tanya?"

Before the first sign of smoke curled under the door, she smelled it.

Boom's done it. He wants to kill us all.

She ran to the bathroom and pressed open the window; misty darkness poured through a slit which appeared much too small for her body to pass through. But it was her only chance. Mobile homes, she had always heard, burned quickly, readily. There would be but a matter of minutes for escape.

Scraping elbows and a number of ribs, she squeezed and forced her body until she was hanging halfway through the window. The aluminum runners cut into her stomach; she moaned, flailed her hands to touch the outside wall for balance—then dropped, negating her fall slightly. Her chin banged against the ground, and she rolled, the breath knocked from her temporarily. For fleeting seconds, the memory of the rape flashed through her thoughts.

Struggling to her feet, she staggered around toward the front door. The yellow-orange glow within the trailer outlined the extent of the fire. And it was spreading.

"Tanya!" she screamed once she had regained her wind.

She tripped, fell to her knees in the loose gravel, then pushed again to her feet.

He's going to burn them. Burn his whole family.

The front door was open.

Was there hope? Had they somehow escaped?

Knees aching and bleeding, she reached the doorway.

And saw Mance.

The scene unfolded before her like a nightmare: the fire, the frightened cries coalescing into stark terror. Mance, both hands clutching the .38, was shouting, "Let 'em go or I'll blow your fuckin' head off!"

His entire body was tensed and trembling. He did not notice her approach behind him. Over his shoulder she saw the two little girls on the floor hugging at Tanya, who looked dazed and disoriented.

Flames had clawed their way from the picture window curtains along the wood paneling on two walls. Boom stood framed against the fire; the look in his eyes held a blackness beyond darkness.

"Let 'em go," said Mance. "I mean it."

"Big mistake, boy. Big mistake."

Boom stepped forward.

"God damn it, I'll shoot you, Boom."

"You best do it, boy. I sure as hell ain't scared of you."

Another step.

Mance fired.

The paneling just above the border of the flames splintered thunderously.

Boom stopped.

Jonella moved past Mance and helped Tanya to her feet.

"Come on, girls," said Jonella. "Hurry." She pulled Tanya toward the door. Boom made a move to block them, and

Mance fired again, this time at his feet. Pieces of fabric from the carpet puffed into the air.

The fire gained momentum.

"Next shot's between your fuckin' eyes," said Mance.

Heat billowed toward the door as Jonella, the girls, and Tanya fled into the misty night.

Boom's fists hung at his sides like hand grenades; sweat beaded his face, and there was no sanity in his eyes.

"Go while you can, boy. But this means sometime I'll have to kill you."

Chapter Six

1

"You got a second, doncha? Oh, where's that notepad? In my purse? No . . . yes — a pen — got one. Right behind my ear. Been a stick of dynamite, it'd a blown my brains out. So . . . OK, you're Mance Culley, aren'tcha?"

The small, wiry, silver-haired woman smelling of cigarette smoke and sporting a raspy, smoker's voice shifted her purse from one shoulder to the other and extended a gnarled hand.

Saying nothing, Mance shook it and found it surprisingly firm. He had seen the woman many times in the past, but did not know her name.

"I'm Bridgette Settleford, and there's no reason on earth why you should recognize me — except maybe my name and the fact that I show up everywhere. My husband was Paul Settleford and he ran the *Soldier-Goldsmith News* — editor-in-chief is what he was — for more years than the sun has risen and . . . Twylla, she's one of my contacts, tipped me off about the fire last night and so here I am checking to see that Tanya, the girls, and Jonella made it to the shelter in decent shape. From what Twylla gathered, you're either a hero or mighty lucky or maybe some of both. That right?"

Mance stepped back from the woman's stream of rhetoric; the wide front porch of the safe house was empty; the late morning sun was pleasantly warm. Mrs. Settleford wore silver-rimmed glasses and bore a somewhat youthful complexion — in fact, she had an attractive face if one overlooked the dark circles under her eyes. Mance judged her to be in the vicinity of sixty, perhaps younger.

"He . . . Tanya's husband, he was gone to—"

The woman flipped the pages of her notepad.

"Honey, I know Boom. Meaner 'n a snake. You're right. He was gone to kill his family. I don't doubt that. I suppose you're wondering why I'm yacking atcha, firing questions and what not. Well, I can explain."

Mance reflexively took a breath.

The whirlwind of a woman had caught him in her gusts. He had no choice but to listen.

"My dear husband passed away six years ago—that tore a big hunk out of my heart, you know. I mourned. Yes, I did. But, oh . . . I couldn't bring him back. Couldn't bring him back, so I got busy. Community service, churchy things and— oh, I'll spare you the details: ladies groups. Do you have any idea how petty and downright shitty ladies groups can be?"

Mance lifted a hand to his mouth to hide a chuckle. The woman barely missed a beat.

"For years I kidded myself. I was staying busy, but, you know, I was *bored*. Better put that all in caps: B-O-R-E-D. As a New Year's resolution I promised myself I was gone start living. I'm a spacey old broad who wants to drink up a few bottles of excitement before they turn out my lights. So, I got a job at the *S-G News*. Hell, they had to hire me, considering what my husband had done for that paper over the years. They made me a cub reporter. But I'm itching for something new, for bigger game—and I've found it."

"You mean, the stuff that happened last night?" said Mance.

"Heaven's no, honey." She leaned conspiratorially close and said, "It's the Rebel Beer murders that've rattled my cage—you wouldn't know anything about them, wouldya?"

Mance shrugged through a microwave of apprehension.

"No, ma'am. Not much."

She squinted one eye at him.

"You're a liar, Mance Culley."

He stared at her in disbelief. He felt naked.

She locked her talon-like fingers on his wrist and laughed a throaty laugh.

"Sit down, honey, and let's get something straight." They sat on the top step; behind them a telephone rang in the shelter. Mance wanted to check on Jonella, but escaping from this woman, he realized, would not be easy.

"I *know* this town," she said. "I *know* its people. What I don't know I'm a phone call away from finding out. You're gone to have to level with me. Something mighty peculiar's afoot these days. All's I want is to pick your brain. Now I can offer you something in return—I can help you by helping your gal and her stepsister."

"How?"

"Never mind that just this second. You listen. Fill in any blanks you can—deal?"

"Yeah, I guess so."

"Long and short of it is," she began, "there's a police cover-up on this Rebel Beer business. I've known Detective Stewart at SPD since he was in diapers. He's never been a good liar. He's hiding something about those murders. I've figured out a few things on my own: first, the murder victims were the same monsters that raped your Jonella—am I right?"

Mance's chest ached; his entire body felt heavy.

"I would swear they were the same. Yes, ma'am."

"Hmm . . . well, I know *you* didn't kill 'em. Detective Stewart is of a mind that some animal may a done it 'cause of the condition of the bodies. I'm not buying it. I'm a no-nonsense old gal. Black-and-white, straight-arrow thinker. I've been adding all this up, and it seems as clear as an Alabama fall day that you have a notion who *did* kill 'em—you or Jonella or the both of you."

"Please don't talk none to Jonella about it," said Mance. "It upsets her."

The woman raised three fingers.

"Scout's honor—yes, I was a Girl Scout leader years ago."

Mance wrestled with a tough question as he surveyed her face: *should I tell her anything more?*

She let him squirm awhile.

"It's all a mystery to me," he said eventually.

She patted his knee in a motherly fashion.

"I reckon you have enough to worry about what with Boom

128

on your tail. Remember this: I know North Street a lot better than you can imagine. I know Scarlett's. Your folks. I know your Uncle Thestis—was sweet on him years and years back—and I know Kelton Austin—that handsome rascal stirs my hormones—and I know the secret behind why he's here, and I know Adele Taylor, too. I know about Fast Track's gambling debts and who framed Punch. I know a thing or two about Sparrow—beyond the obvious fact that he's hootier than a hoot owl. And I know how vicious Boom can be."

Using his knee as an aid, she pushed herself to her feet and Mance followed her lead.

"Something else, too," she added.

Mance met her eyes.

She said, "I know a thing or two about Guillo House."

Then she smiled.

"Mance, when you're ready to talk, give me a ring at the paper. You'll be seeing me around. The head honchos at the *S-G News* gave in to my arm twisting—I'm on the murder beat from now on."

Mance nodded and watched as she stuffed her notepad in her purse.

"You have a good'n," she said, and scooted off to her car.

"She sure is a wacky ole bitch."

"Mance, you shouldn't oughtta say that. Mrs. Settleford's being real good to Tanya and me, finding us a place to stay after we leave here. There're some rooms over in that big house where Miss Taylor lives. And Mrs. Settleford told Tanya she'd help us get some clothes—the fire ruined about everything I had to wear."

Jonella had joined Mance on the top step leading to the porch.

"If you move away from this shelter," he said, "seems like Boom'll just come after Tanya and the girls again, won't he?"

He gazed into Jonella's face; she looked tired and somehow much older. Suddenly she gritted her teeth.

"Tanya can be such a dumbhead—she won't press any charges against Boom for last night. Claims what he did is not his fault. He can't help what he does. But those poor little girls. They'll have physical *and* mental scars over this."

"I shoulda shot him—wish I'd done it when I had the chance."

Jonella sighed. "I wish you had, too, in a way . . . because . . ."

Her body appeared to shudder.

"What is it, Johnnie?"

She stared blankly at the street. "You saved Tanya and the girls—you did. They'd have been killed if you hadn't come. It was brave what you did, but . . . I'm afraid Boom's coming after you."

"I expect he will. What you don't know, Johnnie, is about the voice."

He felt a welling of excitement as he thought about it.

She continued staring at the street, and he said, "When I got home last night I heard it. It told me to go back, to hurry up and go back—it warned me, Johnnie, and it was Sparrow's voice, I just got a feeling it was his voice again, so I'm gone go see him and tell him what happened . . . 'cept, he already knows I bet . . . 'cause of the living dark. He'll protect me just like he went ahead and took care of them two guys that attacked you."

"Mance," she said, turning slowly, reaching out to touch his cheek. "How did our lives get so messed up? What'd we do to deserve this?"

"Hey, we'll be OK. It's not like just me against Boom. Don't you believe what I'm saying?"

"I just haven't no idea what to believe," she murmured.

2

By the weekend, Jonella, Tanya, and her girls had moved into the sprawling, two-story brick house just a stone's throw between Scarlett's and Guillo House. Tanya and the girls occupied the downstairs because another family had recently moved out. Jonella took one of the upstairs bedrooms, a situation which pleased Mance because it gave her more distance from Tanya, and thus more privacy. One of the other upstairs bedrooms was where Adele Taylor stayed. The other two bedrooms were vacant.

With the aid of Bridgette Settleford, who paid Tanya's rent, and Kelton Austin, who loaned Tanya and Jonella whatever furniture they needed, the two young women began new lives. Goodwill Industries provided them with some clothing, as did Twylla, the good-hearted lesbian, who knocked on every church door for donations and generally made herself a nuisance at the courthouse until local officials also did what they could for the unfortunate souls.

Mance visited Jonella on a regular basis, but he found her morose and basically unresponsive to any particular conversational opportunities. Was she concerned about his safety and too apprehensive to talk much? Or had the depression simply deepened? She had not gone back to school or back to work, though she insisted on paying her rent from her waitressing salary. Joining Mance as a frequent visitor to the big brick mansion was Austin, who often sat on the porch with Miss Taylor in the porch swing. Mrs. Settleford made the scene occasionally, continuing to probe and ask questions and irritatingly snoop.

For Mance the days had necessitated feats of tightrope walking as he was forced constantly to balance himself on an invisible line of fear beneath which stalked the figure of Boom. The man had not returned to work; reports held that he had been seen at Jimmy's in Providence, quite drunk. But he had not been arrested, and as far as Mance was concerned, Boom lurked at every corner, every alley. He had become a shadow intent upon enacting a personal revenge for Mance's intrusion into his family life.

Fear growing within him each day, Mance decided to go to the one man whom he believed understood his demise—the one man who could offer him protection. So it was that on Saturday afternoon he entered Sparrow's pawnshop. He was disappointed to find that Sparrow was nowhere to be seen. The man named Rollo, however, was occupying the same chair in which Mance had last encountered him—sleeping, it appeared, but not experiencing visions of a beauti-

131

ful young woman as before.

Strolling through the pawnshop area, Mance heard Sparrow's voice in the distance. He listened closely, straining to determine whether it was the same voice that had called him back to the burning trailer. Yes, he concluded. It had to be. Who else but Sparrow had the psychic ability to project his voice that way? Mance sat down at the soup kitchen counter and toyed nervously with a container of ketchup. Two straggly old white men came in from the back room and sat several stools from him. He nodded hello to them; they returned bleary-eyed, suspicious looks.

Mance cleared his throat. "Is Sparrow around today?"

The two men exchanged glances as if they had been spoken to in a foreign language.

At that moment Sparrow himself burst in from the kitchen, singing in a big, surprisingly fine voice; sweat had streaked his long, blond hair and his flushed cheeks. He was wearing a full-length, white apron speckled and spattered with food and coffee and who could guess what else. He was carrying a tray of clean coffee cups.

The instant he saw Mance he turned off his singing.

"Humph. Orange whimsies fly me to the moon and rocksett bluckle my way to feckso, meckso, peckso. My friend, Mance."

Mance felt a bubble of excitement and joy float up into his throat.

"Yeah, it's me."

Sparrow put down the cups, smiled, and extended a hand.

"You met two of my burdens? This is Roy Dean and Claude. You fellas say hey to Mance here."

They mumbled something; Mance repeated their names softly.

Sparrow grabbed a wet rag and wiped the countertop in front of Mance.

"Hard to keep this place clean," he said. "These days breed filth. It's everywhere." He paused to cast a twitching eye at the boy. "You haven't eaten anything today, have you? Oh, I can tell—I can tell when a body needs sustenance."

Mance was mildly surprised to realize that the man was

132

right.

"No, I really haven't. What's on the menu?"

"Good shit," cried Mance. "We got good shit, don't we, fellas? Same shit every day, but it's good—Brunswick stew and maybe a slice or two of day-old bread. No cornbread, but what the fuck—granids wexit down your barogroove—so there you are."

Mance smiled. "I'll take a bowl if you let me pay for it."

"Ain't for sale. Sorry. My bowls of plenty are furnished by the goodness of the universe."

"Well, OK, I'll take a bowl. No bread."

"Jackpot," said Sparrow. "Dingledodies."

He brought Mance a steaming bowl, then disappeared for five minutes. In the interim, Mance thought about the night he had followed Sparrow down the alley, and he thought about what Punch had said. But nothing could dissuade him from believing that the enigmatic Sparrow was his guardian angel. Jonella's, too.

Roy Dean and Claude cleared out as Mance made progress on his stew. It was good. Maybe too salty, but good. When Sparrow returned it was with a tall glass of iced tea. He shoved it toward Mance and said, "It's sweetened. You won't be able to get it up for days if you drink it, but that stew'll ruin your throat if you don't wash it down with something."

" 'Preciate it," said Mance.

Sparrow leaned his elbows on the counter and scratched vigorously at his sweaty head. "You shot anybody yet?"

Mance nearly dropped his spoon. He couldn't meet Sparrow's eyes. Why would he ask that? he wondered. He knows I haven't. But the boy began talking, hoping he could say what he intended to say, hoping he could find out for certain whether Sparrow indeed knew that Boom was on a killer prowl.

"I was gone to shoot those bearded guys," he said. "Would have, too. But they . . . they bought it. The other night . . . I got the warning and took the gun . . . And I stopped him. Stopped Boom, but you see, now, he's gone be coming for me. Has me scared. I feel like you've helped me. I thank you for it. But I'm scared. Police can't help me. I've talked to them.

133

Nothing much they can do. What's gone happen?"

Sparrow suddenly flailed his arms; his eyes bulged.

Mance thought he was going into one of his weird transformations.

"Chaos," he thundered. "The Final Chaos killed those men. All the dingledodie blood and guts. I saw them in a dream, and I saw you among the flames. Know what I'm sayin'?"

"Yeah. Yeah, I guess I do. It was the fire at the trailer. I heard it . . . I heard your voice."

"The voice of the living dark," said Sparrow, calming down. "You'll help me, won't you?"

"More blood. More filth. These floors need mopping."

"Sparrow? Sparrow, you'll help me, won't you? Boom . . . you'll warn me, won't you? He's coming after me. He's out there. He's out there watching for me."

Mance looked down at his trembling hands; he heard the echo of fear in his voice. Was Sparrow listening? Was this his way?

"The Final Chaos will wash away all the filth, all the blood. Why should I bother?"

Confused, Mance worked up the courage to look unblinkingly into the man's eyes; it was like peering into the ominous centers of two huge storms.

"You have some kinda magic, don't you? Something like what you did to ole Rollo and those pit bulls, ain't that so? It doesn't have to be like what you did at Rebel Beer."

He felt a surge of hope as he witnessed Sparrow's smile.

"Don't worry," said the man, "you got a friend."

3

Mance was late for work when he left Sparrow's. There was no time to dash home and get his .38, one element of his attire which he had worn to work religiously, despite the difficulty he had concealing it. Sting held on for dear life as Mance raced over the tracks and up the sloping street to the warehouse.

Invisible, and watching from the vantage point of an abandoned building, the wolf creature followed the boy's movement. Ears pricked, alert to the boy's sudden apprehension, the creature struck off along his trail. The winter sun radiated through its invisible state, warming its body. It loped eagerly, expectantly, as if picking up the scent of prey and anticipating moments of violence.

After clocking in, Mance stole a second or two to reflect upon his conversation with Sparrow. It was a difficult one to assess. At times the man seemed not to understand what Mance had been talking about; at other times, yes, the Final Chaos, the living dark, Sparrow had stormed his way into the heart of all the darkness Mance was experiencing.

He knows. He has to know.

He'll protect me against Boom.

But Mance felt vulnerable without the .38. He considered running home during the dinner break to get it, but from a perusal of the loading chart, he saw that dinner might be cut short that night.

"Hey, I see Boom ain't wasted you yet."

It was Spivey, grinning and obviously excited and maybe even a little impressed that a co-worker was in imminent danger.

"From what I hear he's too drunk and messed up to hunt down anybody," Mance returned. "Let's get to work—did you see how many trucks we have to load tonight?"

They stopped at the workbench for tin snips and an X-acto knife, the former to cut away metal bands which bound the stacks of boxes, and the latter to slice away loose flaps of cardboard.

They worked diligently for an hour or so before Spivey's curiosity got the best of him.

"How's it feel knowin' some guy'd like to slit your throat or beat your brains out? Nobody's never hated me that much."

"It's no big deal," Mance lied.

"How you sleep at night? Man, it would scare the shit outta me—I couldn't never even come to work . . . I mean, what if just right this second he walked in here to the loading dock and opened up on you with a shotgun? Damn, it's probably not safe to be close to you, is it?"

Reflexively Mance looked up from a pallet of boxes to survey the area for any sign of Boom. Spivey's suggestion had a cold ring of possibility: four-to-midnight shift on Saturday night often meant that only he and Spivey would be on the loading dock—the older men usually weren't asked to work on the weekend.

"I ain't scared 'cause I got . . . protection."

Spivey perked up.

"Hey, yeah, I heard you was packin' a rod—hey, can I see it?"

"Well . . . I—I don't have it on me tonight. Way I look at it, if Boom was gone get me, he's had three whole days to do it in. I feel like he's done forgot about me—it's his Tanya and her two little girls I'm worried about. My Johnnie, too."

Spivey shook his head.

"Takes a real shitload bastard to beat up on his wife and kids, don't it?"

"For sure," said Mance.

They worked through most of their break. Mance had virtually no appetite anyway. He drank three Cokes and strolled among the cavernous shadows of the main warehouse.

Boom could be hiding anywhere, he warned himself, waiting for the right chance.

How would I get away from him?

From the tops of several of the stacks of boxes an agile climber could reach air vents. Mance knew that at least two of the vents led outside; some, however, were dead-end vents. A locked grate shut off passage to the outside.

By the time Mance finished his stroll and returned to the loading dock, he had convinced himself that Boom was not hiding in the warehouse. There was no danger there. Only hard work and sweat.

One more empty truck awaited him and Spivey. They made a game of it, pretending, James Bond style, that if it weren't loaded by the stroke of midnight the evil forces of some belligerent Third World power would detonate a round of explosives, destroying the entire warehouse.

Muscles crying in protest, they beat the deadline with seconds to spare.

The two young men clocked out; Spivey grinned at Mance.

136

"I sure hope you don't get your ass killed—you're a good guy to work with."

"You, too," said Mance.

The first thing odd he noticed was Sting's behavior: the furry creature flashed white up and down Mance's arm, cutting figure eights around his neck, squeaking incessantly.

"What's got into you? You have to piss or something?"

He put the rat on the ground, but immediately Sting raced back up his leg and scrambled to the refuge of Mance's long hair.

The next thing was the movement, the whispering shuffle of feet in the old, abandoned hotel where Punch had been working out. Mance tensed.

Who in the hell?

Through a broken pane, he saw someone in dark clothing.

Then he relaxed. He was no more than ten or fifteen yards from the figure. But this, he concluded, was the proof he had been hoping for. He felt exhilarated.

"Sparrow?"

He kept his voice low.

There was no response at first.

Mance edged to the scarred and shadowy doorway.

"Sparrow? Hey, thanks for watchin' out for me. I'll be OK, now."

Run!

The voice roared through his mind like a freight train.

He jerked away from the door, but not in time; he heard the whoosh of something being swung, something cutting through the air. Then he felt the pain, and the choking sensation as a link of chain coiled around his neck.

And the shock of Boom growling, "You're dead, you long-haired son-of-a-bitch."

Mance fell back. The chain tightened. Mance twisted to one side, and his movement caused the chain, momentarily, to unwind.

Boom grabbed for him, but missed, sprawling forward on the pavement.

137

"Son-of-a-bitch," he hissed.

Grasping his bruised throat, Mance got to his feet and stumbled away. There was enough streetlight to see Boom's face of rage. The man was on his hands and knees; his countenance was that of an animal; a darkness around his eyes threatened to suck the life out of the night.

And Mance.

Boom was wielding what appeared to be a lead pipe, to one end of which was attached a length of chain. The muted light in his eyes spoke of something primitive. The man had been pushed over the edge of some abyss, and at the bottom of that abyss resided the depths of his hatred.

And there he became something inhuman.

Mance saw it all in the standoff moments as he rubbed at his throat, the pain raw and ugly and intense. He wanted to cry out for Sparrow, but the chain had crushed his vocal chords.

"You're dead," Boom yelled.

The man got up. He was limping badly, having, apparently, smashed his knee in the fall. Mance took advantage of the opportunity; he wheeled and began to run. He ran south back over the tracks, his throat on fire. He could imagine flames billowing under the skin.

Sparrow, where are you?

Why had his protector deserted him? Boom had attacked him less than fifty yards from the pawnshop. Why had Sparrow allowed that to happen?

Troubled by the desertion of his guardian angel, Mance ran on, clutching at his throat, wondering if his voice would be permanently damaged, but wondering more whether Boom's savagery would find the victim, the vengeance, the blood it sought.

Mance's blood.

Halfway up the slope toward the beer warehouse, he glanced over his shoulder. At first, he saw nothing. He slowed. He reached to the back of his neck. He spoke in a harsh whisper as if he had laryngitis. Each word felt like a strand of barbed wire was being pulled through his throat.

"Sting? Sting, you OK?"

The rat issued no sound. Mance touched the creature,

138

and he did not move.

Below the boy, toward the railroad tracks, it seemed a dozen shadows moved at once. Was one of them Boom?

Running again, Mance looked ahead to the parking lot.

Damn it, the cops have gone.

The nightly patrol had moved on.

Where? Where can I hide?

There was only one choice. Territory he knew.

He skirted the entrance to the warehouse, slipping around to the parking lot. He stopped once to catch his breath. He felt certain Boom had not followed his movement closely. The gate to the loading dock was padlocked shut; it was, in fact, a new gate, the bloodied one having been replaced, but the bloodstains on the asphalt had not faded entirely. Mance felt his way past the gate and followed the line of a tall hurricane fence until the lights from the parking lot no longer illuminated the area. He was some thirty yards behind the loading dock. Several trucks loomed there casting dinosaurlike shadows. He climbed over the fence and darted to a cluster of vent housings. Into the largest one he crawled, a familiar one, for this was the way in which he had sneaked six-packs of beer and all the pretzels his stomach desired.

Tonight it was a dark, narrow, cold passage to safety.

He dropped from it onto a stack of cases of beer. The warehouse was tomb silent. There were only two lights: one straight ahead some forty yards, positioned above the workbench; the other over the sliding doors which opened onto the dock to his right less than thirty yards from him.

Safe at last, he thought about Sting. He climbed down from the cases of beer; the stack wobbled, nearly toppled. But he negotiated his way to the floor without incident and sought out the workbench.

"Hey, man, you OK?" he whispered, holding Sting out at arm's length so that he could examine him for injuries. Cradling the rat, the boy hunkered down to the floor.

"Can you walk?"

A fiery pain clawed at Mance's throat. His neck muscles had been bruised badly, and he could swallow only with some difficulty.

Sting couldn't move his back legs.

"Jeez, man, you took a beatin', didn't you?"

The rat squeaked a few pathetic squeaks. Mance caressed his head with his fingertips, recalling the day, a couple of years ago, when Uncle Thestis had given the baby Sting—a pink thing resembling a small penis—to him, saying, "Every boy needs a familiar—this will be yours."

"Damn, Sting, am I gone have to shoot you?" he jested. "Guess we're lucky—things coulda been worse."

Boom coulda killed me.

Where was Sparrow? I heard him say run!

He watched as Sting spun around using his front legs only; the back ones splayed out behind him uselessly.

Mance's thought shifted away from the rat. He wished that he could be with Jonella in her upstairs bedroom, in her bed, pressing her naked body against his. She would kiss his bruised neck and the touch of her sweet lips would ease the pain.

Johnnie; am I gone lose you?

The ice cold thought ushered in a sudden, terrifying sound: in the direction of the loading dock a door had swung open. The beam of a flashlight played eerily across the tops of the cases of beer.

"I know you're in here, boy. It's time for you to die."

Boom's voice was filled with menace and a trace of a slur.

Mance's boots slipped on the glazed surface of the floor; he dived behind a sheet of pegboard beneath the workbench.

Weapon. Damn it, I need a weapon.

As Boom's threats neared, Mance scrambled out from under the bench and hurriedly searched among the tools for something—anything. He grabbed an X-acto knife. His heart was beating out of control and his hands were trembling as he thumbed the release button so that the razor-sharp blade emerged from its housing.

"Gone make you die slow, boy," Boom yelled. "You got in the way of me and my family. Made me look like I wasn't a man, god damn you. God damn you, you're gone hurt and die."

The flashlight beam appeared to lead the man's steps toward the workbench area. Heavy, solid steps. Then they stopped.

And through one of the holes in the pegboard Mance saw Sting struggling to move and heard his tiny screams.

God, Sting, please get outta the way.

But it was a futile wish and Mance knew it. Boom's footfalls drew nearer.

"Pullin' that gun on me was a big mistake, boy. You better have it with you tonight . . . better shoot me dead . . . 'cause I'm not leavin' here till I see lotsa blood. Hear me, boy?"

As the man rounded the corner, Mance darted forward to scoop up Sting. He placed him on his shoulder, and the rat dug in his claws and Mance was face to face with Boom.

"Hey, boy," he cried, startled at first. Mance held his ground. Boom, eyes wild and flashing in the halflight, grinned. "Hey, boy . . . found you. You gone die like a man?"

He raised the pipe and chain and began to swing them.

In his left hand Mance clutched the X-acto knife tightly; its blade was short, but he knew it could inflict a horrible wound.

"Dead, boy. I'm gone enjoy this."

Boom lurched forward. Mance ducked a violent swing of the chain, and as he did, he jabbed with the knife, slicing into his attacker's thigh, not deeply, but enough to redouble the man's anger.

Boom staggered backward. He touched at the wound.

Mance circled to the right, looking for an opportunity to elude Boom and reach the stacks of boxes where he might, in turn, climb to one of the vents.

"You cut me, boy," said Boom.

He stared momentarily at the blood on his fingertips as if he had never seen his own blood before. And this time when he rushed at the boy, Mance wasn't able to dodge the chain and pipe. The chain whistled past his shoulder, slapping into the small of his back; he blocked the thrust of the pipe with his left forearm.

He heard a bone snap.

He felt fire. And he cried out in pain, fell back, and rolled. Boom leaped for him and missed.

A surge of adrenaline, some instinctual mechanism—Mance couldn't be sure what it was—kept the boy from passing out from the excruciating pain. He scrambled to his feet and ran,

141

his left arm trailing like a piece of rag.

Behind him, he could hear Boom roar. The shadows surrounding the stacks of beer cases appeared to deepen and thicken. Reality for Mance blurred; he slammed into one of the stacks. There was no choice: he would have to climb, and he would have to do it with one arm. He clamped his teeth on the handle of the X-acto knife and felt for a handhold.

Boom was charging into the shadows. Mance could hear the eerie swish of the chain, though only faintly. The pain in his forearm—*it's broken, I know it's broken*—dulled his senses. He felt weak. Each box he negotiated took tremendous effort.

Halfway up one of the stacks he glanced up in search of a vent opening; he saw one and felt a surge of hope. He was within five feet of his goal when Boom crashed into the stack.

"Son-of-a-bitchin' boy . . . hey, I'm gone kill you real slow."

Mance clutched at the cases; the stack wobbled and swayed. He closed his eyes tightly; his throat and left arm burned. His world swirled.

God, I can't make it.

It was a cold, empty, nauseating sensation.

He opened his eyes and looked up at the vent opening; it appeared miles out of reach.

".. . kill you real slow."

Mance saw the shadows below him rock forward. Boom lowered his shoulder like a pulling guard on a halfback sweep. There was contact. The cases of beer Mance had been clutching slid away from him; the one upon which he had a foothold did likewise.

The stack teetered.

Boom growled.

And blocked into it again.

Mance followed the rasping slide of the cases.

Falling. He was falling. Helplessly. The entire stack was about to crash.

Down upon Boom.

In the fall, Mance momentarily lost the X-acto knife, but he felt Sting tangling his claws in the long locks of his hair—the

142

rat held fast. Mance landed on several cases of beer, one of which split open, sending cans of Rebel Lite skittering, spinning, rolling in all directions. In a daze, he groped for the knife and, luckily, found it.

Then he made out the shape of Boom through a flurry of movement as the man angrily struggled from beneath the weight of three or four cases of beer; apparently he hadn't been hurt badly. Mance could tell by his gasps for air that at least the wind had been knocked out of him.

Was there enough time for another escape attempt?

The fire in Mance's arm told him there had to be—he doubted he could fight off Boom, and it would do no good to call for help. Shouting at the top of his lungs he would not be heard. He was trapped. In the clip of a few seconds, he realized he had two choices: to somehow maneuver past Boom to the main office area and pull the fire alarm; or to scale another stack of cases and hope that he located an air vent to the outside.

He decided to climb again.

X-acto handle between his teeth, he staggered twenty feet to the next tall stack, this one four cases deep and wide and thus much more stable. Boom was on his feet; he speared the boy with his flashlight beam.

"Where's your gun, prick?"

Then Boom doubled over to catch his breath. The light pooled on the floor.

Mance's left arm was going numb; waves of nausea poured through him as he clawed his way up the stack. Sweat burned his eyes, and his jaws ached from clamping down upon the handle of the X-acto knife. But he dared not let go of it—escape was too far away, and Boom too determined to kill him.

Mance pushed on; Boom had straightened and had started to climb the stack. And Mance, wiping the sweat from his eyes, looked desperately at the vent opening above.

Dear God, don't let it be a dead-end one.

His small prayer was the equivalent of no atheists in fox-holes—no atheists in dark warehouses with psychopaths on the loose.

His hold continuously slipping, Mance maneuvered and

struggled, his body virtually dead weight by the time he reached the top of the stack. Resting a moment, he could hear Boom's maniacal laughter and feel tremors as the man gained footholds and scaled the stack.

"Hey, boy—Rebel Beer's just gone find the pieces. Lotsa blood and some pieces of brains and bones and whatever's left."

On shaking legs Mance stood. The vent was then in easy reach, but he would have to pull himself up into it with one arm, and that arm ached and had little strength.

But Boom was not slowing.

Oh, God, I can't do this.

His body wanted to quit.

"Gone enjoy killin' you, boy."

The chain whistled and slapped into the cases of beer on which Mance was standing. And his body found the burst of energy necessary to press up into the darkness of the vent. On his right elbow and knees he crawled forward in the horizontal passage which led some thirty feet before angling up to the roof.

Don't be a dead end. Don't be a dead end, please.

The vent smelled of mildew and sour dust; being in it was claustrophobic. Mance had to take the X-acto knife from his mouth to cough once before pushing on. He knew that if—*God, don't let it be so*—the vent dead-ended or was locked, at least he could fight back with the knife.

Suddenly, light exploded around him. Boom's flashlight froze him.

"Got me a fuckin' coward," Boom muttered, huffing and puffing behind the light. His head and shoulders were at the opening of the vent.

Mance gripped the knife in his good hand and began scooting on his bottom so that he could keep an eye on Boom's progress. The boy rocked his body hard to reach the slant of the vent. Then he felt relief. He reached up and touched a metal grate.

In luck. It wasn't a dead-end vent.

Mance pressed his fist into the grate and tried to lift. He unclenched the fist to get a hold of it with his fingers—and the

144

X-acto knife fell and skittered hollowly down the vent. Boom saw what had happened.

"Too bad, boy. You lost your weapon. Too bad."

He was partway into the vent, moving on his elbows and knees. Mance could feel the vent housing bend and hear it rumble in protest of all the weight it was being forced to bear, but because it was constructed of heavy-duty materials, it held.

Mance pushed again and again at the grate.

"God damn it," he hissed.

The grate could be budged, yet only an inch or two. Mance gritted his teeth and hammered at the metal. Had he not lost much of his strength he could have lifted the grate aside and escaped easily. He grunted and groaned, and he slumped back in defeat. Boom was in the vent; Mance could see the kill in his eyes behind the spray of the flashlight.

I'm gone die, thought Mance.

He pulled up his knees against his chest, preparing, as a last resort, to kick at his attacker.

The vent popped and thundered. Mance heard a growl.

Boom had suddenly stopped advancing.

"What the god damn?" he cried out in surprise, and then he began sliding . . . backward. He glanced over his shoulder, and he screamed. He twisted around; Mance saw his eyes bulge in terror.

Boom dropped the flashlight; he dropped the lead pipe, and he scratched frantically at the slippery surface of the vent.

The flashlight rolled out of sight, plunging the vent into blackness.

Something savage was clawing and biting at Boom. His scream pitched higher and higher as he was jerked from the vent. Mance, shaken, deeply frightened, wheeled again to try the grate, and this time, fear giving him extra strength, he shoved it up and aside.

Strangled screams echoed behind him as he squeezed through the opening and out onto the roof.

To safety.

Part Two: The Hour Between Dog and Wolf

Chapter Seven

1

In the darkness of the van, Mance cradled his useless arm. The fire in it had died down, but the pain, though not as intense, flared with each jolt. It was impossible to position himself where it didn't hurt. How, he wondered, had he ever managed to climb the stacks of the cases of beer—twice?

Fear.

That was the simple answer. With a deranged, not-quite-human force determined to kill you, few physical feats were beyond the realm of possibility. After escaping from the warehouse, Mance recalled little of his trek home. The horrific scenes at the warehouse clicked off in his mind like a series of still photos— they followed him to his room—as did the echo of Boom's soul-sickening screams.

Again, his memory was hazy, but apparently he had passed out in the bathroom. His mother had discovered him. Mothers have, he believed, a special sonar built into their senses to hear when an offspring is in trouble. She had immediately insisted that his dad take him to the emergency room, and so there he was, speeding along in the van waiting for his dad to offer some remark. Secretly hoping, in fact, that he would.

The screams would not fade.

He never dreamed that a human being could make such a terrifying sound. He pressed his right hand to his ear. It felt as if the

149

screams had been trapped there in his head like some small animal.

Sparrow.

Sparrow had saved him again.

He turns into a beast when he kills.

That the man was a killer deeply unsettled Mance, of course, despite the obvious ways in which the boy had benefited. But beyond the murders, Mance found himself trying to envision the darkest side of Sparrow — what kind of a monster did he become when his mind dialed kill?

And the most shattering question of all: if you were to enter the Rebel Beer warehouse right that moment, what would you find? Would it redefine your notion of horror?

Boom's dead.

Or was he?

Should I call the police? Maybe Boom was lying there bleeding to death — but, no, Mance quickly realized that wasn't likely. Sparrow had viciously dispatched Ford and Davis; Boom would not have survived.

What now?

What about the police? What about Sparrow?

Mance squirmed in his seat. Out of the corner of his eye he saw his dad's lips moving as if he were rehearsing something. The man cleared his throat.

"Your mother told me you got'n a fight. You need to say somethin' to me about it?"

Yes, he needed to. Wanted to. At that moment he felt six years old. He felt as if he might talk out all of the horror and press a tearstained face against a parental shoulder. It was a temptation. But he resisted. The helplessness of a very small boy dissolved.

"No big deal," he said. "A guy at work's been picking a fight with me lately."

His dad sighed heavily. A silence followed in which some imaginary conversation took place in the mind of both of them. His dad eventually broke the silence when they pulled into the emergency room tunnel.

"We'll see if we can find somebody to patch you up."

Mance wanted to believe that his dad knew that it was Boom with whom he had fought, that he made a connection between

150

this incident and the one at Tanya and Boom's trailer. Or did the man care enough to speculate on a son who could be in serious difficulties?

The emergency room personnel set his arm, a broken radius bone. It would be in a cast for over a month. The bruises on his neck would disappear in a week or so. But the psychological wound, the legacy of the incident at the warehouse, would take a lifetime to heal.

Mance spent all of Sunday morning in bed; his mother fussed in and out of his room until he had to tell her to stop. Sting lay in his cage, a listless piece of flesh and fur, refusing to eat. Whenever Mance peered in at him, the rat's pink-rimmed eyes merely stared back as if prepared for last rites.

"Sorry, man," said Mance. "Hang in there."

Propped against a couple of pillows, the boy strained to hear sirens. How long will it take them to discover Boom's body? he wondered. The police would, doubtless, come looking for him later. Everyone at Rebel Beer would have to admit that a confrontation between him and Boom had been inevitable.

Would they believe he killed the man?

If, that is, if he were . . . no, forget it, no point in considering further the possibility of Boom's survival.

Boom Browner was dead. He had suffered a violent death.

Tanya had lost a husband, Crystal and Loretta, a father.

And yet, none of those realizations saddened Mance. Such a man did not deserve to live.

Mance closed his eyes; fear held him. He felt desperately alone. He wanted to talk to someone, but not his mother. His dad, he reasoned, would be too busy.

Suddenly he heard a shuffling in the hallway, the unmistakable sound of Uncle Thestis returning from the bathroom.

He's always been there for me. He'll listen.

Mance pushed himself off the bed and went to his uncle's door. Maybe he would know what to do about Sparrow — maybe he would understand.

The boy lifted his fist to knock.

Hesitating, he recalled the falling-out with his uncle over

151

school—*will he want me to say I was wrong?* The fist hung there. The anguish of the moment tore at Mance's soul. Seconds passed. He heard the muzak of commotion downstairs. At last, he shook his head.

And lowered his fist to his side.

"It's Jonella."

His mother was shaking his shoulder.

"Mance . . . she's on the phone. Come on down and talk to her, woncha now?"

He was surprised to learn that he had slept until late afternoon. It was raining. His forearm no longer ached much, but the bulky cast itched with a fire of its own.

Down in the kitchen he tried to carry on the phone conversation over the clatter of the noon hour dishes being washed.

"You OK?" said Jonella, and he couldn't believe how good her voice sounded. It put angels to shame.

"Yeah," he chuckled, "I'll live. Broke my arm and got a bruise on my neck that looks like the world's biggest hickey."

Jonella paused. Something probed at Mance's thoughts like a needle.

"Did Mom ask you to call me?" he said.

"Well . . . she sorta did. I would have anyway, though, because . . . Mance, the police just left here. A detective. He said two patrolmen saw a side door open at the warehouse, and they went in to check . . . and found Boom. He's dead."

Mance swallowed at the news, not that it surprised him, but there was something in the verification that shocked him nevertheless.

"He'll be coming over here," he said. "Johnnie, it wasn't me—it was Sparrow again. And he saved my life. I woulda been trashed. Boom had me trapped, and he—"

"I have to hang up now," she said. "Tanya needs me. She's in pretty bad shape, and the girls don't know what to think. I hear one of them crying. We'll talk when I get a chance. Good-bye, Mance."

"Johnnie, wait—"

The buzz of the dial tone sounded incredibly indifferent.

He replaced the receiver on the hook and turned to find his mother at his shoulder.

"It's Detective Stewart here to see you," she said, her brow wrinkled so deeply that it was almost comical. She wiped her hands on an apron and added, "He's right out by the buffet. Me and your father will be there with you. He, Detective Stewart — he said it would be all right for us to be there."

A heavyset, pink-faced man shook hands with Mance. They sat in front of Tanya's mural — the detective, Mance, and his parents — and Stewart covered everything that the boy expected he would, carefully touching upon the history of Mance's relationship with Boom. Then the tough part.

"Would you care to tell me what happened last night?"

Mance did, but he read in Stewart's squinty gray eyes that the man was trying to force his mind to stay fixed on reality in a case which smacked everywhere of the improbable and unbelievable.

"Did you see who . . . or what . . . pulled Boom Browner from the vent?"

"No, sir. Had to be somebody real strong."

The boy shrugged. Was Stewart buying the story?

The man filled a page of a notebook with notes. For an uncomfortably long time, he said nothing.

"You can't no way think Mance is a killer," said his mother, her face contorted. His dad, gravely silent, touched her shoulder tenderly.

Mance stared into Stewart's gray eyes.

The man closed the notebook and looked, in turn, at each one of them, focusing at last on the woman.

"No, ma'am. Truth is, I don't. What killed Mr. Browner isn't human — it just flat out can't be."

2

Dust rose in clouds, except in those areas beneath a leak in the roof, and there splattery dabs of mud were drying and hardening after the rain two days ago. Mance swept surprisingly well with one arm, especially when he used his broken wing to help steady the handle of the broom.

He wasn't going to be helpless.

Guillo House was providing the refuge he needed away from the circus of reporters that had, in recent hours, descended upon Soldier. He was amazed at how quickly his name had been linked to Boom's death. He was not a suspect, but the assumption was that he had news-making details in his head, a rich load of journalistic ore to be mined.

Wish everybody would leave me alone.

No, that wasn't exactly true.

He stopped sweeping and took a moment to survey the second floor room. God, how he wanted for Jonella to be there with him, but she was taking care of Crystal and Loretta while Tanya attended Boom's funeral up somewhere in Chambers County. The man had virtually no family—Mance wondered whether anyone except Tanya would cry as they buried him.

Returning to his sweeping, he lost himself in the mesmerizing sound of the broom bristles scratching at the dust. He was playing a game, a head game involving the future—a future that had become resolutely bleak. If I could turn back time, he thought, if the big, ole indifferent world would only spin backwards awhile, shucking the days away until he reached that fateful Sunday night Jonella was attacked.

That's where all the darkness began.

And why was he sweeping the floor? Easy. The dust. Jonella hated the dust. It reminded her . . . of all the darkness. Someday he would bring her back here and they would start over. Love each other as they had before.

Johnnie, don't give up on us.

He had called her a couple more times and asked if he could see her and she had told him, "I'd rather you wouldn't," and had given no reason why. And, oh God, hadn't those words stung him. As before, she sounded cold and distant. And frightened?

Through the whispery whoosh of the broom, Mance suddenly heard steps.

The image of Sparrow sprang into his thoughts—Sparrow transforming into whatever dark creature he became before he killed. For the first of what would become many times, he saw Sparrow as a werewolf, man into wolf. But how? The Agent Orange?

154

He heard someone cough.

"Anybody ta home?"

At first he didn't recognize the voice. It was a woman, an older woman. And his mind toyed with a curious notion: *it's Eleanor. It's the ghost of Johnnie's imaginary woman.*

He took a few steps back as Bridgette Settleford, wheezing, pressing a hand to her chest, trundled into the room.

"Thought I might could find ya here. Whew, Lord . . . if you don't smoke, Mance, don't start. I 'bout can't handle a long flight of stairs no more."

Catching her breath, she put her hands on her hips and gently rocked back and forth. Her gaze drifted around the room, and the suggestion of a frown wrinkled her brow.

"Not a happy house," she said. She had a partially rolled-up newspaper in one hand and began to fan herself with it. "Never was a happy house."

Mance shuffled his feet nervously.

"What do you want? I've already told what I know to the cops."

"Oh, course, I'm aware of that. How's your arm?"

"Broke."

A smile flickered at her lips. Then she said, "Appears you'll be out of work a spell. Did you know they've closed down Rebel Beer for the rest of the week?"

Mance nodded.

"Dudn't matter to me — I'm through there. Boss called me this morning and said he was letting me go. I brought too much trouble to the job. I can work for Austin and Fast Track, so it dudn't matter."

"With that broken arm? Can't do any lifting. I heard about 'em firing you at Rebel, and when I did I looked into something for you. There's a good *S-G News* route opening up — North Street, Chrokinole and on east about four, five blocks. It's yours if you want it. I found out you'd been a carrier a few years back. You had a good record."

Mance stared at the floor.

"I don't need nobody to help me get work."

"Oh, course, you don't. But, like I said, the job's yours if you want it."

She started to stroll across the room; he saw that she had noticed what he'd been doing. She glanced at the pallet on the floor and said, "This the passion pit, is it?"

He reddened. And this time, more impatiently, he said, "What do you want?"

She stepped up to him and unfolded a Columbus, Georgia, newspaper: Soldier Wolf Man Strikes Again. It was the headline for the lower half of the front page.

Mance thought instantly of Sparrow; a dark figure lurched through his mind. Was it possible?

"Care to read the story?" she asked. "If you want my opinion, it isn't responsible journalism — sounds more like one of those rags you see at the grocery checkout counter. 'Wolf man' — ever hear such bullshit?"

He shook his head, a no to both of her questions.

"I'm pretty sick of the whole thing," he said.

"What I want, Mance, is what you're not telling the police."

He glared at her, hoping to bluff successfully.

"I've told them everything I know. They feel like some animal killed Boom. Same one that got Ford and Davis probably."

"You believe that, do you?"

He hesitated, wanting to feel for more secure footing. Could he confide in her? Did she already suspect Sparrow?

"Don't know what I believe."

Settleford dropped her eyes to the news story.

"Our little town's freaking out over this. Never seen so many scared folks. Bet your friend, Sparrow, has been selling a few guns, don't you?"

"Maybe. I guess maybe he has."

Her mention of Sparrow's name touched him like a hot brand. He felt that quite likely she noted his reaction.

"Oh, well, then " she said, after studying the news story a bit longer, "I'll let you get back to your housecleaning — lots and lots of it at Guillo House."

She smiled.

At the door to the room she paused.

"Just one more question, Mance: you protecting someone?"

The hot brand returned, searing into his chest.

"Protecting?"

156

"Don't play dumb, Mance. I'm a pretty sharp ole broad."

"No," he said. "Honest to God, I'm in the dark 'bout what exactly's gone on. I'm not sure of nothing."

And that was, indeed, the truth.

3

"Twilight is my favorite time of the day," she said.

Sitting beside her, Kelton Austin gazed into her eyes and feared he might melt and slip between the slats in the porch swing. Adele Taylor's beauty, her warmth—could this woman truly be sixty years old? She did not, to Austin at least, appear a day over forty. He inhaled the aroma of her perfume, a specialty brand from a small operation in New Orleans. There was a touch of cinnamon in the fragrance. He wanted more than anything else to press her warmth to him, to bury his face in that aroma, and to kiss the sweetness of her lips.

As always, she was dressed to the nines, hose and heels, a white, delicately cuffed and high-necked blouse and a black skirt and black necklace and matching earrings. Her hair was of a silver which caught in Austin's mental filter—he woke each morning to the image of it.

"The hour between dog and wolf," he said, and she glanced at him, her expression saying that she had never heard that description of twilight before. "The transition from day to night—the promise of change," he added.

There was something he very much wanted to ask her, something he had been planning for weeks, and this February evening, an unseasonably warm one, seemed as good as any other, despite the pall which had fallen upon the town and the tragedy which had entered Tanya's life.

"Lately, the changes have been so horrid," she said. "Events usher me back to my childhood—to memories I'd rather would remain asleep." She turned her head toward the screened windows. "I feel so very sorry for Tanya. Her husband apparently was a brutal man, and yet she's experiencing a void. She's at a loss to fill it. But only time can do that."

She searched for Austin's agreement.

157

"Time . . . and finding someone to care for, someone whom she can love."

He met her eyes and felt like a sensitive set of scales attempting to weigh her affection for him in grams and decigrams.

Adele lightly squeezed his hand.

"Jonella has been such a marvelous help to her even as she has battled some very serious difficulties of her own. She's wonderful with the girls."

Austin watched as the woman looked away, a pained wistfulness in her expression.

"Those girls," she continued, "they remind me so much of me and my sister, Charlotte, long, long ago."

Leaning back, sensing that the time for his bold request was not right, Austin said, "The VCR you bought for them will get a workout. They'll love it — I only hope that old TV I dug up won't plink out on them too soon."

"I bought them a few tapes this morning — including *Bambi* and *Cinderalla*."

"Good ole Disney."

"Yes . . . Charlotte and I escaped from the hard times of childhood with Disney movies. At the Strand downtown. Though, sadly, there is no Strand anymore. Well . . . what Charlotte and I learned was that the ability to survive was aligned with the ability to fantasize. Crystal and Loretta will have to learn that same lesson. Perhaps I'm merely helping them discover a great truth before they get much older."

Austin felt his breath catch when he saw Adele's mask of distress.

"I'm thankful they don't have to face the future alone — the little girls, Tanya, Jonella. There are some caring people near. Jonella has Mance. To me, the chief sadness, always, is seeing someone who is alone."

She appeared to nod.

Was it time? Could he ask before the question exploded, ripping his heart out?

He cupped both of his hands over one of hers. She smiled at the gesture. But does she understand? Does she have any idea what I'm leading up to? Or how tremendously important these moments are?

"And that's why," she replied, "our friendship is something I value so highly." With her other hand, she patted the top of his. Then she shifted gears. "Shouldn't we be going to Scarlett's? I got so excited buying tapes for the girls that I forgot to eat lunch. I'm hungry."

Her smile widened to a tease; her skin reflected the quiet radiance of the twilight. Everything about her was soft and yet glowing; she was a friend and yet so much more. She was his and yet not his.

"We have some time," he said. "Time." He repeated the word as if it were the most important one in his vocabulary. "But I want . . . I need to have you near me more of the time. I'm never . . . never quite whole when you're not by my side."

She seemed to smile with her eyes. And she said, "We see each other virtually every day—I'm afraid you would grow weary of me if you were to spend more time around me. I'm so fond of you . . . our time together is so dear to me . . ."

Her voice trailed off.

Austin felt a torch of disappointment in his chest. Couldn't she follow his drift?

"Adele?"

She looked at him intently. There was a veneer of confusion in her expression. And suddenly his body seemed foreign to him; it was as if, ghostlike, he had stepped out of his jumpsuit of flesh and bones. He held onto her hand so that he would not float away.

He had to say it. He had to.

Now, his heart demanded.

A bit awkwardly, he found himself getting down on one knee—he hadn't planned to—it just happened. And there he was, looking up at her, nervous, yet beaming, scared, yet pleased in a way to see the surprise on her face.

"Kelton, whatever are—?"

"Please," he said. "I have to do this . . . say some things."

Somewhat embarrassed, she glanced around to see whether anyone was watching. The street was empty; within the house a television show reeled on. A laugh track went off as programmed.

"Adele, . . . I'm so lonely. I've thought carefully about this. I

159

don't come to you as a pauper. The good Methodist folks in Georgia compensated me pretty well all those years I was their minister; the furniture store is just an excuse to stay busy. But you know all of this. What I want you to know as well is that . . . I love you. I want to live with you. I want you . . . would you, Adele . . . would you marry me?"

It wasn't a physical reaction. Not a particular signal in her eyes or her smile. Yet, something in the way she seemed to send out a telepathic response—he was certain, so certain he would have bet his life on it—that she was about to say yes. In the overwhelming joy of the instant, he imagined himself climbing the outside of a building five hundred stories tall. He ascended through clouds. Planes flew below him.

Waiting for her to speak, he was so nervous he chuckled.

She leaned forward, cradling his face in her hands. She kissed him on the forehead. For Austin, it was a giddy, on-a-high-ledge feeling. He couldn't believe how exciting her touch was.

Slowly she shook her head. She bit softly at her lower lip.

Austin began to lose his balance. He reached out to her with his eyes for some assurance. Nerves continued to squeeze involuntary laughter from him. She waited until he had himself under control.

"No," she said. "I can't. I can't marry you."

The words provided the necessary shove. In his thoughts he was falling, wheeling, twisting, in a weird out-of-body dance. A painful roar filled one ear.

He prayed that she was joking.

Wasn't there something in her expression that gave away her ruse?

"Can't?" he whispered.

And suddenly he felt so terribly foolish. He stood and mechanically brushed off his knees. He sat down beside her quickly because he felt that he might—*yes, God forbid, I might*—faint on the spot. In his thoughts, he continued to fall.

"I can't," she said. "I do care deeply for you, Kelton. And someday . . ." Her line of thought broke. "Would you walk with me down the street? I'm not as hungry as I thought."

"Oh, Adele. Forgive me, I've gone about this so badly. Embarrassed you. Made a fool out of myself . . . but I—I don't—"

"No, of course not," she said, touching his soul with the warmth of her voice. "Of course you don't understand. I'm the one who should apologize. But please, walk with me first."

Austin held on to her arm, more for his support than for hers. They walked down Chrokinole Street. Adele hesitated in front of Guillo House.

"I've spent my life alone," she said, "because a certain memory won't release me. I will marry you, Austin, if you'll stand by your beautiful proposal until the day comes when I'm no longer haunted. No longer haunted by Guillo House."

4

More blood.

Mance snapped awake.

More blood, more blood, more blood.

The words seemed to swoop at him in the darkness of his room like predatory birds. He covered his eyes. He buried his face.

Louder.

More blood!

His bed shook. His room shook. His hands . . . his hands felt as if they were coated by the coppery stink of blood.

The voice lost volume.

More blood.

Mance raised his head.

Something in the corner?

Softer, softer. A whisper repeated over and over.

More blood, more blood, more blood.

Sting was squeaking, the first sounds he'd made in several days.

Mance sat up, saw something in the corner, something materializing, rising from the floor like smoke, gaining volume, gaining depth, gaining outline and shape.

It was the wolf creature. Its yellow eyes found Mance's.

More blood.

The voice was insistent. A warning?

The creature was huge.

No

161

Mance stared, breathing through his mouth. His fear splayed out in all directions; it threatened to stretch out of control, pulling on his emotions until they might break.

"Sparrow?"

The sharp outline of the wolf creature suddenly wavered.

"Sparrow? Is that really you? You doin' something weird with your mind?"

That must be it, he concluded. Sparrow using his wild talents — *the living dark?* — to project himself into the boy's room.

But why?

"Sparrow?"

The shape shifted.

Yes, wasn't that Sparrow's long hair?

"Say something."

The shadowy thing in the corner held its human outline momentarily.

"You saved me. From Boom." Mance paused to catch his breath. "Thank you. I was gone come thank you, but . . ."

I was too scared. Too god damned scared.

"Sparrow? Say something."

The wolf creature returned, mushrooming out of the human form.

"Say something, god damn it," Mance pleaded. Sting's squeaks pitched higher. He was dragging his body around and around within his cage. "Please," Mance cried.

Into the boy's mind the creature spoke at last.

More blood.

I want more blood.

It was a variation of the same dream she had experienced for weeks — the animallike creatures chasing her, bringing her down, their bodies repercussions of a primitive lust. But lately in the dreams she had been rescued by . . . someone. Something? In the night terror she would call out desperately for help . . . and it would appear.

She hadn't told Miss Prince about this new dream development. Nor Dr. Colby. It was as if it were a secret she shared with her rescuer, and she feared that if she told anyone else, the rescuer would no longer rush into her nightmare replay of the rape to save her.

She twisted on her pillow.

It was 1:15 according to the clock radio Miss Taylor had given her. A streetlamp seeped light down the window side of the house. Events of the last several days marched through her thoughts like a sinister parade. Staying out of school and tending the girls, she had had time to think, to think hard. And her thoughts circled and circled one conclusion: *I need to start over.*

A clean slate. A new beginning. A different person (persons?) had been given birth within, and she had to get acquainted with that stranger. To see whether she could love the I she was becoming.

It was crazy. Not the craziest thing he'd ever done, but crazy enough. He could easily fall and break his other arm. The old wooden ladder he'd found at the rear of the house whispered a threat. And his first step onto the gently sloping but night-glistened, slippery roof was tentative at best.

He had to talk to someone.

He crept to the window, aware that a passing car or walker would probably be able to see him from the street or front sidewalk. But who would be out in this neighborhood after one o'clock?

I don't give a damn. I've got to do this.

He rapped softly on the window pane.

"Johnnie? Johnnie? It's Mance."

He waited a few seconds. Rapped again more insistently.

And then he could see her, indistinctly at first. A white flash of arms and the window screeched and whished open.

"Are you outta your mind?" she said.

"Yeah, maybe so."

She leaned down close to his face. She smelled different. She had on someone else's perfume. It smelled like cinnamon.

"What do you think you're doing? It's the middle of the night—what if Miss Taylor hears you?"

"Didn't come to see her," he said.

He drank in the lacy strap of her nightie and the lace trail lead-

163

ing to the suggestion of cleavage and to the fleshy eruption of her nipples against the silky nylon.

"What do you want, Mance? Why are you doing this?"

"Can I come in?"

"No!"

"Please. It's kinda chilly out here, and the roof's slippery, and I gotta tell you . . . that I love you and need you."

Her sigh carried a hint of disgust or exasperation as she stepped away from the window to let him enter.

"This beats all," she said.

She slipped on her robe and sat on the edge of her bed. He went over and sat by her.

"I just needed to talk to somebody."

"You coulda done it tomorrow," she said.

"I needed to do it right this minute."

He told her about the episode in his room.

Is that what you came to tell me?"

"Yeah . . . that, and well . . . I love you and want my future to be with you."

"I don't see a future."

"You gotta look at the future, Johnnie. There's gotta be a life out there for us."

"Everything looks dead to me, Mance."

He reached for her hand.

"You been taking your medicine?"

She stiffened and pulled her hand away.

"You better go on home now."

"You're my girl, Johnnie. I just had to see my girl . . . and be with her, you know."

She stared through the shadows at him.

"I don't wanna be," she said.

It wasn't quite Jonella's voice. There was something different about it.

"Don't wanna be what?"

Mance needed to clear his throat, but found that he couldn't. Or dared not. He couldn't believe his own thoughts. There was something alien about them. What was she saying?

"Mance, I don't wanna be your girl no more."

Mance walked through the weekend in a daze. He ghosted from one place to another, bought another jam box with his final check from Rebel Beer, and talked to virtually everyone he knew on North Street and some, in turn, gave him advice:

Austin: "Never give up on love, son."

Fast Track: "Women, ump, ump . . . dey's a kick or a kick in de head."

Punch: "Don't lose your pride over this, hotshot."

His mother: "Jonella's not herself these days . . . she'll come around and y'all be close ta one 'nother again, you'll see."

His dad said nothing.

Bridgette Settleford told him he ought to damn well stop acting like such a wimp.

Sting was getting better; fortunately for Mance, the rat couldn't offer advice.

But Mance was miserable. He felt, in fact, that he was scraping the bottom of his barrel of integrity: on Monday he accepted the job as carrier of the *S-G News* for the North Street-Chrokinole area.

A god damn kid's job.

He had dusted off his ten-speed, swallowed back his humiliation, and by late afternoon of his first day, pedaled into the unflinching present, bound and determined that he wouldn't break down and cry. But, oh God, he wanted to.

He wheeled his sorrow through a Soldier now more peopled with police and police cars than ever before. Detective Stewart was heading up a task force on the so-called wolf man murders, receiving help from the state attorney general's office as well.

None of that was of interest to Mance. All he wanted was to have Jonella love him again. For her to be his girl, and for the shitty world to go merrily on its shitty way and not do anything else shitty to him—Soldier, Alabama, could crumble to dust and blow away for all he cared. All he wanted was to turn back time.

No, that wasn't entirely true.

He wanted one thing more: to silence the voice.

On Tuesday afternoon Mance wandered into Sparrow's. He had put it off for days. It was rainy again, which caused the paper route to take longer to complete because he had to slip a plastic sleeve on every paper. Normally he expected to finish by four o'clock. Today had taken him until five.

He sat at the counter nursing one of Sparrow's patented glasses of sweetened iced tea, waiting for the man to finish dipping up an early supper for his burdens so that some things could be talked over.

"Dingledodie, we'll sure as fuck do it," Sparrow had promised.

Mance had listened closely to the voice.

More blood, more blood, more blood.

Sparrow's voice, wasn't it?

Off and on, the voice, with its persistent theme, would sneak into his consciousness when he least expected it. It was the only thing that detoured his thoughts from Jonella. The voice also served as a reminder that he was protecting a killer. And now the killer seemed to thirst for more.

More blood.

And it frightened and confused the boy, because a question nagged at him: am I responsible in a way for Sparrow's killings? In a way, yes, he feared he was. Yes, obviously he was, he told himself, and so he had come to Sparrow's to tell him . . . to tell him what?

No more blood.

Nearly an hour later Sparrow dragged himself out of the back room and flopped down upon a stool beside Mance.

"Not lettin' the bastards get ya, are ya?"

There was glee and concern and exhaustion and laughter and a preface to tears and something more in his face . . . something like insanity and something like death.

"Guess they broke my arm," Mance offered, feeling nervous, as usual, in the company of this most curious man. His guardian angel and a vicious killer to boot.

"Lots of blood," Sparrow murmured. "Lots of police. My burdens bein' hassled on the street, god damn it. Could a burden cut up a man, tear him into bite-sized pieces? Frizzle ribsit and

166

piss calls on the wikkerdikker, fremdoogle moon, I think not."

"Me neither," said Mance. "I was there." And the boy snickered, though he tried to stifle it.

You were there, too, Sparrow. Why don't you admit it?

"I warned you about the Final Chaos. I warned my burdens, too. It's out there."

Sparrow's face sank grimly. And then he said, "Jesus, I'm thirsty. Do you mind?"

Mance saw that he was eyeing the glass of iced tea.

"No, you need a drink of this?"

He started to slide the glass along the counter, but Sparrow grunted a signal that that wasn't necessary. The man's expression went hard. And the bottom of the glass began to revolve and mutter rapid little scratching, scraping noises.

Mance jerked back.

The glass slid about two feet, leaving a trail of water before stopping in front of Sparrow, who reached for it and drank greedily.

"Thanks, friend," he said. "Whatchoo want to talk about?"

An involuntary shiver tiptoed across Mance's shoulder. And he wondered again how he ever questioned what Sparrow could do — the power of the living dark — the legacy of the Agent Orange. The boy was at a loss for words at first. When he found them, he said, "My girl dumped me."

"That's a dingledodie piss call," said Sparrow, and Mance couldn't be certain whether the man was commiserating or making fun of him.

"I lost her . . . and everything's gone wrong. Gone all to shit."

He feared he might burst into tears.

"It's the way things are," said Sparrow thoughtfully.

Mance pressed himself closer to the man, suddenly desperate to make him understand.

"I'm tired," he said, "and scared . . . and so I gotta say something to you."

He couldn't tell whether Sparrow was listening or not; there seemed to be some engine ticking and thrumming away within the man. His eyes were unfocused like a swirling wind, and Mance figured he was on something — some kind of speed or maybe cocaine. *Or is it the Agent Orange?*

"Get if off your chest, friend," said Sparrow.

And Mance relaxed a notch. It was time. Time to say it.

"The guys that attacked Johnnie . . . and now what happened to Boom . . . you did it for me . . . I see that . . . you been my guardian angel, but it . . . can't . . . it's gotta stop."

The boy looked for a light in Sparrow's eyes. He saw none.

No light. Only pain and the rattle of a man approaching insanity.

"My buddy's name was Angel—killed gooks better'n any of us. Led the unit in kills. And I watched him die—killin' gooks. The Final Chaos took him. Dingledodie. Just like fuckin' that."

Sparrow snapped his fingers.

"No," said Mance, "you're not hearin' what I'm sayin'." He touched Sparrow's shoulder. *There's got to be a way to make him see.* "I want you . . . you gotta stop it." His voice rose higher as he began to shake the man. "Stop the killin'. You gotta stop it. Stop the killin'. No more blood. No more blood . . . no more."

He fell into Sparrow's arms and the tears came. A few old men wandered out of the back area, curious. Then Sparrow pushed him away.

"Stop the killing?"

The man spun off the stool and hustled behind the gun counter. From a rack on the wall he grabbed a deer rifle and raised it high over his head.

"The killing won't never stop," he shouted.

Mance began to cower. He watched, surprised and stunned, as the man scrambled atop the counter, waving the rifle like some Central American revolutionary. His eyes were burning coals. His blond hair seemed aflame, and the scene reminded the boy of a painting he had seen of John Brown the abolitionist.

"This war's never gone end because there's no end to the gooks. That's what the ignorant fuckers at the Pentagon figured wrong." Strings of saliva dangled from the corners of his mouth. "There's no end to the gooks."

Sparrow began to dance. To get down and boogie and to slam out the lyrics to the Rolling Stones' "Start Me Up." The spectacle was at once comic and bizarre and unsettling. Suddenly the man kicked the glass of iced tea, shattering it, showering Mance.

"It's the Final Chaos! The Final Chaos is here!"

More old men gravitated toward the counter. Sparrow raved on.

And Mance, finding an opportune moment, slipped away.

6

Rock bottom.

Mance had hit it. At Fast Track's he managed to cadge two cans of beer from the proprietor in exchange for two basketball picks — Fast Track needed to hit in the worst way. But before the old black man could lay his apprehension about "butcher men" on Mance, the boy exited.

The second floor of Guillo House drew him.

He drank half of one of the cold beers and felt sorry for himself. And missed Jonella so much that his entire body ached. He thought about Sparrow's display of lunacy and was tempted, on the spot, to turn the man in.

He's a murderer.

But he's my friend.

He sat on the pallet — was that the ghost scent of Johnnie that played at his nostrils? he wondered — and took stock of his situation. Compared to oil spills and the environment going all to hell, compared to people in Lithuania struggling for freedom, compared to the pain and sorrow of the rest of the world maybe his troubles were bearable: but no one on the planet could convince him of that.

So what'm I gone do?

"Got to get outta this town," he answered himself.

Yeah. Simple. Rat shit simple.

A plan crystallized in his thoughts. He drank the rest of the opened beer and part of the second. Then he went home and packed a small duffel bag of clothes. Night came on. His folks were too busy with the restaurant to be aware of what he was up to. Uncle Thestis's door was sensibly closed. Sting appeared to be asleep; Mance had not been taking him out lately.

There was one pressing matter. Pencil and paper in hand, Mance plopped on his bed and wrote the following letter:

169

Dear Johnnie,

I'm going away. To Atlanta probably and I'll look for work and when I've been there awhile I'll call you. I got to get away from Soldier before this hellhole kills me. It's all wrong for me and I feel like it's that way for you. I still love you, Johnnie. I know life isn't any kind of movie, but I feel like you and me can have a happy ending. Corny as shit, huh? Well, I can't help it. I want you back as my girl and someday as my wife. It's all I really want. And someday to kiss your rose again.

Love you alot,

Mance, the Fang

He reread it, stuffed it into an envelope, packed a few more things, then hesitated at Sting's cage. The rat was awake and staring up at him. A rockhard knot formed in Mance's throat.

"Hey, . . . you feelin' better?"

Mance bit at his bottom lip to keep it from quivering.

Sayin' good-bye to a damn rat shouldn't oughtta be so god damn tough.

But it was.

"Look, Mom or somebody'll take care of you till you can get around. I can't . . . I can't take you with me, Sting. Not the way you are. Maybe I'll come back for you. I don't know what's gone happen."

He swallowed a mouthful of sadness and forced himself not to look over his shoulder as he left the room.

It was late when he realized that one part of his plan wouldn't work. He couldn't bring himself to take the family van.

But I gotta have wheels. I ain't hitchhiking.

Duffel bag in one hand, his new jam box in the other, he went back to Guillo House and thought about it. There was another possibility. Another vehicle at his disposal. In the darkness of the second-floor room, he decided it was worth a try.

On the way to his destination, he leaned the envelope with Johnnie printed on it against the front door of the big house where even then, he reflected, she was upstairs sleeping. He tried to imagine what she'd think when she read the letter: would she be sad? Cry? Not give a damn?

In the alley behind Austin's store, he climbed into Austin's truck and groped beneath the floor mat. The keys were right there where they always were. The boy glanced at the rear of the store; one muted light was burning.

"Sorry, Austin," he whispered.

On the second crank, the truck sputtered, caught, and he was on his way. Could the ole beast make it to Atlanta? God, he hoped so. It needed a ring job, but it had pretty good tires and new brake shoes. He promised the shadows along North Street that when he got a good job in hot 'Lanta he would return Austin's truck with interest.

It felt good shifting through the gears and slipping out toward the interchange where I-85 painted a black ribbon to Atlanta and beyond. At the turn ramp he glanced over at the inviting lights of the Coffee Kettle, a twenty-four-hour restaurant which served up the best waffles in east Alabama. His stomach growled. He thought about stopping to eat, but decided against it. Gotta make tracks, he told himself.

A green metallic sign read Atlanta 110, and he started to have second thoughts. When he traced back through the events of the past month or so everything returned like some cosmic boomerang to one thing: his quitting school. Maybe if . . . ? He drove another ten miles examining the thought the way his English teacher at school used to look at poems and stories. Maybe if I went back to . . . ? He slowed. Downshifted. Edged to the shoulder. Almost stopped.

No, damn it all. Gotta do it this way.

Pleased with himself at overcoming temptation, he turned up the volume on his jam box full blast and found himself thinking about the only other time he had, in effect, run away from home. He had been about eight. When he announced his intentions to Uncle Thestis, he had expected the man to try to talk him out of it. Instead, Uncle T. had merely said, "I believe it's a fine idea. Boys need to be on their own. Just one word of caution, however. When you get to the state line, whatever you do, don't look back." "Why?" Mance had queried. "Because . . . if you do, you'll transform into a bag of cornmeal and in the noonday sun you'll bake and split open and the birds will pick you clean."

Uncle Thestis, you crazy ole fart.

It was about thirty-five miles to the state line. Where Alabama and Georgia meet, a bridge carries the traveler across the broad Chattahoochee River, and then to the right a bold blue sign welcomes you to the Peach State and a welcome center beckons. Crossing the bridge Mance laughed. He twisted around and gave Alabama the finger and, of course, nothing happened. Until a few feet later.

It sounded like a sonic boom. The truck shook, lurched, shimmied, growled, groaned, moaned, and dropped speed immediately.

"Oh, shit."

It had that stomach-turning ring of major, major trouble. Mance eased the truck into the welcome center. It limped, clanging with the metallic riot that only a broken piston can generate.

"Shit, shit, shit."

The truck rolled dead in the parking lot.

Good-bye Atlanta. Good-bye glowing future.

The welcome center was virtually empty; the spray of the sodium lamps gave the boy enough light to get out and take an obligatory look under the hood. Mostly he found smoke and a hot, wounded engine. It ticked weakly; fluids obeyed gravity. Austin's truck had shut down. Maybe for good.

Mance shook his head gravely. He slammed the hood.

And stared into the yellow eyes of the wolf creature, which was seated there filling the cab of the truck. Its tongue lolled over large, sharp teeth. Mance gasped.

It spoke to the boy. Not directly. No specific words neoned in his mind, but, intuitively, there was something. It was communicating; its message was simple: Mance should go back to Soldier. Back home. Because the people he knew and cared about there might be in danger.

More blood.

Like a cold blast of air, it struck Mance that he had been selfish. He was the only one, apparently, who knew and believed that Sparrow was a killer. The reality of the situation was razor-edged: who could predict when the man would kill again? *Would he kill only to protect me? Would he ever hurt my friends?*

Bewildered, Mance continued to stare at the wolf creature.

172

Sparrow made it appear.

That was his conclusion: Sparrow could somehow — *the living dark?* — project the wolf creature as a hallucination. He was a dangerous man. No one in Soldier was safe from him.

Suddenly the creature began to dissolve; it disappeared like a winter mist. And Mance felt very much alone and stranded. He debated a few minutes between hitchhiking to Atlanta or calling someone to come get him. In the end there was no real doubt. He went to the pay phone at the welcome center and called Austin. He had considered calling his dad, but opted instead for Austin.

The man of books seemed to understand; he wasn't angry. In a sleepy voice, he said, "Can't turn a deaf ear on a man in distress."

Forty minutes later, Austin and Punch arrived in Punch's snappy little truck. When Mance saw them, he thought, *God, they're good friends.*

They turned the episode into something fun, with Austin and Punch swapping tales about the times, years ago, they had attempted unsuccessfully to strike out on their own. They called for a wrecker to haul Austin's truck to the nearest town where it would be salvaged — Mance would pay the expenses. Austin told him not to worry, he'd been needing a new truck anyway.

On the way back to Soldier, each of them confessed to being hungry. They stopped at the Coffee Kettle for waffles. The only somber note was Punch's concern about Fast Track's gambling debts; otherwise, there was laughter, good waffles, and the warmth of companionship that made Mance wonder why in the hell he'd ever wanted to leave.

He felt much better. He forgot about the wolf creature and dark projections of Sparrow.

He smiled at their waitress.

She was almost as pretty as Jonella.

Chapter Eight

1

A week rambled by.

March arrived like neither a lamb nor a lion — more like a homeless dog. Jonella scooped up a fifty-cent tip from the noon-hour rush at Scarlett's. She was thinking about her mother.

Momma never knew who she was.

It was a curious thought. She toyed with it the way one might examine some object the function of which is not readily discernible. And she decided that maybe she was starting to have the same problem. Am I Jonella or Johnnie? she asked herself.

The Jonella in her was older and wiser than the Johnnie. Jonella could take care of herself; Johnnie was more dependent. Jonella was tough; Johnnie soft. Jonella saw only a bleak future; Johnnie still harbored hopes of a future with Mance. Jonella had thought Mance's letter and thwarted escape to Atlanta spoke boldly of his immaturity; Johnnie's heart had been touched — the Rose continued to care deeply for the Fang.

I need to be Jonella, she told herself.

And yet, Jonella wasn't happy. Johnnie basically was.

The two personalities coexisted, but remained on cool terms.

The young woman at the core of both personalities prayed a familiar prayer: *Dear God, don't let me get like Momma.*

As the afternoon wore on, customers at Scarlett's thinned out. Tanya came in with the girls for iced tea and dessert. Twylla was with them, she and Tanya having struck up a friendship. Given Twylla's sexual orientation, Jonella wondered a bit about the large, redheaded woman's intentions, but then — it's Tanya's life, Jonella told herself.

She waited on them, offering a kiss and a hug to Crystal and Loretta; Tanya dressed them in pants so that their burn scars wouldn't show. Jonella had three other customers, two being Kelton Austin and Uncle Thestis, who had started occasionally meeting for coffee about midafternoon. Jonella thought they made a pleasant pair of conversants; she was especially glad to see that Uncle Thestis finally had someone around to talk with him about books and ideas.

The other customer was David Reed. He was tanned and muscular, sporting black, wavy hair, brown eyes, and good looks that could have landed him a role on a TV soap opera were he an actor. He was young, maybe twenty or twenty-one, and managed the Spectrum out on Soldier Road. And he liked Jonella. The problem: Jonella thought she liked him back. Johnnie, however, believed he was a distant second to Mance.

Jonella knew, feared, hoped that David would ask her out one of these days. What will I say? Jonella will say yes; Johnnie, no.

At three o'clock she took a break, her head swimming, life too much with her late and soon. In a far corner, she found Mance's mother and dad, and as she approached she noticed that Royal Culley was patting the back of his wife's hand. Jonella almost didn't join them, but Clarene signaled for her to.

"You back in the groove, sweetheart?"

"Yes, ma'am. Tips aren't as good as before, though. Maybe it's 'cause I look like such a hag these days."

"Ain't a word a truth in that. Is there, Royal?"

The man shook his head and flashed a tired smile at Jonella. There was an awkward pause; Clarene's eyes glistened tears.

"Mom?" said Jonella, self-conscious about continuing to call her that. "What is it?"

"March fifth," the woman whispered. "Karen's birthday. She woulda been . . . I can't remember how old, Royal?"

She glanced at her husband with something like panic in her expression.

"It's all right," he murmured. "Not no call for us to know."

"Oh, but there is," she maintained. "Karen's gone alwis be our beautiful daughter. We can't forget about her."

"We won't," he said. "Could be we oughtta think some about Mance. Don't you see how troubled he is these days? Could be we oughtta be concerned about him."

It was a moment in which Jonella could feel the Johnnie in her scratching and clawing to be heard. She knew she might be stepping out of line – the Jonella in her protested to no avail – Johnnie had to speak.

"Why don't you tell him that? Why don't you ever let Mance know you care?"

Her cheeks suddenly burned hot. She pressed fingertips to her lips.

Royal Culley, instantly ashamed, looked down at the table. Clarene was motionless for a passing of seconds, then nodded.

"I'm sorry," said Jonella, uncertain whether she was speaking for Johnnie as well. In her mind she saw the predatory, yellow eyes of a giant wolf staring at her from within her own darkness.

2

"Something tells me there's a story behind this."

Austin's smile was warm and friendly as he gestured at the silver cup which Thestis cradled lovingly in his hands.

"Yes, indeed," he said. "I carried it along with me this afternoon as a conversation piece. There is a story."

When Jonella appeared on the scene to offer them more coffee, Thestis said, "Would you like to hear it, too?"

The young woman brightened, but was puzzled. "Hear what?"

"The story of this silver cup – my most treasured possession; that is, next to beautiful young lady friends, of course."

"You always have a sweet line, don't you, Uncle Thestis?"

"I try, my dear. I try."

Wiping her hands, she glanced around and decided she could steal a few minutes to hear the tale. Austin pulled a chair out for her to sit in. She thanked him, and then, to Thestis, she said,

176

"I've been wanting to hear this for a long time."

"I'm surprised I've never told you — perhaps I did and you forgot."

Jonella, her chin propped on her knuckles, shrugged happily. She enjoyed being in the company of the two gentlemen.

Thestis lifted the cup, his eyes gleaming diamonds and ice.

"The Senior Fiction Prize at Goldsmith College for 1951 — my gracious, how I wanted it." His head shook wistfully before he continued. "Twenty-five dollars — a considerable sum in those days — and this marvelous cup were the prizes for first place."

He lowered the cup to the table; it was slightly larger than his coffee cup, but by the tenor of his admiration for it, it was as massive as a punch bowl. Suddenly he began to chuckle.

"Two weeks from the deadline for submission, I could not think of a blessed story. My roommate, Perry McCray, had written a most impressive one — a tight little story told in a to-the-bones style. I read it and despaired. It was as good as any Hemingway tale."

Austin interrupted at that moment. "And were you tempted to destroy his manuscript?"

"Indeed I was. Indeed I was."

And Jonella said, "I bet I know what happened: your roommate was such a good friend, and he knew how much you wanted to win the prize, so he decided not to enter the contest."

Thestis rolled his eyes.

"Perry McCray wanted to best me in the worst way. No, we were extremely competitive. I was stuck. I had to come up with something better. But the days passed. My old Royal typewriter clicked and clacked and turned out sheer drivel. Now, you may find this difficult to believe, but I'll swear on William Faulkner's grave that this is the truth. On the Saturday night before the Monday submission deadline, I had a dream."

He paused to admire the cup, to fondle it, to drink in its simple beauty.

"What'd you dream?" Jonella blurted as if fearful he wouldn't complete the story.

Meeting the eyes first of Austin and then of Jonella, Thestis said, "About a wolf."

Jonella felt a cold tightness in her chest; there was a sensation

177

of frost forming in her throat.

"A wolf?" she murmured nervously.

"Yes, a huge wolf. So huge that in the dream I saw it walking through thick woods in which large pines and hardwoods came only to its belly. That was all the inspiration I needed. When I woke Sunday morning, I began formulating a story. I skipped breakfast. Lunch. Perry hounded me to tell him what I was writing. Late afternoon I began drinking coffee and typing away — hot coffee with lots of sugar. I finished the story as the hour approached midnight."

"A story about that big wolf?" said Jonella.

"In a way, yes. It was about an elderly couple living in rural Alabama who claimed that they had been terrorized by a wolf — the same wolf which had eluded the old man's grandfather fifty years earlier. They had a young man, who became the story's protagonist, come to their farm to hunt down the vicious creature. At first the young man believed a real wolf might indeed be roaming the woods and stealing near the couple's home. I loaded the tale with some pretty effective atmosphere and a real sense of menace. But the young man came to realize that there was no wolf, or rather only a wolf in the imaginations of the old couple. It was alive only in their memories actually — but that the creature represented something vital to them: death, perhaps — something with which they had to struggle."

"So what did he do?"

The question was Jonella's, but from the look on Austin's face, it was his, too.

"Well, he went out into the woods and made a kill and brought it back to the couple's house and covered it with a tarp so that only a piece of its fur was showing. They were relieved and pleased."

"But I thought you said there wasn't a wolf?" said Jonella.

"That's quite right. There wasn't. You see, the boy shot a raccoon and put it under the tarp along with a bale of hay from the barn. Oh, it made an imposing-looking kill, with the ridge fur of the coon edging out from the tarp.

"So I submitted my eleventh-hour-inspired tale and . . . well, here's the result."

He lifted the cup victoriously.

"But I spent the money on a new suit for graduation."

Austin and Jonella laughed warmly.

"A good story, Uncle Thestis," she said, hugging his shoulder.

"The cup reminds me from time to time," Thestis followed, "that if you want something, need something enough, the old dream factory in your psyche can produce results if you trust it. This cup is a sacred object to me."

"Your Holy Grail?" said Austin.

Thestis nodded.

Jonella got up. Customers had filtered in.

"Uncle Thestis?" she said, starting to leave reluctantly. "What was the title of your story?"

"Oh, yes . . ." He beamed as if immensely proud of his choice. "I called it, 'Wolf in the Memory.' "

"A good title," said Austin.

"Yeah, cool," said Jonella, and she flitted away.

"Your wolf image is certainly an appropriate one these days — though it strikes a dark note."

Thestis sipped at his coffee. His face hardened.

"The Soldier wolf man . . . such unimaginably horrible killings if rumors are correct."

"I'm worried," said Austin, "not just for the citizens of Soldier — and I don't question that the police are doing everything in their power to apprehend the killer — but I have special fears for Mance. Isn't it curious that he's become entangled in this matter in ways which must make the police suspicious?"

"Yes, of course."

"He's a very confused and troubled young man. It hurts me that I can't seem to help him. Jonella tells me that you and he once were inseparable. Have you been able to talk with him yet?"

"No. But I trust that one of these days he will come to me or perhaps his father."

"What will you say to him?"

Thestis sighed heavily.

He held the silver cup in both hands and looked down into it as if it contained a picture of the future.

"Something will occur to me . . . somewhere there's an answer. My sense is that Mance could be in real danger. I have to trust that something will occur to me. And that the Conqueror

179

Worm will give me time."

3

The maroon sedan drove by slowly; the driver wore a coat and tie and might, had Mance not suspected otherwise, have easily been a salesman cruising the area, sizing up the houses for potential customers.

His heart beating at an uncomfortable clip, the boy rested astraddle his bike, pretending to fold a few more newspapers. He was at the end of his route and had stopped in front of a derelict house which the city had ribboned off because the rakers were about to bring it to its knees.

I'm being followed.

Mance could feel the tick of anger in his throat. For the past week the maroon sedan had, from time to time, ghosted him. Was it someone from the special task force? He couldn't be certain. What did they want? *Am I still a suspect?*

"Hey, boy, when you gone throw away that cast and quit bein' such a pussy?"

Mance had been watching the maroon sedan out of the corner of his eye, but twisted around at the sound of Punch's voice. The black man had dust and bits of plaster in his hair and on his pullover shirt. He peeled off a pair of heavy work gloves and slapped them against his jeans.

Mance smiled at his approach.

"You finally workin' for a living 'stead of sponging off your ole man?"

" 'Bout the size of it — Slow Eddie works the fool outta me. Raking's the toughest kind of day I've ever put in."

"Lot better than this damn kid's job I got. Shit, Punch, soon as the doc cuts this cast off I'm gettin' me a man's job."

"Got to have balls to do a man's job, boy. You grow some lately?"

Mance grinned. "Yeah, along with this finger."

He flashed Punch the bird, and the muscular man laughed.

A car from the city housing department pulled up and a heavyset man with a clipboard got out. Slow Eddie waved a

180

hand at him from near the house, and the official waved back.

Punch said to Mance, "Stick around and watch a master artist at work. Nobody in the state can wreck a condemned house the way Slow Eddie can. He's been raking places for over thirty years—he can collapse 'em on a dime. You open your eyes."

"He fixes super barbecue, too," said Mance. "Best I ever ate. Makes me wish I had some kind of talent besides shootin' pool."

"Yeah, me, too," said Punch. "Something more than using my fists."

Slow Eddie took long, loping strides around the house; he appeared to be moving very slowly and deliberately, but he covered the area in no time.

"What's he doin'?" asked Mance.

"Checking the charges. They gotta be set just right."

Once finished surveying the edifice, Slow Eddie, his face showing no emotion, set a timing mechanism and walked over to join Punch and the boy. The city official kept his distance.

"Thirty seconds," Punch whispered.

Mance took a long, final look at the house: it was a two-story frame job; when new it must have been impressive. Now it was gray-weathered, the roof over its porch having collapsed in a frozen wink. It reminded the boy somewhat of Guillo House, and that, in turn, made him think of Johnnie.

Suddenly there were three nervous pops—like a cap pistol going off—and the house shuddered once—only once—and then fell upon itself, not with a thunderous crash, but rather with what sounded like prolonged sigh of relief.

"She done gave up de ghost," said Slow Eddie. Those words and a satisfied grin combined as his only response.

Apparently pleased with the destruction, the city official got back in his car and drove off.

"Got to go get my hands dirty and my muscles sore," said Punch, frowning at the heap of rubble.

"Ain't it about quittin' time?" asked Mance, noticing how rapidly twilight was coming on.

"Yeah, but Slow Eddie's gone get another hour outta me. He wants my last drop of sweat."

Mance continued watching, his attention given over to the sorrowful pile of boards and shingles and broken plaster. It

181

didn't take much imagination to see the collapsed house as a metaphor of sorts for his life in the last month or so. Fate had wrecked it, brought it down to be picked over and sold for scrap.

Rebuilding seemed, at the moment at least, beyond him.

His foundation was Johnnie — without her he believed he had no real strength. He had called her a few days ago and asked her to a movie, telling her that he had accepted his role as "just a friend." To his pleasant surprise, she had said yes, her voice exuding some of the old warmth he had come to expect from Johnnie. But the next day she had called him — was it the same person? — and had told him she couldn't make it. He had pressed, but then she had grown angry and hung up.

Johnnie, give me another chance.

"How much the *S-G News* pay you to stand around?"

Mance turned toward the source of the harsh cackle. It was Bridgette Settleford leaning her head out of her car, a cigarette dangling from her lip. The boy smiled sheepishly and held up an empty newspaper bag.

"I'm all done," he said.

"I hear you're pretty fair at shooting pool," she followed.

"Can hold my own."

"Meet me down at Fast Track's in ten minutes and I'll kick your butt."

She winked and spun away.

Having nothing better to do, he accepted her challenge. In the gloam of Fast Track's back room, he had to struggle to beat her two out of three games of eight ball. The old gal was good.

"Where'd you learn to shoot pool like that?" he asked her when she had acknowledged his victory.

"Paul had a table down in the basement. I used to practice when I was bored to tears — which was often. Come on, I'll buy you a beer, or does Fast Track obey the law?"

"He sorta bends it for me."

They sat a table in the corner of the bar area. Fast Track's group of old jazz musician friends was blowing some scattered notes, whipping up sounds like batter to produce some mouth-watering treat.

Bridgette had already killed most of a pack of cigarettes; she lit another one and jammed it into the corner of her mouth.

"You want to know who's following you?" she said.

Mance, who had been slouching in his chair, sat up.

"The cops, I guess."

She nodded, blew an impressive rooster tail of smoke, and said, "One of Stewart's boys."

"Why?"

"Just like me, they think you know something."

"They don't still figure I had anything to do with the killings, do they?"

Another puff. More smoke.

"Did you?"

"Damn . . . no, 'course I didn't."

"Who did?"

Mance's shoulders locked. He knew his reluctance to say anything gave him away.

Bridgette smiled through a cloud of smoke.

"OK, I can see you're not ready to confide yet."

Mance grunted his exasperation with her approach. She patted his hand in motherly fashion and said, "I had a private audience with the coroner. Got a detail-by-detail account of Boom Browner's . . . well, I was gone say body, but there wasn't a body left when that so-called wolf man got through with him. Just pieces."

In Mance's thoughts, he saw a man pushing a wheelbarrow and picking up pieces of his friend, Eugene.

"Hey, come on — why you talkin' about this shit?"

He could feel the anger beginning to radiate through him.

"Because I want you to think about it. Because I believe you could stop this wolf man."

"No, I can't!" he cried.

The old men halted their jamming. Fast Track looked up from behind the bar.

Bridgette crushed out her cigarette.

"I want this story, Mance. It's got its hooks in me, doncha see? I think about it all the time — obsesses me I suppose you could say. It's *my* story. Mine. I'm not letting anyone take it away from me."

The bar returned to normal.

When Bridgette caught the boy's eyes again, she leaned forward and said, "Who is it, Mance? Who's the wolf man?"

4

It grew more insistent each day. The voice. More insistent and louder.

More blood.

Must kill.

More blood.

Must kill, must kill, must kill.

Until Mance felt that his head might explode. Until he felt that *he* should be going to see Dr. Colby—Jonella was not the only one needing professional care, he feared.

The only positive note of the week, in fact, was that Sting was getting better. Moving around. Eating. Pissing all over his cage. A couple of times Mance had noticed that someone must have been slipping in to attend to the sickly rat—probably his mom—and a little tender loving care was making a big difference. He reminded himself to thank her one day soon.

By Friday evening, Mance knew that he had to do something about the voice. And the creature. The latter was appearing more and more frequently, sometimes in the corner of his room, sometimes in the dusty shadows of one of the abandoned buildings on North Street, sometimes at the edge of his vision on his paper route.

The creature smelled of wildness and blood. Or was Mance only imagining that?

But why, the boy wondered, was it following him? Why apparently only to him did it deliver its bold confession? What did it all mean?

There was, he had to admit, only one source of answers.

Sting on his shoulder, Mance set out for Sparrow's. What he found was a darkened, virtually empty place. Two of the old men he had seen before were sitting at the counter talking low, sipping at cups of coffee. At first, Mance saw no one else, but as his eyes adjusted to the dim lighting he made out a couple of figures at a table in the corner.

A large, redheaded woman was leaning close to the other per-

184

son, her arm around that person — another woman, it appeared. Mance recognized the redhead as Twylla. The other woman was Tanya.

He experienced a touch of shock as Twylla kissed at Tanya's forehead and cheek. But he recovered quickly. He prided himself on not being repulsed easily — at sixteen, he had witnessed about every form of aberration possible — North Street had it all — not to mention the horror of being close to three murders.

When Twylla saw him, she eased away from Tanya un-self-consciously.

"Can I help you?" she said.

Mance was looking at Tanya, who, when she recognized him, smiled an embarrassed smile. She appeared no older than a young girl, the apprehensive glint in her eyes speaking volumes about her venture into previously forbidden territory.

None of my business, Mance thought to himself. Then another thought: would Jonella be baby-sitting? Or perhaps Miss Taylor?

"I need to see Sparrow," he said.

Twylla was wearing a tank top, soiled and dampened by grease and sweat. Mance guessed that she had taken over kitchen duty that night. Her breasts bulged the tank top, revealing ample cleavage.

"Can't nobody see him," she said, her voice husky. "He's . . . sick."

"Sick? What's wrong with him?"

Twylla shifted her weight impatiently.

"Back in his room . . . he's . . . upset, you know. He gets depressed. It's the Agent Orange. He's feeling pretty poorly. Can't nobody see him."

She wanted Mance to leave. That was obvious. He wondered why she was acting so mysteriously.

"Would you tell him something for me? Would you tell him that when he gets to feeling better I need to talk to him?"

"Sure thing." She warmed a bit. "When he gets down like this, it usually only lasts a couple of nights. He called me in to take care of the burdens. Yeah, I'll let him know you was here."

With a final dart of his eyes toward Tanya, Mance gestured a good-bye and was greeted by the deserted state of North Street.

185

It was deserted, but the murders had brought more lighting to the area, and, combined with a nearly full moon, the street he knew so well projected a false day.

He walked past Fast Track's, resisting the urge to spend the remainder of the evening shooting pool and listening to Punch complain about how sore his muscles were from raking houses; besides, Fast Track had gotten real jumpy of late—he saw the ghosts of butcher men everywhere, prompting him to keep Sweet Lick, his trusty shotgun, on twenty-four-hour alert. Even some of his regular customers were beginning to grumble about the old man's jitters.

Mance kept walking.

There was no light at Austin's. Out with Miss Taylor?

The boy felt an ache of envy. Friday nights used to be special for him and Jonella. Now everything had changed; everybody else in the world seemed to have someone.

Damn it, Johnnie, how do I get you back?

At the corner beyond Austin's he stopped; in more ways than one it was a crossroads. Back down toward the tracks was Sparrow, the man, his guardian angel, who had been sending a vivid image of a wolf creature to haunt him and to whisper of blood and killing. Why? Sparrow's illness—was the man totally flipping out?

Toward Chrokinole Street was the big house in which Jonella now lived. If Sparrow represented darkness and madness to him, then Jonella represented light and love. And a possible future.

Got to see her. Got to.

Adele Taylor met him at the front door, Austin at her shoulder. They were baby-sitting the girls while Tanya was . . . well, trying to get over the loss of Boom, Mance supposed. He asked to see Jonella, and Taylor shot a nervous glance at Austin.

"She's not here," he said.

"I know she's not working tonight," Mance followed.

"No, she's . . . she's out," said Austin, his face registering varying levels of discomfort.

"Out?"

186

"Yes."

"You know where?"

He shook his head, and Mance didn't press him.

"OK, yeah, thanks," he said.

Restless, he walked some more, and with each step he considered the implications of that ugly little word, "out"; the more he considered it, the more his brain felt as if it were filled with thorns.

North Street had been his turf so long that it was easy to forget that Soldier's true downtown was several blocks to the west. There, legitimate, money-making businesses still existed: clothing stores, shoe stores, one jewelry store, a Western Auto, and, where that glitzier downtown bled into Soldier Road, there was even a Dairy Queen.

Mance decided to treat himself. Hell, it had been a tough week—no sign it might get better either.

Sting loves ice cream and hot fudge. Why not buy the little bugger a sundae to celebrate his recovery?

At the end of the long walk, Mance ordered two hot fudge sundaes and sat with Sting on one of the picnic tables where they could nibble at their treat and watch the traffic filter through the Dairy Queen drive-through.

"Don't eat so damn fast," he warned the rat, "you know how ice cream gives you headaches."

Sting soon had a hot fudge beard and tiny balls of the vanilla ice cream on the ends of his whiskers.

"You're a pig, man."

He laughed at the ice cream-eating machine as it tipped over its sundae cup to wallow in the gooey concoction.

"Hey, Sting, ole buddy, you and me gone make it, ain't we?"

No, he wasn't very certain of that but no point in being pessimistic, he reasoned. At least there wasn't until he saw David Reed's new, black Camaro growl into the drive-through.

With Jonella in the bucket seat next to him.

Chapter Nine

1

Somehow he staggered back to North Street.

His mind was playing a game of refusal; each time he called up the image of the black Camaro and David Reed's smiling, satisfied face and that of the young lady, his passenger, Mance's mind pasted someone else in her place—*anybody* else. But not Jonella. Not his Johnnie.

He had escaped from the Dairy Queen without her seeing him—*it's her, goddammit, I know it's her*. It was, he decided, better that way. What would he have done had she seen him? Wave? Stop them for a pleasant chat? Hey, how you doin'? Nice car. Oh, and by the way you son-of-a-bitch that's my girl.

Or bust in Reed's head?

Seeking oblivion, Mance walked along the tracks and thought wistfully of jumping in front of a train roaring through and having his molecules squished, spreading them from Soldier to Phenix City or the state line. Jonella would be sorry then, sorry she dumped him, sorry she caused him to be so distraught that he threw himself in the path of the implacable night monster.

But, no, after groveling in the imaginary scenario for a few minutes—and enjoying it the way only a teenager can enjoy being miserable—he concluded it was a "dumb kid" thought. What good would getting squished do? Getting squished like . . . well, like Eugene?

Then Reed would have Jonella all to himself.

He wandered by the Holiness Temple and across the street to

the old abandoned hotel where Punch had established a make-shift gym. The hotel lay far enough from the streetlamps that it hugged darkness within except for the slant of moonlight. Despite its dust and emptiness and neglect, the hotel made Mance feel . . . welcome.

He needed to be alone.

Lifting Sting free from his shoulder, he entered the first floor, and in the silver-blue spray of moonlight he could barely piece out the shape of something hanging from the ceiling. He bent down to place Sting on the floor.

"Jesus, what? — "

Sting gave no indication of wanting to leave the protection of the boy's hand, a hand which, like the rest of his body, had tensed sharply, causing his arm to tingle beneath its cast. Seconds passed slowly like floating bubbles.

"Punching bag," he whispered, after the shadowy bulk no longer carried the horrific suggestion of a body.

By degrees, his muscles and nerves relaxed. He chuckled at himself. He stood.

"I'm seeing things, man," he said to Sting. "Go on and take a piss or something;"

Mance began to circle the room aimlessly. He felt he could smell lingering odor of Punch's workout sweat. In every corner, darkness nominated candidates for threatening entities: demons and fanged creatures and a myriad of night things capable of creating terror.

"Maybe it wasn't Johnnie."

His voice sounded as hollow and dusty as the room.

"Maybe it . . ."

His body started to quake. His throat constricted. Tears came like convulsions. He gritted his teeth and fought to choke them off. After a moment or two he won the battle. Or rather anger won out over sadness.

"Johnnie, I want you back!" he shouted.

His words echoed as he bumped into the punching bag, then began to butt his head against it.

"Please, Johnnie, please."

The heavy bag pushed back.

And became David Reed.

"Bastard, she's not yours."

He lashed out with his right fist, and the impact felt good, and images and actions reeled free: a punch to his competitor's forehead, several to the stomach, one to the chin, one to break his nose, two more to crack ribs. Punch after punch after punch until the boy, panting and groaning and still fighting back tears, collapsed to his knees. His right arm burned and throbbed.

"Not yours," he said, his voice no more than a raspy whisper.

He was sweating and trembling and fearful that the tears would reclaim control.

Sting was there squeaking apprehensively.

"Oh, shit, man," the boy said to the rat. "God, I feel so damn . . ."

A half sob wracked his upper body. He took a deep breath, found Sting, and placed him on his shoulder. The rat burrowed into his shelter. On shaky legs, Mance pressed to his feet.

And saw the wolf creature.

It was sitting on its haunches not fifteen feet away. It appeared to generate its own light, an aura of sorts, because Mance could see it clearly.

The sight of the beast sobered him instantly.

Weren't those Sparrow's eyes?

The power of the living dark?

Mance wasn't frightened; in fact, there was something pathetic in the eyes of the creature, an unspoken pleading.

Must kill . . . must kill.

Those eyes again. Mance studied them, and suddenly his own heartbreak seemed trivial. The creature had reached into the boy's soul and touched his sympathy as if it were a living, breathing thing.

Mance cleared his throat and said, "What do you want?"

It was weird speaking to the creature—just a hallucination sent by Sparrow—that's what the boy kept telling himself—and yet, it seemed so real. The dust-laden first floor of the hotel had transformed into some shadowy realm beyond his understanding.

Must kill.
Must kill.

"No," said the boy. "No, Sparrow. There's been enough. No more killing."

His whole body tingled. Did the apparition understand him? It moved a few feet closer.

"Hey, damn, what you want? Stay back. What you want?"

Mance was having some difficulty breathing. His heart was beating the way Sting would race around his cage on one of his crazy, frenetic days.

Help me.

"What?"

Help me . . . help me.

Sparrow's voice? The man was asking for help? The Agent Orange — was it driving him to kill?

How? I mean . . . you gotta see a doctor, right?"

You help me.

Mance laughed softly, nervously. This can't be happening. I'm talking to something that ain't real.

"Hey, no . . . I mean . . . how? I can't help you. What could I do?"

His voice quavered, the rhythm of the words halting.

Stop me.

"Stop you?"

Stop me . . . stop me . . . stop me . . . must stop me . . . must, must.

The creature's voice rumbled and rocked in the boy's mind; he clutched at his ear, but the insistent, heartrending words continued until he cried, "How? I don't know how. Sparrow . . . I don't know how."

And then sadness vanished from the face of the creature. It snarled. There was silence as it shifted its weight and appeared to flex its muscular body impatiently.

Mance stepped back.

"How?" he repeated, suddenly fearful of what the creature would do next.

Find a way.

It was like a swan song of anguish. Mance could only watch, captivated, as the wolf creature burst into a thousand motes of dust, the particles shimmering briefly in the moonlight before merging with the larger darkness of the room.

Fast Track had Sweet Lick handy.

The gun was loaded and ready to protect him from butcher men. Knowing the nature of the gambling game, he expected them any time. Some night after he closed up they would come. More than one probably. Two or three. Maybe a whole pack of them.

Fast Track was sweating.

He poured himself a glass of ice water and garnished it with half a lime. His little jazz ensemble had beaten their way through the up-tempo stuff and were now, as closing time neared, laying out some of the softest, sweetest, most mellow sounds that God ever allowed a body to hear this side of heaven.

They would go to heaven—Fast Track was convinced of that—all five of them: Frankie "Bad Boy" Wilson on trombone; Delbert "Footsie" Rutherford on sax (the best between Soldier and New Orleans); Big Ben Smith on the stick; Willie "Glowball" Brown on bass; and Chester "Dog Man" Dowdell, the oldest piano player in the state, maybe the world—somewhere between 95 and 105 years old. Of course, no one much kept records on the age of old black men in Alabama.

The musicians were rubbing shoulders with the night. Footsie was coaxing sounds so mellow that even Fast Track's water tasted like a stiff and satisfying drink that would burn your gut yet set you free. And Fast Track needed that—oh, yes, he did.

Set me free, Lawd, Lawd.

He had not, for years at least, been a religious man, but recently, sometimes when he did not expect them, prayers would spring to his lips, incoherent ones, but prayers nevertheless. And in the cash drawer, yes, if you looked closely, in the slot where he kept twenties, there was a crucifix on a string. He had gotten into the habit of fingering it after every transaction.

Surveying the partial darkness, he saw only three customers. All black. All old. White folks had their own bars. The older, white street people, those with no family, would be at Sparrow's. So it went. Fast Track believed he was offering a service to the blacks of the community: a reasonably clean place where they could come, have a few drinks, talk or rag each other, and feel the soft notes of a music that was pure silk.

"Glowball, hey dare. Glowball," he called to the bass player.

There was an awkward halt to the music. Laughter among the group. Playful exchanges of "nigger chit" as they liked to term it among themselves.

"How 'bout 'Sugar Sunrise'? Milk hit ta tears—get me down low. Scratch hit out."

That was the irony of this music: when you were feeling down, it took you even lower until you reached bottom and then . . . well, you started feeling better. The piece he requested was his favorite. Glowball and Footsie had nailed it to the wall a few months ago when the group was improvising. Man, it was sweet. And Fast Track had asked Glowball, "What's dat sugar sound?"

And Glowball, who enjoyed tacking a title onto their compositions, had said, " 'Sugar Sunrise'—sweet notes to meet the day."

Glowball smiled.

"You got it."

Dog Man stroked a note that, to Fast Track's ears, was the equivalent of the sensation of sugar on the tongue. He grinned. For ten minutes, he forgot about everything else in the world: butcher men and betting slips, Sweet Lick, the recent violence at Rebel Beer, and the fact that his son, Punch, was dating an older woman that evening—a slut named Wyomie Dyson.

Sugar Sunrise.

He could feel it deep in his bones. A good ache.

But all too soon it was over. The group began to break up like low morning clouds before the sun spears through. The scattering of customers shuffled to the door, most fearful of the angry face that North Street wore those days.

Fast Track almost begged everyone to stay.

He feared this was the night. Butcher men night.

Humming nervously as he cleaned up, the old black man wondered how the devil had poisoned him. That's what gambling seemed to him to be—a slow poison. Seated at the bar, he poured over his betting slips and his tally sheet and his most recent tab.

$8,123.00.

In the red.

He couldn't pay it. No way. He'd have to sell the lounge.

But he had refused to, asking the nasty boys in Montgomery for another week or two to come up with the money. He hadn't let Punch know exactly how deep the hole was that he had fallen in to. A pit. A fiery pit. With the devil laughing at its rim.

Football. Basketball. All the sure things had not panned out. Ten-point favorites had won by eight. Tempting underdogs had gone belly-up. Numbers flashed in his thoughts like fireflies, and he would try to guess where their light would materialize again.

Parlays and point spreads. Teasers and pushes.

$8,123.00

God hep dis po' sorry ole nigger man.

He pressed a thumb into the corner of his eye to discourage a tear. He locked the front door and turned off all the lights except the neon beer ads in the window. In the back room, he racked up the pool balls and put them away.

He heard someone at the back door.

He saw the doorknob twist slightly.

O'dear savior Jesus, dis is hit.

He scampered to get Sweet Lick, and when he returned he braced himself some twenty-five feet from the back door, barrel leveled about where the heart of an intruder would be. More than one—the cowards would send more than one. And he would make a hole in them. Self-defense.

The back door was unlocked.

Why were they fidgeting with it? Just to scare the shit out of him? Make him suffer?

He waited. Something thumped against the door. There was a groan.

A minute passed. Fast Track tasted the lime from his ice water. He smelled a foul odor. Garbage in the alley?

"I gots dis gun," he said finally, the waiting unbearable.

He went to the door.

Everyone said butcher men were cowards—now he knew it for a fact.

He heard someone whispering. Someone asking for help?

194

Dear savior Jesus, dis is hit.

He wiped the sweat from his upper lip, took a deep breath, and opened the door.

There was a mournful moan as he jumped back and the body of old Rollo slumped at his feet.

It took a good deal of effort and ten minutes or more to lug the drunken Rollo back to Sparrow's.

"You ole fuck," Fast Track growled. "Scar't de runny shits owda me. Ole drunk fuck. Donchoo know where de back a da pawnshop be? Ole fuck."

Several rounds of pounding on the back door brought Twylla, clad in a robe which flapped open even as she reached for Rollo. Fast Track could see the creamy fullness of her breasts despite the meager light.

"Dis one's your'n," he said.

Twylla hissed in exasperation as she bulldogged Rollo through the door.

"Thanks," she said.

Fast Track tipped an imaginary hat and took one more look at those breasts before Twylla managed to corral them with a tug at her robe.

And he was fantasizing about sinking his face between those full, luscious breasts and going blugga-blugga when, on the way back through the alley, he could just make out a figure waiting for him in the shadows.

3

"That you, Fast Track?"

The old black man hesitated.

"Who dare?"

His heart was a trapped and very frightened animal, but he thought he recognized the voice. Whoever it was, being cautious—as if he feared meeting a butcher man of his own.

"Me. It's me. Mance."

The boy stepped fully into the light.

195

Fast Track blinked to make sure; his heart was slowing, but not much.

"I done thought you was a butcher man, boy—shore am glad you ain't."

"No, it's me."

"Whatchoo want?"

"I was . . . I was following someone. I was afraid that—"

"Ole Rollo?"

"Huh?"

"Dat's who hit was. He lost. Drunk. I took 'im home."

"Oh . . . I was afraid he would . . . have you seen Sparrow, or . . . or anything strange?"

"No'um. Jist ole Rollo. Ole drunk fuck."

To Fast Track, the boy appeared unusually apprehensive, and that, in turn, fueled his own fears.

"OK. Well, I'm headin' home. See ya."

He stood a moment or two longer, then dissolved into the darkness of the alley.

Fast Track was shaken, tired; his eyes peopled the shadows with all manner of beast, each one intent upon savaging him before he reached the protection of the lounge.

And even there, was it safe from the creatures of the night?

4

"Punch not around?"

Mance was lining up a combination shot: seven ball into the thirteen for a cut into the end pocket. A smooth stroke. A solid clack. But the thirteen rimmed out.

"Dis boy losin' he touch?"

Fast Track chuckled deeply, then added, "Punch, he gone to Providence. Can't hep hisself. Can't get dat woman owda he mind."

Sizing up another practice shot, Mance said, "He still trying to make up with Chantel, huh? I got the same damn problem with Johnnie."

"Lease you didn't get yo'self married ta her like Punch done wid Chantel."

"No, but Johnnie and I, we been together long enough it seems like we could be married. Now maybe she's got somebody, you know, somebody else."

"Dat why you puppy dawg sad?"

"I'm not sad—I just . . . I just want her back."

Fast Track chuckled again and waddled off to check on the Saturday night crowd, which, unfortunately, was not a crowd at all: a half dozen customers, most of them regulars. Though it was early evening, the jazz group was already into the mellow stuff.

Mance followed the slow exit of Fast Track; he knew the old guy had a lot on his mind. He was scared just as he had been last night in the alley. Butcher men. That's why Sweet Lick was leaning near the back door. The sight of the shotgun reminded Mance that he needed to keep his .38 out of sight. He had decided to carry it again; it was tucked inside his jacket, and it gave him some comfort against the knowledge that Sparrow, in the guise of the wolf creature, was eager to kill.

Help me.

Stop me.

I can't, Mance told himself. Sparrow would have to help himself. *I don't know how to help him.*

Find a way.

There was one possibility: he could go to the police and warn them that Sparrow was about to kill again. He could call Detective Stewart, or locate officers Lawrence and McCants; they practically lived on North Street these days. They could arrest Sparrow and take him in and see that he got help—Sparrow could plead insanity in the murders of Ford and Davis and Boom. No judge and jury would give him the death sentence, would they?

He missed two more practice shots as he toyed with what he should do; his thoughts acquired shades of darkness. He could imagine the wolf creature stalking Reed's Camaro, dancing a predatory dance that would end in blood and Jonella would . . .

"Chalk up, hustler, I want revenge."

The boy glanced up; a slow grin spread across his face at the sight of Bridgette Settleford, an ever-present cigarette defying all laws of gravity as it held on tenuously

197

in the corner of her mouth.

"You're on, lady."

Maybe it was a lack of concentration, maybe Bridgette was just lucky, but she beat him soundly the first two games of eight ball. Each drank a beer, and Bridgette puffed her way through three more cigarettes.

"Well," she said, not displaying any real joy over her victories, "I know Fast Track's worried about butcher men, but what's with you? Your piss-poor shooting have anything to do with Jonella seeing David Reed?"

It was a hard pinch at his emotions.

"Maybe," he said. "Maybe it's more than that."

Because it was. And his comment started the curious old gal pursuing the issue which obsessed her.

"Our hirsute friend the wolf man?"

"What's 'her suit' mean?"

Bridgette cackled. "Means hairy. Like a stud's chest. Least, that's what I'm told."

She rolled her eyes and did a bump and grind, and Mance had to laugh softly at her playfully lewd actions. Then she said, "Do you know what Detective Stewart told me about the wolf man?"

Mance shook his head. He really didn't want to hear. But, of course, she continued anyway.

"He—it—whatever—doesn't leave clues. No footprints. Or tracks. Nothing. Experts who have examined the body—or the parts thereof—of the last victim—dear Mr. Browner—claim an animal most likely caused death. And yet, it had to be an animal that could rear up on its hind legs and maneuver every bit like a human. What do you make of that?"

She blew smoke rings and speared them with the point of her cue stick.

"I don't make nothin' of it. Except it's strange, sure. Some kind of psychopath, but maybe he . . . I don't know."

Bridgette squinted at him. She had picked up the scent of something.

"Maybe he what?"

Mance shrugged.

"Maybe he can't help it," he said quietly.

He won the next two games; they agreed to call the contest a draw and, mercifully, Bridgette did not probe further into what had prompted the boy's observation.

"Did I tell you," she piped up as she put away her cue, "that I've renewed my friendship with your uncle? Such a sweet man. Sorry I waited so long to give him a call. And I found out something: he misses you, Mance."

"So?"

"So . . . look, you're feeling like shit. He's a great listener and—"

"No, I've got Punch or Austin to talk to."

"Appears Punch is gone, and Austin is dog-faced mooning over Adele Taylor. Thestis would be delighted if you shared your troubles with him—he's not well, you know."

"You sound just like Johnnie and my Mom."

Bridgette winked.

"Pretty good company, I'd say."

"Anybody ever call you a busybody?"

The woman laughed.

"Hell, yes. That and a lot worse, believe me."

5

Mance killed time at the pool table for most of the evening; when Glowball took a break from fondling the strings of his bass, the boy clobbered him in three quick games of eight ball. Maybe I haven't lost touch, he told himself. Glowball bowed to the master.

Fast Track gave Sting a generous saucer of beer and, after slurping it dry, the rodent lush lapsed into a semicomatose state and required assistance to climb back onto Mance's shoulder.

The evening grew late by degrees as the boy waited for Punch to return from Providence; Punch had lost *his* woman, so Mance naturally assumed he would lend a sympathetic ear to the situation with Jonella. He might, in addition, be able to offer some advice regarding Sparrow and the insistent murmurings of the wolf creature.

But midnight neared, and the boy was tired and Sting was snockered, and who could tell when Punch might choose to stagger in—and would he be sober enough to talk anyway? Lately the man had maintained that he was putting a cork on his heavy drinking and that he was getting in shape, anticipating that the review board would reinstate him as a member of the Soldier Police Department.

"One for de road?"

Fast Track had noticed how disconsolately Mance had wandered up to the bar.

"No, guess not. Better get Sting home 'fore he pukes on my shoulder."

"You gone shoot somebody wit dat litt'l gun?"

Mance smiled weakly.

"Gone shoot the big bad wolf, maybe."

"Dat no shit?"

Patting the bulge under his jacket, Mance said, "No shit," and walked out into the night.

And found the wolf creature waiting for him.

It was sitting in the middle of North Street like a statue of some Confederate general. The street was empty, the sidewalks free of people, and no stray dogs scavenged the gutters. A full moon bathed the scene in an eerie, hollow light.

Stop me.

Help me.

Mance stared at it; he reached for the .38.

Find a way.

"No!" the boy suddenly shouted.

He dropped his hand and began to run toward home.

"Leave me alone!"

Running harder.

A police car was cruising up near Scarlett's. For a fleeting moment, he considered flagging it down.

He eventually slowed to catch his breath. Sting had awakened and had knotted his claws in Mance's hair and was hanging on for dear life.

Panting, the boy turned to see whether the creature had followed.

He scanned the street.

A breeze caught an empty beer can and sent it skittering along the gutter.

There was no sign of the creature.

Fast Track totaled out the register. He frowned at the meager take. This wouldn't feed the bulldog. No way. This wouldn't keep the butcher men away.

He began to hum 'Sugar Sunrise,' and it made him feel good — surprisingly good — yeah, Glowball was right: sweet notes to meet the day. Yeah, he could make it.

Ole Fast Track, he can do hit. He gone make hit.

He survived growing up black in Alabama, had lived through years of segregation and gut-twisting prejudice — why fear something like butcher men? They could only murder your body, not your dignity.

His thoughts shifted to Punch.

A good son.

If only he could get back on the police force, his life would gain a fresh start. If only things could be resolved with Chantel, a strong, proud woman who, rightfully so, wouldn't tolerate his drinking, wouldn't accept less than the man Punch could be. If only.

Fast Track wanted to do something to help his son. But what?

He yawned.

He needed more sleep tonight. He was too old to stay up half the night.

Lawd, let me rest.

His hip was bothering him. Bursitis? Or just tired old bones?

Limping into the back room, he surveyed the work to be done: cases of beer needed to be moved up front, the floor needed to be swept, and his inventory required some attention.

But he was tired.

"Sugar Sunrise" was on lips. He hummed it, and the humming graduated to a whistle, and the whistling lifted his spirits. And the whistling gained volume, and he felt energized enough to move a few cases of beer before a noise at the back door halted him.

A thud. A scratching.

The unmistakable sounds of Punch coming home drunk. Or was it ole Rollo? No, the redhead with the heavenly breasts would keep him off the streets tonight. It had to be Punch. But just in case, Fast Track reached for Sweet Lick.

"Punch?"

He heard a liquid, slavering noise.

After last night's episode he had locked the back door and had kept it locked.

There was a second and pronounced thump at the door as if someone had lowered a shoulder into it.

"Give yer ole man a blessed minute, wouldja?"

Sweet Lick braced against his side, Fast Track swung open the door.

Something (someone?) that had been crouching rose to its feet, but remained far enough from the door not to be distinct.

Fast Track's heart went cold.

Butcher man.

It wasn't precisely the shape of a man; he couldn't see a face distinctly, nothing except the eyes, yellow and predatory.

Sweet Lick in hand, Fast Track stumbled backward. He wasn't going to give in without a fight. No, god damn it.

"Get out," he said, the fear in his voice thick and rough. "I be callin' de po-lice on ya. Get out. I tole ya I needs mo' time."

Shotgun aimed at his visitant, he tried to calculate the time and distance to the phone at the end of the bar. But he was too scared to think clearly.

"Get out, fo' I call de po-lice."

The yellow eyes continued staring at him, but the dark and indistinct figure made no move to attack. It apparently had no gun, or at least Fast Track couldn't detect one.

"I needs mo' time," he said, more to himself than to the figure.

Suddenly he turned and scrambled as quickly as his old muscles and bones would allow. The receiver of the phone jerked as he punched 9-1-1 and cried for help, expecting any one of the next moments to be his last.

Officers Vanetta Lawrence and Clay McCants responded.

Neither, however, wanted to.

In obvious disgust, Lawrence said, "I bet Punch is drunk and threatening to beat the hell out of the old man."

"Could be if we drive slow Fast Track will take care of things with that shotgun he keeps around," said McCants. From behind the wheel, he glanced at Lawrence and added, "Routine B on B—I get a little sick of it. How 'bout you?"

He knew she wouldn't answer. He knew his allusion would anger her: "B on B"—black-on-black violence—it was McCants's not so subtle way of tossing racism into a tenuous relationship.

You white bastard, she thought. While she had no regard whatsoever for Fast Track and his son, for anyone on North Street, in fact, McCants had a maddening way of lumping all blacks together. Teaming up a black woman and a white man simply hadn't worked, however innovative it might have looked on paper. McCants repulsed her. She didn't trust him. She often fantasized that in a life-threatening situation, she would be deliberately slow in backing him up.

McCants wheeled the patrol car into the alley.

"Bulldoze the whole fuckin' block is what I'd recommend. God damn riffraff from one end to the other."

Lawrence was forced to smile inwardly at that image; she agreed entirely with the sentiment.

The car lights flooded the narrow alley.

"What the shit was that?" said Lawrence. Something large and . . . well, not quite human-looking had been evident in that first thrust of light, and then it had . . . disappeared?

"Reflection of some kind," said McCants, though the sudden dryness of his mouth betrayed a doubt or two.

They pulled up within twenty feet of Fast Track's back door.

"Weapon?" said Lawrence, staring at McCants for his judgment on the potential seriousness of the call. "Could be something dangerous."

"No," he said. "No, hell, I can handle this with my stick."

"You'd love to be provoked, wouldn't you?" she said, her eyes flashing hatred. "So you could beat in a nigger's head."

He grinned. "Officer Lawrence, sometimes I'd swear you're psychic."

When Fast Track returned to the back area, the mysterious

203

figure was there, still indistinct, still menacing, still watching.

"I ain't scar't uh you," the old man boldly lied.

Sweet Lick felt heavy, much too heavy; sweat trickled steadily down Fast Track's face, blurring his vision.

Those eyes. The figure's eyes. He had seen no eyes quite like them.

"I ain't 'fraid a usin' dis."

He shook the end of the shotgun as if it were a switch and he were threatening a misbehaving child.

Had he called the police? Suddenly he couldn't recall.

What difference did it make?

There was a butcher man at the door, and if a butcher man wanted to get you, no one could stop him. And if you knocked off one butcher man, another would appear, and then another. And another. The stream of butcher men would never run dry.

It was one of the laws of gambling.

The night seeped in through the door.

This was a standoff; Sweet Lick and butcher man.

Somewhere a clock was ticking—but where? In some abandoned room in his thoughts? In a memory of the old homestead on the muddy bottomland where each spring Pilgrim Creek would flood?

"You can't scare—"

Lights strobed, catching, for an instant and a lifetime, the figure in the alley. The sight of it burned a hole between Fast Track's eyes. The light revealed something savage. The old man's mind staggered, stumbled, and he fought to regain his mental balance.

It looked like a giant wolf.

Before it dissolved into thin air.

Fast Track heard a car engine, heard the susurrus and static of a radio, and heard car doors slam.

The first butcher man entered, as Fast Track knew he would, and the butcher man said, "What's the trouble here?"

Another butcher man followed at the shoulder of the other, this one smaller and black.

A black butcher man—no, it was a woman: the fact registered dimly before Fast Track pulled the trigger.

Officer McCants, nightstick in hand, looking almost comically surprised, cringed as if the explosion hurt his ears. The dark blue of his shirt beaded red in a rough circle. He was knocked back two steps. And before he collapsed to his knees, he stared down at his shirt as if he had simply spilled a cup of coffee on himself and was merely stunned and a little disgusted.

Officer Lawrence unholstered her service revolver in a clean, efficient sweep of her hand, just as she had been taught at the police academy. Her eyes widened as if she were on a roller coaster heading down that first big hill.

Fast Track pulled the trigger again.

And her face was gone.

Seconds ticked away.

In shock, Fast Track hunkered down by McCants's body, carefully avoiding the ever-widening pool of blood. McCants was on his stomach, his fingers continuing to clutch the nightstick. The old black man, his heart chugging and misfiring like an engine on the verge of stalling, nudged at McCants's shoulder as if he were trying to awaken him from a deep sleep.

"I needs hep," he said. "You gots ta hep me. Butcher man comin'. He be comin'."

McCants did not respond.

Neither did Lawrence.

Out in the alley, the scratchy voice of a police dispatcher crackled the air.

A figure filled the doorway.

Fast Track glanced up.

And the wolf creature reached for his soul.

205

Chapter Ten

1

During a rhetorical upswing in the Reverend Earvin "Magic" Moore's funeral oration, Mance blinked to attention. Moore, beloved pastor of the Soldier Holiness Temple, had a voice like a jetliner taking off. When under way, he could shake the building, shake your soul, and shake contributions out of your wallet or purse. He could bring the message. And as Mance reentered reality, he could see Moore's fat jowls wobble as the man said, "In Ephesians 6:12 we read, 'For we are not contending against flesh and blood, but against the principalities, against the powers, against the world rulers of this present darkness, against the spiritual hosts of wickedness in the heavenly places.' "

The long, narrow confines of the Holiness Temple rang with his thunderous words; there were scattered amen's, and outside, the rain continued. It was a Friday, and it had started raining the night before, dumping four inches by morning; now, early afternoon, another four or five inches were predicted.

"Our brother Johnson died at the hands of this present darkness."

More amens and a buzz of other exclamations from the predominantly black gathering. The Reverend Earvin Moore shifted gears, leaving the bumpy trail of Scripture for the superhighway of contemporary issues such as gambling, where his understanding of human weakness could roar.

Mance tuned out again . . . except for a thought about a lingering phrase from the Ephesians passage which had been iterated by Moore: . . . this present darkness. Like the living dark? the boy wondered. Because in his heart he believed that's what had killed Fast Track: the living dark—the wolf creature sent into the night by Sparrow's wild talent.

Because . . . Sparrow could no longer control it. The creature was out of control.

Find a way.

But maybe there wasn't a way.

Except one.

He pushed the thought aside and glanced around. As was typical of black funeral services in which a sprinkling of whites attended, the blacks amassed at the front, while the whites chose to occupy a pew or two at the rear. The place was packed; friends, relatives, apparently from all over the state and parts of Georgia, had assembled—the turnout surprised Mance. Common in the black community, there had not been an immediate burial; time had been generously allowed for mourners to reach Soldier and pay Fast Track their last respects.

Mance recognized only a few black faces, but nearly all of the whites: among them, his mother and Uncle Thestis, Austin and Miss Taylor, Twylla and Tanya and the two little girls, and Bridgette Settleford.

Oddly enough, Mance could not locate Punch among the crowd of seventy-five to one hundred people. He did, however, notice Jonella; she was wearing a dark blue dress he hadn't seen before and she was beautiful. Dazzling. Stunning. At least, to Mance, she was.

God, I can't quit loving her.

As they had filed in before the services began, she had offered him a smile and he had experienced a melting sensation, and though he meant no disrespect to the memory of Fast Track, his mind flitted to thoughts of Jonella. And the rose.

And touching her breasts and kissing her pillowy lips.

Would she ever be his again?

His.

The Reverend Earvin Moore was creating the image of Satan being much like a bookmaker who takes on our daily gambles knowing we will eventually lose to him—the odds are in his favor. A clap of thunder intruded — Moore smiled knowingly as if he had planned the phenomenon — and then merely turned up the volume of his powerful voice.

Mance felt uncomfortable. He had borrowed his dad's suit jacket; it was too large in the shoulders and made Mance feel like a little boy. His only white shirt, one left over from junior high school days, was too tight around the collar, and every time he dug a finger along it, Sting squeaked a protest; Mance feared that someone would hear the cranky rodent and throw a fit that he would have the audacity to carry a rat into a church. To a funeral service. The nerve.

But what the congregation didn't realize was that he had spent part of the morning shampooing Sting, blow-drying and brushing his white fur until it shone. So let them think what they like: he had a clean rat, cleaner than some people's children. The week had been tough enough without having to consider social amenities.

Monday morning Detective Stewart had visited with him. More routine questions, most centering on the night of the triple murder. Understandably, they had hauled Punch in, but he had an airtight alibi — sleeping off a drunk at Jimmy's in Providence. So neither of them became a suspect, but . . . the authorities were growing more and more frustrated and the good folks of Soldier more and more apprehensive. On Tuesday, Officers Lawrence and McCants were laid to rest. The news media were all over; Scarlett's became their unofficial headquarters, and while Mance's dad was grateful for the extra business, he hated that it had come as a result of the deaths of Fast Track and the two officers.

North Street had been virtually shut down all week. Mance had pedaled by the lounge a couple of times, and the sight of it had saddened him. Austin had kept his store open, but no one much came looking for used furniture — most people in Soldier saw North Street as a forbidden zone. Sparrow's place, however, remained ever the same; Mance basically stayed away from it, but he had seen old men trickle in and out of it. He had seen Twylla through the window. And once, he had seen Tanya there. But not Sparrow.

". . . Satan knows a sure thing when he sees one, my friends,

208

make no mistake about that."

Mance tried to concentrate on the sermon, he really did. Jonella stole his concentration; she was in the row in front of him and seated a few folks to his right. She seemed pleased when she became aware he was staring at her.

Locked in a loving gaze, Mance at first did not notice when someone came through the door and was guided toward a pew by one of the young ushers. It was Sparrow. Mance experienced a burning sensation in his chest; Sparrow was wearing a sport coat (patches on the elbows) and tie, a wrinkled shirt, jeans, and loafers. He might have looked like a slightly hip college professor except for his eyes and the sallowness of his face and the way the rain had plastered some of his long hair to his forehead. He seemed scared — his expression, the timid way he approached the pew — and yet those eyes. The yellow cast of them. Had they always been that color?

The eyes of the wolf creature.

Of course.

Mance felt sick.

How did Sparrow dare come to Fast Track's funeral? How could he do it?

Suddenly there was silence; heads bowed; Moore launched into a prayer. Mance could hear heartfelt sobbing up near the front. It touched him. It broke through the disgust and loathing he was feeling toward Sparrow.

There was a rustle of music. Fast Track's jazz group had set up in one corner. They began to play "Sugar Sunrise," and many in the gathering rose as Moore invited them to file past Fast Track's open casket. Mance knew there had been speculation surrounding the condition of the old man's body — how badly torn up was it? Had the face been damaged too hideously for viewing? Apparently not, but some in the audience held back, his mother, Twylla, Tanya, her girls, and Jonella among them.

But Mance moved forward mechanically.

He saw that Sparrow had joined the somber procession.

Cold-blooded nerve, Mance thought.

A few black women wailed pathetically as people filed along uncertainly. After several minutes Mance reached the foot of the casket. He felt Sting squirm. The casket was lined with some kind of blue, satiny material, and in the midst of it was Fast Track in a dark suit looking as if he were snoozing deeply but at any second might awaken and wonder why in the hell so many folks were parading by him when all he wanted was some peace and quiet.

Peace and quiet.

At last he had plenty of that.

His debts had been paid off. In full.

Mance stared down at him. The man's skin seemed more purple than he had recalled. Aside from one long scar (the mark of claws?) on the left side of his throat and a smaller gash at his temple (which had been powdered over), his body showed few signs of what must have been a savage attack.

Fast Track, man, I wish I coulda stopped that creature. Coulda stopped Sparrow.

He wavered there. Regret, sadness, deep sorrow washed over him. His knees were weak. He braced himself against the casket and was about to push on when he heard shouting. With everyone else, he turned automatically toward the back of the church.

The mass of people appeared to convulse; there were loud murmurings and a parting of humanity to reveal Punch as he stumbled forward. He was obviously drunk; he was crying and talking gibberish. And he was waving a shotgun.

The scene was over in a matter of seconds, but those seconds had razored edges. Pushing his way through to the casket, Punch had a weird fire in his eyes, a determination that emerged from the fog of inebriation. He was soaked from the rain, with the knees of his trousers muddied, his shirt unbuttoned, a tie looped around his neck like a snake.

"Pop," he cried. "Pop."

Someone reached for the gun, but Punch pulled it away, swinging toward the crowd as if he were bent upon firing. There was a scream and muffled shrieks. Mance believed his friend was about to kill—the death of Fast Track had snapped his mind.

Everyone stood back, giving him plenty of room. Everyone except the Reverend Earvin Moore, who approached him cautiously.

210

"How may we ease your suffering, son?"

Punch wheeled on him, and the crowd gasped.

"Let me be," he said.

He was staggering, but he held on to the shotgun as if it were his only reality.

For Mance, the moments were hard and cruel; beyond Punch's shoulder, beyond Moore, he could see Sparrow, and in the derelict man's face was horror of the Final Chaos.

"Don't shoot nobody," Mance called out.

The exclamation surprised the boy as much as it did everyone else. Punch's not-quite-focused eyes glanced his way.

"I got Sweet Lick," he said.

Mance stared at the shotgun. It appeared to be a brand-new one; the police had, no doubt, confiscated the real Sweet Lick. Punch had bought a new gun and had some kind of purgative violence in mind.

"Don't shoot nobody."

Several people clambered out the back door. Most stayed put, mesmerized by the unfolding scene.

"I won't," said Punch.

The tension within Mance eased.

"Please put the gun down, my son," said Moore.

"It belongs to my pop," said Punch, looking around as if he suddenly realized that everyone had misinterpreted his actions. "I wanted him to have it."

He turned and gently laid the shotgun in the casket, its barrel resting on Fast Track's stone cold shoulder.

"There you go, Pop. Ole Sweet Lick in case there's any butcher men where you're goin'."

Mance held his breath as the scene concluded. Various individuals surged forward to embrace Punch; there was a collective sigh of relief, and Mance made his way out to the sidewalk, where a soft rain was falling beyond the protective overhang.

He was in a daze.

Until a hand touched his.

Jonella's pretty face suddenly swam before him.

"I'm sorry, Mance. I know Fast Track was your friend. I'm sorry."

"Thanks," he said, not quite certain what to say.

She smiled, opened her umbrella, and started to leave.

"Could I walk with you?" he said.

"Sure."

So together they negotiated North Street in the light rain. Mance listened as Jonella talked about Adele Taylor and Austin—was marriage a possibility?—about Crystal and Loretta—on the surface they had recovered, but—and about Tanya—yes, there was something between her and Twylla, and yet Jonella believed it was not her place to raise any objections: love is where you find it.

His heart pounding in his throat, Mance said good-bye to her at her apartment house; every fiber of him wanted to hold her and kiss her. But he settled for a smile.

Minutes later, a poncho draped over him, he pedaled through his route, reality sinking its claws into him, drawing a sort of emotional blood. Fast Track was dead. Officers Lawrence and McCants were dead.

And Sparrow was alive. And the wolf creature was out of control.

Both of them had to be stopped.

The rain intensified, acquiring a chill, and that chill added to the tough question seeping into the boy's thoughts: Am I the one who's going to have to stop them?

2

Early evening at Scarlett's.

The rain continued. Nearly eight inches had fallen. Torrents of water gushed through the gutters on North Street. But Mance knew that it would take more than a flood to wash the street clean of what had tainted it. Death was impervious to any such phenomenon.

"Adele's very frightened," said Austin. "She believes I'm in danger if I persist in living at my store. Naturally I reminded her that if we were married, we would be together—neither would have to fear for the other."

Mance was sitting across from his friend. He had slipped into some dry clothes after completing his paper route and was sipping at a cup of hot chocolate. Because of the bad weather, Scarlett's had few customers for dinner.

"You'd make a good couple," said Mance. "You know, you and Miss Adele."

The boy was watching Jonella, who had just started the evening shift. She looked terrific in her waitress outfit; in fact, he couldn't keep his eyes off of her.

"Thanks for saying so," said Austin. "One of these days perhaps we will marry. The past, it seems, is standing in our way. The present, too, I suppose."

From there, the conversation took detours from the issue neither much wanted to address. They talked of the rain, of Tanya, of Mance's paper route, and of the possibility that he would have his cast removed next week.

Mance stopped following Jonella's every move.

"We're all going to miss him," said Austin. "Punch most of all, of course, but I can tell that Fast Track meant a great deal to you, too."

The boy nodded. "Austin, what can I do," he said.

"What do you feel like you need to do?"

"Well . . ." He hesitated as his thoughts spun wildly, landing on words that surprised him nearly as much as the words with which he had confronted Punch. "I . . . wanna talk to Uncle T., to Uncle Thestis, you know."

"Then do it," said Austin, smiling warmly, a shock of white hair spilling over his forehead.

"It's gone be tough. We ain't talked in a long time."

"You need to talk with him about this wolf man business? About the murders?"

"Yes, sir."

"You obviously believe he can offer you some good advice."

"Yes, sir. He . . . always has. I don't hardly ever follow it, but . . . this time's maybe different because . . . I'm scared."

Something in Austin's big, soft eyes said he understood.

"Room for one more?"

The throaty voice came at them like a gust of wind.

It was Bridgette Settleford. Austin smiled and waved her over. She sat down with a wet squeak and took off some of her rain gear.

213

"Two ducks drowned out in the parking lot," she cackled.

Mance really didn't want her to sit with them, and she knew it, but she trailed the boy these days like a bluetick after a coon — not a woman to give up easily. Inevitably, the discussion wove its way to the murders.

"Only angle on it is this: Fast Track was scared. He had called the cops believing a butcher man was after him. When Lawrence and McCants arrived, he thought they were the real thing. It was a matter of waste them before they waste you. The wolf man closed the curtain with his own nasty little final act, and so we're left where we were before: who's this wolf man? And why . . . why would he kill someone like Fast Track?"

The second question was directed at Mance. He dodged her inquiring glare and pushed away from the table. He had made a decision, and he wanted to share it with Jonella.

She was pouring a pitcher of iced tea into a tray of glasses when he caught up with her.

"Johnnie?"

"My *name* is Jonella," she said, keeping her eyes on her task.

"Oh . . . yeah, I mean, Jonella."

"What is it?"

Over the slosh of tea and ice, he said, "I've decided I'm gone go talk to Uncle T. — you were right all along. I was, you know, too stubborn I guess not to do it sooner."

He waited for her to express how pleased she was.

"I think it's a good idea," she said, registering no special gladness, and brushed past him toward the kitchen.

Is this the same girl I walked home from the funeral?

She left him empty and puzzled and wanting all the more to confide in the man who had meant so much to him as a child. In the hallway outside his uncle's door, he reached beneath the hair on his shoulder and rubbed Sting's back for good luck.

He took a deep breath and raised his fist to knock.

3

She heard a knocking.

Or did she imagine it?

The sound echoed along the walls, moving from room to room.

Here's a knocking indeed!

She had studied that play. She had understood the rhythm of darkness in *Macbeth*.

Knock! knock! knock!

Who's there, i' the name of Belzebub?

Was she, too, at hell's gate?

The flame of the candle held her in its web of silken glow. Jonella had come alone to the second floor of Guillo House. It was late. The darkness beyond the windows was palpable, the air still moist from all the rain. Small puddles of water had formed around the room, but, surprisingly, the pallet—the one she used to share with Mance—was mostly dry. She sat down upon it and wondered why she had come.

And who she was.

She stared into the flame and sighed deeply.

I'm Johnnie.

And I miss Mance.

She pressed three fingers inside her blouse and felt for the outline of the rose, and though she couldn't be certain, she believed she had touched it, for the tattoo always seemed slightly warmer than the other skin in the area. It was there, above her heart.

Make love to me, Mance.

Make love to your rose.

She closed her eyes and imagined him there with her, imagined his eager, puppy dog hands fumbling with the buttons of her blouse. She could feel and hear his warm, excited breath. His hands were jerky, not really efficient, but his actions aroused her. And the clasps of her bra presented a time-honored mystery to him, and so she helped him. It fell away, and she giggled softly at his moan of anticipation.

On her back, she slipped out of her jeans smoothly; it was a "wet panties" projection, and the description fit her own, and so she removed them. Mance had scattered his clothing with fire drill rapidity and was kneading at her breasts, fitting his mouth over first one and then the other as if they were ice cream cones.

He was erect and clumsy, and when he tried to mount her, he bruised her thighs and she pushed at him, seeking a more com-

215

fortable position, and she struggled because she knew she was losing the edge on her arousal and . . .

A new scene evolved.

She was no longer young Johnnie, a girl waiting for and wanting her first sexual experience. She was Jonella, and her body knew much more . . . knew that it needed more and wanted more. And Mance had disappeared, replaced by some dark, faceless figure.

He had tied her down by her wrists and ankles. And he was hovering over her like a shadow, like a cloud of sexual energy, building and building, and his touch, not quite a human touch, and his kiss, not quite a human kiss.

But they burned, and fired her arousal until she squirmed and yet did not want to be released from the binding. She could taste his approach. He started at her ankles, a warm, light touch. Waves of her arousal lapped along her skin ahead of his touch. Along her calf and to the soft side of her knee. It was the touch of a butterfly and the touch of hot steel. Higher and higher it moved until it was inches from her wetness.

Where it paused.

And the ache she felt was almost too much to bear.

His lips sought hers, and the kiss was deeper, more complete than any other she had ever experienced, taking her desire into realms she had not imagined, spiraling and lifting . . . but then he pulled away and began kissing and sucking at her breasts and touching and caressing and still hovering so close. She could feel his warmth above her. And she wanted it, but she was held down.

Her legs bucked, her thigh muscles taut, and she struggled for position, and she called eagerly for him.

But again and again when he drew near entering her, his touch and his warmth would halt their advance. She cried out in frustration.

Again and again and again.

Suddenly Jonella jerked free of the fantasy projection.

"Momma," she said.

Sweat had beaded along her hairline. She fought to catch her breath. She closed her eyes and colored stars swirled. She was a different Jonella. And the sexual frustration had evolved into a different form of wanting — not Mance. Not David Reed. Not

216

even the dark fantasy lover. But something more.

She felt the need in the pit of her stomach, and she wanted desperately for someone else to understand that need. Into the shadows she whispered, "Eleanor?"

Whatever walks here walks alone.

"Eleanor, I need . . . need help."

What I need is here. In Guillo House.

Her voice pitched higher.

"Help me!"

Jonella, flesh into ghost.

What's happening to me?

Guillo House listened.

The walls moved, shifted; she heard a rustle, a scratching.

A snarl.

"Someone help me," she said, exhausted, scared.

I am all alone.

She began to shiver.

She was too frightened to lift her candle and leave the room and walk down those stairs and out of Guillo House and back to reality.

Something here needed her as much as she needed it.

"Eleanor?"

The shadows invited the shaping of a form.

Confused, Jonella shifted to her knees; the candle flickered; she held her head, her eyes darting about the room trying to see, to determine precisely what was occurring.

"Where am I?" she called out, tears thorning in the corners of her eyes.

In the center of the room the wolf creature materialized.

Jonella gasped, but she did not scream.

She stared into its yellow, primitive eyes.

Those eyes held answers.

"Where am I?" she begged to know.

WhereamIwhereamIwhereamI?

And the wolf creature spoke one word into her bewildered mind.

Lost.

"When they all gone leave?"

"Not till the wolf man's caught. Better just get used to 'em."

"Marge Jenkins tole me one of the Mont-gomery channels was down on North Street with their cameras, and you know who they interviewed?"

Mance looked at his mother disinterestedly.

She whispered, "That Sparrow fella," and nodded as if to confirm the bizarre truth of it.

"Sparrow?"

Trying hard to imagine Sparrow on camera, the boy was struck by the cold irony of it all: they were interviewing the killer and didn't realize it.

"Marge also said some folks from that TV show, 'Strange America,' well, they's plannin' to do a show 'bout Soldier and the killings. Bridgette Settleford says they probably gone want to talk to you." She hesitated, carefully, and with a mother's sharp eye, observing his reaction. "You know somethin' 'bout this you hadn't tole the police?"

His words came out tinged with more anger than he had intended.

"I don't want to talk about it."

It was a slow Sunday afternoon, two days after Fast Track's funeral. His mother was taking a break from the register, and, having seen Mance deep in thought, felt she might offer him some motherly comfort.

"They say Punch has skipped town," she said.

"Maybe he just wants to get away from this stinkin' place for a while. Can't blame him for that."

"Can't run away from your troubles," his mother followed, giving her words a little air of wisdom the way you might put spin on a tennis ball.

Using the prongs of a fork, Mance dug at the persistent itch beneath his cast. It was just one more thing to make him miserable these days.

"Where's Johnnie?" he asked.

He noticed she wasn't on duty and that was unusual for a Sunday afternoon because she almost always chose to work then.

Seated across from him, his mother, her chin resting on her knuckles, arched her eyebrows. There was a flicker of concern in her expression — it seemed as if her forehead had given birth to a new wrinkle or two.

"She didn't come in yestiddy either. Tole me she plain didn't feel good."

"She's sick? What's wrong? Why didn't you tell me?"

"Nothin' you could do — it's in her head," she said, tapping knowingly at her temple. "I'm 'fraid she's gone strange. Oh, I got to run. . . ."

She bustled away to the register, leaving Mance to contemplate the abyss of his own thoughts.

Gone strange.

Oh, Johnnie, sweet Johnnie. He wanted to help her, but he realized that he needed help himself. He hadn't knocked on his uncle's door the other day. His courage or pride or something had failed him — he needed something special to make him seek out his uncle once and for all.

Feeling restless, he considered exiting Scarlett's, jumping on his bike, and heading north on one of the county roads — maybe ride as far as Taloa Springs, the small community known mostly for its mental institute. Two summers ago he had pedaled up there to watch the inmates mow the grass and clip azaleas. Hell, he reasoned, it might even lift his spirits to see folks who were in much worse shape than he was.

"This seat taken?"

"Huh?"

It was his dad, who hesitated a second, then sat down.

"You awful damn tired of that cast by now, ain'cha?"

"Yeah. It itches like sin."

Mance studied the lines of exhaustion in his dad's face: Royal Culley was looking old, and yet along with the lines of exhaustion and the lines of age were lines of strength. Like a fortuneteller reading a palm, Mance read that face: he read love, he read regret, and he read a desire to help.

"Suppose we ain't been close of late," said the man. And Mance noticed that he had slipped a slender photo album onto the table. "Truth is, over the years I've given most of my attention to Karen — Uncle Thestis was always there for you. Karen,

219

she was a daddy's girl, you know. And you, well, you thought Thestis was a shiny new quarter all your own. And he sure was. Maybe I was even jealous of him." He shrugged. "Thing is now, your mother, she says you been wantin' to talk to him but can't bring yourself to do it."

"Dad, listen, I —"

"No, I got to finish. Your mother, she wanted me to say something to you, convince you to go to him. Hell, you know I don't got the right words — a son should oughtta be comin' to his father, but . . . I understand." He fumbled with the album, and Mance saw what it was.

"You recognize this?"

"Yes, sir, I do. It's my old picture album from grade school. Mrs. Kinder's homeroom."

His dad nodded.

"You didn't have many friends in them days — that kinda used to worry me some."

"I was too little and skinny. Kids picked on me."

Thumbing through the pages, his dad stopped at a section headed by a bold script which read, For That Special Friend.

Mance knew what was there without looking.

His palms prickled. Ironically, his dad had come up with the magic formula.

Turning the book around so that Mance could see the picture, his dad said, "I'm supposin' that special friend still is. Oh, he's got a few more years on him, but, hell, ain't we all. Go see him, OK?"

Mance looked down.

At the smiling, molelike face of his Uncle Thestis.

Then he glanced up, something catching in his throat.

Silence wrapped around the two of them.

He found what he needed in his father's eyes.

"Thanks, Dad," he said. "I'll do it."

5

It wasn't easy.

Before he knocked on his uncle's door, he listened outside of it, building up his courage one final time. He could hear the man humming. Without even seeing him, Mance knew what he was doing: polishing that silver cup.

How many times growing up had he been asked by his uncle to polish that cup?

"Rub up my silver, Manson?" he would say. And afterward, had he done a good job: "Oh, it shines like the promise of tomorrow."

The promise of tomorrow: was there such a thing?

He knocked.

"Entree."

Nervous, the boy stepped into the dimly lit room; his uncle Thestis fitted into an easy chair the way a peanut fits into its shell. But he looked somewhat diminished; he had lost weight, and his arms had loose folds of skin and his hands appeared to have formed permanently into claws.

Yet, at the sight of Mance, the man's face lost many of its wrinkles, dropped many of its flags of pain.

"Uncle T.?"

"Well, goodness . . . Manson, why . . . why, come on in."

He was clearly surprised, but pleasantly so.

The boy's chest tightened; his uncle looked very ill.

Is he gone die?

"Mom wanted to know if there's something, you know . . . anything particular you wanna eat for supper this evening?"

His uncle saw through the phony remark immediately — Mance knew he did — but it broke the ice.

"Come on in and sit," the man gestured. He was, as Mance had imagined, holding his silver cup. "Let me think a moment . . . hot lemon tea and unbuttered toast. Yes, I'd like that. Tell her, though, not to go to any special effort for me."

Sitting on the edge of a hard-backed chair, Mance said, "OK. Yeah, I'll tell her."

He glanced at the silver cup, hoping it would provide some inspiration. But he felt extremely awkward. There seemed no smooth way to bridge over the weeks in which they hadn't spoken to each other.

His uncle smiled shyly. "Quite a rain we had, huh?" he said.

"Yeah. Somebody said over nine inches."

There was a lull in their exchange, the mind of each racing to generate further small talk.

"Your mother tells me Jonella has been under the weather. I do so worry about that child, though, of course, she isn't a child but rather a lovely young woman."

"I feel like maybe she's still depressed," said Mance. He wanted suddenly to leave—or at least part of him did—part wanted to stay and confide and ask for help. "We don't . . . we aren't goin' together no more. Guess Mom probably told you."

"Yes, yes, as a matter of fact, she mentioned that. And I'm very sorry to hear it. You belong together."

"Yeah, me, too—I mean, that's what I feel like. Maybe when she gets over bein' depressed . . ."

And his uncle saw that it was a painful topic, saw that he had come to talk about something else.

"North Street has more patrol cars and news people than regular folks these days. It's tragic that our little area had to be the scene of such horrible events."

They exchanged general comments about the deaths of Fast Track and the two officers. They talked a bit about Punch, but the conversation seemed to Mance to be going nowhere. On the verge of leaving, he was stopped by his uncle's almost casual observation:

"You know something about this wolf man, don't you?"

Mance shrugged.

Hot ant tracks found a trail into his throat.

"And you came here to talk about it because you've always eventually come to me with your difficult problems . . . for the wisdom of Gottfried Sücher, right?"

A smile caught Mance before he could elude it.

"That detective guy from your weird stories?"

Mouthing a drumroll and a "ta da," Uncle Thestis gestured that yes, indeed, they were one and the same.

"I got a tough one for him," said Mance.

Wincing in pain as he shifted his weight, the man leaned forward in anticipation. In his best imitation of Orson Welles, he replied, "The tougher the better for Herr Sücher."

"Maybe I better get you that tea and toast—this could take awhile."

It did.

Through the evening and into the grip of night.

Mance began this way: "I feel like I know who the wolf man is."

Uncle Thestis listened carefully to every word, interrupting only occasionally for clarification of a detail. Mance told all. And when he had concluded his narrative, he said, "I feel like maybe I'll have to kill him."

Uncle Thestis frowned.

"If he's the murderer, he has to be stopped—yes, most certainly."

"What's going on, Uncle Thestis? What's the living dark? Is Sparrow crazy? A psychopath? What is he?"

The man sank back, took a sip of tea, ground his teeth at a stab of pain, and then said, "Perhaps he's a werewolf."

"Werewolf? You mean like in horror flicks? Does Sücher know 'bout werewolves?"

Uncle Thestis smiled broadly.

"Herr Sücher knows everything there is to know about werewolves."

For the next hour or more Mance was given an anatomy of werewolves, a compendium of information as Uncle Thestis punctuated his presentation, asking the boy from time to time to retrieve a volume of supernatural lore from one of the incredibly messy shelves.

"According to the tradition, it's the most accepted way to send a werewolf shuffling off this mortal coil."

Those were the man's final words of explanation.

Mance, cradling the silver cup, said, "Silver bullet? Yeah, I'd heard that. Sounds like a pile of shit to me. You believe all this? There ain't really such things as werewolves, are there?"

"I believe in mankind's *need* to believe in them."

Mance thought a moment.

"Something's gotta be done about Sparrow right away," he said.

"Let me think on it," said Uncle Thestis.

"There just ain't much time," the boy insisted.

And his uncle nodded in dark agreement.

Chapter Eleven

The Conqueror Worm issued a calling card during the night. Pain ripped through the bowels of Uncle Thestis, a biting and tearing as if piranhas were there engaged in a feeding frenzy.

He twisted awake.

Give me time, Conqueror Worm. Give me time.

He needed it now more than ever.

More fully conscious, he switched on a lamp and saw that it was 3:00 A.M.—a good hour at which to die, he'd always heard. He went to his easy chair and nestled into it as comfortably as the pain would allow. He squirmed, and someone watching him might have been reminded of a mother hen ruffling her feathers and positioning herself over some eggs.

The angry pain took two more bites, and then, apparently satiated, released him until a later feeding time. And for that he was thankful. Reprieve from the pain gave him a chance to think . . . and remember.

Guillo House.

As a child running with the small girl away from the snarling, growling thing in his mother's bedroom—no, she wasn't his real mother, yet hadn't she filled the role to his heart's content?

He never saw the source of the primitive sounds.

But Adele had.

Drumming his fingers on the arm of the chair, he let his thoughts wander from the darkness of memory into a soft, warm light, and at the center of that light, pure and beautiful and desirable, was Adele Taylor.

The only woman he had ever truly loved.

He remembered her touch; he remembered how gently, how lovingly she deflected his intentions; and he had, ironically, loved her all the more for it. She had told him love was not an option for her—or, at least, not marriage, not a family. At the center of her self-denial was Guillo House and a fateful night.

Had Kelton Austin changed all that? Or did something continue to keep her from surrendering her affections completely?

I've never stopped loving you, Adele.

It was his secret, and it rested there in the corner of his heart, much like one of his jars of marbles hidden deep in the closet. Not even Adele herself knew.

It's always been you, Adele.

The thought embarrassed him somewhat: a man of advancing years harboring a hopeless love as he stared death in the face. Shouldn't he be devoting his energy to the real present? And to the sharp-toothed problem with which Mance was struggling?

Yes, he knew that he should be.

And thus he began to replay his conversation with the young man, sifting among the details, evaluating, doubting, testing, balancing the possible and the improbable, and when he had finished, he concluded quite confidently that Mance was wrong: there was no werewolf—not in the traditional sense—and Sparrow was no killer.

But the description of the wolf creature haunted Thestis.

A wolf in his memory. Dangerous? How so?

Only one person—one woman—knew the answer.

Suddenly, he felt a jolt of fear which made him bite down hard. The pain within stirred. He saw Mance's wolf creature, imagined it threatening Adele.

Half a cry sprang to his lips.

Give me time, Conqueror Worm.

For Adele. For Mance. For all of us.

* * *

Mance waited at his bedroom door for some indication that his uncle was preparing for his morning bath. It had become a daily ritual, midmorning, for the man to shuffle into the bathroom and fill the tub with scalding hot water and lower his pain-racked body into it. And there he would soak for an hour or more.

Plenty of time for Mance to do what needed to be done.

Turning momentarily away from the door, the boy noticed Sting's rapid pattern of squeaks.

"You don't think I oughtta do this, right? Tough shit, I'm gone to."

It was a last resort. But would it work?

While some thoughts formed muddy pools, others were crystal clear: he knew, for example, that his uncle entertained serious doubts about his theory that Sparrow was the wolf man; but, as well, he himself questioned whether werewolves existed.

Men into wolves? No way.

And yet: *I've seen the power of the living dark.*

He had witnessed what kind of borderline human being Agent Orange had turned Sparrow into.

"Damn it, Sting, he's gotta be stopped. If he's not he'll kill again. He killed Fast Track, a harmless old man. Who'll be next?"

Anyone on North Street.

Possibly even Jonella.

Something intensely cold stabbed into Mance's chest, and in the aftermath chill he felt that he was doing the right thing. He had called Spivey, who, in turn, had called his brother who dealt in gold and silver junk jewelry and had access to a small smelting operation.

A door clicked.

Mance held his breath. In one sense, what he was about to do was wrong—it would hurt his uncle—but in another sense, ultimately more hurt might be prevented, tragedy averted.

Sparrow had to be stopped.

Would a silver bullet do the job?

Mance forced himself to believe. It was time to believe in something.

There. Another click. His uncle was in the bathroom. Mance stepped out into the hallway, listened, heard bathwater running, and checked any final doubts.

Slipping into his uncle's room, however, he felt like a common thief. Or worse. He glanced around as if he were unfamiliar with the surroundings, his eyes brushing across everything except the one object which had seduced him to such a violation of humanity.

God damn it, I've got to stop Sparrow.

But his hands were trembling, his legs unsteady. Each breath sucked hot needles into his lungs.

Was that someone in the hall?

Panic bubbled into his throat.

There it was, resting proudly atop the dresser among photos and other leftover effects of his uncle's desire to hang on to the past: the silver cup.

A fresh wave of panic: *when I touch it, will it burn me like the fires of hell?*

How would he ever be able to explain the theft?

I had to kill the wolf man.

I had to.

He cursed softly, reached for the cup—and it felt solid in his grasp.

But as he left the room with the cup in hand, he imagined the room screaming a protest which would have awakened the dead.

3

Lyrics throbbed in his head: "Break On Through" by the Doors, his favorite group years ago—that same song was roaring through his thoughts the day he shipped out to Nam.

What was that "other side" Jim Morrison sang of?

Sparrow learned in Nam: it was the land of the dead, of bloodied, mutilated bodies, of dreams drowned in blood, and now, deep into the spring night, watching over the sleeping bodies of his burdens, he was again reminded of the other side.

Something from that nether realm was approaching.

He had said good night to Twylla. Having recovered from his brief illness, he no longer needed her to tend to the burdens. She had returned to her home for battered women, though Sparrow had wanted her to stay, wanted her to give their relationship another chance, for he believed he loved her.

Teasingly, he had always maintained that he could "convert" her to being a heterosexual, but his efforts had failed. She had a new love. Let her go, he told himself.

Your burdens need all your love.

In the shadowy back room sleeping area, Sparrow moved among the cots and pallets. The burdens tossed and turned fretfully; they acted like a herd of cattle catching a whiff of an approaching storm or of wild animals. Some moaned in their half sleeps; others rose for a drink of water or a piss call.

Tonight there were ten or twelve of them—all old white men except for one old white woman, a poor soul Twylla did not have room for. Sparrow had taken her in; she was mostly deaf. From her he had learned that the daughter she had been living with had broken up with her husband, thus creating a dislocation. The woman, Dora, was let out to fend for herself. And could not.

Roy Dean and Claude, in gentlemanly fashion, had fixed her a comfortable cot, replete with pillow and the best blanket to be found. Her eyes had twinkled appreciation, and she had muttered some wet and garbled words of thanks.

Sparrow surveyed all of his burdens in a sweeping glance.

Fear churned and rattled in his stomach like a small engine about to stall.

Dingledodie fuck. What's going on?

Often his burdens would be restless; there would be the echoes of phlegm-filled coughs and an occasional pain-induced cry or even a strangled, nightmare-charged shriek. But tonight was different. Some had asked for a night light, so he had obliged, rigging up a mechanic's hooded light and nailing

228

it to one wall.

That light thickened the shadows.

When the burdens would roll over to glance at him for reassurance, he would see a death glare in their eyes like road animals caught in the spray of car lights. The sight made him shudder.

To calm his apprehension, he hunkered down near old Rollo. But he noticed that the pathetic derelict had wet his pants, the pungent odor of urine rising from him like gasoline fumes.

"Rollo, man, what the fuck?"

He shook the old guy, though he could see that his eyes were open.

"Why'd you piss your pants, man? We had a long piss call — you ole dingledodie, what the fuck?"

A sliver of light captured Rollo's face. Tears were sliding down his cheeks.

Sparrow's upper body tensed.

"Hey, man? Frizzlemydick — hey, man — what the fuck? Why you cryin'?"

"Is it coming?" asked Rollo, his voice tear-choked.

"Is what coming?"

Sparrow's hands felt intensely cold — just as they used to on patrol in the jungle — not cold feet, but cold hands, hands that threatened not to be able to operate his weapon.

Rollo clawed at Sparrow's wrist.

"It's coming, isn't it?" And he turned his face toward the back door, which opened onto the alley.

Sparrow found it difficult to breathe.

"Go to sleep, Rollo."

Momentarily the man tightened his grip on Sparrow's wrist.

"It's coming from . . . from the neverwhere," said Rollo; then he nodded, released his grip, and lapsed back down. But he did not close his eyes.

"Go to sleep," said Sparrow, unable to repress a touch of anger in his voice.

As he stood, he heard a sprinkling of exclamations from the sea of shadowy bodies.

"What's wrong?"

"Is Rollo sick?"

"I'm cold."

"I'm scared."

"Is it morning yet?"

Sparrow raised his hands to calm the waters.

"Go to sleep. All you. All you ole dingledodies go to sleep. Hear me?"

Silence claimed them grudgingly.

Sparrow waited.

And wondered why he was trembling.

He decided that he would sleep in the back area to keep watch in case some of the burdens grew apprehensive during the night and needed him. From his cellar room—the "hole," as he affectionately termed it—he retrieved his M-16, a memento from that "police action" in another world which had stolen his sanity and replaced it with the living dark.

Rifle in his lap, he slumped against the wall, the hooded light directly above him. Some of the burdens eyed him, a delicate fire burning in their faces, then turned hesitantly toward the embrace of sleep.

Sparrow kept one finger on the trigger of the loaded gun.

He glanced over at the quiet form of ole Rollo.

It's coming, isn't it?

From the neverwhere.

Break on through to the other side.

His eyelids suddenly heavy, Sparrow invited the pulse of the night to fill his ears. In the wash of gray light, he found himself slipping into a void, hanging there by a silver thread.

It's coming.

Whose voice was that?

"Angel?" Sparrow whispered. "Christ, man, is that you?"

The void had swallowed him.

"Angel? Where are you, man? Christ, I thought the gooks got you."

I'm in the neverwhere.

Sparrow opened his eyes; gladness leaped into his throat: was it true? Angel? His ole buddy had come back, come back from the other side? From the neverwhere?

"Angel?"

The burdens swung awake in a chorus of anguish.

Something was prying at the back door. The rasping sound of claws, of wood splintering.

"Angel? Hey, man, what is it?"

Some of the burdens were crying; most were huddled together like war refugees.

Sparrow pushed himself to his feet; his hands burned like ice on the rifle.

"Angel?"

And then a voice.

It's the Final Chaos. The Enemy.

A rush of wind. The roar of a jet taking off. A rumble of thunder as something crashed through the back door.

It had no distinct form.

It was all darkness and claws and fangs.

Sparrow couldn't move.

The Final Chaos was stalking his burdens . . . and he couldn't move.

They screamed and cowered as if being threatened by a tidal wave. The Final Chaos flooded into the shadowy room, creating its own sickly aura, a pale yellow light, diseased and putrid. And the enemy remained indistinct as it lurched into the midst of the shrieking souls.

One of the burdens rose to meet the invader.

Shadows pitched and coiled. Sparrow opened his mouth to call the burden back, but no words escaped, only a spray of spittle. The burden raised a fist and hammered it into the formless thing.

There was a scream of agony which leaped beyond the background swell of cries, and in the meager light Sparrow could see that the burden's right hand had been ripped away; blood fountained and the burden dropped to his knees, face contorted in horror.

"Help us," someone pleaded.

231

"Dear God, it's here," cried another.

"Sparrow, stop it . . . stop it . . . stop it."

"We're all gone die."

"Nooooo!"

The word thundered from Sparrow like a grenade exploding.

But the Final Chaos continued its slow, deliberate movement, and Sparrow's legs resisted the command to work; his fingers were solid rings of ice upon the M-16.

The burden whose hand had been torn away began scuttling backwards like a crab as two other burdens courageously stepped into the path of the attacker. A claw extended like the tip of a hungry whip and raked across the face of one of them, laying open his cheek in a ribbon of skin and bloody flesh which ran from ear to ear and claimed the man's upper lip. He issued a guttural scream and fell away; his comrade slugged at the beast with both fists before a vicious sweep of claws cut a swath from his right shoulder to his left hip. Clothes peeled away; skin and flesh and muscle appeared to dissolve as if they had been dipped in some volatile chemical; ribs snapped; the stomach cavity opened, and a hot, steamy mass of blood and undigested food spilled into the shadows. The burden staggered and fell forward without more than a shocked gurgle and a helpless flailing of arms.

"No," Sparrow whispered, but still could not move.

The Final Chaos shambled toward the old woman, who was sitting up on her cot, her head pivoting from side to side as if merely confused—her eyes, her face, gave evidence that on the road to terror she had passed a point of no return and her mind had ceased functioning.

Roy Dean and Claude were there, Roy Dean wielding a jagged piece of milk bottle, Claude bracing a broom handle against his chest. Screams and shouts and a frenzy of desperate movement continued.

Deep within the shadowy block of the Final Chaos, a growl gained momentum until it sprang forth like the roar of a lion, momentarily keeping the men at bay. Then Roy Dean jumped forward as if he were attempting to tackle the dark force. In an uppercut motion, he swung the piece of glass at the center of the approaching darkness. But something caught his wrist; Sparrow heard one bone snap, then the wrenching and grating of a shoulder socket being destroyed. Roy Dean whimpered. And he could do nothing to impede the swing of his arm as the Final Chaos twisted the elbow back upon itself and the jagged edge of the glass met his chin and plowed a deep groove through his lips and nose before disappearing behind one of his eyes.

"You son-of-a-bitch," Claude shouted as he saw what the Final Chaos had done to his friend. Broom handle pathetically poised, the old man charged, ramming the handle at his shadowy nemesis with all the force he could muster. Sparrow looked on helplessly; with the exception of Rollo, all the other burdens had scattered to relative safety.

Time slowed as the point of the handle appeared to strike its mark, but then a nervous pop reverberated throughout the room; the handle shattered; Claude stumbled, twisted to one side. Sparrow heard him cough twice, and then the man was angling toward him. When Sparrow saw him, the shock sent a burning sensation through his body; the hands that had been frozen in a death grip upon the rifle began to thaw: the broom handle had impaled Claude just below the heart. He crashed to his knees at Sparrow's feet; he was trying to say something, his lips working around a bubble of blood; but no sound gained purchase.

Sparrow read those lips: "Help me," the man was pleading. "Help me stand up."

Then gouts of blood strangled him.

The Final Chaos had changed directions; it was coming for Sparrow.

Face enemy with your bare hands.

Wasn't that Angel's refrain?

Sparrow dropped the M-16; it clattered on the floor, and the pale yellow aura of the Final Chaos shrank into two intense yellow dots. Two eyes. Predatory eyes.

Then it was old Rollo's turn for heroics; he lunged forward, windmilling fists almost comically. But his challenge was met even as Sparrow cried out for him to keep back. Claws dug into Rollo's mouth; there was a nerve-rivening snarl as the beast's fury concentrated, and Rollo's face tore open with the hollow sound of a watermelon splitting.

"Noooo!"

And the scream blazed a fiery trail, burning his lungs and throat and mouth and lips.

He woke, jolted by his own cry.

The burdens jump-started; some pressed tentatively to an elbow and looked at him questioningly, others tossed and groaned and cursed their aching and weary bones, and perhaps a few others mumbled prayers.

Only a nightmare.

The relief was so overwhelming that all of Sparrow's senses became acute: he could see the face of each burden in his mind's eye; he could feel the raspy breath of each; he could hear the beat of each heart, and he could taste the bitterness of their fear.

Because the Final Chaos was out there.

No, there had been no bloody massacre, but it was out there.

Come, it said.

It's time, it called.

Into the neverwhere, it insisted.

And Sparrow knew that he had to meet it just as he had on the battlefield.

He waited until the burdens had calmed; he helped them get glasses of water; he helped one take his high blood pressure medicine; and he guided several to the bathroom for piss calls.

Walking among the cots and pallets, he slowed near old Rollo's cot and instinctively reached down and brushed his fingers across his shoulder. Rollo's face was intact; there were no tears, but the old guy surprised him by saying, "You gone go?"

Something tickled in Sparrow's throat—it was fear. Undiluted, raw fear.

"Yes, I have to," he said, trying his best to keep his voice even.

"Well," said Rollo, "you got a friend."

Touched by the remark, Sparrow squeezed the old man's shoulder. And when the hum of an after-midnight silence had spread over the sleeping area, he listened to the call of the Final Chaos.

Come . . . it's time . . . into the neverwhere.

Sparrow hefted his M-16, then set it aside as he sensed the presence of Angel at his shoulder . . . *face your enemy with your bare hands.*

Yes, he would: bare hands and the power of the living dark.

His hands had chilled again as he stepped through the back door and out into the darkness of the alley, and yet the rest of his body was sweating, sweating profusely as he always had in the jungle, an all-consuming sweat. It was draining him, weakening him, though it was not a particularly warm spring night. His throat felt dry, and, curiously, he imagined his bones to be as brittle as matchsticks.

Angel was there at his shoulder. Angel's ghost.

The Final Chaos continued to call, drawing him like a magnet down the alley and around the corner to a string of abandoned buildings.

It's a trap.

Angel knew such things. His ghostly voice halted Sparrow in his tracks.

Were they beyond their perimeter? No one had an accurate map. The gooks controlled the darkness.

"Help me, Angel. Stay with me, buddy," Sparrow whispered.

Where you going?

"Into the neverwhere," Sparrow replied, the words leaping like a surprise into his thoughts.

And, God, he was scared. He felt naked without his weapon. But he had the living dark—he could use it against the Final Chaos if he kept his nerve.

He shuffled past two buildings, reaching the doorway to the old hotel—*the neverwhere;* a sodium lamp offered light above him, but pitch dark glared at him from within.

"Angel? Hey, man, stay with me."

He turned, searching for some evidence of his companion's presence. But there was none.

"Angel? God damn, where are you?"

It's a fucking trap.

The voice was there and then gone like a star winking out in the skies above Soldier.

Cautiously, Sparrow stepped into the hotel. Two steps. Three. And as his eyes started to adjust, he saw something which caused him to jerk around, intent upon fleeing the scene. But a force held him, and suddenly he was lifted bodily by his shoulders and spun and tossed to his knees.

He cried out, and dust rose and filled his nostrils. He clambered to his feet and stiffened into a karate stance. To his right was the solid block of darkness formed by the punching bag.

"God damn you!" he shouted.

The eyes stung him. Yellow, predatory eyes.

Twenty feet from him, framed by darkness, was the wolf creature.

Sparrow's hands began to shake uncontrollably.

Settled on its haunches, the wolf creature loomed implacably. Into the consciousness of Sparrow it spoke: *must kill.*

"Not goin' down without a dingledodie fight," Sparrow muttered.

Balling his hands into fists, he forced himself to concentrate. The powers of the living dark stood against the Final Chaos.

The moment had arrived.

He shut his eyes tightly and sent a lightning stroke of terror at the heart of the creature. The dust stirred into whirling devils. The building groaned as the air pressure plunged. But the force which had scattered stray dogs and humbled every other foe he had encountered failed to affect the wolf creature.

Its eyes, unblinking, seared Sparrow's flesh.

Redoubling his courage, he concentrated again, sending every ounce of the powers of the living dark he could muster.

"Run, you bastard," he murmured. "Run."

Again and again and again he loosed the psychic powers of the living dark upon the wolf creature, but its eyes reflected no fear; its body did not quake.

Tears welled and began to stream down Sparrow's dusty face.

"Run," he whispered.

The wolf creature shifted its position. High in its chest it growled. Its eyes focused, threatening Sparrow like a knife at his throat.

Must kill.

It was a blast of fire and sound and wind.

Sparrow staggered back, and then he did something he had never done before in the face of an enemy.

He ran.

3

Two nights later.

At the front door of Sparrow's pawnshop, Mance checked his .38—five cartridges, each coated with silver. Good ole Spivey—and Spivey's brother. He owed them one.

But would it work?

Jesus: silver bullets and werewolves and the living dark.

It was hard to know what to believe. Except this: Sparrow had to be stopped.

Would Uncle Thestis understand? Would he forgive him? Yes, he knew who stole his cup, though he had not, as yet, said anything about it.

The front area of the pawnshop was dimly lit. It was after ten o'clock; he imagined the burdens had been put to rest, and that was good. They wouldn't interfere with his plan, which was to calmly pull the .38 on Sparrow and tell him that he had to surrender to Detective Stewart. It would be the end of the wolf man. No more killing.

And if Sparrow did not cooperate?

Silver bullets. All five of them. To still the beating heart of the wolf man.

He found the front door locked, and no amount of pounding at it could raise anyone. Odd. Sparrow never failed to heed a knock on his door. At the back door, Mance tried again, and this time one of the old men let him in, and when he demanded to see Sparrow, he was directed to a side room.

Impatient, Mance started to knock, but then decided instead to ready the .38 and barge in. Surprised screams greeted him from the darkened room. He fumbled by the door for a light switch.

Two more screams, softer this time, as light filled the room. They were in bed, naked, atop the sheets. Twylla and Tanya.

Twylla, her breasts dangling heavily, grabbed a sheet from the end of the bed and covered herself and her lover.

"What the goddamn hell you doin'?" she said, her jaw tight with anger.

Mance raised the .38, but for a few seconds all he could think of were Crystal and Loretta. Who was their mother these days? Then the thought extinguished itself.

"I want Sparrow," he said.

"Sparrow's sick again. You better get the fuck outta here before I call the cops."

"No," said Mance. "No, I gotta have Sparrow. Now."

With the aid of the .38, he won the standoff.

Clad in a robe, Twylla led him away from the room; over his shoulder, he glanced once at Tanya, but her face was turned toward a wall.

"He's down there," Twylla said, pointing to a small door which obviously led into a basement. Mance motioned her away and pushed open the door; a nearly palpable blackness welcomed him.

"Sparrow?"

From behind him, Twylla said, "He's in bad shape . . . he's had a bad scare."

Then she reached past him and switched on a small watt bulb which revealed a phone booth-sized room, and there, seated upon a dirty blanket and leaning against a concrete block wall that seeped greenish water, was a man who somewhat resembled Sparrow—the long blond hair, the beard; and yet the face. The eyes.

Here was a man who had returned from hell.

The face had been crumbled like a paper bag; the eyes were dark, gouged openings. Madness rested in the hollows of the cheeks. He did not blink at the sudden fall of light. Is he blind? Mance wondered.

Surrounding the man was a cache of guns and ammunition.

"Leave me alone," said Sparrow, and the voice was a skittering of claws. "I have to finish the job and fremsit on baromsett mickledickle fly me to the neverwhere moon dingledodie fuck."

"Get up," said Mance, doubting suddenly that there was any point taking this man to Detective Stewart. "You're giving yourself up."

"You're fucking crazy," said Twylla, but Mance turned on her and gestured for her to stay out of the way. Meanwhile Sparrow creaked to his feet.

Mance's hold on the .38 was tenuous.

Thoughts tiltawhirled. His motivation was petering out like the slackening of a spring rain.

I gotta do it for Johnnie. For everybody on North Street.

"We're going to see Detective Stewart, and you're going to give yourself up and confess about the killings. You can plead insanity and maybe they won't 'lectrocute you, and I'm sorry I gotta do this 'cause you were my friend . . . my guardian angel and you saved my life, but, see . . . you're a werewolf, I think . . . and you're gone keep killin' if I don't stop you."

Sparrow stood, zombielike, and yet something flickered in one eye: a tiny fire indicative of some wild desire to complete a dark ritual to which he was compulsively bound. Twylla slipped into the shadows, and the burdens stirred apprehensively. Some begged to know what was happening.

"Tell 'em to shut up," said Mance, his nerves beginning to fray.

Sparrow raised his hands.

"Everything will be all right," he told them, his voice scratchy and weak.

Mance started marching him toward the front door.

"I'm sorry," said the boy. "I don't got a choice."

Sparrow shuffled ahead; Mance fought to hold the .38 aimed at the man's back. He never heard Twylla approach from behind with the sheet, though he felt the rush of air as she tossed it over his head just before she pulled him backward.

He fell hard on his butt, dropped the gun, and began swinging his fists frantically, striking the sheet but nothing else. In the span of seconds it took the boy to extricate himself, Sparrow had made his way to the back door. But once out in the alley, he stumbled to a halt.

Waiting for him was the wolf creature.

Must kill.

Terrified, Sparrow dived behind a couple of trash barrels. And cursed his cowardice.

Locating the .38, Mance scrambled to his feet, but had to fight off the harpy attack of Twylla; she kicked at him and raked at him with her long fingernails. In desperation, he swung at her with the butt of the gun, catching her on the cheekbone just below her right eye. She issued a deep groan and fell away.

Mance dashed for the alley, regretting that he had had to hurt the woman.

Can't let him get away.

And the cold necessity washed over Mance as if he had leaped into an icy stream: he had to shoot Sparrow. It was the only way. The silver bullets. The legend come true.

He had not expected to see the wolf creature in the alley, had not expected Sparrow to transform so quickly.

Sucking in his breath, he tried to steady himself; the creature was twenty yards from him, almost inviting death.

Mance raised the .38 in the two-hand grip he had seen on television.

"Sparrow . . . I got to do this."

But in a twitch of movement, the wolf creature turned and began loping away down the alley toward the railroad tracks.

"Stop, goddamn it," Mance yelled.

In no hurry, the creature continued.

Mance fired, and the explosion numbed his right ear.

Then he gave chase because he had missed his mark. Around the corner he raced, but seemed to gain no ground on the creature. He saw it hesitate in the doorway of the old hotel.

Mance fired again, certain this time that the shadowy creature must have been tagged.

Three bullets left.

He beat a breathless path to the hotel doorway and ducked within its darkness.

Help me.

Find a way.

Help me . . . help me die.

The voice of the wolf creature hammered him to a standstill.

Sparrow wants to die.

Yes, he had run, but it must have been an instinctive move. Now, in the shape of the wolf creature, he was begging Mance to kill him, to end the misery of the living dark.

Suddenly, as Manse looked into the eyes of the creature, he felt a shattering sadness. It would be a mercy killing.

"Oh, God," he muttered. "I'm sorry, Sparrow."

Help me die.

"I will."

The lobby of the old hotel was dark and silent; only the yellow light from the eyes of the wolf creature gave it illumination. On its haunches the creature waited not thirty feet away.

"Sparrow . . . I'm sorry, Sparrow."

Mance aimed the gun, closed his eyes tightly, and squeezed. The first shot ricocheted off a far wall; the boy's hands jerked. The next two shots hit something solid, and there was a thunk as something heavy thudded to the floor.

"Sparrow," Mance whispered as lowered the gun. "Sparrow . . . I had to."

Through the sting of tears, he looked for the eyes of the wolf creature and did not see them. The deed was done.

The .38 dropped from his fingers.

And for a score of minutes Mance stood in the darkness, the silence of it broken only by his low sobbing.

Sparrow heard the shots.

Back inside the sleeping area, he passed among the restless bodies of his burdens; he was bidding them an unspoken good-bye. Unfinished business awaited him. They sensed it; a few clutched at him, and he touched them warmly.

He knew what a coward had to do.

For an indeterminable ticking of seconds, he thought of Mance and admired his courage: perhaps he had faced the Final Chaos without running. Perhaps he had discovered a stronger form of the living dark.

He would need it in the neverwhere.

Had those shots destroyed the Final Chaos?

Sparrow doubted it.

"Go back to your room and sleep. You need rest."

It was Twylla; her hands were warm.

He reached out to touch her cheek, and she kissed at the corner of his mouth, and the tingling sensation there was more than he had felt for hours.

"Take care of my burdens," he told her. He paused, then added, "Don't let the bastards out there get ya."

At a glance, she read the pages of the unfinished business he had in mind. There was no point in trying to stop him, though she was tempted to.

He entered his small cell like a prisoner and closed the darkness in with him.

Before he lifted the revolver and wormed the barrel into his ear, before he pulled the trigger and decorated the walls with blood and flecks of brain tissue, before the Final chaos claimed another victim, before the living dark pulled him down into a cold embrace, he had one last thought: *dingledo-die fuck.*

4

Mance shivered as he sat in the front seat of Detective Stewart's big black Ford sedan.

I killed Sparrow.

And for that he was deeply sorry.

Admitting the murder had been deceptively simple. When he had confessed to Stewart, it reminded him of an incident back in the seventh grade, in Mr. Edmiston's history class, when he had been suspected of cheating.

Suffering the pangs of a guilty conscience, he had gone, voluntarily, to Edmiston, a kindly bachelor with a stern face veneering a warm, rich sense of humor, and he had said, "I cheated on your test."

At the time he had feared being kicked out of school. Instead, Mr. Edmiston had offered him a chance to redeem himself: "You'll want, I'm sure," he said, "to take another exam to demonstrate to yourself that you're capable of doing well without cheating."

Mance had agreed.

Strangely, taking that second exam was like taking Stewart to Sparrow's body—to demonstrate to himself what he was capable of doing.

In a way the analogy seemed trivial, even absurd. But for the boy it worked.

"Here," he said, as the big Ford eased by the old hotel. Two SPD squad cars accompanied them.

Stewart had been sober and deep in thought during the ride; Mance imagined that he was trying to decide what charges would be filed against the boy.

Will they go easy on me?

"Show me where the body is," said Stewart, and it struck Mance as a ridiculously unnecessary remark. But it had the ring of police procedure, so he gave it no further thought.

One of the accompanying officers, his regulation flashlight tipped in red like the end of a huge cigarette, entered the hotel first. Stewart stepped aside for Mance to go in front of him.

The silence and dusty darkness had curiously been cleansed of threat.

"He's back there," said Mance. "I shot him twice."

The investigation took but ten minutes.

And left Mance emotionally deflated.

243

There was no sign of Sparrow's body. No blood.

Only a large punching bag heaped on the floor with stuffing leaking out from two sizable bullet holes.

Twylla cradled Sparrow's head in her lap, unmindful of the blood oozing onto her robe, but she knew, of course, that he was dead. That he wanted it that way. She did not cry, though she held him lovingly and embraced her own regret that she was never able to return his affection.

She kissed his bloody forehead once and whispered, "The demons won't haunt you no more, sweet Sparrow."

Chapter Twelve

1

And no demons haunted Mance, either.

He was free of them.

A week after the death of Sparrow, he felt that a tremendous weight had been lifted from his shoulders. The world was bright and shining; the future was clear and bursting with possibilities. The wolf man was dead.

Yes, it had been embarrassing to lead Detective Stewart to the old hotel only to find a bullet-riddled punching bag instead of the body of Sparrow. But the next day Mance had learned of Sparrow's suicide—and the boy had felt redeemed. In fact, things had worked out perfectly: there would be no murder charge, though Stewart had confiscated the boy's .38—*I won't need it no more*—and North Street was safe again.

Which meant, best of all, Jonella was safe.

And, yes, Mance had experienced many moments of regret about the death of Sparrow. The living dark, such a positive force in some ways, had turned the man into a monster, a monster which had needed to be stopped. Sparrow had not been responsible for his acts—the violence within had been directed outward—the man who had been kind to the homeless had been driven to kill.

It was a strange and sad world sometimes, and sometimes

it deeply confused Mance. But on this particular spring afternoon, it was a hopeful world. His broken arm felt as good as new, and while he hadn't given up his paper route, he had designs on more manly work; in particular, he had talked with Slow Eddie some about becoming a "raker," knowing the black man was shorthanded because Punch continued to absent himself from Soldier. Rumor had it that he was in Birmingham drowning his sorrows daily over the death of Fast Track. No one knew whether he would return.

Primary in Mance's thoughts, however, was the upcoming Soldier Spring Festival, a two-day wingding featuring local arts-and-crafts displays, a barbecue, various fund-raising activities, country-western music, a syrup-sopping, and a ragtag carnival. He had never missed attending one of these motley affairs, and for the past two years Jonella had accompanied him and they had had a bitchin' time there.

From his vantage point in a corner at Scarlett's, the boy waited patiently for Jonella to take her afternoon break so that he could offer her a glass of iced tea and pop the question: wanna go to the festival with me?

What if she turned him down? He had to consider that possibility, but lately she had acted friendlier to him, though he had noticed a pattern of one day friendly and the next day cold. Women—who could figure 'em?

Curling onto his shoulder, Sting sniffed the air, sorting through the good smells of Scarlett's buffet. Mance absently stroked the rat as Jonella came into view; she filled the tight skirt of her uniform in delicious ways. A stray lock of hair spiraled down to touch softly at one eyebrow. God, she looked sexy. Picking up some empty plates from one of the tables, she caught his glance and flashed him a smile. Warmth smoldered around the boy's heart as he smiled back and gestured for her to join him. She shook her head, but a few minutes later, wiping her hands on her shapely hips and brushing back the unruly lock, she approached his table.

"You want me?" she purred.

What a question.

"Too much," he said, feeling as if he were being microwaved. Then he regained some composure. "It's 'bout your break time, isn't it?"

She looked over her shoulder at the central dining area.

"Yeah, I think maybe it is. OK if I sit here?"

"Sure. Yeah, I was gone ask you to."

She sat, and having propped her elbows on the table, she leaned forward, smelling of some wonderful mixture of cinnamon-scented perfume and sweat.

"You really look terrific," he added.

She rolled her eyes.

"Look a mess, you mean—and I know it."

She wiped her fingertips at a sheen of sweat along her hairline. "It gets downright hot in here."

"Want some iced tea?"

"No, I'll be fine," she said, wrinkling her nose and fanning herself.

God, I still love her, Mance thought. Has she really quit loving me?

Then she said, "I heard you tried to shoot Sparrow."

Uncomfortable with the topic, Mance shrugged. "Yeah, well . . . turned out he done himself in . . . so, no more wolf man."

"You had to be pretty brave to try that," she persisted.

Were her eyes inviting him to keep caring for her?

"Yeah . . . or pretty stupid."

They both laughed nervously; it was a good moment. Mance felt giddy locking into Jonella's gaze. He watched as she bit at her lip and a mischievous glint twinkled in one of those beautiful eyes.

"You going to the festival?" she asked. "You and Mr. Sting?"

And she giggled softly and Mance dipped his shoulder so that she could reach out and stroke Sting's head.

"I was . . . but maybe only if . . . if you would go with me."

She smiled a seemingly neutral smile, and for a treacherous string of heartbeats Mance had no idea what she was going to say. A clatter of dishes and other restaurant noises pulled her attention away from him, but when she spun back she said, "I'd like to, yeah. Maybe this year you'll win me a stuffed toy."

In a sudden rush of movement she was up, smiling over her shoulder as she gave him a sweet little wave and returned to work.

Mance sat back feeling as if the gods had just issued him a fresh and sinless soul. The floor disappeared beneath him, and for a timeless moment his feet rested upon a layer of clouds.

"Well, ain't love grand?"

Lost in warm projections, Mance failed to notice Bridgette Settleford chuckling at him a few feet away. He was thinking of his futile efforts at last year's festival to win Jonella a stuffed animal—this year, he vowed, would be different.

"Hey, you plan on comin' back from the twilight zone anytime soon?"

Puffing at a cigarette, Bridgette sat down across from him and cackled raucously.

Embarrassed, Mance waved away a cloud of her smoke. "Don't you know those firesticks are killing you? Damn, no fresh air anywhere."

"Some nice perfume just sittin' here," Bridgette countered. "Looks like you and Miss Jonella gone get back together. Good goin' friend. But, hey, don't worry about my health—I mean, I don't have a whole notebook of things to look forward to 'fore I die—just a good cigarette and a good mystery . . . and a friendship or two." She hesitated. "Has Thestis been down?"

Mance shook his head. "You expecting him?"

Bridgette offered a shy yet knowing smile. "We have a date if you want to know all the poop. You see, Thestis loves a mystery, too."

"No more mysteries on North Street," said the boy.

"That so?"

248

Mance shrugged. "The wolf man's dead. It's the end of your story. All the newspaper people and the other freaks can get outta town."

"You sure about that?"

"What are you sayin'? Sparrow's dead. Blew his brains out. Why won't you believe he was the wolf man?"

Bridgette puffed thoughtfully, then cocked her cigarette hand against her temple. "Sad case, wasn't it? I hear that Twylla's gone try to keep his shop open so all the ole derelicts have a place to go. And Tanya—you know, I suppose, that she and her two little girls moved in with Twylla at the safe house—well, she's gone help out."

"Tanya moved in with . . . ? Hadn't heard that. Not surprised, I guess. None of my business no ways."

"Sparrow . . . very strange, very sad case," Bridgette continued. "Yes, he was a suspect. Even Detective Stewart admitted that. But . . . Sparrow wasn't the killer. Stewart agrees with me. Our wolf man is still out there somewhere—that's what I believe. And I'm not typing thirty at the bottom of my story until I find out who it is."

Mance smiled, though he couldn't mask his frustration with the woman.

"Believe whatever the hell you want. Sparrow's dead, and there won't be no more murders. You'll see."

2

Mance couldn't understand what they saw in each other. Uncle Thestis had some class, some dignity to him; Bridgette Settleford, on the other hand, was rude, crude, brash, obnoxious, and smoked too much. And why did she continue to insist that the wolf man was on the loose? Just to stir up more interest in her news stories? Probably.

Lingering to watch Jonella's mouth-watering body negotiate the dining area, the boy noticed Kelton Austin and Adele Taylor together. They were laughing over big glasses of iced tea garnished with a sprig of mint, and they seemed a perfect couple. The sight of them sent Mance on a slingshot trip into an imaginary future: yes, of course, he would be married to Jonella—there would never be anyone else for him. And they wouldn't live in a mobile home; they would have a real house and real grass that he would mow on weekends. All day he would work hard (at a good, high-paying job), his thoughts always on what awaited him that evening: a good supper, some quiet moments with his Jonella before retiring to the bedroom where she, in her evolving sexiness, would cause him to thank his lucky stars that he was a man and had married her.

Children? Yes. How many? Two or three. A son or two to roughhouse with. Maybe a girl, too, one as beautiful as Jonella, and when she became a teenager he would have to beat the boys away. One day, when his children were old enough, he would tell them the strange tale of the spring of 1990, when the living dark came to Soldier. His narrative would touch upon Boom Browner and Fast Track and a most peculiar man named Sparrow. Perhaps he would also mention the silver bullets.

Yeah, it would be a good life.

But it was time to get started on his paper route.

North Street was quiet; not even patrol cars cruised it any longer. Pedaling past Austin's, the boy drank in the peacefulness. At what was once Fast Track's lounge, he slowed; it was vacant, the bar and floor gathering dust. The neon beer-ads had lost their jangle. A large real estate placard in the front window announced that the property was for sale. Mance missed Fast Track. He missed Punch. Would he ever come back to Soldier?

A heaviness on his heart, the boy pedaled on before stopping again, this time at Sparrow's. Through the window he could see a few old men—Sparrow's burdens—and a sudden stab of sorrow took his breath away. There had been no service for him; Twylla shunned any kind of military funeral, opting instead for cremation and a very private ceremony.

I'm sorry, Sparrow . . . you had to be stopped.

He pushed on and completed the route—it was time to put all the horrors behind him, time to wipe the slate clean and get on with his life. Time to win back Jonella. And yet one task dangled threateningly above him like the sword of Damocles: He had to make things right with Uncle Thestis.

It was not a task he relished; the necessary words would be hard to find.

Later that evening he found a pleasant diversion: walking Jonella home from work. The old apartment house where she lived seemed very empty with Tanya and the girls no longer on the first floor. Adele Taylor still occupied one of the upstairs rooms, but to Mance the building seemed haunted. On the walk, Jonella chattered on and on about how Adele and Austin had taken her under their wings; she expressed no bitterness toward Tanya, however.

"Things change, Mance," she told him at the door. "Who knows why."

She gave his hand a warm squeeze and his cheek a soft kiss, and he wanted to grab her and hold her and take her up to her room and make love to her. But his mind flashed a warning: *go slow.*

She told him she was looking forward to the festival and then she slipped inside and the front door transformed into some magical boundary he could not cross. Aching all over emotionally, he sauntered home.

And up to Uncle Thestis's door.

When the old guy greeted him, Mance couldn't help noticing how careworn he looked. Was he losing weight? Yes, quite a lot of it.

"Guess you know why I came," said the boy.

"Of course I do," said Uncle Thestis, his overstuffed chair surrounded by several dozen jars of marbles. "To help me make a final tally. You see, I had your dad set all my jars out for me the other day—I've just been waiting for my counter to come."

"We ain't done this in a long time, have we?"

Memories began to surge through Mance's thoughts.

"No, no we haven't. And I regret that. But why

251

don't you and I have a final reckoning?"

And so they did.

It took hours as Mance, sprawled on the floor, counted and Thestis, pocket calculator in hand, recorded the count, interrupting the proceedings occasionally to mark the moment they reached the one thousand, two thousand, and three thousand plateaus. During the process, he talked about life, about finding the center of one's self and clinging to it, and he touched upon a score of other topics. Mance listened, feeling years younger . . . and liking the feeling.

Marbles finally all counted, the boy yawned and stretched.

Uncle Thestis winced in pain.

Mance studied him.

"I took your cup, your silver one," he said, knowing full well that his companion was aware of the fact.

"Yes, well . . . there comes a point when our trophies at last we lay down. I'm rapidly approaching that point, and, furthermore, I believe you never would have taken that cup without a very, very good reason."

It was the opening Mance needed. He recounted everything from the theft to the instant he fired at the wolf creature, mortally wounding the punching bag. At the end of his story he waited for Thestis to respond.

The old guy laughed.

"Nailed that punching bag, did you? Oh, my . . . that's a good tale."

"You forgive me?"

"Course I do. You thought you were doing what you had to do. Hard to fault that. This makes better sense to me than when you quit school."

Would his uncle ever let that go?

"Least now the wolf man's gone," Mance followed.

Thestis raised his eyebrows.

"Bridgette Settleford doesn't think so."

"You feel like she's right?"

Frowning through a stab of pain, Thestis said, "I'm leaning that way, yes. You know, they say the past is a ghost which always comes back to haunt us. Could be that wolf man is one such ghost."

"I don't understand none of that."

"Oh, I can't say it's very clear to me either. But soon . . . soon it may need to be. I'm worried, and I want you to do something for me."

Mance shrugged. "Sure. What?"

Thestis leaned back in his chair and drummed his fingers on the armrest. "Stay out of Guillo House by yourself."

"Guillo—? That where this ghost is you're talking about?"

"Could be. Could be the house itself is what created the ghost in the first place. . . . I just can't say for certain."

3

Today she was definitely Jonella.

Or was she "Miss X" instead?

Her mirror ruled out Johnnie. The difference was the face—Johnnie had a peach-smooth face and pillowy, pouty lips, and a mischievous glint in one eye. Johnnie was heart-breakingly close to being a little girl again, and it was John-nie, of course, who liked Mance. He was nice enough, but not a man—he was still too interested in juvenile pursuits. But so was Johnnie. Imagine looking forward, for instance, to a hokey local festival?

Johnnie wore just a touch of makeup: petal pink lipstick and corn silk blue eye shadow and an apricot blush. It kept her face fresh and innocent, and she had the body to match: a teasing combination of curves and sharp angles, and every move that body made spoke of inexperience and sexual insecurity.

On the other hand, there was Jonella, and as the girl in the mirror smiled, she became Jonella, no question about it. The face was harder, more mature, the lips thinner, re-strained, the eyes wary and penetrating, better able to see the whole of reality than the eyes of Johnnie. No little girl here. An emerging woman. A woman who longed for the right kind of man and who pictured herself in an expensive restaurant or dinner theatre in Atlanta rather than at the Soldier McDonald's.

She wore magenta lipstick and matching eye shadow and a ripe and dark blush; every blemish had been discreetly hidden. The face spoke of one who knew the ropes, whose innocence had been torn away from her. A sensual body added to the impression, sexy in a comfortably experienced way—soft and seemingly accessible, and yet a body secure, feeling no real need to have most men desire it.

Jonella admired her image. She stood before the mirror clad in a white half slip and a new Lace Sofistique soft cup bra, also white, with a blossoming rose filigreed delicately on each cup. She inspected her cleavage and smiled: *Miss X would not approve.*

Which was true.

In recent days Jonella had become aware of a third personality, a hidden observer, an older woman, rather a combination of her mother and Adele Taylor, and this personality did not particularly like Jonella, finding her cold and aggressive, favoring the warm innocence of Johnnie instead.

Miss X was schoolteacherish and independent, wanting what was best for both Jonella and Johnnie, but wanting, most of all, for the two personalities to get along—she had to ride herd on them the way a mother rides herd on two sisters who can't ever seem to keep from fighting.

Buttoning the blouse of her Scarlett's uniform, she wished she could stay home and lounge on her bed and read and listen to music and write down all those projections about the future, about being a powerful, strong-willed woman and getting whatever she desired. Or go to Guillo House and just sit and think by herself. The wish caused her stomach muscles to coil: she wanted fierceness, she wanted to open herself to some wild force which would make her free.

Not like Momma.

Not like Johnnie, either.

If Johnnie were to take the day off, she would waste it watching soap operas or shopping at the mall or mooning over Mance or some such mindless activity. In contrast, Jonella wanted to improve her mind; she had plans to go to summer school and get back on track for graduation in a couple of years. Maybe sooner.

Even Miss X applauded her for that.

Suddenly she glanced at her watch and saw that it was ten till eleven. She was scheduled all week except Friday for the eleven-to-seven shift so she had a shot at tips from both the lunch and dinner hours. She finished preparing herself and then descended the stairs in a clipped, womanly pace.

At the front door she experienced a curious dizziness. Something was wrong. She lingered on the porch, realizing she would be late but feeling powerless to move.

I am the center of a circle of fear exceeding its boundaries in all directions.

She had no idea where that line had come from. Something she had read? Clutching at her purse, she wondered why, suddenly, she felt so apprehensive. In one ear she could hear the voice of Miss X cautioning her that she should inform Dr. Colby of these recurring episodes of panic and an altered sense of self.

But, no, she told herself, she would be all right. It was a bright, pleasant spring morning. Alabama was exploding green; the azaleas and dogwoods were blooming and why on earth should a young woman be frightened?

She walked toward Scarlett's whistling softly.

Until she noticed the cloud.

It appeared to be the only one in the sky. At first blush it displayed no peculiar features—just a billowy, rounded cloud, white with a gray underbelly and shaped like nothing in particular. Except perhaps . . . a face.

Yes, a face. The face of an old man with hoary eyebrows and puffy cheeks and angry wrinkles on his forehead. A face from some painting she had seen? Yes. Michelangelo's Sistine Chapel.

It was the face of God. Michelangelo's God.

Jonella lowered her head and quickened her pace.

A small, black terrier barked at her. Or was it warning her?

She looked up, hoping her angle on the cloud would change its countenance, but it did not. The cloud was following her. God was following her. God wanted to punish her. But why?

Then she heard God's voice.

Thou let those men rape you. Thou shalt not let men rape you.

"No," she cried. "No, it wasn't my fault."

She tried to run, but her low heels clopped unsteadily and tossed her off-balance. She nearly fell. And behind her the terrier barked again, and she thought she heard words embedded in the barks—words echoing the cloud-God's angry denunciation.

"Please, no—none of this is my fault," she said aloud, not caring whether anyone heard her—in fact, not being aware of anyone else on the street.

She hurried on and the cloud-God kept pace; she pressed her hands to her ears so that she wouldn't be able to hear further denunciations. God had singled her out on this fine spring morning. He was going to punish her for her sin unless she could do something to redeem herself. A welling of tears smudged her mascara.

At the back door of Scarlett's, Miss X attempted to calm her.

And once inside, Jonella could no longer see or hear the cloud-God or the terrier.

"I'm safe," she whispered to herself.

Miss X agreed, but cautioned her again to see Dr. Colby.

"I'll be all right," Jonella told herself. "I'm strong. I know who I am. Tomorrow I'll be better. I'll make it through today, and tomorrow I'll be better."

Jonella was an hour into the shift when Scarlett O'Hara spoke to her.

It caused her to drop a plate filled with chicken-fried steak, mashed potatoes and gravy, and green beans. The crash brought tears to her eyes and Mance's mother to the rescue.

"Heavens, sweetheart, this ain't nothin' to get teary 'bout," she said, patting the girl's wrist. "You shoulda seen how many plates I dropped in my hash-slinging days—oh, Lordy." She surveyed Jonella's face. "Sweetheart, is somethin' eatin' at you? Bad cramps? A fight with Mance?"

Jonella shook her head and jutted her chin and got a, by God, hold of herself and worked another half hour before she started thinking about what the portrait of Scarlett O'Hara above the fake mantel had said to her. But, no, of course, the portrait hadn't spoken—that was only a creaky motif from some old Gothic novel you would find in Uncle Thestis's collection of weird books.

They want to break you down.

Yes, those were Scarlett's words spoken as clearly as the noonday sun shines.

They?

Jonella glanced around.

What secret information did Scarlett have access to?

I know their thoughts.

Jonella gasped. There. Yes. Scarlett was speaking to her again. And as Jonella moved from table to table, from customer to customer, she listened. Scarlett told her about the bearded man in the plaid workshirt.

He wants to put his hands all over your body. He wants to be rough with you and force his manhood on you and hurt you, press you down and hurt you and make you feel dirty just to satisfy himself.

Jonella blinked; she turned her face away as she refilled the man's iced tea glass and then moved to the next table where two elderly women, silver-blue hair and dressed to the nines, sat mired in sotto voce conversation until she neared, at which point they fell suspiciously silent.

They hate you. They know you're wearing your prettiest

257

underwear and they're envious of you and are watching for you to make a mistake. They want to see you lose your job. Lose your mind.

Jonella could barely breathe. Her stomach roiled.

She fought to make it through the afternoon. When Kelton Austin and Adele Taylor came in toward the dinner hour for a piece of peanut pie, Scarlett's voice, which had not uttered a word for several hours, materialized again.

Don't trust them. They ask how you are, but they want you to lose your mind. Don't trust them.

It took every ounce of her mental energy to survive without screaming until her shift ended. Drained, she said good night to Mance's mother, who advised her to get some rest and drink prune juice. Mance was near the register and asked if he could walk her home; she hesitated, let her eyes meet Scarlett's, and the proud southern beauty spoke into her thoughts.

He'll bring you down.

"I'd like to walk home alone," Jonella told him.

Mance and his mother exchanged looks of mild surprise, and Jonella released herself, feeling like a balloon floating directionless into a threatening sky.

Lost.

She felt tethered to the candle she had placed in front of her. Shadows paraded across the wall every time she moved; she sat on the pallet with her back against the wall and thought about Eleanor.

Eleanor had loved and feared this room.

Loved and feared Guillo House.

Jonella wondered, most of all, what remained from those days and nights in which the delicate sadness of Eleanor wafted through this room like a fine perfume. Was it a dark force? Guillo House's resident ghost?

Whatever walks here walks alone.

Lost.

And its voice spoke to her, and, at first, she fought it.

258

"Why do you say I'm lost?"

Lost.

But she knew she was. She had lost herself. Somehow in the tragic events of the winter, the mirror of self had shattered.

"What can I do? Help me. What can I do?"

Her shoulders heaved with the ache of her heart.

Come home.

"Come home? But where *is* my home?"

Come home.

"Where?"

She waited. But neither the voice nor the presence of the darkly seductive force returned. Exhaustion prodded at her. She relaxed her body; she felt a warm fullness in her stomach. And then it happened, though it could easily have been a trick of her imagination: silver threads began to emerge from her stomach and extend into the shadows as if they were seeking something to entwine.

Jonella closed her eyes and lapsed into sleep, and when she woke—she had no idea how long she'd slept—the silver threads had disappeared and panic touched at her like pinpricks. She looked down at her body, the candlelight bathing it in a golden glow, and felt that something was wrong: she imagined that her blood had turned to electric current and was pulsing through her veins.

Not mine, she thought.

My body is not mine.

I don't exist.

There is no me.

4

"I'm glad you're who you are."

It was hard for Mance to know what to expect from Johnnie these days. She was liable to say the damnedest things. There they were tossing pieces of bread into the duck pond at the center of the city park, site of the Soldier Festival, when Johnnie up and said, "Mance, do you ever get tired of being who you are? I sure do. I don't think I like Jonella anymore."

She was breathtakingly beautiful, wearing a yellow sun dress dotted with small daisies; it clung to her body like a comfortable glove, and the low scoop of the neckline hinted at the promise of softly mounded breasts, and if you were close and happened to catch a glance at the right angle you could see the rose tattoo above her left breast. And Mance was proud and happy and absolutely delighted to be with her; they had come over in his dad's van, Mance having cleaned the interior so that his queen would ride in relative cleanliness if not in luxury.

"I mean," he continued, "I wouldn't want you to be nobody else because . . . because I like the somebody you are."

She looked at him, her expression warmly bemused; then both of them laughed at his bumbling efforts to follow her line of thought. She reached for his hand, and the contact sent a silken ribbon of ecstasy flowing through him. Hand in hand, they strolled through the arts-and-crafts area, stopping here and there to examine duck decoys, and macrame displays, and a local artist's attempts to capture the dispossessed aura of Alabama landscapes.

With Johnnie by his side, there was no one else at the festival. The whole affair seemed to have been laid out solely for them. The sights, the sounds, the smells—everything seemed to be in league to bring his girl back to him.

"I want popcorn," she suddenly announced. "Doesn't it smell great?"

It did, and so did she—that ever so seductive scent of cinnamon and something else; Mance tried to find words—*so do you,* he wanted to say—but applause nearby created too much static.

"What's going on over there?" Johnnie asked after Mance had brought her a tub of popcorn and a soft drink for each of them.

"A storyteller, I guess. He was here last year, remember?

260

From Goldsmith College."

They pushed their way to the inside of a semicircle formed near a tall, mustached, blond man sitting on a stool on a makeshift stage. At the man's feet were a half dozen fuzzy yellow ducklings, his ploy being that the kids in the crowd would be entertained by the ducks while he told his story to the adults.

"I have a tale for you that I like to call 'Tender Haunting'—it's set during the War Between the States, and it's about a young Confederate surgeon and his love for a nurse whom he meets at a field hospital."

Mance asked Johnnie if she wanted to stay around to hear it, and she nodded that she did. The storyteller, dark circles under his eyes, retrieved an escaping duckling or two and launched into the tale. And a marvelous tale it was—a tale of hospital horrors and pathetic cases, and yet a tale of the evolving love of the surgeon for the angelic nurse who stayed by his side during the most difficult situations. It was a tale of unrequited love, and a ghost story as well. For, in the end, the surgeon discovered that his lovely helper was but an apparition, the wife perhaps of some soldier who had fallen in battle, perhaps a soldier that very surgeon had tried gallantly but unsuccessfully to mend.

Tender Haunting.

The tale having been told, Johnnie pressed her head against Mance's shoulder, and he slipped his arm around her small waist and held her and wished that the storyteller had a dozen more such stories. But the man gathered up his ducks and waved, and the crowd applauded and slowly bled away to other diversions.

"Wanna see what's at the carnival?" Mance whispered to Johnnie.

In response she took hold of his forearm and gently turned it until the fang tattoo appeared; then she raised the arm and planted a soft, warm kiss there. An imaginary feather tickled the boy's groin, and an involuntary shiver raced up his spine.

Love, indeed, was grand.

It could have been the colored lights or the bouncy music or the sheen of the horses, or perhaps the touch of Mance as he sat behind her, his arms holding her snugly. She was a little girl again, and her mother was telling her, "You don't have to be rich to be happy, you just have to like yourself. You have to find your happiness inside."

Up and down the merry-go-round horses pranced, frozen in their timeless gallop, and she thought that she did like herself—not Jonella, but Johnnie—and she thought that she loved Mance and would one day marry him, and she would never end up like Momma and she *would* find her happiness inside.

She felt Mance's lips against her ear and his hands sliding from her stomach closer to her breasts, and then she happened to look over her shoulder and noticed that they were being followed. Foaming-mouthed horses mounted by adults as well as kids were right behind them and, yes, closing in.

Bring you down.

Stifling a shriek, she shut her eyes, hoping they would go away.

Mance must have felt her body tensing because he whispered, "What's wrong?"

Through clenched teeth she said, "I have to get off. Please, I have to get off."

"Johnnie?"

She struggled, tearing his arms away from her as if they were kudzu vines. "Mance, please."

Fortunately the ride was easing to a stop when he swung off, nearly crashing to his knees as he reached for her, lifting her free as their horse descended in its mechanical rhythm.

"Hey, you OK?"

He pulled her to one side as laughing children bumped them and boinged away like pinballs.

For a moment she bent over, then began nodding, her eyes blinking rapidly.

"God, you were freaking out, Johnnie."

The world spun a three-quarter turn; she clutched at Mance's wrist, tasted salty, bitter popcorn in the back of her mouth, but then felt better.

"I think I got dizzy," she explained.

"Yeah . . . yeah, that was probably it," said Mance, not really convinced.

Behind her the merry-go-round pulsed to life again; this time, however, Johnnie felt fine. She smiled at the thrum of the lilting music. Taking Mance's hand, she said,

"OK, Fang, time to win me something."

The dart game had a deceptively easy cast to it: six burst balloons in a row and you won a big prize. At Mance's side Johnnie drooled over inordinately large stuffed bears and elephants and dogs.

Mance blew five bucks, never popping more than four balloons at a stretch.

"Let's try the milk bottles—I'm better at that."

Johnnie's touch eased his frustration; to Mance she seemed like a beautiful and delicate butterfly, and he couldn't imagine loving her more.

At the milk bottle booth Mance took a deep breath and fingered his wallet.

"Try your luck, son. Win the little lady a nice prize . . . yes, sir, a *nice* prize."

The greasy attendant slid his eyes up and down Johnnie as he emphasized the word "nice."

Mance plopped down some bills.

"What the f—? Hey," the attendant exclaimed, "there's a . . . there's a tail in your hair."

Eyes bulging, he pointed a cigar at Mance's shoulder.

Johnnie giggled.

"It's Sting," she said, and reached up to the back of Mance's neck for the rat. "See? He's our good luck piece."

Staring at Mance in disbelief, the attendant said, "You mean you keep a gawdamn rat in your hair? Jesus cripes

. . . they're dirty, nasty buggers."

"Not as dirty and nasty as some *people*," Mance responded.

The attendant shook his head and chomped down on his cigar. "Jesus cripes," he muttered.

"Pet Sting for luck," Johnnie suggested.

And so the boy did.

But it didn't help. Each time, he managed to topple only two of the three bottles, never a clean strike.

"So-o-o close, son. Try'er again," the attendant encouraged.

"Wait, I know," said Johnnie.

She returned Sting to his lair.

"I've got just what you need — a good luck kiss," she chortled.

"Are you serious?" said Mance, smiling sheepishly as he looked around to see whether anyone besides the attendant was watching.

"Sure, honey, give 'im a smack, a big smoocher."

And she did.

A long, full-on-the-mouth kiss with her glorious body pressed firmly against his and her tongue playfully exploring and teasing and causing his blood to rush in two directions at once.

When she had finished, the attendant murmured, "Jesus cripes," and scratched at his crotch. And Mance had trouble focusing on the milk bottles. He deflated his lungs and gripped one of the softballs and felt that he could squeeze it like a tennis ball. He imagined throwing the ball so hard that the blowby wind would sweep the bottles from their stand.

However, it failed to work that way.

Ten bucks deep into embarrassment Mance grinned miserably at a despondent Johnnie.

"Sorry, sweetheart."

But the attendant came to the rescue, motioning him over for a confidential word or two.

"Son, I just happen to have a Friday night special on my

medium-sized stuffed animals. Ten crisp green ones sets you up for a real reward—that's some kinda pretty little gal there. Make her happy, and a dime to a dollar says she'll make you happy."

He winked salaciously.

Mance dug out his wallet. Again.

But seeing Johnnie's reaction to the stuffed dog, well, he thought maybe it really was worth the twenty dollars total he had buried in those milk bottles.

"I'm gone name him Stubby," she said as they strolled away.

She pressed a wet, joyous kiss onto his cheek, and he wondered when he had ever seen her quite so happy.

They meandered through the carnival as if it were faintly unreal, like a movie set or an illusion, and eventually they ended up on a picnic bench under the park pavilion, where a yellow bug light burned dimly. Twilight had transformed to night with seductive rapidity.

Johnnie hugged at the stuffed dog and cooed to it as if it were a baby.

"You wanna have kids someday?" Mance asked her. The combination of darkness and the yellow spray of the bug light gave her what to him was an angelic glow. His question came out of nowhere; and, of course, there was no chance to retrieve it.

"Kids? I hope so, yes. I'll settle for Stubby right now."

"You'll be a good mother."

"How do you know that?"

"Oh . . . I just feel like you will be. I guess you got good practice taking care of Crystal and Loretta."

"Two little darlings," said Johnnie, but she said it with an air of regret, and Mance took it that she preferred not to talk about them, or, inevitably, about Tanya.

"Lot's happened in the last couple of months," he followed. "You know, bad stuff."

Then he chuckled nervously at the understatement. "But everything's gone be better. . . . I mean, the killings will stop. The wolf man's dead, and it sounds kinda funny, you know, but I'm real sorry Sparrow's gone. And I miss Fast Track, too, and who knows if Punch'll ever come back. One good thing is that Uncle T. and I, we, we're friends again, and I hope he doesn't get any sicker."

He heard Johnnie stifle a sob.

"Oh, Jesus, I'm sorry," he said. "Shouldn't be talking about all that stuff. I'm sorry, Johnnie."

She was rocking gently, the dog crushed to her breasts.

"Mance?"

"Yeah?"

"Do you think . . . do you think I've changed?"

He was relieved, realizing that she hadn't even been listening to his downbeat review of Soldier's darkest weeks.

"Changed? Well, yeah, . . . some. You couldn't help but change some, Johnnie. I mean . . . look at all . . . I've changed some, too, except . . . I ain't changed how I feel about you."

Blinking away the birth of a tear, she forced a smile.

In the distance a country-western band had cranked up.

"You know what I would like?" she said, leaning her head toward him until it rested against his shoulder.

"What would you like, sweet Johnnie?"

"To dance."

"You're kidding?"

"No. A slow dance. Dance a real slow dance and just not think anymore tonight."

"Right here?"

She shook her head. "They got a band over at the bandstand."

"But it's that damn redneck music."

"So? You can't slow dance to Metallica."

Mance grinned. "You got me there."

The band played every tear-jerking, cheating-hearted, down-and-out tune it could muster, and Mance choked back his repulsion at the music because he was holding the woman he loved as closely as the rhythm of his own breathing.

He held Johnnie; Johnnie held Stubby.

"I love you so much," he told her.

"Momma used to love to dance," she told him.

By the time the band called out "last dance" Mance actually began to feel that country-western music was tolerable.

Thank you, Randy Travis.

Moonlight followed them to Johnnie's apartment house.

They sat in the porch swing, and she kissed him eagerly and told him that she wished she could take him upstairs with her because her bed seemed so empty some nights.

Mance felt the deepest ache he would ever feel in his life.

"But I think I'm gone save myself for Mr. Right," she teased.

"Any chance that could be me?"

"A chance. A chance it's Mance." And she laughed at the rhyme and touched his nose with the tip of her finger and enjoyed the fact that she had aroused him so much that he had to keep repositioning himself in the swing so that his jeans wouldn't cut off his circulation.

"Johnnie, you're the only thing I want in the whole world," he said, hating it that his tone sounded so melodramatic. But, damn it all . . . he had to say what he had to say.

"The world's a big place. How do you know there isn't something—or someone—better out there?"

She kissed his throat.

He felt miserable and happy, deliriously happy, all in the same breath.

And he held her until he knew that he must leave.

Far into the night.

Chapter Thirteen

1

After he had said good night to her, he decided he could not go home—too much adrenaline (and whatever else) was pumping to calm down enough for sleep. The unfocused nature of life had, as a result of one long, wonderful evening with the woman he loved, clicked into focus.

Ripping out an imitation of the soul singer, James Brown, he moonwalked a few feet and exclaimed, "I feel good."

Sting stirred.

"Know what I'm sayin', little buddy? I feel *good*."

He felt that he could run a mile in under four minutes, that he could high jump seven feet or clean and jerk a thousand-pound weight. Or swim across Catlin County Lake and back and challenge the gators and snapping turtles and cottonmouth moccasins with his bare hands.

He felt good.

Afraid of nothing.

Not even Guillo House.

And I want you to do something for me.

The memory of Uncle Thestis's request came unbidden like a sudden spring shower.

Stay out of Guillo House.

It seemed a challenge, and in his feeling-on-top-of-the-world mood no challenge was going to be left unmet.

"Gone take a different way home, Sting. May have to do some ghostbusting."

He grinned. Johnnie's good night kiss lingered on his lips like the touch of something pleasantly warm on a cold winter's day.

Nothing could have kept him away from Guillo House.

There was the hint of a chill in the air as he bounced up the front steps to the old mansion and found his approach slowed suddenly. He recalled the night that Sparrow had first appeared to him as the wolf creature; that night, in anguish, the boy had cried out for help. For solace. And the wolf creature had appeared.

But with Sparrow gone, Guillo House was haunted only by its own history, its own disrepair, and its own resident pigeons. Atop the roof, they were cooing in a deep-throated chorus, their outlines nebulous against the moonless night.

"No ghosts here," Mance whispered.

Sting squeaked apprehensively.

"Wanna see if anybody's home?"

The boy reached around and gave the rat a calming stroke. Then he playfully knocked at the door despite the all-too-evident fact that the door to Guillo House had not been locked for years and no inhabitants greeted callers for years.

Mance was having fun.

Right up to the moment he heard the voice.

Want death, it said.

2

It took awhile to wake uncle Thestis.

Out of breath from running, Mance found the man asleep in his overstuffed chair, a book open in his lap, and the reading lamp burning. It was 3:00 A.M. But he listened to Mance's account of hearing the voice of the wolf creature.

No mistake. It was the wolf creature.

"Is it Sparrow's ghost? Is that what it is?"

Mance was shaking; he had hunkered down in front of his

Uncle and was speaking in a quietly raspy tone like that of a sinner in the confession booth.

"I wouldn't think it is."

The man's heavy-lidded eyes narrowed, then a lance of pain or perhaps a confusing thought spawned a frown.

"Tell me again about this . . . this vision you had," he continued.

"God, it was awful."

"You're sure it was Jonella you were seeing in it?"

"Yeah, it definitely was . . . and, God, she was screaming. She was in pain. There was something after her. She was upstairs . . . you know, in Guillo House, and she was screaming and crying and in pain, and then something happened . . . something weird . . . and the thing that was after her . . . disappeared."

Uncle Thestis's frown deepened.

"Anything else? Think hard, Manson, this is very important."

"I was just standing there by the door, and it was like I was having this very vivid dream . . . mostly about Johnnie . . . and Guillo House . . . and the wolf creature. God, it's come back, Uncle Thestis, the creature's come back."

He pressed forward, and his uncle took him gently by the shoulders and felt the fear coursing through him. It was like holding on to an idling engine.

Seconds passed. A minute or more.

"What else? What else do you remember?"

Mance took a deep breath, having gained a measure of control over the shaking and his mental chaos.

On the screen of memory he let the vision replay itself.

He cringed at Johnnie's torment.

"What else, Manson?" his uncle prodded.

The boy's mouth had lost most of its saliva; he licked his lips.

Yes, there was something more. He concentrated.

"Threads. There's a whole lotta threads . . . strings, you know."

"What color were they?"

270

"White or, or maybe silver. Yeah, silver. It's like they glowed in the dark."

"What did they come from?"

"From . . . I don't know. They got all wound up into one big thread and that's when Johnnie stopped screaming."

His uncle patted the boy's knee.

Mance looked into his eyes.

"What's it mean? If the voice . . . if the wolf creature isn't Sparrow, then who . . . or what is it? Where does it come from?"

On his uncle's face, the boy could read a special moment, one in which a man who thirsted for proof of something otherworldly, for a direct encounter with the unknown, was about to drink deeply.

The man allowed the suggestion of a smile to play at his lips.

"Sparrow," he said, "called it the living dark—I have no better name for it, but in time . . . soon, very soon, in fact . . . I think we may all learn where it comes from and to where it must return."

3

Mance spent the next several days thinking hard about Uncle Thestis's remarks. The central question: what was he *not* saying? The old guy had picked up the scent of something very unusual, something of which he had some knowledge—something, no doubt, from the realm of the occult.

For Mance, the most difficult part was adjusting his thinking to admit that Sparrow had not been responsible for the wolf creature, or, in turn, the murders. Something else was involved. But what? Worst of all, it continued to speak into his thoughts: *want death*. The boy could often *feel* its presence, usually at night but sometimes during the day. The darkly insistent messages typically evoked fear in him, but on occasion he heard the same plea for help from the wolf creature which he had heard weeks before.

271

Want death.

The words struck him as enigmatic.

Did the creature want death in the sense that it wanted to kill? Or did it seek death for itself? What motivated the creature? Was it simply a wild, unpredictable force which somehow had been brought to life and would continue wreaking havoc on Soldier?

Did I call it to life at Guillo House?

It was a cold thought.

By midweek, such thoughts survived to plague the boy despite a change in his work situation. Quitting his paper route, he began to sweat away his days as a raker for Slow Eddie, acquiring sore muscles and calluses and a new respect for physical labor—he had never worked this hard at Rebel Beer. But Slow Eddie was a good boss; the money was decent, and it felt like a man's job.

His relationship with Jonella remained on a feast or famine course—one day she would be affectionate and warm and the next day cold and distant. One day it would appear that she loved him, the next day that she couldn't stand to be around him. Regardless, Mance felt he would never stop loving her. In a few years, he believed, he would marry her; he had to be patient.

And yet . . . the present frightened him. What if the creature threatened Johnnie? Could there be any truth to the vision he had received several nights ago? Was Johnnie in danger?

His mind troubled, Mance went out that evening and walked down the center of the railroad tracks as he had as a small boy. Locked in thoughts of Johnnie, he was a quarter of a mile from downtown when the wolf creature spoke.

Want death.

Help me.

Want death.

Help me . . . help me . . . help me . . . find a way . . . find a way.

At that moment, Mance knew somehow with absolute certainty that the creature had killed again.

He raced to Scarlett's, but Johnnie had already finished her shift; Uncle Thestis and Bridgette Settleford were together, and, as usual, Bridgette flashed interest in what the boy was up to. He told her nothing. At Johnnie's apartment house he found, to his relief, that she was there, safe, listening to music and reading. She dismissed his concern as silly and that was that.

He left.

His wanderings brought him next to Austin's.

After hearing Mance's account, the white-haired man said, "We all have to understand that our lives are changing—this, this . . . *something* has come into our lives to frighten us, but mostly to change us. The medieval alchemists understood such changes. The period between the cutting away of the old and the growth of the new is a period of black mourning— what the alchemists called *mortificatio.*"

"I don't know what you're saying?" he confessed.

Austin smiled.

"I'm scared," the man followed, "and yet . . . excited. I can't explain, but Adele will. In a few nights you will be invited to come to Guillo House with us. Adele has a story to tell. I've come to believe it relates to your wolf creature."

"But we can't wait," said Mance. "If you know about the wolf creature, you gotta do something now before it kills again . . . I think maybe it already has."

"The time isn't right. And there's much we don't fully understand about this . . . this dark force. We would only place ourselves and others in more danger if we tried to do something without being sufficiently prepared. Please, son, you have to accept that."

But it was difficult to.

Frustrated, Mance bid Austin good night.

The darkness was calling.

Into the familiar alley the boy made his way. Sting tangled his tiny claws in Mance's long hair; the rat was alive to the boy's fears, to the change in his body chemistry.

Help me.

Find a way.

Want death.

The wolf creature was near.

Mance could sense it.

Behind him? The boy turned, but saw nothing in the dimly lit alley.

Someone following him?

He couldn't be certain.

Toward the end of the alley, where the shadows took a sharp left and angled under the overpass, Mance smelled something which burned his nostrils. He followed the putrid odor into a weed-choked plot of ground that was too far from the alley to receive illumination.

At the very heart of the odor the boy tripped over what felt like a tree root or some stray piece of trash which someone had illegally dumped beyond the alley. Holding his nose, he felt at his feet and discovered loose dirt.

And the rotting flesh of a human arm.

On his knees, Mance pitched backward. The scream rose out of his chest like a geyser, tearing from his lips with such force that it strained his neck and facial muscles. Warm vomit spilled from his mouth, and he collapsed to one side, not unconscious, but in a twilight realm of horror which numbed his senses.

He remembered nothing more until a flashlight beam speared his eyes.

He heard Bridgette Settleford as well as another familiar voice. Strong arms helped him to his feet; he couldn't quite decipher what the two of them were saying, speaking as they were in a hushed tone.

Once back in the alley, Mance pulled away from the arms which had guided him from the half-buried body. When he saw who was accompanying Bridgette he gasped in surprise.

"Punch?"

"Yeah, boy, it's me . . . looks like you found more trouble."

"Suppose I oughtta apologize for following you," said Bridgette. "Your uncle sorta tipped me off. When you came into Scarlett's like you'd been chased by all the hounds of

274

hell, he told me something was up. And I thought Punch might be interested, too."

"You came back," the boy said to Punch. "I felt like you wouldn't."

"I had to, boy. My mind won't never rest till I find out who killed Pop. I had to come back to Soldier."

For a few moments the three of them were silent; night insects and a distant tree frog belied the horror with their characteristic sounds. To them all was normal.

"Who is it?" said Mance. "Who's been buried out there?"

He was shivering as if the temperature were below freezing.

"I don't know, but I'm sure as hell not so curious as to want to dig up the body and see. From this point on Detective Stewart's in charge of this business," said Bridgette.

"It was the wolf creature," the boy muttered. "It's back . . . and somebody's got to destroy it."

Part Three:
The Living Dark

Chapter Fourteen

1

The body was that of Rollo.

But only one thought pulsed through Mance's mind: *it might have been Johnnie.* Even as Detective Stewart questioned him, visions of her in pain, being attacked by the creature, made it difficult to follow what he was saying.

Rollo had been savaged.

And though Stewart retained his suspicions, and though he grilled the boy for several hours, he knew, intuitively, that he was not confronting a psychopathic killer.

With just the two of them alone in his office, Stewart, weary from weeks and weeks of coming up empty on the case, asked, "What's out there? Your story sounds crazy as all hell — even the psychiatrist the state brought in to talk to you says it's crazy. But you know more about this killer than anybody else does. How, I can't say. It's beyond me. But you do. Between you and me, son — throw out the police business — between you and me, I have to know what's going on."

There was pleading in his eyes.

And Mance was tempted to tell him everything.

Stewart reluctantly accepted the silence. He sat down on the edge of his desk and rubbed his jaw. He looked old and deeply troubled.

Feeling genuinely sorry for him, Mance straightened himself in his chair.

"I only got one thing more to say," he said.

"I'll take it," said Stewart, his interest pricked.

"Well . . . I feel like . . . like it's 'bout over."

2

Several days later Mance was still not certain why he had expressed such a view to Stewart. Perhaps he merely wanted to offer the man some hope. Or could it have been that the boy sincerely believed that the end was in sight?

Regardless, when the weekend rolled around, Soldier had returned to its former state of chaos: a fresh wave of officers cruising and coat-and-tie fellows snooping, of newspaper types and morbidity-inclined curiosity seekers. The situation reminded Mance of flies being drawn to a fresh road kill.

But when Saturday night arrived, he forgot about everything except the promise of learning more about the wolf creature. Darkness had set in by the time he called on Johnnie.

"You ready for this?" he said as he met her at the door to her room. The hallways of the apartment building caught his voice and gave it a muffled resonance. Johnnie looked as pretty as ever, though there was a betrayal of puffiness beneath her eyes.

Has she not been sleeping well? Mance wondered.

Has she been dreaming of the wolf creature?

Taking his hand, she smiled and kissed him on the corner of his mouth. She smelled great, and in that instant of her closeness Mance wanted nothing more than to turn her around and take her to her bed and make love to her, and to forget about wolf creatures and buried bodies and Guillo House.

"Adele and Austin have gone on," she said. "They told me Uncle Thestis has been invited—do you think he'll come?"

"I sorta doubt it. He's been holed up in his room all afternoon. Didn't want to see anybody except Bridgette Settleford.

I've got no idea what he's up to. Could be he's feeling bad. Whatever sickness he's got, it's not gettin' better. My mom and dad are after him these days to see a doctor, but he won't do it."

Johnnie squeezed his hand and they started down the stairs. On the way to Guillo House, Mance noticed the approaching clouds; a cold front was moving in from the west, probably bringing rain to Montgomery right that minute.

The two of them said nothing until they reached the porch of Guillo House, at which point Johnnie tugged at him. "Are you scared?"

Suddenly he realized he was. What were Adele and Austin going to tell them? Would it lead to the destruction of the wolf creature?

"Yeah, some," he admitted. "I'm afraid of what might happen. Afraid something might hurt you."

He wanted to tell her about the vision, but he knew that it would frighten her.

"I think it's sweet that you're concerned about me. It's Adele and Austin I'm worried about—they've been very troubled about something, and I sure want things to work out for them. Did you know that they want to get married?"

"Yeah, that's what I keep hearing."

They hesitated, the long, dark stairway looming in front of them. From the second-floor bedroom the spray of lantern light encouraged them.

"They're waiting for us," said Johnnie.

Mance held her hand firmly.

"Let's go," he said.

Adele and Austin welcomed them warmly. Austin's lantern gave off a comfortable glow, causing the dusty, otherwise dreary room to seem almost hospitable. For Mance—and he hoped for Johnnie, too—it would always be a special room, but for the first time he fully realized that it had a dark history, a history Adele was about to share.

She was wearing pants and a plain blouse and sandals; Mance had never seen her so casually dressed, nor had he ever seen her face so pinched and tired. Austin appeared similarly tired and drawn. As a couple, they had covered painful miles, and their relationship was evidently destined for additional pain and suffering.

The scene was set: half the room illuminated, half besieged by shadows; Mance stood holding Johnnie's hand, and across from them stood Austin, nervous, apprehensive for Adele, who stepped forward, her gaze surveying the room before she looked directly at the boy and said, "I believe I know something about the creature, the one that has been communicating with you, the one responsible, it seems, for the deaths. It must appear unconscionable to you, but I've said nothing to the authorities about this. First, because I can't be absolutely certain that the creature is what I believe it is, and second, because . . . because I've been so deeply frightened, knowing that circumstances could force me to face the past."

She paused to reach for Austin's hand before continuing.

"This wonderful man has given me the strength and courage and support I need to put a foot in this house, this room, once again. He claims to want to marry me, and I have told him I would happily marry him if, once and for all, I could rid myself of a powerful fear—a fear that what my mother experienced in this room would somehow be revisited upon me or the people I love."

She glanced at Austin, who smiled his encouragement. Out of the corner of his eye, Mance noticed that Johnnie was totally enthralled by Adele's words. On the roof, the pigeons cooed and shuffled their delicate feet along the ridgeline, fluttering as the wind rose.

"It was a warm night," said Adele, plunging suddenly into the narrative she had come there to relate, "much like this one, only warmer, and I believe it was early summer, and a storm was approaching, heat lightning flashing on the horizon. And—"

"Wait." It was Johnnie who interrupted her. "Shouldn't we wait for Uncle Thestis? Shouldn't we see if he needs help getting here? He should hear this, too, shouldn't he?"

"I don't feel like he'll come," said Mance. "I can tell him the story later."

Austin nodded, then pressed Adele to continue.

"My mother's name was Renèe—in French that means 're-born.' She was a beautiful woman, graceful and quiet, dominated by a certain dreaminess or moodiness which could make her difficult at times to live with. My father was a salesman and, naturally, spent a considerable amount of time on the road. We lived here during the thirties—hard times, and yet we owned this house. My grandfather, Joseph Guillo, had willed the house to us. At first, I loved it, but then . . ."

Edging forward, Austin wrapped an arm around her waist and whispered something to her, and she touched his face, obviously appreciating his supportive gesture.

"It was 1939," she continued, "and I was ten years old. My father was away on a business trip. My mother and I had returned from Cassadaga, Florida, from a spiritualists' camp there where she went for several days every summer. She liked to receive readings from one particular woman in the camp, and sometimes she would go to séances in the back room of the auditorium while I stayed in the lobby of the grand old hotel and read or played on the spacious porches. Going to Cassadaga was about the only luxury my mother would afford herself. My father cast a cold eye on her interest in spiritualism, but he never tried to keep her from her yearly sojourns."

Adele paused as the grip of memory tightened.

"She fancied having some psychic ability—seriously considered becoming a medium. That is, I recall her asking me once what I would think of having a mother who was a medium, and I told her that would be swell." Adele chuckled and added, "I used that word quite often in those days, but after my mother asked me that question she said, 'Adele, my dear, you have the sensitivity to become a fine medium yourself. Would you like to take the necessary training?' I very quickly said no. The idea frightened me. I believe Mother was disappointed at my response."

Mance and his companions watched as the woman lapsed momentarily into a thoughtful silence. Shadows parted like weird vegetation as she began to stroll around the room, her eyes brushing areas of empty space as if she were mentally reconstructing what had been the furniture layout years ago.

"I was sitting on the bed with her that night. She smelled of cinnamon. I had noticed that she seemed unusually nervous, though frequently she displayed signs of anxiety. She would sometimes pace the room and study . . . study the design of the wallpaper."

Adele reached out and rubbed her palm against the cracked and dusty plaster.

"The print was quite nice, blue and silver stripes or bars, but Mother, in her more anxious moods, would find that the design had transformed into prison bars and would believe that she had become imprisoned in the room."

Johnnie, apparently unnerved by the woman's account, inched closer to Mance, and he put his arm around her, much as Austin earlier had comforted Adele.

"Excuse me," said Adele, "I don't mean to digress. It's just that so many pieces of memory are being swirled around in my thoughts. . . . I'll get to the central part of the story directly. You see, there was a man here in town — I can't recall his name if I ever knew it — he stayed at the hotel downtown and he was some kind of private investigator or security officer. He was quite rough-looking, but apparently rather charming, or so a number of the women in Soldier believed. He liked Mother, and though she put off his advances, he was undeterred by them or the fact that she was married. Mother grew rather frightened of him, for his persistence embraced certain veiled threats that he planned to come and claim her. I realized a few years later that she feared he would attack her."

"He came that night — is that what happened?" Johnnie broke in.

Adele turned to her and slowly shook her head. "I never saw him or even heard him, but Mother did . . . or imagined she did. She experienced a moment of such intense terror, and yet her main intention was to protect me and not herself. We were on the bed, and I was clinging to her waist and just as Mother imagined that someone was about to enter the room, I felt something . . . drawing out of her stomach. And then I saw it — not ten feet from the bed: a gray but largely colorless form . . . the form of a huge wolf. I screamed and hid my eyes."

Mance listened and felt empty.

"The wolf creature," he muttered tonelessly.

"Yes," said Austin. "We have every reason at this point to believe it is the same one. Reading as much occult literature as I could lay my hands on, and building from Adele's description of what occurred that night, I would say that the wolf is a projection of the etheric body. Adele's mother, in effect, called it forth from within her as a protective spirit of some kind—she must have imagined it, and the force of her imagination caused it to materialize."

"Is all this true?" Mance asked.

Austin glanced at Adele, smiled weakly, and said, "A few years ago my church in Georgia asked me to leave because word got around that I was harboring an interest in the occult. One Sunday, my last one as pastor there, I admitted to that interest because I could no longer deny that the occult had acquired as much validity in my thinking as my Christian faith. And I would say one thing more: unusual forces were at work in drawing me to Soldier, and with all my soul, I believe I was meant to come here . . . to find Adele and to help lay to rest this ghost from the past."

"But how?" said Mance. "How can you destroy the creature or make it go away?"

"It won't be easy," said Austin. "What we believe is that Adele's mother had primary control of the creature because, well, because she created it. Since it's been alive and living in the walls of Guillo House all these years, it will be extremely difficult to control or, certainly, to destroy."

"We think there's a way," said Adele, but her voice betrayed lack of confidence.

Mance, however, was lost in his own forest of thought.

"Then . . . I'm responsible . . . isn't that right? The night I was here . . . after Johnnie was attacked . . . I came here and I called out for help, and that's when the wolf creature . . ."

"Yes," said Austin. "Probably so. You see, the wolf creature, as I said, is a protective spirit. Occult literature suggests that mothers have a special capacity to create such spirits—

it's quite likely that because you were in an hour of need, the creature heeded your call."

"For a while," said Mance, "it *was* a protective spirit . . . like a guardian angel, but then it started killing on its own: Fast Track and now ole Rollo . . . in a way it killed Sparrow, too."

"This is what we fear most. That it has developed a life of its own, that its more primitive, predatory instincts have taken over—as a result, there's no way of knowing who its next victim might be."

"Why hasn't it come after one of us?" said Mance.

"Merely because—and here I'm speculating—we're your friends, and the creature may be less inclined to attack those closest to you."

Mance looked at Johnnie, then at Austin.

"But it could start, couldn't it? You're saying you don't know what it's going to do next."

"That's where you can help," said Adele. "The creature communicates with you—what does it say?"

"Before Rollo was killed, it spoke to me, and it said, 'Want death . . . help me . . . find a way.' "

Adele turned to Austin and he nodded gravely.

Johnnie, who had been listening to every word, gently pulled away from Mance and took a step toward Adele.

"What happened to your mother? After she called the wolf . . . what happened?"

Adele was about to respond when Mance heard something on the stairs.

"Listen," he said.

The tiny group fell silent; the shadows seemed to thicken. They began to hear footfalls, heavy and slow ones, which sounded more ominous with each passing second.

3

At first, they did not recognize him.

He shuffled through the door, and the shadows conspired to help conceal his identity. He was wearing a ratty-looking fur coat, a holdover from the late twenties, and a black felt hat which he removed the moment he entered the room. His large, sad eyes tended to bulge, but what arrested the attention of Mance, Johnnie, Adele, and Austin was the shaven head, the baldness gleaming like a miniature moon.

"It's Uncle Thestis," said Johnnie, delighted to see him.

"No," said Austin, "it's Gottfried Sücher."

And, indeed, both of them were right.

"Pardon my lateness," said the man bearing a striking resemblance to Peter Lorre in the role of Dr. Gogol in *Mad Love.*

Then he appeared to stumble, and the four of them rushed to his side and guided him to the pallet.

"Here," said Austin, "here, sit and rest yourself."

On his uncle's face Mance saw a mask of pain, and yet a bright determination to see things through.

"Why did you dress up like this?" asked Johnnie. She and the others hunkered down around him and Austin drew the lantern closer. Uncle Thestis, despite the warmth of the night, insisted upon keeping the fur coat on; sweat beaded on his bone-white, bald head.

He smiled a crooked, Peter Lorre smile at Johnnie.

"To play my final role. To draw inspiration from the character of Sücher. Before the Conqueror Worm takes me away, I have one last desire."

He paused, and when the man looked at Adele, Mance could see a glint in his eyes; yes, his uncle had once loved Adele. Still did.

"How much of the story have you told?" he asked her. When she had iterated the details, he glanced at the others.

"There's more to the story. Adele has been guarding my secret . . . several secrets, but what we're faced with demands that everything be told. If not, we may have no chance against the wolf creature."

There was a nearly imperceptible movement forward as each listener showed an eagerness to hear the man's additions to an already strange tale.

"When I was a boy of eight or so," he began, "my parents abandoned me and my older sister, Rosamond. She moved in with a family on the other side of Soldier, and Adele's parents took me in. For a time I lived here with them and Adele and her younger sister, Charlotte. And on the night which Adele had told you of, I was here, too, but Adele's mother told me to take Charlotte and go hide in the attic until the danger had passed."

"So you never saw the creature?" said Johnnie.

"No, but I have no real doubts about its existence, nor have I any real doubts that it has returned. I should have seen earlier, when the killings began, that such a possibility had presented itself, but it seemed beyond belief. I rejected the notion. But no longer."

"Adele's mother," said Johnnie, "is she the rest of the story?"

"Yes." He hesitated, sweeping the room as if recalling details of it, much as Adele had. "Again, in this dreadful room. Mother—I have always thought of her as my mother because of her kindness to me—had acquired a gnawing fear that the creature would turn upon her and her children. One night—Adele and I were here with her—she tried to call the creature, but . . ."

It appeared at that point the remainder of the narrative would go untold. Uncle Thestis was in pain, and his mental as well as physical exhaustion were exacting a toll.

"In the midst of her attempt," said Adele, continuing the story, holding Thestis's hand in hers, "she fainted. She woke momentarily and complained of a severe headache. I told Thestis to run get a neighbor for help. Mother died before help came—a brain aneurysm, we were told."

No one spoke for nearly a minute.

"We should see that Thestis returns to his room right away," said Austin.

Together, Mance and Austin tugged the man to his feet; he had tears in his eyes. Adele kissed his cheek. Johnnie buried her head in Mance's shoulder.

"But what now?" said Mance. "The wolf creature, it's gone kill again. What can we do?"

"Not we," said Adele. "I see that the responsibility is mine. Mother knew that I possessed some psychic ability, ability

I've consistently denied and repressed. As Austin says: It's time. It's time for me to call the creature home."

4

After saying good night to Johnnie and Adele at their apartment house, Mance and Austin concentrated upon helping Uncle Thestis home. Obviously in pain, he winced at every step, each passing second an agony.

"I wish he hadn't tried to join us," said Austin.

"But he wanted to tell the rest of the story," said Mance. "I feel like I understand a lot more about what's happened."

"Poor dear Adele," Austin murmured, "if only I could give her more assistance. What she has in mind will require a mountain of courage."

"Can she do it by herself? Can you call the creature home like she says?"

"I honestly don't know," said Austin.

Uncle Thestis groaned as they reached the rear entrance to Scarlett's, and there they were met by Bridgette Settleford and someone else seemingly lurking in the shadows.

"I told him . . . I told him he was too sick to do this. I pleaded with him . . ."

Bridgette was upon them, pressing at Uncle Thestis, and Mance could see how much she cared for him.

"He'll be considerably better when we get him off his feet," said Austin.

Relinquishing his hold, Mance fell away as Bridgette moved in to help Austin; together they guided Thestis through the back door to the kitchen; Mance's dad switched on a light and held the door for them.

"I didn't see it was you," said Mance.

"I was worried," said his dad.

"Yeah, Uncle T.'s overdone it, but he felt like he had to . . . to help us with what we've got to do."

"It wasn't Thestis I was worried about—it was you."

His dad's hand felt like magic on his shoulder.

"I'm OK, I guess. This is all so freaky . . . so strange. Dad, you ever believe in the supernatural or the occult?"

"No, I'd say I don't put much store in them. If I can't hold something in my hand or give it a kick, then for me it just don't really exist. But I've talked to your uncle and he thinks something mighty peculiar's loose in Soldier. My concern is . . . well, I don't know what all you've got yourself into, son. Just promise me this: be careful, would you?"

The others had left.

Mance hunkered down in front of his uncle, who was nestled in his overstuffed chair, still wearing the fur coat and black felt hat, still very much Gottfried Sücher. Mance had made his uncle a cup of tea, and after the man had taken a sip of it, he appeared to revive.

"Now you've heard the whole story," he said to the boy. "What do you think?"

"That I wished I'd heard it sooner. Thing I feel is that I'm sorta responsible, you know, for all that's been goin' on. For the killings. I didn't mean to . . . but Fast Track and Sparrow . . . I might as well have shot 'em with a gun. I killed 'em, didn't I?"

"You came in contact with the invisible forces of the universe, with the dark, primitive forces within each of us."

"I want to be the one," said Mance, suddenly feeling a surge of energy and desire which surprised him; it was like the hit of an upper. In that moment, he felt that something deep, deep inside which had been imprisoned had been given its freedom: a fierceness, a courage he never knew existed. "I want to be the one to meet the wolf creature. It shouldn't have to be Adele. Would you help me do it, Uncle Thestis?"

A sparkle woke in the man's dark, heavy-lidded eyes.

"I will," he said, tapping fingers at his heart. "Herr Gottfried Sücher will."

In his best Peter Lorre imitation, he cocked an eyebrow and curled his lip into an ironic smile.

Scarlett O'Hara was never confused.

She always spoke her mind freely and authoritatively, and that was the case when Jonella, who had been dominated by the personality of Johnnie all evening, was sitting on her bed listening to music on her radio and thinking about Adele's story—and about Renèe and Guillo House.

The voice of Scarlett O'Hara beamed through on the radio with stunning clarity.

Come home, it said.

Johnnie becoming Jonella knew what it meant. Miss X warned her not to go.

Jonella thought: I have to go where I belong.

Sneaking out was easy; the unlit candle was her companion. The darkness at the front door of Guillo House was intense and touched with such animation that it seemed alive. Inside, Jonella brought the candle flame to life and trod the stairs.

In the second-floor bedroom, Renèe's room, she sat on the pallet and waited.

Reborn.

Something prowled the walls of Guillo House.

She could hear it panting; she could hear an occasional growl or snarl.

Jonella smiled to herself; she felt that she belonged.

"Renèe," she said, "I'm here."

"Mother," she said, "I've come home."

Chapter Fifteen

1

Rain danced hard on the roof of the abandoned house, a two-story mansion with a pseudotower and wide, yawning doors that opened into a broad foyer. Despite the fierceness of the downpour, there were few signs of leaks. But the house injected the boy with a mild discomfort: it reminded him, structurally and atmospherically, of Guillo House.

On the edge of Soldier, the sorrowful old edifice had been marked for destruction, and thus Slow Eddie and his crew of Mance and Punch had been called upon to bring it down. Rain had brought the major phase of the raking to a halt. The charges needed drier weather, so attention was being given to salvaging the better wood within: the solid oak flooring and stair railing.

"I've never ever been so sick of a town as I was of Birmingham—you know what I mean?"

The boy half nodded at Punch's remark, but he wasn't listening carefully. He felt the presence of the wolf creature. Everywhere. At Scarlett's. In his room. On North Street. When he was with Johnnie.

Want death.

The voice, at once pathetic and frightening, hammered at him day and night until he wanted to scream. There was little relief from it. Worst of all, there was blood in its tone, a persistent suggestion of a warning that if something weren't done to free the creature from its misery, it would kill again. Soon.

Mance worried about Johnnie.

Mostly it was her proximity to Adele Taylor which troubled him: both women, he believed, were in danger, living alone in that apartment building so close to Guillo House.

"You ain't hearing a word I'm saying," said Punch.

Crowbar in hand, Mance was tugging at a section of flooring.

"Sorry," he said, "I got a lot on my mind."

"You and me, let's take us a break," Punch suggested.

And so they sat on the bottom step of the stairs, drank from Punch's thermos of water, and stared through the open door at the rain.

"Since I ain't got nothing better to do, you might as well tell me what's messin' with your head," said Punch.

"Well . . . it's the creature."

"Oh, Lord. That again. Boy, you really got yourself believing that, donchoo?"

"I know it, Punch. It's super weird, yeah, but it's . . . it's real."

And he shared his current fear, opening himself so that the black man could sense something nailed down and writhing in agony within the boy.

"Bridgette Settleford, she thinks it's a man, and so do I," said Punch. "I'm gone track him down 'cause he murdered Pop. Settleford, she's been good to me. Loaned me some money. She understands how much I wanna catch this guy."

"I understand it, too," said Mance. "You think I don't want the killings to stop? Next one could be Johnnie."

"Next one could be *you,* boy."

"Maybe so. I can't go crawl in a hole and hide because of that. I got to face the creature."

"I can help you," said Punch. "You tell me where to find this guy and I'll handle him."

Mance shook his head in frustration. On the boy's shoulder, Sting squeaked his displeasure with the movement. The boy said, "Punch, you just don't understand . . . this thing isn't something *human.*"

"OK, OK . . . let's say you're right. There's gotta be some way to kill it, ain't that right?"

"I feel like there is, but I got to face it alone. Don't want your help. Don't need it."

"Fine. OK, fine. I see how you feel. Just remember this: whatever's out there, whatever killed Pop, I want it . . . I want it dead. That's 'bout my only reason for wakin' up every mornin', you got that?"

Mance looked away.

The rain fell harder.

2

"She had the softest hands ever given to a woman. Whether she was washing my face or soothing me after a nightmare or putting medicine on a scrape, those hands were gloved with the stuff of heaven."

Thestis Sinclair paused to sip at his tea. He wondered if the rain had set off the present round of pain. In the silence and comfort of his room he had been toying with what old men call the pearls of memory, unstringing individual pearls and rejoicing in each one. Here a memory of Renèe's hands, there one of Charlotte's laugh. Or Adele's smile.

He knew he was dying.

The Conqueror Worm had taken up permanent residence with him. Waiting. Waiting for the right moment. And so Thestis had decided to engage this ultimate foe in conversation, sharing memory and dreams and fears.

"Conqueror Worm, before I leave this strange and sad and yet somehow hopeful world, I want these old eyes to behold a few things: first, the end of the wolf creature; with that, much should follow—the lifting of fear from the relationship of Mance and Jonella and the freeing of Adele to marry Austin."

He closed his eyes.

"Austin loves her, Conqueror Worm. He will gilt the edges of her final years. She deserves that. So beautiful. Like her mother."

The effort it took to speak, to reflect, exhausted him. He set his teacup on the lampstand and whispered, "We'll talk again, Conqueror Worm."

When Mance slipped into the room, he felt something tear loose in his chest. Panic raged like a fire through his mind: *Uncle T.'s dead.*

But he wasn't.

Evening had come on, bringing an end to the rain. Mance could see that his mother had brought Thestis some dinner, but hardly a bite had been taken from it. Bending down, the boy touched the old man's knee and, like magic, it seemed, he woke.

The relief of the moment dizzied Mance.

"Have you come to talk about the wolf creature?" said his uncle, pressing himself more fully awake. A smile stole across his face.

"Yeah . . . yeah, it's always in my head."

His uncle shifted in the chair, groaned, blinked away the pain, and then searched for the smile which had fled. "I've been thinking about the creature," he said.

Mance brightened. "And you've got a plan to stop it?"

"Perhaps."

"We gotta do it as soon as we can . . . . The creature, it follows me, it keeps talking to me . . . . And I'm scared for Johnnie."

"You and I will go to Guillo House. I don't want . . . I can't bear to think that Adele will face the creature. You and I will go together."

"How will we destroy it?"

"I'll be there with you. I'll tell you everything you'll need to know."

Excited, his heart trip-hammering against his rib cage, Mance said, "Can we go tonight? Before something happens . . . can we?"

"No, I—I need strength." His voice weary, Thestis leaned back. "I need a few days to gather strength. Then we'll go. I promise."

Mance wanted to protest.

But there was something so tenuous, so fragile, in the man's face that he held back his words.

3

"His name is Stubby," said Johnnie.

Crystal and Loretta giggled.

"Why's he called that?" said Crystal.

She's going to be beautiful when she grows up, thought Johnnie.

"Because of his real short legs—stubby legs." And she bounced the stuffed dog across the bedspread.

"See my toy?" said Loretta, thrusting a green figurine of some kind toward her.

"Oh, let me see that. What is it?"

"It's a Ninja Turtle," Crystal broke in as if translating a foreign aspect of culture. "I've got one, too."

Johnnie examined the caricatured turtle figure.

"Pretty strange stuff . . . don't you have dolls? When I was a little girl, I had a coupla dolls."

"Did you have the Disney Channel when you was a little girl?" asked Crystal.

"No, but I liked the Disney movies, especially the old ones like *Cinderella* and *Snow White.*"

"Momma's gone take us to see *Dick Tracy*," Crystal followed, "and Twylla promised to take us to Six Flags in Atlanta."

"Sounds like fun. You like living with Twylla?"

She knew she shouldn't probe; it wasn't a fair question.

Crystal nodded slowly; Loretta imitated her sister's nod, only making hers more vigorous.

"Would you ladies like a glass of Coke, or is it too close to your bedtime?"

"Momma lets us have Coke all the time," Crystal assured her.

"Yes," Loretta echoed, clapping her tiny hands.

So they journeyed downstairs to the kitchen of the main

apartment, which, since it remained vacant, Johnnie and Adele used on occasion. The three of them sat at the kitchen table and sipped at Cokes on ice and nibbled at stale cheese puffs and giggled a lot.

"Momma and Twylla went to Victoryland," Crystal abruptly announced in the midst of the girlish chatter.

"Yes, I know," said Johnnie. "To see the greyhound dogs race. Maybe they'll bet some money on them and come home rich. What would you do if you had a whole lot of money?"

She directed the question at Loretta who, as a three-year-old, could only giggle, roll her eyes, and glance at Crystal for help.

"I would buy . . . I would buy, hmm," Crystal began, raising her voice self-importantly and rocking back and forth. Then her voice trailed off, and she said, "I would buy us a new daddy."

Johnnie felt a hot rush of sadness. She patted Crystal's hand and led the two girls back upstairs.

"Did you know we have the house all to ourselves?"

"Where's that older lady?" Crystal asked.

"She and her friend have gone to Montgomery, so you guys have to protect me and Stubby, OK?"

Loretta tugged at her. "OK," she said.

"Can we play Starship Future?" said Crystal.

"Sure, but you'll have to teach me," said Johnnie.

Crystal laughed and Loretta, in a delayed reaction, joined in.

"No," said Crystal, "it's a video game. I have it in my big purse bag."

So the two girls settled in on Johnnie's bed, their attention glued to starbursts and neurotically happy, blippy background noises. Johnnie decided not to make it a threesome. Bunkered by pillows, she relaxed and enjoyed watching their absorption in the game.

She was feeling good about herself.

She was Johnnie. Johnnie liked baby-sitting with the girls; Jonella did not.

It was a moment in which Johnnie could imagine being married. Yes, to Mance. She could imagine, without too

297

much difficulty, that Crystal and Loretta were her daughters; she could imagine how in later years they would have serious talks about boys and school and life in general.

Jonella would not.

Jonella might never marry. She would go to college and probably become a business executive and make tons of money and travel all over the world. And yet not be very happy.

What did Jonella want?

She was spooky. Why else would she like to go to Guillo House all alone at night? Johnnie thought suddenly about Renèe: *Jonella's like Renèe.*

Yes, they could have been sisters.

The minutes passed, and she imagined her wedding day: she would spend hours preparing herself to look as beautiful as possible for Mance. She would attend to every detail: it would be her day. She would not invite Jonella to the wedding. She would invite only close friends.

But who will give me away?

For the first time in years she found herself truly missing not having a father around. The thought of there being no one to give away the bride buzzed at her like an annoying insect. The thought grew darker. *It's Momma's fault.* No, that wasn't fair. She pushed the notion aside. Perhaps Uncle Thestis would give her away. Or Austin.

Hugging Stubby to her stomach, she closed her eyes and imagined her wedding night—she smiled at the thought of Mance, who, no doubt, would be as nervous as she. What would it be like? What kind of man would Mance become?

Deep into reflection upon those questions, she snapped back to reality when the bulb in her lamp next to her bed flickered twice and then plunged the room into darkness.

"Hey," cried Crystal. "What's going on?"

"Power's out, I guess," said Johnnie. "Wait a moment, and it'll come back on."

Apprehensive, Loretta crawled up to snuggle against her.

"It's OK, honey. Don't worry," said Johnnie.

Crystal continued playing her video.

"Loretta's just being a fraidy cat. See, the dark doesn't

298

scare me."

As Loretta tightened her grip on Johnnie's arm, Johnnie reached for her stuffed dog.

"Stubby will protect us," she said.

"Momma," said Loretta. "I want Momma."

"Momma's not here. Jonella's our momma tonight."

"That's right, honey. Your momma will be here soon, and she'll take Loretta home to be in her own little bed. How will that be?"

"My bed," the tiny girl murmured.

Crystal's video was no larger than a purse, but it put off enough multicolored light to provide a soft, eerily muted illumination for the room. The blips and boinks and jangles fingered into the partial darkness; Johnnie felt comforted by the sounds.

She stroked Stubby and rocked Loretta. Eventually Crystal tired of her video game and wormed her way toward Johnnie's lap.

"Maybe you didn't pay your 'lectric bill," Crystal offered.

Johnnie chuckled at the remark.

It's coming.

She froze.

The girls were silent. But she had definitely heard a voice. A warning tone. She waited as the girls squirmed.

It's coming.

Johnnie sat up straight: the voice, which apparently only she could hear, seemed to have come from the stuffed dog.

When the girls began giggling and pinching at each other, she shushed them.

"What's wrong," said Crystal.

"Quiet."

"Is it Momma?" Loretta asked.

There was someone or something on the stairway.

And Johnnie knew what it was and what had disrupted the lights.

"Oh, dear God," she whispered.

"What's wrong?" Crystal repeated.

"Both of you stay right here a second."

Johnnie got up and went to the door; she could see most of

299

the stairway, and while she caught no movement, no visible sign of the creature, she heard a snarl.

Shutting the door, she tried to calm herself.

Protect the girls. I have to protect the girls.

A growl. The skitter of claws on the bottom stairs.

Johnnie felt numb.

"Oh, please God," she whispered, but it sounded more like a whimper.

"Jonella, come be with us," said Crystal. "Loretta's crying."

And she was, softly, pathetically, and it tore at Johnnie's heart. She flattened her back against the door and concentrated all of her apprehension. And thought of Mance.

Help us. Help us, Mance. Help us, please.

Sting was in his cage nibbling on a salad of cheese and lettuce. Mance was on his bed listening to a tape of Metallica. "Eye of the Beholder" was thrumming and grating in his ears, but its message of hungering after independence caught in his mental screen. Yes, he wanted to do things his own way, be free of all entanglements except the ones he chose.

He imagined being twenty-one, having a good job, a nice car, and, of course, a wife. . . .

Help us. Help us, Mance. Help us, please.

The boy jerked forward. He swallowed hard and glanced around. He punched off the tape.

No mistake about it—that was Johnnie's voice, and it had spoken into his mind just as the wolf creature commonly did.

"Johnnie," he whispered, as if she were near enough to engage in a conversation with him. Then the immediacy of the moment struck home.

"Damn it, she's in trouble."

He began to move as quickly as he had ever moved in his life.

She had herded them to the door of her closet.

"Is something after us?" Crystal cried, her voice pitching

300

higher with fear.

Loretta was sobbing, her small arms locked around Johnnie's neck.

Setting the little girl down, Johnnie said, "Listen to me. Listen, Crystal." She fought to maintain an air of calmness, but was losing the battle. "I want you to get in the closet and stay there until I tell you to come out."

Thirty feet beyond her she could hear the wolf creature; it was nearing the top of the stairs, its panting thick and eager.

The girls reluctantly, fearfully, obeyed her directions.

"Stay here—please stay in here."

She wanted to tell them everything would be fine. Don't worry. No one will be hurt. She shut the closet door, then went to the door to her room and locked it. Suddenly she felt so weak that she dropped to her knees.

Johnnie began to fade; Jonella came surging through, taking control, finding strength to face the creature.

Mance leaped up the front steps of the apartment building. He knew that Johnnie was baby-sitting Tanya's girls; in fact, he had planned to stop by to check on them and spend some time with Johnnie once her duty was over.

He also knew—feared—why Johnnie's paranormal call had reached him.

The wolf creature.

It was turning against the ones it had once protected.

Up the inside stairs two or three at a time he drove himself.
"Johnnie!"

It was dark and silent, but as he reached the top of the stairs, the wolf creature wheeled around; its yellow eyes seemed to create an aura surrounding its face.

Want death.

Mance clenched his fists.

He had no weapon to combat it with, and in that instant of helplessness, he thought of his Uncle Thestis, and he also thought of Sparrow, the man who contended that you had to confront your enemy with your bare hands.

"It's me you want, you bastard!"

The wolf creature growled low.

Mance prepared himself for its attack.

But instead, the creature turned and stepped through the closed door of Johnnie's bedroom.

Momentarily stunned, Mance could not move.

A scream from within the room animated him; he charged the door, crashing into it with his shoulder; the wood whined and popped, but the door held.

"Johnnie!"

Again and again he slammed against the door until at last a section of it splintered loose so that he could reach through and unlock it.

"Johnnie?"

She was standing by her bed, and, amazingly, she was holding the wolf creature at bay . . . or was it merely choosing to spare her and the little girls?

The wolf creature spun around as Mance opened the door, and into the boy's mind it shouted, *Want death.*

It was as if someone had driven an iron spike into his brain; Mance clutched at his ears and staggered backward. Consciousness slipped away toward a vanishing point.

But before the world faded to black, he watched as the wolf creature's fury unleashed itself on Johnnie's room and the hallway; claws extended, it lashed the walls and floors and door. Plaster dust and splinters churned into the air, and yet in the midst of the chaos Johnnie stood firm, though her face registered fear.

Mance sank to his knees.

Dust and noise swirled around him, and, second by second, he let go of reality until his senses recorded nothing more.

4

Jonella did not go to work the next day. She spent the morning cleaning up her room and the hallway as best she could. Adele and Austin, both very interested in her account of the wolf creature's attack, helped her. They were astounded and not a little frightened by the deep claw marks. Austin assured Jonella that the plaster could be repaired, but that a new door would have to be purchased and the floor would, no doubt, bear its scars for years and years to come.

"We're just thankful that you and the girls were not physically harmed," said Adele.

Tough as their small selves would allow, Crystal and Loretta handled the situation reasonably well; they had not, fortunately, caught sight of the creature, and thus would not retain its nightmare image; yet, the sounds of the attack, and the tension of being huddled in the dark closet not knowing exactly what was taking place, would add to the stockpile of horrors produced weeks ago by their father's abuse.

Tanya became very distressed when she came to pick them up. Jonella couldn't blame her for that. There would be no further baby-sitting at the apartment, and Jonella doubted that she would get to see Crystal and Loretta for some time to come. It was not something, however, which troubled her much, because it was Johnnie they both adored anyway.

When Mance had come to, he had pleaded with Jonella to move out of the apartment to someplace safer, but she had found that a ridiculous notion. Where could one hide from the wolf creature? She reasoned that if it desired to find her, it would, regardless of her maneuverings to avoid it.

After calling in to Scarlett's and asking for a day off, she pondered how to spend the time. She was Jonella, not Johnnie, and thus felt a need to be alone and yet to blend with humanity and learn more about how her innermost self related to other people. She wanted to test herself, and discover a more concrete sense of identity.

I am Jonella.

I want to be free.

Empty-headed Johnnie, she believed, did not understand that longing for freedom. She never would. Nor would she ever understand Jonella's need to make contact with that inner fierceness, that primitive, elemental strength every woman possesses.

But Renèe understood.

Restless, Jonella decided late morning to go to the mall.

303

She dressed up, applying makeup which would give her the look of a slightly older woman. In her mirror, she saw that older woman—not Johnnie or Miss X, but Jonella. She liked what she saw.

Soldier offered a shuttle bus service to the hospital and to the mall, and so she rode the bus and pretended along the way that she was journeying to some distant city to start a new life. Perhaps Atlanta. Or Chicago. Or San Francisco. Or New York. Yes, why not New York? Or even Hollywood. Perhaps she would become an actress or a successful businesswoman. But the latter would require college. Fine. She would finish high school and go to college and study business.

She felt good about herself as she entered the wide walkway of the mall and heard the siren song of each glitzy, colorful shop. She smelled hot pretzels and chocolate chip cookies and roasted nuts and a dozen perfumes and nostril-burning whiffs of bad body odor. She dodged elderly mall-walkers clipping along in expensive tennis shoes, and a pack of small boys, half black, half white, raced past her, and she saw two young women pushing baby carriages and she told herself that they were wasting their lives.

She met scores of faces, but she did not look directly at any one of them. She felt no need to know them; there was something comforting about swimming amongst strangers in this sea of unreality.

On a whim, she decided to try on shoes. In and out of numerous stores she wended her way, finding pieces of the "new me" with each outlandish style. She easily rebuffed the flirtations of the salesmen, some of whom were barely older than herself.

At the window of a men's clothing store, she paused to admire her reflection. *You are beautiful and free.* But it was there, for just an instant, that the yellow eyes of the wolf creature appeared. She gasped, then wheeled around. It was not visible; yet she felt its presence. She glanced back at the window display and stared full in the face at a male mannequin decked out in a three-piece suit. Its flesh-colored complexion appeared waxlike, with streaks around its mouth

304

where the skin seemed to have melted. Its eyes were dark and frozen, its lips too feminine.

It was hideous.

A mild panic rising within her, Jonella pushed herself from the display. She looked again for the wolf creature, picked up no sign of it, and then sought out the eating area. Though not particularly hungry, she believed that some lunch would restore the balance of reality. At one of the many fast-food places, she ordered a chicken sandwich and lemonade. She sat at a table in the vaulted atrium, and with each bite she felt better.

The wolf creature was near.

But if she concentrated, she could force it to keep its distance.

I am beautiful and free and strong.

I know who I am. I am not lost.

She began to study those around her. They were mostly women of all shapes and sizes and ages. There were men, too, some old, talking obviously about the past. She wondered why there were so many kids—why aren't they in school? It was early April. Was it spring break? She could not remember.

Sitting there finishing her lunch and dressed as she was in a nice outfit which Adele had bought for her, it was easy to imagine that she was a successful businesswoman, an owner perhaps of one of the shops, a boutique or one of those expensive import shops. Yes, and she was being admired by . . . a man whose face was melting.

By dark, frozen eyes.

Jonella looked at her hands. They were trembling. But she hoped, she prayed, that when she glanced up the male mannequin in the three-piece suit would not be sitting there three tables away, staring at her as if considering a move to join her.

No, the mannequin wouldn't be there. Would not. Would not. Would not.

But it was.

Later, she remembered nothing about leaving her table, about scrambling away, crashing into an old man and knocking him down, about finding her way somehow, crying and moaning, to the bus stop outside the mall; and about riding home with a dozen pairs of eyes staring at her and the heavyset black driver who helped her off.

Nothing.

Early evening, Adele had come by to check on her, at which time the fog of unreality began to lift.

"Hold on," Adele told her. "This will all be over soon."

But Jonella found little reassurance in those words. For most of the evening, she barricaded herself in her room, certain that the male mannequin had followed her from the mall. The wolf creature had sent it.

No one understood her fear, she believed.

No one could.

Except Renèe.

But to communicate with her, Jonella knew she would have to enter the lair of the wolf creature. Would the creature allow it? Would its claws and sharp teeth finally turn upon her?

No, it wants death.

She was developing an understanding of the wolf creature. But she needed to know what Renèe knew.

The flock of pigeons had increased in number. They showered down from the roof and stumbled over one another to gather along the porch railing and coo and preen and watch her like mythological birds in a tale from Ovid or some such classical author.

The pigeons. So many of them.

She felt uncomfortable as they followed her entrance into Guillo House.

In Renèe's bedroom, her candle pushing back the darkness, Jonella felt much better, and yet it suddenly occurred to her that she did not know how to call the dead.

She sat on the pallet and stared into the candle's flame.

"Renèe," she whispered, "I have come to talk to you. Are you there? Can you hear me?"

306

In the distance, she heard the pigeons rustle. Guillo House creaked and groaned. A breeze skittered down the chimney. But there was no response from Renèe.

Jonella closed her eyes. She concentrated.

The warmth tapped the base of her spine. She experienced it first as a tingle. Its spread was slow but firm, like a massage. Jonella relaxed. The presence of the woman who had passed beyond life filled her.

Who are you?

Startled at first, the young woman thought she had only imagined the voice.

Who are you?

"I'm . . . I'm Jonella. And I . . . I need your help. Are you Renèe?"

"Yes."

"I know your story. Your daughter, Adele, told us what happened here. The wolf creature . . . it's a threat to everyone. It has to be stopped."

The voice of Renèe fell silent, though her presence remained strong.

"Will you tell me how . . . how it can be stopped?"

The warmth seemed to mushroom into an almost visible aura. Jonella opened her soul and listened.

5

Mance admired the skill that Punch had acquired: Slow Eddie had taught him well. The old house, at Punch's command, tumbled upon itself in a thorough yet sorrowful crash as the charges sounded off like clockwork. Dust billowed and the thunder echoed from the moments after the final stud and joist and shingle had fallen into the lazy, pyramidal heap.

Slow Eddie backed the truck close to the heap, and they began to load it.

Mance's thoughts, however, were not on the work; there was a bandage on his forearm where a splinter from Johnnie's bedroom door had stabbed him. He touched the bandage as a piece of substantial evidence that the wolf creature's attack had actually taken place.

A shudder ran through him as he replayed selected images from the scene.

It wants Johnnie.

The thought made him feel cold and empty.

But most of all, he tried to tackle the ultimate puzzle: why didn't the wolf creature kill them? It certainly had had within its grasp an opportunity to do so.

It doesn't want to kill.

That was the obvious conclusion.

It wants its own death.

Or was it setting a trap? Would it vent its fury at Guillo House?

Mance believed that only one man had the answers. Only one man could help him face the wolf creature and end its menace.

It was Good Friday.

That evening after work, stiff and sore and still feeling dusty and gritty despite having showered, Mance found himself in his uncle's room, preparing to hear his words of wisdom, hoping those words would create the necessary magic to make the darkness light.

Uncle Thestis, clad once again in his Gottfried Sücher costume, could barely hold his eyes open, not because he was tired, but rather because of the pain. He breathed with the tenuousness of a man on a high wire, each breath carefully calculated to bring him to the next one.

Mance shared every detail of the wolf creature's attack on Johnnie, and when he had finished he surveyed the failing man for signs of encouragement — would he know what must be done?

"I have to face the creature now. Now, Uncle T. I have to face—"

His uncle raised a hand feebly to interrupt.

"Herr Sücher, you mean . . . Your uncle has passed on. Herr Sücher has remained behind."

Mance played along; matters beyond his uncle's fantasy

308

were pressing in on all sides of him.

"When do we go to Guillo House?"

The boy's question was a test. There could be no further waiting; the wolf creature had to be dealt with. Uncle Thestis could surrender to his fiction, but the present had to be confronted unflinchingly.

The old man suddenly bulged his Peter Lorre eyes; a smile flickered. It was as if he welcomed Mance's challenge, his insistence upon bringing the nightmare to a close.

Lifting a glass of water to his lips, Herr Sücher cocked an eyebrow knowingly. His theatrics seemed to give him a modicum of energy, energy to look the boy squarely in the eye and say, "Tomorrow night. Tomorrow night the days and nights of the wolf creature reach a glorious conclusion."

A leap of joy caught Mance high in his chest. He smiled broadly.

"You serious? Tomorrow night, for sure?"

Herr Sücher nodded, staring down at his bone white hands, his eyelids drooping. Mance shook his knee.

"Tell me what we'll do—how will I destroy the creature?"

Silent, as if considering the question for the very first time, Sücher sighed, then winced in pain. Then he said, "I'll be with you. I'll coach you. Bring your courage. I'll tell you what you'll need to know when the time comes."

Disappointed at first, Mance found a handle for his emotions. He would trust his uncle—the man had never let him down. The only thing that mattered was eliminating the wolf creature, preventing it once and for all from harming Johnnie, banishing it forever from their lives.

"It wants to die," he said. "The wolf creature wants death."

Sücher raised a cautionary finger. "You must never, never deceive yourself into believing you understand the nature of an elemental, of a projection of the etheric body . . . for such things ultimately are beyond knowing. At best, we can exercise but a modest control over them."

"The wolf creature . . . I know it's dangerous, I've seen what it can do, but, you know, sometimes I feel sorry for it. Responsible for it, too. I called it out of the walls of Guillo House. It's been like a companion ever since . . . like a part

309

of me I didn't know about before."

"Be warned," said Sücher, "that which appears to be the soul's companion can turn and tear out your throat."

"Yes, sir."

Then Sücher leaned back, summoning enough energy for parting words.

"I must rest now . . . Tomorrow night . . . tomorrow night we shall deal with our dark visitor."

Downstairs at Scarlett's, Mance ate a late evening snack and thought about Johnnie. With the wolf creature removed from their lives everything would return to normal.

Johnnie would be forever his.

In another year or so they would be married. They would move to a new town. Start all over. Maybe Montgomery. Or Auburn. Or Taloa Springs. They would leave Soldier to the ghosts of memory.

"You must be thinking about your lady love, 'cause that sandwich can't be that good."

Bridgette Settleford cranked up a smile and sat down.

"You don't mind if I join you?"

Mance swallowed a mouthful. "Go ahead."

"Your Momma said you've been upstairs chewin' on your uncle's ear."

Mance shook his head. "Not my uncle. Herr Sücher."

He said it with a straight face, but Bridgette had to chuckle.

"I love that ole bird," she followed. "Loony but sweet as sugar. How was he feelin'?"

"Not so good, I'd say."

"Damn," she hissed. "I hate like hell to hear that."

Wary of her motivation, Mance decided to say as little as possible.

She studied his silence a moment and then said, "Sources tell me the wolf man paid Miss Jonella a visit last night."

"You ain't gone let this story die, are you?"

She leaned forward; her eyes narrowed. "Not on your life, I'm not."

"Why?"

"Listen to me," she snapped, "curiosity is all an ole gal like me has left. If there's a wolf man, I have to get a look-see at him before they lay me in my grave."

Mance offered no response. Her presence was discomforting.

She lit a cigarette and relaxed back into her chair. "Don't suppose you'd care to let me in on what you and your uncle have planned?"

He looked at her, then looked away as smoke curled in tendrils between them. "Why should I? You'll find out somehow anyway."

She threw back her head and cackled. "You're right, my friend. You're absolutely right. Call it a newspaperwoman's intuition, but I have a feeling my story's gone end at Guillo House."

Chapter Sixteen

1

I've never lived.

Adele Taylor stared into her makeup mirror and wondered how the years could have gone by so quickly and how she could have existed without embracing life more fully and more passionately. She pressed her fingertips at an age spot near one eyebrow; it was brown with a darkening nucleus, the kind of spot which more and more frequently these days she had difficulty concealing.

I'm turning into an old hag.

What did Kelton Austin see in her? she asked herself. She had lived such a cloistered life, a self-imposed cloister; could she truly be a stimulating companion for him? Would he be tremendously disappointed if and when they married? Wouldn't his books provide him with much superior company?

Tracing fingers along her chin and down across the netting of wrinkles on her neck, she tried to recall when her skin had been smooth. Once upon a time she must have been desirable to touch—did Austin find her that way now? Would their marriage have all the intimacy that he would need?

Her fingers continued their tentative journey, slipping inside her robe and into the valley between her breasts; tugging the robe open, she examined those breasts and frowned at how much they appeared to sag, looking more like the drooping dugs of an ancient woman than those of a woman clinging to her sexual attraction.

Would Austin want to fondle them?

She shut her eyes and closed her robe.

I am a sixty-one-year-old virgin.

Oh, but of course, there had been many opportunities to remedy that. Long-ago opportunities. Thestis Sinclair, for example, had wanted her. Boys in college, too. And during the many years she had worked as an administrative secretary at Goldsmith College, men had expressed an interest in her. Yes, one man in particular. She had been in her late forties at the time; a faculty member, some ten years younger than she, and rather handsome, began pursuing her one spring quite in earnest. Flattered, yet determined to keep his attraction in perspective, she attempted to turn the relationship into something more platonic.

The man insisted on something more.

And so it happened that one evening she found herself on the first floor of his apartment building, having been invited to his place for dinner—he had promised an Italianate feast—but at the bottom of the staircase she realized that if she climbed those stairs she would later leave him having allowed intimacy to develop. She would have forced herself to live.

It seemed in some ways an odd analogy, but facing the wolf creature would also force her to live, force her to confront the past, to come to terms with something dark and threatening within herself as well as with an elemental creature her mother had called into being, an unpredictable creature fully capable of ripping her to pieces.

She would have to call the creature to Guillo House.

She and Austin had agreed that that must be the way.

Feet of clay—I have feet of clay, she chided herself as she took a deep breath and raised her eyeliner brush. Austin would be by in less than an hour to take her to Scarlett's for breakfast. The tip of the brush tickled her eyelid; she blinked rapidly, then concentrated upon the task at hand.

Until the face in the mirror changed.

A tiny squeal of fright escaped from her lips.

The yellow eyes and most of the face of the wolf creature filled the mirror, ghostlike, or like an image from a dark fairy tale.

Come home.

Adele pushed away from the mirror but had trouble unlocking her eyes from those of the wolf creature.

Come home.

And in that moment she knew that the wolf creature would be waiting for her at Guillo House. There would be no need to call it.

Come home.

She would try. Home to her deeper self. Home to overcome her fear of the creature, home to complete her mother's unfinished business.

But her mother had died in the process.

I won't die, because I have never lived.

The face of the creature dissolved. It took nearly every ounce of her energy to finish applying her makeup and to get dressed.

Over coffee at Scarlett's, she told Austin of the creature's call.

"It's in control," she said. "We're not."

He patted her hand.

"It's time," he said. "Whether you call it or it calls you. Nothing has changed what you must do. Tonight. I'll go with you as far as the situation permits."

"I need courage," she said.

"You have it, my dear. I feel it. Draw upon it."

"I've never lived, Austin," she followed, fighting off a welling of tears. "My life is a life almost lost."

He smiled and the touch of his hand upon hers was firm and reassuring.

"Tonight," he said, "we win it back."

2

Come home.

The flow of her period was the heaviest it had ever been. The odor of her own blood nauseated her, and the voice of the wolf creature drummed in her ears. Her senses grew more acute by

314

the second.

Johnnie stayed in the employees' cubicle of a rest room at Scarlett's until she had calmed herself, until she had changed her tampon and convinced herself that she could face the world.

Come home.

More than anything else, she wanted to be a little girl again, to play with her dolls, and to pretend that one day she would have a home—a real home. Not the chaos of living with her mother, or living with her stepsister, or living by herself, but the feeling of wholeness which only a real home could offer.

Not Guillo House.

Come home.

"It's not my home," she whispered to herself.

Yet, perhaps it was.

Perhaps only the wolf creature understood that.

With a fresh pair of eyes, she struggled back to work.

"Sweetheart," Mance's mother exclaimed to her, "you remind me a trifle more every day of our Karen. Lands, you surely do."

Johnnie forced a smile.

To herself she prayed that the wolf creature would be silent the rest of the day. Its call was painful. It touched her in ways that completely unsettled her.

"Where's Mance?" she asked, suddenly wanting him to be near.

"Oh, lands, he was up pretty early, shoveled down some breakfast and took out on his bike. He has the day off, so's who can guess where he'll end up."

Disappointed, Johnnie nodded.

There were customers to wait on.

She walked into the dining room, giving wide berth to the portrait of Vivien Leigh—she had no desire to hear the wisdom of Scarlett O'Hara just then.

3

Taloa Springs was a pleasant, yet dying southern hamlet several miles from Soldier. As he biked through the derelict downtown, Mance felt good. Tonight he and his Uncle Thestis — or Gottfried Sücher — would face the wolf creature and exorcise it from the lives of all it had disrupted.

Despite some lingering soreness from house raking, he had an energy level which surprised him: was it the promise of freedom from the living dark? Was it hope? And why, he wondered, had he been drawn to Taloa? Something within had seemed to insist upon it.

He pedaled on to the edge of the town, not slowing until he passed the black, corrugated-iron gates of the Taloa Springs asylum for the mentally ill. The sprawling facility of whitewashed brick was surrounded by well-kept grounds dotted with islands of azaleas and dogwoods. To one side of the central building a fairy-tale lake replete with a pair of swans seduced the boy's eye.

A few patients meandered on the grounds, most choosing to sit on benches situated under the canopy of water oaks. But Mance gave no attention to them; instead, he stashed his bike in the ditch and leaned against the bars of the imposing fence which boundaried the asylum.

The lake was perfectly calm.

How could such a pleasant place be the refuge of so many tormented souls?

Were they able to appreciate all the physical beauty at their fingertips?

Mance watched the pair of swans and thought about Johnnie.

Come home.

Instantly his grip on one of the bars tightened. At first, he thought it was Johnnie's voice calling him as she had a few nights ago. But no.

Come home.

It was the wolf creature.

He felt as if suddenly he had been thrown off-balance. The creature was calling him. Was it somehow aware of what he and his uncle had planned?

Come home.

The scene began to change. Some of the beauty had been stolen. Mance knew he must return to Soldier. The wolf creature awaited him and his uncle.

Home.

His home would be wherever he and Johnnie would choose for it to be. Taking one last look at the lake and grounds, he climbed upon his bike and quickly put Taloa Springs behind him.

Cutting through the wind and spring warmth, he was thankful that Uncle Thestis or Gottfried Sücher would be there at his side when he entered Guillo House to answer the challenge of the living dark.

4

The man who had become Gottfried Sücher talked slowly, every word exacting a heavy price in agony and pain.

"Remember what I told you," he said.

Bridgette Settleford had come to visit him that Saturday afternoon because her journalistic instincts told her something was up.

"I will," she said, "and there's someone else who needs to know."

He tilted his head wearily to one side. "You have been a good friend."

Bridgette's eyes sparked like a flint on stone.

"Oh, Herr Sücher," she replied, "had I gotten to know you months earlier we could have generated some heat."

He grinned at that.

But pain quickly rubbed it from his lips.

"I've reached the end," he said, his tone darkening.

"Have you seen a doctor?"

"Yes. It's cancer. I refused the treatment — why forestall the inevitable?"

"I'm so sorry. I know what you mean to folks around here."

"My only regret . . . is missing out on tonight," he stammered.

Bridgette sighed heavily and thought about the death of her husband years ago.

"Is there anything I can do for you?"

He was silent and virtually immobile; his face was grim. Then something hopeful, something almost imperceptible flickered in his eyes.

"I want to see . . . Adele and Jonella."

Starting to rise, Bridgette said, "You've got it."

He followed her movement, saying, "Thank you. . . . I hope you get your wish. Good-bye."

She smiled, then leaned forward, removed his black felt hat, and kissed his bald head.

"Good-bye, Herr Sücher."

5

Adele entered the room while Johnnie waited in the hallway.

"Please smile for me," he told her.

She tried, but tears nearly prevented one from stealing across her face.

"Will this do?"

She pulled up a chair and sat near him.

"You never stopped being beautiful," he said.

"Oh . . . thank you, but I feel old and ugly . . . and wish I had more courage."

"Adele," he said, concentrating on her face, transforming it to the one he knew years and years ago, "You know . . . that I've loved you."

"And I've always cherished that love. Austin tells me love is the only response to evil."

"A wise man . . . with heart and soul enough to win your love."

There was a moment of awkward silence.

"Must you go to Guillo House?" he asked.

"Yes."

"I had a dream last night," he followed. "There will be . . . a resolution." He paused to fill his lungs with enough breath to finish. "I dreamed of a *tertium non datur*—the third outside of logic. There will be . . . a resolution."

Adele nodded. Then she hugged him and said, "You have another friend waiting to see you."

318

He released her. "Good-bye, Adele."

Tears choked her soft reply.

At the door, Johnnie embraced her.

Herr Sücher smiled at Johnnie's approach.

"How are you?" he asked.

"Scared," she half whispered. "I don't understand what's happening to me. I feel bad."

Her words seemed to catalyze the man, and for a score of heartbeats he was Uncle Thestis again. Thumb rubbing against forefinger, he said, "I give you the world's smallest violin."

For Johnnie, tears and a smile came in a rush. Embracing the man, she murmured, "Please don't die."

"Oh," he said, "the Conqueror Worm has waited long enough."

"Nothing will be the same without you."

"No, but that's a foolish thing to say. . . . You live your life . . . the best you can . . . and love our Manson . . . he needs it."

"I will," she said.

Then panic stabbed at her as he faded in her hold. His head lolled to one side. She immediately pushed away and ran downstairs, heart in her throat, wishing she could save him.

6

Mance could hear a siren as he crossed the tracks and headed up North Street. Blue-gray clouds promised rain before the afternoon ended. The voice of the wolf creature had echoed in his mind all the way from Taloa Springs. Herr Sücher, he believed, would assure him that nothing had altered their plan.

The wolf creature would await them in Guillo House.

Come home.

Yes, home.

Where the evil would be laid to rest.

Pumping his legs, Mance scaled the slope; sweat soaked his long hair, and Sting signaled his displeasure.

The pulsing bank of orange lights caught Mance's attention.

The ambulance was parked at the rear of Scarlett's.

A white, cold fear numbed the boy. He watched helplessly as

paramedics wheeled his uncle to the ambulance.

"You can't do this to me," Mance whispered to himself, and then in a matter of moments he was there pushing aside one of the paramedics.

"Hey, kid, what the hell are you—?"

"I've gotta talk to my uncle. Please, man, I gotta talk to him."

Reluctantly, the paramedic allowed him to crawl into the back of the ambulance.

Mance found his uncle strapped down, his head resting on a hospital pillow. His eyes were closed; his face possessed a death-mask tightness. Hovering over the man, the boy felt his anger rise.

"You can't do this to me. You can't do it, goddamn it. You promised you'd go to Guillo House with me."

The man blinked awake. He was no longer wearing his hat or the fur coat.

"You don't need me," he said, his words slurred.

"Yes, I do. I don't know how to destroy the creature. You have to help me."

The man shook his head. He swallowed with an audible click.

"Your love for Johnnie," he said, "is all you need."

Mance stared at him, suddenly feeling every emotion possible, yet finding it impossible to express them. It was at that moment Sting chose to scamper down the boy's arm and onto the dying man's chest.

Through his pain, the man glanced at the rat and chuckled.

"He thinks I'm a big ole hunk of rotting cheese."

Mance could barely see his uncle through the curtain of tears. He retrieved Sting, and then the paramedic pulled the boy away.

The ambulance doors closed.

And the sound had the finality of death.

320

Chapter Seventeen

1

It began to rain soon after dinner that evening, ending a few hours before midnight. In her room, Adele waited, reliving the sad moment of parting with Thestis Sinclair and wondering why the gods should occasionally decree that a man love a woman and receive no love in return.

It was cruel.

She stood at the window watching the night shake itself free of the rain, knowing that she had to concentrate upon the present and not the past. Austin would be by in a matter of minutes — Guillo House and something dark and fierce awaited.

She stepped out into the hallway and noticed that Jonella's door was closed, the room lightless, and she was thankful that the girl must be asleep and would not have to be involved further with the wolf creature. Back inside the room, Adele thought of her mother.

"Mother, it has taken me fifty years to do this," she whispered. "It's time."

When at last she heard Austin on the stairs, she nearly panicked; her heart raced, and her breathing became shallow and ragged.

"It's a Gothic night for Gothic deeds," he told her at her door.

The hard lines of fear in her face told him that he had miscalculated. His comment, designed to lighten the moment, had been inappropriate.

Embarrassed, he reached for her hand.

"You are strong, Adele. I know you can do this."

She forced a smile.

"Is there any chance you could substitute for me?"

He returned her smile, delighted to see her attempt to shift the mood.

"I love you," he said. "And would it accomplish what we need to have accomplished, yes, I would take up your role in a heartbeat."

She kissed his cheek, and they walked down the stairs and out into the thickening mist. On the front porch of Guillo House, Austin lit his lantern.

"Diogenes used his lantern to search for an honest man," he said. "We'll use this one to begin our search for a new life together."

Involuntary shivers coursed through Adele like currents of electricity. She took the lantern from Austin and said, "I'm ready," and wished that her voice had carried a more confident tone.

He embraced her firmly.

There was nothing more to say.

The shadows parted for her on the way up the stairs; she turned once to look back, but saw only an indistinct form. Lantern on the floor beside her, she stood in her mother's room and cleared her thoughts of everything except the wolf creature.

It was a combination of will and imagination.

A concentrated focus on her solar plexus.

She glanced up, and at a broken windowpane she saw several pigeons appear. She could hear scores of others on the roof above her. But she held her concentration. Time passed, though how much she was not aware.

The silver cord of ectoplasm which began to extend from her abdomen gave her a feeling of almost unbearable lightness. Yet, every muscle in her body was taut, every nerve activated; perspiration dampened her face.

Two pigeons winged through the room; she gritted her teeth

322

and regained control of the moment. The silver cord thickened and became more substantial.

She had come home.

And the core of her being invited the wolf creature to evidence itself.

Her body shuddered and quaked; images flooded her mind, threatening to drive her mad. Her face contorted; the silver cord twisted, eagerly seeking the etheric projection that had to be absorbed.

Courage, she told herself. For Austin. For the future.

She heard an echo of Thestis Sinclair's assurance: There will be a . . . resolution. I dreamed of a *tertium non datur.* . . .

She saw its eyes first. Large, penetrating, glowing with a predatory eagerness, they burned into her thoughts. The shadowy form of the wolf creature materialized by degrees, becoming more and more substantial until its hugeness rested on its haunches within twenty feet of her.

The silver cord began to draw; the muscles of her abdomen were being strained to their limit. The wolf creature resisted, but the cord possessed surprising strength; the battle of wills unfolded, heading, it appeared, toward a standoff.

Shutting her eyes tightly, Adele clenched her fists; tears rolled from her eyes. Her soul reached for the enemy; shadows shifted.

And the universe within that room exploded in a ghostfall of wings and light.

2

Mance had never seen so many pigeons.

He entered Guillo House from a back door, having overcome the sadness and anger he had felt when his uncle had been taken away. He had spent most of the rainy evening in his room. Johnnie had tried to console him, but had only partly succeeded. Without his uncle at his side, he had doubted whether he could face the wolf creature.

Your love for Johnnie is all you need.

But was it?

Midevening his dad came to his room to tell him that the hospital had informed him over the phone that Uncle Thestis appeared to be failing rapidly.

"Do you want to see him again tonight, son?"

"No. There's something else I have to do."

A question begged in his dad's eyes: can I help?

"I gotta do it — just Sting and me," said Mance.

And his dad had honored that request, and when the rain ended, the boy made his way through the gathering mist; he had seen Adele and Austin at the front door of Guillo House and thus had detoured to the rear.

He had climbed the stairs not knowing quite what to expect, drawn like a moth to the pool of lantern light which had spilled out from the second-floor room.

The pigeons swept past him like a torrent of water.

He heard a woman scream, and above that scream he heard the growl of the wolf creature.

Every heroic impulse within him came alive.

In the room, he found Adele cowering by the lantern; the shadows strobed with the flutter of the pigeons, the birds having been animated by the *genius loci* of Guillo House and the elemental energy of the wolf creature.

Mance turned.

Want death.

The claws of the wolf creature sank into his shoulder. Blood welled through his T-shirt in dark ribbons. It might have been the sight of the blood, or the rush of fear, or the promise of sorts that he had given to his uncle, but something galvanized Mance into action. He attacked the wolf creature with a physical fury he little realized he was capable of.

He fought, and in the tight circle of his battle he lost awareness of everything except the claws and fangs and brute strength of the wolf creature. Sometime during the clash, Austin had entered the room to rescue Adele, leaving the lantern burning brightly.

Bleeding from his shoulder and thigh, Mance continued his valiant yet ultimately pathetic attempt to defeat the creature. A blow to his chest sent him rolling against a wall; a fresh streaming of blood seemed to feed the creature's desire to tear the boy to pieces.

Slamming off the wall, Mance had the wind knocked out of him. Doubled over, he twisted his head around in time to see the creature closing in on him. Uncle Thestis was wrong, he thought, realizing that if a miracle of sorts did not occur, he would be killed.

Love had not been enough.

It was at that moment Sting, jostled, tossed about, and clinging desperately to Mance's long hair, decided he had had enough. From the boy's shoulder, he leaped to the floor and skittered straight for the wolf creature, scampering between its legs.

Surprised by the rat, the creature wheeled around to give chase. In the lifesaving interim, Mance dragged himself forward until he reached the door.

And there his dad's hands gripped him by the shoulders.

3

In the misty darkness in front of Guillo House, Mance heard Adele crying and Austin attempting to console her. She had faced the creature, and though she hadn't defeated it, she had gained a small victory over her own fear.

"We need to get you home, son, and look at those cuts and scratches."

Mance's dad hunkered down with him, touching at his torn shirt.

"OK, yeah," said the boy, his heart sinking because the task of stopping the wolf creature had not been completed. They had tried and failed; he was glad that his Uncle Thestis had not been there to witness it.

Help me, Mance.

"Wait, Dad."

The boy glanced over his shoulder, every nerve alive, and saw the muted dot of light punctuating the second floor.

Help me, Mance.

It was Johnnie.

Her call was clear and direct; the fear in it cut at him like the edge of a razor. He sensed that she was on the second floor, but why was she there?

"Son, no—"

"Johnnie needs me."

His wounds slowing him down, Mance struggled to the rear of the house, hoping to find some kind of weapon to take with him. What he found instead was someone training a flashlight upon the weathered siding of Guillo House.

Bridgette Settleford turned at the boy's approach.

"The wolf creature . . . it's in there, isn't it? I have to see it," she said, "before the house is destroyed."

"Johnnie's up there and she needs help," said Mance.

In the spray of the flashlight's beam, he saw a broken branch about the size of a baseball bat. He grabbed it and dashed into the house, only vaguely aware that Bridgette had followed.

Help me, Mance.

There was no way he could have prepared himself for the scene that greeted him.

She had become Jonella.

And she felt as if a lightning bolt had struck her brain. Her body pulled at the creature, and the lantern light acquired a blinding intensity. She threw back her head and screamed and felt the creature's savage resistance, felt the pulse of its blood within its veins, felt the primitive strength it had gained over the years.

But also felt its need to die.

Want death.

The threads of her being wrapped around the creature and began to draw the form of the wolf closer and closer, inch by inch, and with every inch the shadowy form began to dissolve.

Jonella rocked forward and concentrated; it was as if her body were sucking the essence of the creature into her abdomen, into the central fire of her being, where it would be trapped forever.

The room shuddered.

Plaster dust spun free, and in the lantern light created an eerie, false snowstorm.

Jonella gave forth one final, agonized scream of determination; the wolf roared, and the lantern extinguished itself.

But not before Mance had grabbed Jonella's wrist and pulled her into his arms.

"I want to see it . . . I have to see it," said Bridgette from the hallway. She shined her light upon them, and Mance said, "It's gone . . . the wolf creature's gone."

But the woman moved past them into the room where the dust continued to swirl.

"I have to see it," she muttered.

Weakened by loss of blood and the shock of seeing Jonella absorb the creature, Mance spent the remainder of his energy carrying the young woman he loved from the culminating scene of horror.

At the back of the house, Punch appeared seemingly from nowhere.

"I've set the charges," he said. "This is the end of the wolf man."

"Punch . . . Bridgette's still in there!" Mance exclaimed.

"Jesus Christ, no. Go around front and get everybody back from the house—we've got maybe thirty seconds."

And he tore away from Mance and Jonella and into Guillo House.

They huddled at the edge of Chrokinole Street like the survivors of a holocaust: Adele and Austin and Mance's dad. Jonella, becoming Johnnie once again, pressed her face into Mance's shoulder and cried softly.

The night rang with a series of sharp explosions.

Guillo House, framed within the mist of Easter Sunday, seemed to shudder; there was a loud popping and the wrenching noise of the foundation giving way.

Mance watched in disbelief.

Oh, God . . . Punch, Bridgette.

All at once the house appeared to deflate, and then as it crashed inward, producing a chorus of sounds, each of the stunned witnesses could hear the moans and cries of something ghostly, something unearthly rising above the chaos, swinging blind and blackening into the moonless air.

And when the old mansion came to rest in a sorrowful, tragic heap and Austin and Mance's dad surged forward hoping against hope to find Punch and Bridgette alive, the only life to emerge from the rubble was a dusty and quite upset white rat.

Chapter Eighteen

1

Four weeks later.

It was a glorious May morning.

Mance knelt at the freshly laid stone marking the grave of his Uncle Thestis. Not far away was the grave of Bridgette Settleford, and the boy had also spent a moment there and had offered a warm thought to her as well as to Punch, who was buried next to Fast Track in the small cemetery for blacks a few miles down the road.

To the stone and the mound of earth extending from it, Mance said, "I feel like we beat it, Uncle T. I mean . . . the living dark. We beat it. You'd been proud of Johnnie. She was the one."

Silence surrounded him like oppressively humid air; for a minute or two he spoke no further words—but images of the man who donned the role of Gottfried Sücher to help solve an occult mystery flashed in a comforting sequence.

"God, I'll miss you," said the boy.

And he rose and walked back to the van where his dad was waiting.

"You OK?"

Mance sighed and nodded slowly.

The death of Uncle Thestis, inevitable as it was, struck the boy harder than any of the other tragic events. Perspective, however, was what the day called for. On that eye-bursting, bright morning, there was much on the positive side of the scales: Adele and Austin had married and were on their honeymoon in Florida; Mance's parents were planning to take the following week off to drive to the Smokies in Tennessee; Tanya had found a life free from fear of the person she loved; and Mance was on his way to bring the young woman he loved back to Soldier. Back home.

Over recent weeks he had grown closer to his dad, and on the trek to Taloa Springs they talked, warm, benevolent-spirited, father-to-son talk, and the good feeling lasted even as they passed through the gates of the Taloa Springs asylum.

2

The asylum boasted a wide back porch and whitewashed wicker chairs and a view of a well-tended garden and the lake. To Mance, everything appeared somehow too serene. But when he saw Johnnie leaning against a white column waiting for him, the setting was suddenly perfect.

Pale, but still beautiful, she was clutching Stubby to her breasts and staring up at a single, puffy cloud.

"Johnnie," he said, approaching her, "we've come to take you home . . . back to Soldier."

She threw herself into his arms with a squeal of absolute delight, the stuffed dog dropping, neglected, to one side. She felt good in his arms — and, oh, God, he loved her so much — though the pleasant cinnamon fragrance was gone, replaced by something slightly pungent.

Pushing away, she studied him carefully.

"You cut your hair . . . oh, what's gone happen to Sting? Why did you cut your hair?"

She was giggling, and she cupped a hand over her mouth, and Mance couldn't believe how good it was to see her.

"I cut it 'cause I'm gone back to school . . . to summer school. Gone work for Slow Eddie, too, but Johnnie, I'm gone finish high school and make something of myself — for you."

She kissed at his lips, a giggle-filled peck. She seemed pleased as she reached down and picked up the stuffed dog.

"What's in your bag?" she asked.

He lifted the canvas satchel from his shoulder.

"A big snake," he teased.

"Oh," she shrieked, "something moved."

Mance dangled Sting by the back of his neck and Johnnie cooed and fussed over the rat.

"Got something else, too," said Mance. "Hope they haven't melted."

They sat in a pair of wicker chairs and Johnnie tore at a colorfully wrapped box. Her shoulders appeared to slump when she looked down at the rose-shaped chocolates. She said nothing, but her gesture spoke for her: she took Mance's arm and gently kissed the fang tattoo.

Placing a finger beneath her chin, he leaned toward her and kissed her lips.

"You ready to go home if Dr. Morris says it's all right?"

"Yes. When I get scared, Stubby talks to me. I'm not friends with Jonella no more. She's strange. I hope they keep her here."

"We'll forget all about this place," said Mance. "Don't talk like that. Things will get back to normal pretty soon."

Johnnie led him out into the flower garden, where bees darted about. She squinted up at a single cloud and said, "See his face?"

Mance looked but saw only a billowy, white cloud.

"It's Uncle Thestis," she followed. "He's been here all morning."

An attendant came to take her back inside.

"I'll be back for you after lunch," said Mance. "Dad and I gotta talk to Dr. Morris." He wanted to add, "I love you," but there would be time for that later, he reasoned.

"I'm happy for you, son."

He and his dad waited in an imposing outer office, a high-ceilinged, whitewashed, and intimidating room.

"It's gone work out," said Mance.

They were ushered into Dr. Norris's office, a dark, heavily paneled room where a small, silver-haired man soberly greeted them. He seemed to be holding his head back as if it would topple from his neck should he lean forward.

He got right to the point.

"What we initially diagnosed as mildly acute schizophrenia in Miss Withers we now believe is more severe and quite possibly chronic."

In a calm, measured voice he traced Johnnie's medical history, citing Dr. Colby's records, test results, observations, and therapy sessions, and he speculated on the causes of her demise, emphasizing trauma and touching briefly upon hereditary factors. As he spoke, he habitually studied his fingernails. He might have been talking about any patient at the asylum. He might have been talking about a potted plant, there was such cool objectiveness in his tone.

"She can't be released now."

The conclusion of his spiel was a spear in the chest for Mance.

"But she's OK," the boy countered. "She's not . . . not crazy or nothing. She's just . . . my Johnnie."

Morris launched into a summary of potential treatment.

"You have to let her come home," said Mance.

His dad touched at his elbow.

"Son . . . please."

Morris folded his hands and stared directly at the boy.

"She wouldn't be able to make it. At this point a relapse should especially be avoided."

"I want to see her again," said Mance, still convinced that Morris was wrong.

"I urge you to accept what I've recommended," said Morris.

Mance could only shrug, his thoughts locked in a cold swirl.

An attendant advised him that he would find Johnnie down by the lake.

There was a young woman there, not Johnnie, but rather Jonella; there were no swans on the lake, and an attendant stood watch some thirty yards away.

"Johnnie?"

The face was similar, but the eyes—no, too wild, too unfocused for Johnnie.

She turned and stood on one leg, grasping one foot and pulling it behind her.

"If I stand like this," she asked, "will the flamingo hunter shoot me?"

Everyone, Mance realized, had been wrong about the living dark: Sparrow and Uncle Thestis and Adele and Austin. Everyone who had tried to understand it had missed its true nature. The living dark was in Jonella's eyes.

"Would you like to see what I can do?" she asked him.

He noticed that the attendant had let his attention wander.

It materialized there at the edge of the lake for no longer than a few seconds: the wolf creature. It seemed smaller, less frightening, and much more insubstantial. Jonella laughed, and in another few seconds had reabsorbed it.

Mance caught her arm and looked into her eyes.

"I'll wait till you get better. I'll wait as long as it takes."

She was puzzled by his words.

Mance took her into his arms; he felt something so painful flare inside that he could hardly bear it.

"What can I do?" he pleaded.

At first, she struggled to free herself.

"What can I do?" he said again.

There was a flicker of something in her eyes and around her mouth. A sudden softness.

He waited until that something generated words.

He held her and listened.

"Love me when I'm Johnnie," she whispered.

And for a few seconds longer, the world belonged to them.

A breeze lifted, and the dark surface of the lake momentarily rippled light.

Dear Reader,
Zebra Books welcomes your comments about this book or any other Zebra horror book you have read recently. Please address your comments to:

Zebra Books, Dept. WM
475 Park Avenue South
New York, NY 10016

Thank you for your interest.

Sincerely,
The Editorial Department
Zebra Books